TERESA F.

I live in sunny Weston-super-~~~~~~~~~~~~~ ~~~ ~~~~ onto my Surrey accent where I was born and bred. For years I persevered with boring jobs, until my two boys joined my nest. In an attempt to find something to work around them, and to ensure I never endured full time boredom again, I found writing.

I am at my happiest baking cakes, putting proper home cooked dinners on the table (whether the kids eat them or not), reading a good romance, or creating a touch of escapism with heroes hopefully readers will fall in love with.

You can follow me on Twitter @Teresa_Morgan10.

Plus One is a
Lucky Number

TERESA F MORGAN

A division of HarperCollins*Publishers*
www.harpercollins.co.uk

Harper*Impulse* an imprint of
HarperCollins*Publishers Ltd*
77–85 Fulham Palace Road
Hammersmith, London W6 8JB

www.harpercollins.co.uk

A Paperback Original 2013

First published in Great Britain in ebook format by HarperImpulse 2013

Copyright © Teresa Morgan 2013

Cover Images © Shutterstock.com

Teresa Morgan asserts the moral right to
be identified as the author of this work

A catalogue record for this book
is available from the British Library

ISBN: 978-0-00-755967-1

Automatically produced by Atomik ePublisher from Easypress

This book is dedicated to Elizabeth Charles (aka Junkfoodmonkey who writes professionally as Becky Black) and Star Ostgard (aka Shadowwalker). Without their encouragement I would never have started my writing journey. They've been tough on me at times, to the point of tears, but they have taught me so much and thickened my skin for the real writing world. Without them I would not have created this book.

And rather than miss out names and upset anyone, I would also like to thank all my good friends and family who have put up with me... I mean supported me in fulfilling my dream of becoming an author – you know who you are!

Thank you x

Chapter One

Sophie Trewyn needed an excuse. A good one. A week to go and she was still no closer to a decision. She hated being a coward, but she couldn't face this alone.

"Sophie, what's up? You're quiet tonight." James frowned at her as he drank his pint.

Roused momentarily from her reverie, Sophie picked up her wine glass. "It's nothing. I'm tired." She plastered on a smile.

They were sitting in the garden at The White Lion, where everyone – from Accounts to the techies on the factory floor – went on Fridays for a drink after work. Luckily, it was a warm, July evening, so they could sit comfortably outside. Otherwise the small pub, with its low ceilings and wooden beams, would be swelling under the strain of its increased patrons.

"Who's keeping you up at night? Someone I know?" James nudged her playfully.

"You know I'm not seeing anyone." She sipped her Chardonnay and tucked a wisp of hair behind her ear.

"Yeah, I mean, who'd want to go out with you? Pretty, intelligent –"

"Oh, please." Sophie blushed.

"Okay – forget the intelligent bit."

Used to his teasing, she laughed. James and Sophie were

design engineers, specialising in robotics. When she'd started at the company ten months ago, he'd taken her under his wing, becoming the older brother she never had and even introduced her to his girlfriend, Kate.

"Does Kate know you think I'm pretty?"

"Kate thinks you're pretty! She wants to set you up with one of her boring accountant types." Then, grinning, showing off boyish dimples, he added, "I keep telling her they'll be too outgoing, even for you."

She jokingly slapped him on the arm, finished her drink and excused herself, heading for the ladies. When Sophie pushed open the door she found a stunning young woman, cursing into the mirror whilst delicately dabbing the corner of her eyes with tissues. Sophie meekly smiled and hurried into a cubicle. Having enough worries of her own, Sophie didn't need someone else's problems, too. The woman continued her tearful rant to herself in front of the mirror. "Commitment-phobic bastard. You can do better than that arsehole, Bella. Adam arsehole Reid's loss, not yours!"

Sophie knew that name. Relief washed over her as she heard the door swish and Bella leave, and hoped she wouldn't be upset for too long. Men these days were not worth it.

With the amenities to herself, Sophie tidied her ponytail and reapplied some lip-gloss. Working in a male-dominated office, she preferred to keep a low profile, hair worn back, minimalist make-up. Sophie wanted to be noticed for her work, not the skirt she wore.

She stared into the mirror as Bella had just done, her head clouded with excuses to make to her best friend Cassie, and how she'd deal with Cassie's anger – albeit over the phone.

Coward.

If only it had been Kate who had set Sophie up with one of her friends ...

8

Or maybe she could feign a terrible illness?

God, why'd she let it go this far?

Because I thought I wouldn't be going home alone. She'd had months to find someone, and she hadn't thought it would come around so quickly.

She sighed heavily. This was ridiculous. She couldn't stand in a pub loo worrying all evening, James would wonder where she was.

Walking towards the picnic bench, Sophie noticed fresh drinks on the table and someone sitting in her seat. The man – with mouth-watering good looks – had removed his jacket and loosened his tie, laughing with James.

Adam Reid – Bella obviously long forgotten.

His name often came up when James discussed his weekend jaunts with his mates. How could such good friends be the opposite ends of the spectrum? Unlike his friend, James wasn't a naturally smart dresser. Adam looked sophisticated with his crisp, white shirt, a contrast to James' faded dark blue polo shirt that hadn't ever seen an iron.

Adam glanced at her as she approached. He had short, sandy blond hair, expensively cut. She'd heard some of the women in the office talk about him being a real head turner. They weren't wrong. *Poor Bella.*

Poor Bella? More like poor Sophie.

Oh, please don't have a trail of loo paper stuck to my shoe like some Andrex puppy trailing tissue behind it.

She subtly tried checking her blouse was tucked into her trousers, and quickly brushed a hand over her hair. Why hadn't she untied it? She could understand why Bella had been upset. This man was a catch.

"Sophie, this is Adam Reid."

She nodded and smiled. "I know." She'd attended a couple of meetings which he'd been at, and could count – on one hand

9

– how many words she'd spoken to him.

"Oh, sorry, I'm in your seat." Adam stood up, and Sophie had to look up into his blue eyes. They shook hands. He had a firm, professional handshake. She could feel the warmth from his palm in her own.

She shuffled along the bench as some of their colleagues moved from the table, and she gestured to Adam to sit. As he did, she caught a whiff of his aftershave and heat instantly rushed up her neck.

"Adam's an account manager in Sales and Marketing," James said. Hence, he looked smart and she and James didn't. Working in the design department allowed them a more casual dress code. *He must think we're a right pair.*

"I know that, too," she said, placing her handbag on the table. Some said he was the best in the marketing department supporting the company's biggest clients. Sophie wasn't going to forget his cool, confident attitude in a hurry. Adam Reid had dominated the meetings she'd sat in a couple of times. His smooth, deep voice, combined with his good looks, had made it very hard for her to concentrate on what he'd been saying. James once told her Adam had started on the factory floor. She doubted he ever got his hands dirty now, but it hadn't stopped her watching his strong, masculine hands, and picturing what they could do.

He rubbed his thumb along the condensation on his pint glass. *Stop looking at his hands.*

"Sophie works with me," James said to Adam.

"I'd worked that one out, James." Adam winked at her. "Aren't you lucky working with such a bright spark?"

"Someone has to work with him. I drew the short straw," she said, nervously smiling back, finding it very hard to meet his eyes and not blush. The bottom of her wine glass was easier to look at. "I've managed to put up with him for almost a year." Adam chuckled.

"Hey, you two!" James laughed and reached for his pint, but knocked Sophie's full wine glass over, spilling the contents on her handbag.

All three of them jumped to their feet. Cheers and laughter came from a neighbouring table. James righted the glass.

"Oh, hell, sorry."

"James," she huffed, as she scrambled to empty her bag onto a dry part of the table and shake it out. Some of the contents fell through the gaps of the picnic table and onto the ground. She mumbled a curse. Luckily her bag had got most of it, not her clothes - the last thing she needed, especially in front of Adam.

Adam reacted quickly, grabbing clean paper napkins from another table and soaked up the wine.

"What's this?" James picked up a card, battered and now soggy, from underneath the table. Sophie tried to snatch it, but he held it away from her.

"A wedding invitation." James looked at Sophie, then Adam, his eyebrows raised. "For next weekend."

"James, please give it to me." She tried reaching for it again, but he raised it so she couldn't grab the card.

Sod him for being so tall.

Lowering his arm, he read further. "'To Sophie Trewyn and guest'. You never said anything about this."

Sophie wanted the ground to swallow her up. *Please don't let this be happening. Not here.*

"No, because I'm not going," she said coolly.

"Why? Aren't weddings supposed to be fun? All that free food and drink." He playfully grinned. "Isn't that right, Adam?"

"Yeah, so I've heard." Adam shrugged. "I'll go get Sophie another drink."

James nodded, and before she could say not to bother, Adam

11

had walked off.

"So?" James sat down, giving Sophie an interrogating look.

Sophie, relieved that Adam had gone to the bar, rolled her eyes and sat back down at their table. She pulled tissues from her jacket pocket and started wiping her bag. "I have a mountain of stuff to do and I can't afford to take the time off from work either."

"Rubbish!"

"And well, they're not really close friends or anything."

Who are you kidding?

"It's an all day invitation, so you must mean something to them," James said.

Sophie looked down, unable to meet James' gaze. It galled her to admit this, even to James. "I'm not sure I can face going on my own."

"Oh." James' smile dropped. "You don't have an 'and guest', do you?"

"You know I don't," she hissed.

"Well, you should still go. Might find yourself a nice man."

Sophie cringed, but hoped her expression didn't show. "James, I'm too busy with work."

"Really?"

"Yes."

"Bollocks."

Sophie let out a sigh, glancing around the pub garden. Could anyone hear? "It's complicated." Then she lowered her voice, "I don't know if I can handle the 'why is a pretty girl like you still single?' speeches."

She remembered the family gathering last Christmas, all tucked around the dinner table about to tuck into the turkey. Her Aunt Veronica, with too much sherry inside her, started harping on at her. 'Isn't it time you found yourself a boyfriend, rather than follow that career of yours?' She hadn't let it rest all day. Her

12

insides turned cold, even now. Not to mention the endless 'So how's your love life these days Soph?' from a variety of younger, male cousins. 'Still single, eh?'

Irritated, she snatched the wedding invitation from an unsuspecting James. She didn't exactly date much, but she couldn't admit that, could she? It wasn't that she was shy. In fact she used to be much more outgoing ... and why she had thought that she might have found someone to go with her. The months had whizzed by and her only social outlet was The White Lion on a Friday night. It was her own fault. She should have gone out more, accepted James and Kate's invitations.

"I'd go with you, for the champagne and food of course!" James said, smiling. Sophie clicked her tongue. "But as you know I'm going –"

"Yes, to that bloody meeting in Manchester." Most of her colleagues were going next Friday and tonight they'd been talking about extending it to the weekend. Sophie wished she was attending. It would be the perfect excuse. But she'd actually booked the time off ages ago in preparation for the wedding. Months ago she'd psyched herself up, telling herself that she could attend it. Now it came to actually going, her confidence had gone. "Besides, I don't think Kate would appreciate you going away with me for a weekend."

"True. She likes you a lot, Sophie. But even Kate might find that difficult to swallow." He laughed. "But what if Kate went with you?"

Sophie smiled, understanding James' offer, though not particularly enamoured he was still pressing the matter. "You're sweet. Thank you, but it's not really a case –"

"Soph, come on. Would you go if you had someone to go with?"

"Um ..." Yes, she would. But did it sound pathetic? She frowned. Adam walked towards them carrying a glass of wine and a greying dishcloth.

"Sorry, queue at the bar," he said, handing Sophie her glass. She wasn't sure if it were true, yet was glad he'd taken his time.

James suddenly beamed. "Adam, you'll go with Sophie, won't you?"

Sophie nearly spat out her wine.

"What?" He stared at James, shocked – or horrified even? – stopping mid-wipe with the cloth.

Sophie waved her hands in protest. "Seriously, it's not that big a deal. I'll cancel." She took a gulp of her wine, Dutch courage was really required now.

"No, no, no." James placed his hand on hers and squeezed it. Once he had an idea in his head, he didn't stop or even listen. "Adam, you'll do it, won't you?"

Sophie glanced around again, hoping no one would take any notice. Good job they weren't in the office otherwise she'd be the talk of the whole building. She imagined the sniggers.

"Just go along so she doesn't get all those awkward and annoying questions, you know, like 'why aren't you married yet? You're working too hard at that office.'"

Sophie laughed, and even Adam couldn't hold back a smile. James sounded exactly like an old lady, not dissimilar to her Aunt Veronica.

"Well, I'm not sure," Adam stammered. Unable to look Sophie in the eye, he picked up his pint.

Sophie sobered. Maybe he'd do it for someone prettier. And smarter. She hardly compared to Bella. Automatically Sophie brushed her hands down her trousers. She couldn't blame him. Adam was well out of her league. He played Premiership; she was way down in second division.

"Adam, honestly, don't listen to him," Sophie said, pointlessly dabbing the cloth over the table. "You don't have to. I'll say I'm not going."

"Rubbish!" James interrupted. Sophie quickly glared at him. "James –"

"Go on," James cut in, ignoring her. "You'll charm the socks off the wedding guests." He grinned.

"Sophie looks quite capable of standing on her own two feet," Adam said, giving her a smile. It wasn't huge, but enough to make her heart flutter. He'd just made her feel like a million dollars. Maybe she should wear more makeup into the office after all.

Stop it.

Adam was right though, what was James suggesting? She didn't know Adam from … Adam. *Oh, God.*

"You'll be helping a lady in distress."

"I'm not in distress!" Sophie slapped her hand down on the table.

"Ah, James, shall we go get another pint?" Adam said, giving James a stern look, then his expression softened. "Sophie, would you like anything else?"

She shook out her bag and started putting the contents back into it. "Um, no, thanks."

***

"What do you think you're doing?" Adam scowled at James. He'd never heard of anything so ludicrous in all his life. They both ducked the low doorframe as they entered the pub. The warmth hit them, dry and stuffy compared to outside. "Not only did you just put me in a very awkward situation, the poor girl's embarrassed."

"Come on, Adam, she needs a date. Just go along, charm the guests, keep them off her back. You never know, you might enjoy the weekend." James leaned against the bar. "And Bella's no longer on the scene, so what's the problem?" Adam winced. Bella had

15

wanted more than he was prepared to give. He was too busy with work. And his father expected nothing short of absolute dedication.

Adam ordered the drinks when the barmaid arrived, trying to think of arguments for not doing it. There were plenty.

"We hardly know each other."

James nudged him and laughed. "When has that stopped you before?"

"That's different! Besides, what have you told her about me?" Adam looked at him questioningly.

"Only what everyone else knows." James held up his hand defensively. "If she's ever listened to me jabber on," James winced, "then she might think of you as ladies' man."

"Oh, just wonderful." Adam shook his head.

"Look, you know I would have gone with Soph, but I'm at that damn meeting in Manchester – and you're not." James paused. "And even if I could, Kate loves Sophie, but I'm not even sure she'd understand this one. Come on, help a mate out," James said, rubbing his hand through his unkempt hair. "Do it for me? You're the only guy I can trust to do this properly."

"I don't know." Adam slid his hands into his pockets. Why hadn't he stayed at the office this evening? He'd taken the opportunity to leave on time, rarely able to join the workforce down the pub on a Friday. Now he regretted it. First Bella, and now this.

"So, how good is she...at engineering?" Adam said hesitantly.

James frowned. "She's a bloody good design engineer. Thomas will be making her chief engineer at this rate – obviously some time yet, she's only young."

"So we don't want to lose her?" Adam's forehead creased. Would helping Sophie actually benefit him, even if only in company matters?

"No, but what's this got to do...? Adam, I'm asking you as a friend."

16

"I know, but I might need to call in a favour." He shrugged.

"Man, it's always about work with you. Well, you're probably both suited. The woman works all hours," James said. Then more sternly, "But she's the sort who'd help a friend out if that's what you're thinking."

"I don't know what I'm thinking. This is a stupid idea."

"She's great. You'll love her. You two might even hit it off." James sounded hopeful. Adam scowled.

"We've talked about this before. You know it's not for me, settling down. Not everybody wants what you and Kate have."

"How do you know if you don't try it? Dating a woman who's not afraid to chip a nail might do you good."

"Date?" Adam sighed and run a hand through his hair. The barmaid put the last pint on the bar and Adam paid her.

James continued frantically, realising his misplaced word. "I'm not asking you to sleep with her. In fact you'd better not - I'll bloody kill you! Sophie's a nice young lady, who needs treating properly." James looked at him knowingly but Adam's returned expression was horrified. "But truthfully, I think something's up."

"Oh, great."

"She needs someone there for moral support, for some reason. Like I said, she helps friends out, that's why I can't believe she's seriously thinking of not going." James nudged him. "Haven't I got you out of a few scrapes? If you're helping Soph out, you're helping me out," James added, looking pleadingly at him. "You're the only one I know I can trust."

Trust. There it was again. If James wasn't such a good friend …

The barmaid handed Adam his change and he sighed. "All right, all right, I'll do it."

James slapped his back and grinned. "You won't regret it."

"Famous last words those."

"Sophie is lovely."

"You keep saying that, but she's not really my —"

"The problem is you can't see beyond a woman's looks. You wait until you get to know her. Trust me."

Adam rubbed his forehead, and they headed back to the pub garden. "Why do I get the feeling I'm going to regret this?"

***

Well done, James. The one thing she would have liked to have kept buried deep in her handbag, was now the topic of the most embarrassing conversation at the pub.

Coward.

This could be the answer to her fears; only Adam Reid... *Really?*

While she worried about what James was telling Adam at the bar, she said hello to colleagues, not really listening to them and what they were up to at the weekend.

What would she be doing this weekend? Thinking about packing, or plucking up the courage to call Cassie?

Why hadn't James stuck with asking Kate? Or one of her accountant friends? Oh, no, he'd asked Adam Reid from Sales and Marketing — a department she wasn't even familiar with, as her job rarely led her there. All she knew was everyone dressed in smart, slick suits and looked immaculate. They talked about sales figures, advertising campaigns and the big picture, while she and James knuckled down to the hard work behind the scenes.

She glanced around the pub. Some of them were here.

Sophie swallowed, conscious her throat was like sandpaper, and sipping her wine didn't help.

James and Adam walked towards her and sat down in silence.

What had James told him?

All nice things, surely? He's a friend. Though, how well did

18

James know her, really? So they worked together five days a week, and went to the pub on a Friday evening, but Sophie didn't speak much about home, and what awaited her there. They talked shop most of the time, discussing their latest design project, or she let James fill her in on his weekends with Kate and friends.

"As I was saying," James looked at Adam, as if passing a silent message between them, "Adam will go with you to the wedding."

"You don't have to."

Adam smiled, in an 'I don't mind' kind of way. "So where's the wedding?" She became very aware of his blue eyes piercing through her at knee melting capacity. Good job she was sitting down.

"Cornwall, where I grew up. I'm supposed to drive down Thursday morning," she said nervously. "It would mean taking a couple of days off."

"See, mate, it'll be fun –"

"Shh, James," Sophie hissed.

"Okay, fine," Adam said, ignoring James. He frowned, combing a hand through his hair. Sophie could see he was still thinking about it. Had James bullied him into this?

"So, you will come with me?" She kept staring at the table, looking at James, anything but meeting Adam's eyes. Admittedly, this could be a good solution, although he still sounded hesitant.

"Yeah, I could do with a weekend away."

"You'll both have a scream!" James said, eagerly. "All you got to do is pretend to be her boyfriend."

They both stared at James and spoke in unison, "Boyfriend?"

Chapter Two

Adam walked up the stairs towards Sophie's flat with some anxiety. He'd never been nervous picking up a woman for a date in his life. *It's not a date.* God, James' pep talk all week had him jittery. He took a deep breath, adjusting his jacket collar, about to ring the doorbell, when the door opened unexpectedly and he jumped, staring at Sophie.

She looked different to the bland engineer he'd seen on Friday. For some reason, he'd expected to see her in the same style of plain – and unflattering – trouser suit. Instead, Sophie was wearing a fitted summer dress, cut just above the knee, revealing an appealing figure. Her chestnut hair hung loose, shaping her face and there was colour in her cheeks. Hell, he'd been wondering what he had got himself into, but maybe this weekend wouldn't be too bad after all.

"Sorry, didn't mean to startle you," he said, clearing his throat, and straightening his tie. "I thought I'd come help you with your bags."

"Oh, uh, thanks," Sophie said, putting down the case outside the door, and grabbing a small holdall and her handbag.

"We agreed – eight a.m.?"

"Yes. For some reason I thought ..." She shrugged.

What? He wouldn't show?

"Doesn't matter. You're on time."

She wouldn't look him in the eyes and seemed nervous as hell – especially the way she fumbled to get the key into the lock.

"Here, let me." He gently took the keys out of her hand and locked her front door.

"Thank you," she said as he gave her bundle of keys back.

"Not a problem." Adam picked up the case, then frowned, feeling the weight of it. "We're going for the weekend, right? Not the week?"

"I know, I know." Sophie winced as she spoke. "I couldn't think what to take, and decided to pack for every eventuality."

"You are normal then," he said, smiling, as he walked down the stairs to his car with Sophie following.

"What?"

"I wasn't sure the woman I met Friday was the sort to pack everything but the kitchen sink." She had appeared to be a minimalist, not the type to lug a tonne of make-up about with her.

Her expression sobered.

Great, Adam. Before you start teasing her, maybe you should wait until you get to know her better. It had been his intention during this week, but got too caught up with work – he'd had two days out of the office sprung on him, after all. Now he was glad he'd insisted on driving when making the arrangements; it would give him something to concentrate on and he'd keep his mouth shut.

"I didn't mean ... well, you look great."

"Oh ... thanks," she said, combing a hand through her hair, then smoothing her dress.

Adam looked at her speculatively. James was certain something was troubling Sophie. The last few days, whilst mulling it over, he'd been assured by James, over and over, this weekend would be good fun and that he would appreciate the break from work. But Adam was still not comfortable with this whole plan. How

21

far would the pretending have to go?

Hopefully it would be a case of standing to the side, making idle chit-chat. As James had said, if he couldn't sweet-talk a few old dears ...

Adam hid a grin as he placed Sophie's luggage in the boot. He'd noticed her stunned expression as she looked at the huge car – a brand spanking new BMW. He'd thought this would be more comfortable for the journey, and they could arrive in style. If Sophie wanted to impress someone, this would do it.

His expression sobered. What if it's too flashy? This wasn't the car he used for work. Sophie didn't know who Adam really was. To her he was just some account manager. Only James knew his secret – had kept it for ten years, too.

Hell, he hoped he hadn't over-done it – first impressions and all that. He needed to put her at ease, not make her think he was some poser.

"Hang on." He shut the boot. "Let me get that." He strode around and opened the passenger door for Sophie, smiling. She stared at him, opening her mouth, then closing it.

"Thank you," Sophie said, settling into the black leather seat. "I can see why you insisted on driving - beats my poky little car."

Adam chuckled, shutting her door. He took off his suit jacket and hung it up in the back. Once seated, he smiled at Sophie, receiving a fragile smile back before she looked down into her lap, then out the window. He really needed to reassure her he didn't bite.

"Right, Cornwall it is then," he said, starting the car.

"I said I'd pay for the fuel, and I mean it," Sophie said in a worried tone.

Adam thought best not to disagree. Not that he would let a lady pay where he could help it. But maybe she was fretting because, although James had talked him into this, she didn't want to look like she was sponging off him. For the sake of her pride, he wasn't going to argue with her – yet. Besides, it had been his choice to bring the gas-guzzler of a car compared to using hers. Was she worried about the expense?

"Don't worry about it for now, we'll sort it out later. There's a full tank. Let's enjoy the weekend, yeah?" He winked and she smiled again, lighting up her face.

"Okay. But you're doing me a favour, so I don't want you out of pocket."

"For services rendered?" He grinned at her, then turned his attention to the road.

Luckily, Sophie giggled, realising he was teasing her. "Yes, something like that."

She stayed quiet while Adam drove. He wondered what to discuss. Cornwall wasn't a trip around the corner; they had a good four to five hour journey ahead of them – providing traffic was good. Would they have enough in common to talk about or would they be stretching out conversations on the weather for the next few hundred miles?

"It's a very nice car, by the way," Sophie said after ten minutes, breaking the silence. Internally, Adam cringed. At least they weren't discussing what a nice day it was.

"We could have used the convertible, but it gets a little uncomfortable after about an hour." From experience, he knew most women didn't enjoy the roof down; it messed up their hair, especially if going some place they'd dressed up for. And Sophie was dressed up. Besides, he wouldn't have got his golf clubs plus all the luggage in the boot.

"Oh."

Now you do look flash. Shut up.

"Depending on the traffic, we'll stop after half way," Adam said, glancing down at the clock in the dashboard. "But tell me if you need a stop before then, otherwise I'll carry on." He didn't want her sitting there, too scared to ask him to stop, desperate to stretch her legs – and what fine legs they were, too.

You promised James you'd behave.

"Okay."

"You're very quiet, Sophie."

"Oh, I thought you'd want to concentrate on the road," she said.

"I don't mind. If you want to talk, talk."

"I'm happy listening to the radio."

"I can put on a CD," he said

"No, radio is fine."

He adjusted the volume of the radio. Not too loud they couldn't hear one another, but wanting to make sure they could listen to it. Did he usually worry this much? She seemed on edge. It's not every day that a stranger picks you up and takes you away for a weekend.

They listened and commented on the morning broadcast. Occasionally, he'd catch the subtle scent of her floral perfume and glimpse to see Sophie staring out of the window. What was so bad about this wedding? Or was it him? He didn't usually have a problem charming women. Was she intimidated? Shit, what *had* James told her about him?

Well, if he was going to do this, he was doing it properly. Adam certainly hated looking like an idiot. He didn't want them turning up to this wedding and it being obvious that they didn't know one another. He wanted them to step out of this car and look like a couple. This journey would be a good time to work out the finer details, and get to know the shy engineer better.

"Should we get our story straight?" Adam asked, breaking the silence that had fallen between them.

"Story?" Sophie replied, frowning at him.

"Yeah, how we met and all that. Am I going to get the third

degree?"

"Hopefully not, but maybe we should have matching stories. Sorry, I didn't think," Sophie said, laughing nervously.

According to James, she was supposed to be a brilliant designer and could put Thomas Robotics ahead of all its competitors. Maybe talking about work would bring her out of her shell.

"It shouldn't be too difficult. We both work for the same company," he said, concentrating back on the matter at hand. "What about Ted Phillips' retirement party a few weeks ago?"

"Did you go?"

"Yeah, didn't you?" He frowned. Thinking about it, he didn't recall seeing her there, because if she'd been dressed like this, he'd have noticed – wouldn't he?

"Um … no."

"Why not?"

"I was out with friends, I think."

She's lying. Friday nights at The White Lion was about her limits as far as Adam knew. He didn't think she had other friends outside of work.

"How was it?" she asked, looking at him. "Did many people go?"

"Yeah, a good night." Adam chuckled. "James got up and sang his rendition of *You've Lost That Loving Feeling* to a couple of ladies who work in Accounts."

"He never told me."

"I don't think he remembers."

Sophie laughed. "Well, we can still say we met there."

"Okay, Ted's retirement party." He nodded, liking her laughter. There was honesty about it. He would like to hear it more often. It meant that she was relaxing, too.

Adam concentrated on the road, looking in his wing mirror and moving the car into the outside lane, although he wanted to get a better look at the woman sitting beside him.

Plenty of time. He had all weekend. And his job was to stay in close proximity – *oh, what a shame! Not.*

"I've got my clubs in the boot," Adam said, first thing entering his head, his mind wandering to the hotel. Golf was something he did to relax and entertain important clients.

"What?" Sophie frowned.

"I checked out the hotel facilities. They've got a golf course."

She looked at him, almost mortified. She didn't think he'd be trying to escape her every given minute, did she? That's not why he'd brought them. He thought it might be a place they could escape to.

"I know nothing about golf."

"Then I'll have to teach you." He grinned. Now there's a heart-warming thought and a subtle way to get close to this woman.

"To be honest, I'm pretty useless at any sport. You'd need longer than a weekend."

"My contract is only for this weekend." He raised his eyebrows, giving her a mischievous smile. "If you need me for longer, we'll have to renegotiate."

"Oh, um, I didn't mean –"

"I'm kidding!" Adam chuckled. "I was going to suggest the tennis courts – they have those, too, but it looks like you'll be using the pool."

"Yes. I can swim." She chewed her lip.

Okay – so she didn't look keen on going swimming either. Probably the idea of them going together. She didn't come across confident in her own skin – but why? He'd give her privacy, if that's what she wanted.

Changing the subject, Adam filled Sophie in about Ted's retirement party and the conversation moved on, allowing them to get to know one another better.

He stumbled over an old girlfriend's name, internally kicking

26

himself as he quickly washed over it. One thing he'd been trying very hard to avoid; past girlfriends – he had a few. He could see it had set off alarm bells inside her head, her eyes widening.

"You don't have a girlfriend, do you?" Sophie asked him, hesitantly.

Adam shook his head. "No, don't worry."

"For a minute there I thought I'd put you in some awkward predicament."

"Well, actually James got me into this predicament, because it was his idea." Then, more seriously, he said, "But if I had a girlfriend, I wouldn't be here. I'm not that kind of guy, either."

"Of course not. Sorry."

Her cheeks flushed pink – the English rose look suited her. What would she look like ...? Adam swallowed, burying his inappropriate thoughts. Where did that come from anyway? He didn't need to be thinking along those lines. He'd promised James. Besides, she wasn't even his type.

"I hope you don't feel bullied into this," she said, frowning.

"I wasn't bullied. I can't be made to do things I don't want to do. We should have some fun, right?"

He hoped she could have fun. Something had stopped her from wanting to attend this wedding. Now Adam was with her, maybe she could enjoy herself. If that's what she needed – company? Or would Adam add to her stress? They were strangers after all.

Sophie turned in her seat and Adam kept his eyes on the road. Occasionally he glanced and smiled at her. It was working; she was relaxing.

"I hope you don't mind me being nosy, but ..." Sophie stopped.

His eyes narrowed. "What?"

"I don't mean this to sound as bad as it does, but you're an account manager… and this car..?"

Adam relaxed. "Not exactly standard issue company car?"

"No."

"Long story. Might tell you one day. Might not." He winked and tapped his nose. "It's a secret."

"What? You'd have to kill me after?" she said, giggling, then sobered.

Adam noticed her anxious expression, and chuckled. "Sophie, you're safe. I promise. I wouldn't hurt you – James would murder me for a start." He wanted to put her at ease.

He decided to stick with work topics. "Hey, the other week, I was in Bracknell stripping down one of our old QB13's."

"Oh, now you are showing your age," she said, unable to hide a smile. "They're an old model, way before my time."

"I was on the shop floor making them." He narrowed his eyes. "And I'm not that old. I'm thirty-three."

"Oh, definitely old," she said, sarcasm lacing her words.

"Experienced." In many things. Adam liked the fact she was flirting.

Sophie coughed and sobered, her cheeks flushed. "So why were you st-stripping it down?"

He pretended he hadn't heard her stutter over the word stripping. "Well, it was either that, or they'd have to wait three days for our engineer," he said. Had Adam taken it too far flirting back, or did he look like he was bragging? Shit, he felt like he was treading on eggshells. He wanted her to loosen up, get to know him, even like him. It felt important.

Of course it was important; they needed to at least get on this weekend to be remotely believable.

"Why?" she asked.

"He was on holiday." Adam grinned. "And our other engineers were busy with other projects."

"When things go wrong, they go wrong at once."

"Exactly. We couldn't get anyone else there sooner."

She giggled. "I can't believe you got your hands dirty."

"Me neither. But I didn't want to break our service agreement."

"Ah, yes, very costly," she agreed.

"Yes. And I wanted them to purchase the new QB20s. Wasn't going to be likely if they had to halt their manufacturing line for three days." Adam chuckled, and Sophie laughed with him. Yeah, and he'd won the contract.

And maybe he was worrying about nothing. They'd become comfortable with one another inside the car, all tension had ebbed away. But what would happen once they set foot on the grounds of the hotel, meeting Sophie's friends and family? Adam's stomach churned. Then he'd really have to turn up the charm. A whole different experience awaited them. Would he be believable enough for her? Or would they see through him?

No, he'd be fine. She was pretty, after all – not much pretending required there. But he would be pretending. Sophie didn't seem like his usual girlfriends. And they worked under the same roof. He needed to tread carefully. Do enough to keep her friends at bay, but not too much to send mixed messages to Sophie.

"So who's getting married?" Adam couldn't believe he hadn't asked this question.

"Oh, a second cousin of mine."

"Family?" Adam's eyes widened, he nearly swerved the car. "Are your parents going?"

"No." She shook her head, and chuckled. "They'll be on holiday." Relief waved over Adam and he relaxed.

Adam pulled into the services around eleven o'clock, suggesting an early lunch. They'd been on the road three hours, and his stomach growled, reminding him he'd skipped breakfast.

They stood in silence, waiting to be seated in the small roadside restaurant on the A303. They were shown to a table and their orders taken.

"So what does your father do?" Adam asked.

"Pardon?" Sophie looked at him, frowning.

"What does your father do? And your mother? Where do they live?" Adam asked as the waitress arrived with their meals. Sophie smiled her thanks at the waitress, then met Adam's gaze. Her dark brown eyes flitting with worry.

"Why do you want to know about my family?" Sophie's voice was hesitant.

"Well, have I met them or not? We need to decide."

"Oh, right. I didn't think of that, either." Sophie sighed, resting on her elbows.

Neither had James when he'd come up with this harebrained idea – 'just pretend you're her boyfriend.' Adam started making a mental list of the things he was going to 'thank' James for when he returned.

He waited, patiently, watching her deep in thought. She frowned, fiddling with a paper napkin.

"Is it easier if you haven't met them?" she said.

"Probably. Not really a lie then, is it?" Better to keep this fabrication to a minimum. Believable too, if they had only been seeing each other a few weeks.

Sophie agreed.

"But I might need some background about your family," Adam said. "I mean, it's not like you wouldn't have talked to me about them."

Sophie picked up her fork and sighed. "Okay, I'll fill you in."

As they ate, Adam listened to Sophie explain she'd grown up in Cornwall, and her parents were still living there, although currently on holiday. They had booked a once in a lifetime trip before the wedding had been announced.

"They're probably in Hawaii as we speak," Sophie said, after sipping her coffee. "Sunday, I think they fly to New Zealand."

30

"Nice."

"They decided to retire last year. They owned a couple of restaurants but sold up last autumn," Sophie said. "So, what about your parents?"

"They're in Surrey." Adam didn't look at her. Hell, what should he tell her? He finished his coffee, aware she was watching him, waiting.

"Um... shall we say I haven't met your parents either? Being a bit early in the relationship."

Adam met her gaze and nodded. "Yeah, good idea. I'm not really close to them."

"Oh, I'm sorry."

Now what would it look like if she found out the truth?

He sighed heavily. "They're divorced." That was true.

She finished her cappuccino. Adam felt relieved she was too polite to ask about the gory details – albeit they'd separated fifteen years ago.

"I'll get the bill then." Sophie clutched her purse.

"Wait." Adam grabbed her arm, stopping her rising from the table. "You've got chocolate on your lip." He reached out and gently rubbed the top of her lip with his thumb, removing the smudge.

Sophie flinched, rising out of her chair. She looked mortified, rubbing the same spot on her lip with her own finger automatically. She sure knew how to blush.

"Uh, thanks."

Shit, had he done it again? Moved things too quickly? Had he frightened her?

Once she'd paid, they were back in the car and on the road again. They'd stopped for no longer than an hour.

"Nearly there," Adam said, pointing to the sign on the motorway, 'Welcome To Cornwall'.

"So how did you escape Cornwall and wind up in Surrey?" he

asked, lowering the volume on the radio.

"Oh, I did my degree in Guildford," she replied. "I came straight out of Surrey University and landed this job at Thomas Robotics."

"Do you go home much?"

"Sometimes. My parents tend to visit me though. They like to stay in London, see a play, shop in Oxford Street – that's more my mother rather than Dad."

"Your dad carries the bags," he said.

"Yes, and holds the credit card."

"Of course." Adam chuckled.

After half an hour of winding through the narrow country lanes of Cornwall, their journey ended as they pulled into the drive of Tinners Bay Hotel. A large, five star contemporary hotel was positioned on the hill of Tinners Bay, like someone had sunk a luxury cruise liner into the hillside. It stood three storeys high, with balconies on the top floors to admire the golden sandy beach below.

Adam took a deep breath and cool, salty, sea air filled his lungs. The wind whipped up Sophie's hair, so she turned to face the oncoming wind and looked out towards the ocean.

This was it. Now they started pretending.

Lying.

As they approached the entrance, with the glass doors opening and the doorman greeting them, Adam instantly noticed Sophie slow down. Adam held out his hand, gesturing Sophie to go first. They entered the circular atrium, white and fresh, with the contrast of rich orange and blue furnishings. It had a definite seaside resort feel with bold stripes of colour and plenty of natural light.

Adam gently nudged Sophie in the small of her back to get her walking again. He kept his arm around her as they made their way towards the reception desk, following the porter with their luggage. She nervously glanced around, possibly searching for anyone who would recognise her. He gave her a reassuring squeeze.

"Miss Trewyn. Part of the Staplehurst wedding party," Sophie said to the receptionist.

"I'm sorry, Miss Trewyn. Your room isn't quite ready yet. Please accept our apologies; we had some problems this morning and housekeeping is catching up," the receptionist said with a professional smile, looking up from her computer screen. "Why don't you go through to our lounge and have a complimentary drink? I'll arrange for your luggage to be taken to your room once it is ready." The receptionist had the porter secure their luggage. "If there is anything else you may need, please see our concierge, who will be more than happy to help you."

Sophie slowly nodded, mumbling a thank you.

Adam frowned. She'd come such a long way in the car, opening up, laughing with him, even flirting. Now she'd turned back into the shy, nervous wreck he'd picked up this morning.

"Thank you," he said to the receptionist and grasped Sophie's arm to lead her through to the lounge.

"No, Adam." Sophie placed her arm across his chest to stop him entering the room. "I can't do it."

"Of course you can."

"No, I can't. This is ridiculous. No one will believe it," Sophie replied, her voice low. He could barely hear her. "Let's drive home."

Adam's jaw clenched. There was no way in hell he was driving home. He needed a drink. Strong one, too. He softened his mood, and touching her chin, made her look at him. "I promise, I'll be convincing. I'll be with you every step of the way."

"Adam, I don't doubt you can charm the spots off cheetahs." She nervously fiddled with an earring. "But I don't think they'll believe I'm seeing a guy like you."

Adam chuckled and wrapped his arm firmly around her waist to pull her closer, liking the way she felt against him. Soft. Warm.

33

"Of course they will."

"It's a big lie we are trying to pull off so I can save face," Sophie whispered. She tried to step away, but he kept her held firm against him, so they looked close – like lovers? That's what she wanted, wasn't it?

She hesitantly put her arm around his waist. "I can't believe James talked me into this."

"Look, at first I wasn't too sure about this either, but James is right. We can do this. Hey, we might even have fun." Adam even liked the idea of the challenge.

"But it's foolish. More on my part than anything. I'm lying to my friends and family."

"Sophie, I promised James I wouldn't let you down and I won't. They will never know." He held her hand, and tugged gently. "Now let's get that drink. You may not want one, but I do."

Sophie took two hesitant steps, stopped, bit her lip, and looked him in the eye. "Adam, I'm still not sure about this."

Adam, trying to keep a lid on his impatience, caught someone heading towards them out the corner of his eye and pulled Sophie even closer. His hand pushed back her hair, his thumb brushed her neck, as he whispered into her ear, "Too late."

He breathed, taking in the scent of her hair – coconut, reminding him of Caribbean beaches and the sun. Before he could register the sensation it provoked Sophie had released from his hold, allowing an older woman in her sixties to hug her.

"Sophie! Sweetheart, so glad you could make it," the woman said loudly, her voice echoing through the bar. She kissed Sophie's cheek. "How was the drive down? Not too much traffic I hope."

"Aunt Veronica, lovely to see you." Sophie's smile stiffened. Adam swallowed. "This is my boyfriend, Adam."

Chapter Three

"I'm so sorry about Aunt Veronica." Sophie sighed as Adam opened the door to their room.

"Oh, she was fun." Adam followed her in, surprising Sophie with his relaxed tone.

Veronica had been their first encounter with *family*, and Sophie was amazed at how well Adam had fallen into his role. She'd felt terrible about the lack of warning, but what could she do? If she'd hesitated, it would have made her look a fool. She'd jumped straight in with both feet – either sink or swim.

Adam had swum. He'd kept his arm around her, giving her a gentle squeeze without a flinch. She'd become as stiff as a board in his arms and tried to relax, focussing on the scent of his after-shave, the warmth of his body close to hers. Considering she'd only known him a day, it felt natural to lean into him. Sophie started to feel safe, protected. She didn't want him to let her go. With Adam beside her, she could do this – face her demons. He would be her pillar of strength for this wedding.

And, oh my, was Veronica impressed with him – and who wouldn't be? – beaming away, occasionally cupping his cheek.

How embarrassing!

But it had worked. Veronica certainly believed Adam was her boyfriend.

Did Adam even encounter his girlfriends' families? Was he used to it? She doubted it. He'd sounded nervous in the car when she'd mentioned the 'family' word and confessed he wasn't close to his own.

Sophie was grateful she didn't have to lie to her parents, face to face, about Adam. It was bad enough she'd have to answer some questions over the phone, as they knew she wasn't seeing anyone. And Aunt Veronica liked to chat so it wouldn't take long for the family gossip to reach them.

"Can you afford this, Sophie?" Adam said, breaking Sophie's thoughts. Sophie had been staring out the balcony window, watching the beach below, never tiring to see the ocean. He walked around the luxurious room, admiring its rich blue colours and lavish décor. The luggage had been delivered, as promised by the receptionist.

"It's paid for by the bride's parents – Natalie's parents. Her father owns the hotel." Then added quickly, "That's why I insist on paying for the fuel."

Adam narrowed his eyes, with mischief across his face. "You didn't tell me your family were rich," he said, raising an eyebrow. He acquainted himself with every detail in the large room.

"Not really. The bride's father is a rich man, yes. But I won't be inheriting any of his money. Natalie and I are only second cousins."

"Drink?" He pulled a small bottle of white wine from the mini-bar and offered it to Sophie, who shook her head. He put the bottle back. "Shame about Natalie's father."

She eyed him suspiciously. "Why?"

"Hoped he'd own a factory and need robotics." He grinned.

"Okay, now I'm seeing the real Adam Reid. Mr Workaholic." She placed her hands on her hips, mockingly.

Adam shrugged. "Worth a try. Thought I could have picked up a sale while I was here ... nothing ventured, nothing gained."

Sophie clicked her tongue. "You said you needed a break. Forget about work. Besides, I'm sure the M.D. of Thomas Robotics wouldn't thank you for the extra effort."

Adam opened his mouth, as if to say something, but nodded instead. "You're right, I do need a holiday."

Sophie removed her jacket and stared at the bed. It was huge - a super king, dominating the room, a dark blue quilt covering it. Oh, hell, she hadn't thought about sleeping arrangements.

"Look, I'm sorry about the bed. I didn't think about it when I confirmed. You can take it; I'll have the chaise longue," she said, gesturing to the long, royal blue couch beside the balcony.

"You can take the bed. I'll sleep on there."

"No, I insist. I dragged you down here. It's the least I can do."

Adam chuckled, removing his tie, and unbuttoning the top of his shirt. "I've slept in much worse places than a sofa in a five star hotel."

"Really?" She smirked, trying not to be distracted by his sexy, laid-back state as he removed his cufflinks and rolled up his sleeves, revealing strong, tanned forearms. She had to get used to this. "You don't look the sort to rough it."

"I used to camp – as a kid."

Luckily, he didn't unbutton any more of his shirt, though Sophie really wanted to see what he was made of underneath. Oh God, this weekend was going to be intense. Day one and already drooling over him.

He appeared so relaxed and she needed to calm down, before he thought she was a nervous mess.

"Well, in that case, if things get pretty bad, you can always pitch a tent on the golf course."

"Things won't get bad," Adam said, sounding more serious than Sophie had intended her joke.

Sophie smiled. "Good." She turned and started to lift her case, thinking unpacking would probably be a better way of spending her time than watching Adam – though he was very hard not to watch. She wouldn't get bored, that was for certain.

"Here, let me help you." Adam grabbed hold of the handle, his arm brushing hers, and lifted the luggage onto the stand beside the wardrobe.

"Thank you," she said, knowing she should move out of his personal space, but found herself entranced by him. Sophie unzipped her case and started to hang her clothes. Adam did the same, emptying his own case.

"No problem." He gave a genuine smile and that small gesture lifted her heart. The perfect gentleman. Would she get used to being in his company all weekend?

She hadn't been prepared for how nice he would be, having it in her head you couldn't trust the ridiculously good looking ones; they only knew how to hurt you, cause damage. She'd been fretting about whether they would get on, whether the conversations would go down like lead. But on the journey here, he'd done everything right. She imagined him arrogant, yet he'd been charming. The impression she received from James was Adam had a different girl on his arm every time James saw him. She wondered whether he was the sort to settle for one girl...like Sophie.

Not that Adam would be even remotely interested in her. Of course he wouldn't. Scruffy engineer on the arm of an immaculate account manager – *I don't think so.*

But then, maybe Sophie had him all wrong, and she shouldn't judge him on what James had said. They're men after all. They see things in completely different ways. Maybe he just hasn't found the right woman to settle down with...

Head out of the clouds, girl. You've watched too many chick flicks!

She remembered his touch in the roadside cafe, wiping the chocolate from her lip and she'd panicked, not prepared for how good his touch felt, how she liked it. She needed to get control of her irrational response to this man. But was it irrational? He was absolutely gorgeous. It took every inch of self-control not to touch him, smell him – or kiss him.

Get a grip! The man's doing you a favour, the least you can do is stop gawping. Everything is imaginary.

Although there was no need to pretend now, in the safety of this room, no one observing. They were acting normally around one another. And it felt nice. She could be herself, not worry what others were thinking – except for Adam. She'd probably always worry about what he thought.

As she grabbed another hanger from the rail, she remembered last night, fretfully packing, going through her wardrobe and trying everything on, worrying because she'd be hanging on Adam's arm. She had to look the part. Adam had class. She was grateful her mother had insisted on all those shopping trips, because what good clothes she owned were thanks to Mum.

"By the way, you're out with the boys tonight," she said. Adam looked at her with surprise. "Sorry," she cringed, "I'm going out with the girls."

"You don't need to apologise. It'll be good to meet the groom and the best man."

Sophie's expression dropped, and she busied herself, continuing to unpack her case. "Yeah, yeah, it will."

Perfect opportunity right there. He has to know the truth.

She'd tell him once she'd showered.

***

While Adam finished hanging his shirts in the wardrobe, he churned over something Veronica had said.

39

"Ah yes, your boyfriend – the one you haven't told us enough about."

Veronica spoke as if she'd heard about him, as if Sophie had been dating him for a while. They'd only agreed to this last Friday. He needed to talk to her. She wasn't telling him everything.

Adam didn't like being lied to and if this was to work...

A knock at the door broke his train of thought. He looked towards the bathroom where the shower was still running.

As the knock repeated, harder, he shook his head, hurrying to open the door.

"Oh, you must be the boyfriend." A young woman grinned, looking Adam up and down as she leaned against the doorframe. She looked similar in age to Sophie, with short, black, bobbed hair and a pretty face. In her arms she held a long, burnt orange, satin dress wrapped in clear plastic. "She wasn't letting on much about you, when we spoke the other week."

Adam's eyebrows knitted. *The other week?*

"Adam," he replied, holding out his hand. The young woman shook it, moving a little closer towards him, her large, blue, confident eyes fixed on him. He smiled.

"Cassie." The woman grinned back. "I'm a friend of Sophie's, although technically we are related in some way, but it's far too complicated to explain." Cassie spoke fast, rolling her eyes. She tried glancing over his shoulder. "Is Sophie there?"

"She's in the shower at the moment. Do you want to come in?"

"Oh, no, no, so much stuff to do, being the chief and all. Janice – the bride's mother – is sending me on all sorts of errands."

"Chief?"

Cassie laughed. "Hey, not as in Indian," she did a little impression patting her hand over her mouth, "but as in bridesmaid."

Adam nodded. "Ah, I see."

Cassie held out the dress in both arms. "Okay, well, as I said, busy, busy, busy. So this is Sophie's dress. Tell her Aunt Rose will adjust it further if it needs it."

More aunts. Adam needed to keep up.

He took the satin dress from Cassie, looking at it, frowning.

"She didn't tell you she was a bridesmaid?"

Adam's eyes widened as he looked at her, but he shook off the surprise.

"Probably slipped her mind," he said, shrugging calmly. "She's been under pressure at work lately."

"Bloody hell, where'd she get you?" Cassie playfully nudged him, giving him an appreciative glance up and down. "Please tell me you have a brother."

"Sorry, only child."

"Bum!" She snapped her fingers, then gave a wicked smile. "Sophie's far too modest for her own good. I approve already." Cassie winked at him and Adam couldn't help but smile. "Boy, you'll knock the socks off Simon."

"Simon?"

"Simon. You know, her ex-boyfriend?"

Adam stared at Cassie blankly. His expression sobered and his stomach dropped into his gut. Cassie cringed.

"She didn't tell you about Simon, either? Okay, Cass, you've said enough." Cassie backed away. "Shit! Okay, tell Soph I said hi, and I'll see you both later." She called out as she walked down the corridor, "We're all meeting downstairs in the bar at eight."

Adam closed the door, shaking his head. Bubbly girl, although he had the impression there was a screw loose. He hung up the dress in the wardrobe with the rest of Sophie's things.

So she's a bridesmaid? And there's an ex-boyfriend.

James, what have you got me into?

"Who was it?" Adam turned to find Sophie in one of the hotel bathrobes, with her hair wrapped up in a white towel. Her face shone, her cheeks were rosy from the steam. He swallowed, imagining her body moist, fresh and naked underneath.

"I heard voices," she said.

"Cassie."

"Ah, yes, sorry. Should have explained about Cassie. She's completely off her rocker, but a really sweet friend." Sophie chewed her lip, then hesitant, she asked, "What did she want?"

"She came to drop off your *bridesmaid* dress."

"Oh, um, I was going to tell you. Honestly, I was."

"You were coming to this wedding with or without me," Adam said, frowning with confusion. A shot of anger pulsed through him. Had she tricked him into coming away with her? James had been the one who'd talked him into it – so he couldn't get mad at her. Not yet.. "You were never going to cancel, were you?"

Sophie met Adam's gaze and then quickly looked at the floor, shoving her hands into the robe's pockets.

"And I've been trying to work out something your aunt said earlier, about you mentioning a boyfriend but not going into detail. Then Cassie said she'd talked to you over a week ago about *me*. We only arranged this last week. So how do they know about *us* already?"

Sophie sighed and dropped onto the chaise longue, wrapping her arms around herself. "They all assumed from the beginning I had a boyfriend, so I played along with it. I thought, by the time the wedding arrived, I might have found someone to come with me, and then I wouldn't have been lying."

"But you didn't find a boyfriend, did you?"

"No, because I didn't even try. Hardly going to find him down The White Lion on a Friday night." She looked up at him and then shrugged her shoulders. "Which I'm fine with. I don't need or want a boyfriend. If they hadn't jumped to conclusions…"

"It seems a bit much to cancel, especially as you're part of the wedding party. They're your friends and family. They'd understand. You don't seem the type of person to let people down." James always spoke highly of Sophie – she was always the one who was there to the end, getting a project finished. She'd had a nerve to call *him* a workaholic earlier.

She didn't look at him, staring out the balcony window. Any anger he had been feeling vanished with the devastation he'd seen in her face. Adam sat beside her.

"That's not all of it, is it?" He rested his hand on her shoulder and resisted pulling her into him, fighting the desire to inhale the scent of soap lingering on her. "Simon is the real reason you didn't want to come to this wedding?"

"How'd you know –?" She instantly turned to meet his eye. "Oh, let me guess, Cassie and her big mouth?"

Adam watched her closely. He squeezed her shoulder. Something was eating away at her. He had a knack of knowing when someone wasn't telling him everything – usually applied to sales negotiations. He was also good at keeping his own secrets. But he needed some answers for this weekend to be effective. And he certainly didn't like seeing her this anxious. They'd come a long way today, and he'd only just started seeing her relax.

"Sophie, for this to work, I need to know what's going on. I can't play along if I don't know everything."

Sophie nodded. "I wanted to tell you. I needed to find the right moment. It felt so…" Sophie sighed, met his gaze and then stared at her hands in her lap.

He waited patiently.

"Simon's the best man," she said.

"And?"

"And the reason I didn't want to come here on my own."

Chapter Four

"Sophie, are you ready?"

"Just finishing my make-up!" Sophie called from the bathroom.

Adam looked at his watch. They had five minutes yet, but what was it that took a woman so long? He smiled to himself, rubbing his brow. She might be a plain Jane in the office, but it didn't mean that she'd make less of an effort to look nice. *Let her take her time.* She wouldn't be the first woman to keep him waiting... and unlikely to be the last.

She's probably anxious too. He could feel his own nerves with the idea of going downstairs and performing. Especially now the stakes were bigger for him, up against an ex-boyfriend.

"Okay, I'm ready," Sophie said, emerging from the bathroom, clipping her small, glittery handbag closed and putting it over her shoulder.

Adam cleared his throat and smiled, staring at her transformation. *Wow.* She wore more make-up than she'd been wearing today, or down the pub when he'd first seen her. She was definitely dressed for a night out, not to blend in with her engineering colleagues. If her appearance this morning was a surprisingly pleasant change, tonight she was devastatingly sexy, intending to create a stir – a midnight-blue, strapless dress clinging to her figure perfectly, cut above the knee, heels and jewellery. She looked like a woman he'd love to have on his arm.

"How do I look?" she asked, smoothing her dress.

Did James – and the rest of the design team for that matter – even realise they had a beautiful woman in their department? Why would she hide herself in the background?

And she really did have great legs.

You made James another promise, remember. Stop thinking about her.

But was her effort for him, or Simon? And why did that thought grate upon him?

Sophie shook her head. "Oh sorry, what a typical thing to ask. You don't have to answer it."

Realising he'd taken too long to respond, he said, "I was going to say you look good." Which was an understatement, stunning was more like it, but Adam decided it was best to keep his thoughts to himself. He needed to play this cool where Sophie was concerned.

Sophie let out a laugh. Something, or someone, had really hit her confidence, and he wanted to know why.

"So, how do I look?" Adam asked, straightening his tie and adjusting his black jacket.

"You know damn well how good you look."

He gave a sly smile and they walked out of their hotel room.

***

As the lift door opened they could see across the atrium and into the bar. A small crowd waited for them. Sophie took a deep calming breath, trying to not let her nerves get the better of her. She glanced at Adam. He appeared relaxed. She should do the same. She had a very handsome, competent man holding her hand – literally. She'd be fine. Relax.

"Sophie!" Cassie shouted across the bar, waving at them.

"Here goes nothing," Adam whispered in her ear, wrapping his arm around Sophie's waist, pulling her closer to him. To everyone watching it probably looked like an affectionate whisper, a kiss. She slid her arm around him. She realised she had a tight grip on his jacket, and loosened it.

No need to show everyone the whites of your knuckles.

"Hi, everyone, this is Adam." Sophie made her introductions, noticing Adam still kept his arm around her, keeping her close. She really liked it – so reassuring. "Adam, this is Cassie, who you've already met. She's Natalie's cousin and a friend of mine."

"Hello, handsome. You're sure you haven't got a brother?" Cassie winked at Adam, grinning at him. He laughed, shaking his head. "I've known Sophie for years." She mischievously pinched Sophie. "Any secrets you want to know, I'm the person to tell you."

Adam looked at Cassie with intrigue. "Secrets… okay."

Sophie scowled at her.

"Only kidding!" Cassie held her hands up and backed off, winking again at Adam.

"This is Natalie, the bride." Natalie gave a little wave. "Gareth, the groom." Gareth shook Adam's hand firmly. "And…" Sophie hesitated, "this is Simon, the best man."

He hadn't changed, not really. Still the broad shoulders, muscles defined by his hard work as a builder. He owned a construction company now. When she'd met him, he'd always been sporty, so his physique had been impressive. He hadn't lost it. Dark, short hair and mischievous eyes; distinctive looks that got him a long way, especially with the girls. She could see why she'd fallen for him – yet now he didn't seem so attractive. Now she knew what he was capable of.

"Hi." Simon shook Adam's hand, too. Sophie noticed Simon made little eye contact with Adam, watching her instead. She couldn't look him in the eye, instead ignored him, talked with the other guests. This was harder than she thought. She'd managed to avoid him for so long, but it still wasn't any easier. Thank God she had Adam standing beside her. Her pillar of strength, her superhero – minus the tights.

"We're waiting on the mums and then we'll leave you boys in peace." Cassie joyfully slapped Simon on the back.

"Good," Simon responded, as two older couples approached the crowd.

"Those are the bride and groom's parents," Sophie whispered in Adam's ear, now clutching his hand. It felt strange, but he'd squeeze it occasionally, like a silent message, telling her everything was working. She was grateful for it. She still wasn't happy about this lie and was still wondering whether they would pull it off, but she had to stop worrying. Why wouldn't her family and friends believe it?

They *were* accepting it. So start believing, too.

The parents joined the group, Cassie making the introductions and Adam shook hands with each of them, giving his friendly smile.

As Adam talked, Sophie watched the group fall for his charm. Every now and then he'd make subtle loving gestures to her, squeezing her hand or stroking her arm, which she played along with. Adam pulled off the act superbly; however she felt nervous and hot. Did it show? She didn't want to give the game away.

A part of her wondered if the heat radiating from her was due to him. It had been a very long time since she'd received these sorts of loving gestures. But she had to remember it was an act. She just hadn't anticipated how great it would feel.

Listening to the women whilst Adam spoke with the men, Sophie felt something stroke her lower back, brushing across her bottom. She wasn't sure where it came from, what or who it was. She subtly checked. Adam's hands were clearly where they should be, one holding her hand, the other gesturing as he spoke. So, was it Adam? Had he done so before taking her hand? No, she was sure he wouldn't do anything unless it was necessary. He knew exactly how far to take this and wouldn't cross any lines – not that they'd discussed the lines. Maybe they should have? He'd made his whispers look like kisses, brushed her hair, but nothing he shouldn't do. He wouldn't take liberties – in the whole day she'd been with him, he'd always been a gentleman.

She glanced around to see Simon wink at her. Adam hadn't noticed a thing. Or had he, choosing to ignore it? Maybe Simon had brushed past her accidentally, although it had felt deliberate.

"Right, come on, girls, taxi's outside," Cassie said. "Time to leave, otherwise the others will wonder where the hell we are."

"Will you be okay?" Sophie whispered to Adam.

"Of course," Adam replied. "I'll wait in the atrium for you later. Enjoy yourself, sweetheart." A sly smile spread across his lips as he spoke the word 'sweetheart'. No one else would have spotted it but Sophie, who playfully narrowed her eyes.

"You'll be back before me, will you?"

"More than likely. You're out with Cassie and I can't see her coming home early."

Sophie giggled. She hesitated, staying within his hold. *This is where you would ordinarily kiss him goodbye.* She moved towards him to plant a kiss, a peck on his cheek, but he moved, making sure her lips met his.

They hadn't discussed kissing! Why hadn't they discussed kissing?

If hot with nerves before, she was on fire now. His soft but determined, warm lips pressed against hers. The heat rose in her cheeks.

He held her close and moved his lips to her ear. "Don't give the game away – always on the mouth." Again, he could have been whispering sweet nothings. His warm breath on her neck sent an electric pulse of pleasure down her spine. How was she going to last a weekend with him and not make a fool of herself?

He brushed her hair back gently with his fingers and then let her go. She looked him in the eye, giving him a smile.

Was it normal to want to kiss him again?

"I'll see you later," she said, hesitating.

"Come on, love birds!" Cassie grabbed Sophie by the arm, and pulled her away from Adam. "Adam, I promise I'll bring her back in one piece." She chuckled mischievously. "One drunken piece."

Adam smiled at Cassie, shaking his head. Simon approached Sophie and Cassie, his back to Adam and the other men, putting an arm around each of their waists. He let go of Cassie, but kept hold of Sophie.

"Don't worry, Sophie, I'll keep Adam out of mischief. You can trust me."

Trust?

There, again, his hand on her bum! She glared at him, releasing his grip, stepping away, closer to Cassie. She glanced at Adam. Could he see?

Worried her expression showed her anger, she faked a smile and waved at Adam, then linked an arm through Cassie's and Natalie's.

It felt alien to have Simon anywhere near her, dragging up old feelings, torturing her all over again. Simon would never be forgiven.

***

Adam watched the women leave the hotel, giggling and talking. He disliked how Simon had wrapped his arm around Sophie like he had some privilege. It didn't take a psychologist to work out

Sophie didn't like it – he'd observed her irritated reaction to Simon.

Simon clapped his hands then, rubbing his palms together, walked towards the group of men. "Right, gentlemen, I've got the perfect place for us to start off the night."

"Simon, a quiet night was the plan," Gareth said, frowning.

"Nah, what's the fun in that?" Simon replied, grinning, revealing perfect teeth.

Teeth Adam could quite easily break. He was only just getting to know Sophie, but already he had this primeval instinct to protect her against this man. Simon had to be the reason why Sophie wanted to cancel on this weekend.

"Don't fret, Gareth. We're staying in the town, wouldn't want to bump into the girls," Simon continued. "But this is one of your last nights of freedom. You need to let your hair down, mate."

Gareth wasn't happy. Adam had his own impression of Simon forming now, and it wasn't a good one. It was a gut feeling, but he could be wrong. Sophie hadn't reacted to Simon by flying off the handle, so it was best to play along. To be the perfect boyfriend.

Chapter Five

The music drummed loudly in the packed club. The rammed dance floor bobbed like a choppy sea, dark silhouettes moving against the multi-coloured lights.

Sophie watched from the table, perched on a stool and swayed to the music, sipping her drink. She used to love dancing, but now she feared the hassle of it. A girl couldn't just get lost on the dance floor. It was practically a cattle market, with men watching the women like farmers picking a prized cow. She didn't fancy that bit any more. Yes, she would probably meet a nice enough guy, eventually, but how many others would she have to waste her time on before she found him? How many might hurt her?

However, if she'd conquered the fear, gone out more, rather than just down the White Lion on a Friday evening, she wouldn't have needed Adam here this weekend to hold her hand.

"So, come on, spill the beans - where'd you find him, Soph?" Cassie said loudly, leaning against the tall table they'd all circled around. Natalie sat next to Sophie, grinning, waiting patiently to hear her gossip. Cassie sipped her wine, then turned back to another girl, nudging her. "Sophie's got one hell of a man. Drop. Dead. Gorgeous."

"Cass, please." Sophie fought the urge to tell her friend the truth. After the wedding, in a month or so, she could admit it, if she had to.

"Come on, where did you meet him?"

"At work – we were both at some guy's retirement party and hit it off." Sophie took a sip of her own wine. She wanted to gulp it down, but knew she needed to keep her head straight. She hated lying to her friend, a good friend whom she wouldn't normally keep secrets from. But if she confided, and the lie got out, she'd look more of an idiot. So would Adam. It was best kept between her and Adam.

"You hold on to him, girl."

"Yeah, he's a good one," Natalie said, raising her glass.

"I intend to," Sophie replied, swallowing the lie as she swallowed more of her wine. Although somewhere lurking in the back of her mind, a small voice wished she could keep Adam. That kiss had really been no more than a peck, like lovers kissed, but she could still feel the pressure of his lips against hers and hoped she'd feel it again. More than likely she would. Lovers had to kiss, right?

But they hadn't discussed kissing – she hadn't even thought about it. She hadn't been kissed in a while and she hoped it didn't show. Adam had said 'experienced' in the car, and she doubted he was only talking about his job. A man like Adam knew how to make a woman tremble at the knees just by smiling at her.

Sophie's mind wandered back to Simon and his display in the bar earlier. Seeing Simon again had put her head in a spin and brought back memories, as she'd feared. Some good, but mostly bad. After all this time she still found it hard to face him. Had he brushed past her accidentally or deliberately? When they'd been about to leave, that had been most definitely deliberate.

Had Adam noticed Simon's hand on her backside? She'd wanted to say something to Simon right then, but knew it wouldn't be good to make a scene. This was Gareth and Natalie's weekend. But what was he playing at? It had been over four years since she'd seen him. She'd been successful in avoiding him, thanks to her parents insisting on visiting her, rather than Sophie coming home.

Was he jealous and therefore trying to make Adam jealous? Sophie resisted laughing to herself. Adam wasn't going to get jealous - but would he act that way for her, for this weekend's performance?

But then jealousy wasn't a quality she liked. So she hoped Adam would rise above it and not show any reaction, making him the better man. He was a better man.

A much better man who she couldn't have. *Pretend, remember?*

She sipped her drink. Luckily, Natalie and Cassie had dashed off to the ladies', leaving her alone with her glum thoughts.

"You're not for me, Sophie," Simon had said. Excuses of course, but had there truth in them? He'd thundered into her life, then back out again, like a storm. "We're not right for each other like I thought we were. You don't know how to love."

She didn't know how to love. Apparently, she was... *No, don't go there.* She obliterated the words from her mind and finished her wine to loosen the tightness in her throat.

If only she could prove him wrong. But for real. Not with pretend boyfriends.

He doesn't need know it's fake.

Simon's touch had surprised her, too. She was shocked at how much she didn't like it any more. She didn't remember Simon being like this before – not really. A flirt with the ladies, yes. But acting like an arse now certainly wasn't going to help improve her feelings towards him. Was Adam getting on with him? She shouldn't worry. Adam looked like a man who could handle himself and besides, Gareth was there. He'd be fine.

Natalie squeezed through the busy club and stood beside her at the table. "Save me from Cassie," she said, swaying, shaking Sophie from her thoughts. "I swear, she drinks like a fish and cannot be removed from the dance floor without heavy machinery!"

Sophie giggled at her friend, who had a hideous fluorescent pink veil stuck in her hair – it was a good distraction from her bleak thoughts. Her smile dropped as she saw a woman go up to the bar, luckily ignoring Sophie.

Zoe.

"I didn't invite her here tonight," Natalie whispered. "She still lives locally. Probably meeting friends."

"Good." Sophie grabbed her next drink lined up on the table and took a gulp of it, turning her back on the woman. Zoe was another reason why she didn't like coming home.

"But she might be coming to the wedding – only the evening do though," Natalie nervously confessed, wincing. "Sorry."

Sophie shrugged and took another gulp of her wine. Maybe getting drunk was the answer. She would blank the woman, pretend she didn't recognise her – unless she had Adam on her arm, of course. *Oh, now she liked that idea.*

"Shall we go to the beach tomorrow morning?" Cassie said, intruding drunkenly into their conversation, nestling between Sophie and Natalie.

"Uh, I don't know..."

"Go on, Soph. It'll be a laugh. We'll all go. Smarmy Simon did suggest it and you can show him what a fool he was to let you go – you know, drape yourself over Adam in your very best bikini." She grinned at Sophie, then hiccupped.

"I didn't bring one." Compulsive liar, now.

"You can borrow one of mine."

Sophie swallowed. Cassie's idea of a bikini was three triangles and bits of string, or the equivalent thereof – and she had the boobs to fill them.

"Sounds like a great idea! We can kill a couple of hours, top up our tans and play volley ball," Natalie said.

Sophie could have slapped Natalie – metaphorically of course. *Get out of this one, Batman.*

She'd feel more comfortable on the beach in a bikini if Adam wasn't there. She secretly prayed for rain tomorrow morning. *Note to self: wake up early and do rain dance.* As long as sunshine arrived for Saturday, Sophie would be guilt free.

"Agreed. So, are you two dancing or what?" Cassie bellowed over the loud music that suddenly seemed to get louder. "You'd better not be daydreaming about lover-boy."

Sophie laughed, shaking her head.

"Come on, this is my favourite song. Let's dance." Cassie pulled her from the stool, grabbing Natalie with her other arm and any other friends on her way. "I've seen a TDH on the dance floor." Sophie and Natalie looked at each other, frowning. "Tall, dark and handsome. Come on, then we can hit the tequila!"

Oh, bloody hell.

***

"Simon says, another beer!"

Gareth shook his head slowly.

"Gareth, don't be such a lightweight," Simon slurred. "It's Simon Says, remember?"

Gareth looked tired and unsteady on his feet, the bar supporting him. Adam had been doing him a favour most of the night, hiding the copious number of pints Simon had tried to feed him.

"He's had enough. We don't need him in hospital for alcohol poisoning two nights before his wedding," Adam said, trying to make a joke about it. But it wasn't working. Gareth sat on one side of him at the bar and Simon stood on the other. Only the three of them now. The fathers of the bridal couple had long since retired.

They'd come out for a few and then headed back to the hotel. Various friends of Simon's and Gareth's had also been and gone.

"Ah, he'll be all right," Simon said, elbows resting on the bar. "Simon says, another!"

Adam held up his pint glass and shook his head. "No, I'm fine."

"Lightweight," Simon muttered, catching the attention of the barman and holding his glass up to him, nodding.

"So, how'd you meet Sophie?" he asked, turning to Adam.

Adam swallowed his mouthful of Cornish ale before answering. He'd been waiting for this question all evening. "We met at an office party."

"Yeah? What do you do?"

"I'm an account manager." That's all Simon needed to know as far as Adam was concerned.

Simon nodded, as if he knew what that meant. Adam tried not to smirk.

"You know we were once an item, don't you?" Simon smiled arrogantly and Adam badly wanted to wipe the grin off his face.

"Yes, so she said." Adam met Simon's eyes. Simon was probably too drunk to realise Adam was watching for a reaction, not intimidated by him. But Simon seemed confident, continuing to talk about her, like he knew her better than anyone. He did know her better than Adam – but that would change by the end of this weekend.

"Yeah, she's a smart girl." Simon nodded as he said the words. "Smart girl. Shame I didn't realise it back then." The barman handed Simon another pint of ale. "But things got too heavy. Talking about marriage, kids, that sort of thing." Adam kept his surprise in check. "But we were younger then. It's different now." Simon slapped Adam on the back. "You got a great girl there, Adam. Hold on to her."

She's a woman. A beautiful woman.

Adam nodded, keeping his eyes fixed on Simon. "I intend to."
Especially if it's the only way to keep your hands off her.

As he took a sip from his beer, Adam glanced at the entrance to the wine bar, noticing two women come in. Straight away, Simon headed over in their direction and started chatting them up, encouraging them to join him. Simon wasn't ugly and he knew it, so it wasn't long before the two women were at the bar with him. Simon had his arm draped over one girl's shoulder, the other encouraged to stand beside Gareth. She gave Adam a flirtatious glance, but he kept his cool. *Not interested.*

Simon nudged Adam. "Now the fun begins."

The woman made her move on Gareth. Flirting, playing with his tie, hair, ears.

Adam didn't pick up girls for the night any more. Yes, it was usually how it started, getting chatted up, but he liked to at least get a number, take them to dinner – a date. His relationships were short, but not that short. Gareth certainly wasn't interested – he was batting the woman off as if swatting flies.

"Look, lady, you're nice and all, but I'm not interested." Gareth stood up from the bar, walking away, escaping the woman. "I'm getting married Saturday." Angered and flustered, he paced the bar, then pointed at Simon. "If this was your idea –"

"Oh, come on, Gareth. Make the most of your freedom before they lock the ball and chain around your ankle for good. Simon says –"

"I don't give a monkeys what Simon says! I told you." Gareth lunged; Adam instantly reacted, stopping him from shoving Simon.

"Hey, hey, come on." Adam stood between the two men, watching Gareth, but with Simon in view as well.

"Gareth, lighten up, it's a bit of fun."

"Simon, why don't you drop it," Adam said, turning towards him, trying to control his own anger. Gareth needed him to keep his cool. "Gareth obviously isn't interested."

"Why don't you sod off out of it, Adam?"

"No. You sod off," Gareth said, moving out of Adam's grasp and shoving Simon. "I'm sick of Simon says." Adam grabbed Gareth's arm and pulled him back, putting an arm around his shoulder. The drink was talking for these two. Simon held his hands up, unfazed by his friend's attempt to attack and shook his head, smirking.

"Why don't we head back to the hotel?" Adam patted Gareth on the back and led him towards the door. "The ladies should be getting back soon, too." He raised his eyebrows at Simon, a subtle warning to let them pass. Simon stood aside, still drinking his pint.

"Hey, if you two lightweights don't mind, I'm going to hang about here."

***

"Cigar?" Adam took a cigar out of his inside pocket and offered it to Gareth as they walked along the narrow road towards the hotel. Simon had handed them out earlier and now he was glad he'd held onto the two he'd taken. Adam only smoked the occasional cigar, normally amongst clients, but now seemed a good time.

"Thanks." Gareth took the cigar, putting it in his mouth and Adam lit it, then his own.

They had a climb ahead of them, but he could see the hotel lit up on the hillside. The tide was up, the waves crashed onto the beach. The moon illuminated their narrow road as the streetlights were at a dull minimum.

"Thanks, Adam, for back there." Gareth thumbed behind him, slightly out of breath and then slung his free hand in his pocket. Adam watched Gareth walk, drunkenly weaving along the pavement. He didn't need him falling over and getting a black eye – or worse. Try explaining that to the bride. And the wedding photographer. He put his arm on the man's shoulder, subtly supporting him.

"No problem. Don't need two best friends falling out before the big day. And over a couple of birds!" Adam laughed.

"Oh, please don't tell Natalie."

"I won't." Adam shook his head. He gave a sly smile at Gareth, who smiled back, shaking his head.

"And that means don't tell Sophie either. You know how women talk." Adam's eyes widened. "Hey, Natalie will be fine with it really. We trust each other, you know? But she's likely to kill Simon. So until after the wedding, right?" Gareth laughed. "Or I'll be left without a best man."

Adam chuckled, puffing at his own cigar.

"I know he can be an arse at times, but why'd he have to pull a stunt like that?" Gareth ran his hand through his hair, then placed it back in his pocket. "I'm getting married, for Christ sake! Just because he can't keep his knob inside his pants..."

Adam raised his eyebrows, intrigued. He'd thought about seeing if Simon could shed some light on why Sophie was acting oddly, but had chosen to leave it be. Sophie wouldn't have been happy having him delve where he shouldn't go. And besides, what would he have looked like? The jealous boyfriend? He didn't want to look as if he had anything to be jealous about. That would wind Simon up more than anything. Gareth might be able to give him some insight to the bloke, what Sophie had been attracted to. Because at the moment he couldn't see why Sophie, as smart as she was, had fallen for Simon. Gareth was right; the man was an arse.

"Maybe he doesn't know you as well as you thought."

Gareth laughed. "Yeah, I should have known, really. Simon only looks out for number one, after all. And thinks with his dick most of the time."

"So why is he your best man?" Adam asked, scratching his head.

"From what I see, you're nothing alike."

Gareth shrugged. "I've known him so long. We grew up together. We've always been 'best friends'. But he changed when he hit puberty." Gareth chuckled and Adam watched with interest. Gareth continued, "I'm not sure when exactly, but all of a sudden girls came into the equation. He became very popular with the girls and it gave him a new kind of confidence."

"So why'd you stick around with him?"

Gareth shook his head, exhaling the smoke of his cigar. Both men's breathing had become heavier with their climb. "I don't know. We each had our own set of friends at uni, and we were studying different things – only natural." Adam nodded, listening to Gareth. "But after uni, we met up, hung out, went to a match together, that sort of thing. I started seeing Natalie one summer and through us, he met Sophie. I suppose, when it doesn't come down to girls, he's all right really. We've bailed each other out occasionally." Gareth looked Adam in the eye. "You must have a friend that gets on your nerves at times, but you still wouldn't be without."

Adam thought of James, who'd got him into this mess. A part of him was already planning on how to kill him. And a small, ridiculous part wanted to thank him. James had started at the company as an apprentice at the same time Adam had stepped off the factory floor and into the offices. He'd been glad to meet someone close to his age and interested in similar things. They might be chalk and cheese, but along the way they'd become good friends. Yeah, James drove him mad at times, but he'd become a very good, trusted friend. Not an arse like Simon though. He was more like Gareth actually, his life settled with Kate.

"Yeah, yeah, I do, actually." Adam smiled.

Chapter Six

"Hey, how'd it go?"

Sophie approached Adam, finding him waiting in reception as promised. He stood up from the leather sofa and she reached up, giving him a gentle kiss on the lips, remembering what he'd said. Heavens, did that feel good – and odd. Luckily, the alcohol in her veins meant she didn't care. She relaxed when he smiled. Then she frowned, noticing he was on his own.

"Where are the others?"

"Gareth has gone up to his room, and Simon isn't back yet. We left him to it."

"Oh."

"I'll tell you in the morning." Adam glanced over to spot Cassie talking to a group of people, and she waved at Adam.

"More family and friends arriving." Sophie took Adam's wrist and glanced at his watch. "Do you want to be introduced?"

"Can it wait?" He wrapped his arm around her waist and pulled her tightly towards him.

"Yeah, it can wait." Relaxing into one another felt natural, but was it alcohol fuelled? Whatever, it did feel rather wonderful, like she had her safety net back. Sophie waved back at Cassie. "I'm tired, too."

"Then let's go to bed." Sophie looked at him. He subtly chuckled.

"You know what I mean."

They headed towards a pair of lifts and Adam pressed the call button, keeping Sophie close to him. She rested into him, tiredness creeping into her bones, wanting to drop the pretence in front of her friends and family. To her relief, the lift door opened and they stepped in.

Adam pressed their floor button, and turned to face Sophie. If she could feel it, he could too – all eyes were on them. The lift doors started closing and he slowly leaned towards her, his eyes meeting hers. He moved towards her gradually, glancing to her lips, his slightly parted.

Sophie's heart raced. Watching his blue eyes, then his lips. *He's going to kiss me, really kiss me. We haven't discussed this!* The lift doors closed. Adam pulled away with a wink. Sophie breathed out.

But the lift didn't move. The doors pinged and started to open. Adam, startled, instantly planted his lips on Sophie's, pulling her into an embrace, one hand stroking her cheek. Sophie hesitantly ran her fingers through his hair, kissing him back, softening into his hold.

"Oh, sorry!" a man said. A middle-aged couple stood there awkwardly as the doors fully opened. "We'll wait for the other lift."

Sophie pulled out of the kiss, her cheeks red hot. Then, she spied Simon with two women, one clinging to each arm, walking towards them.

"All right, Adam? Sophie!" Simon called out, kissing one of the women, groping at the other. Both women giggled, their hands were all over him. Sophie scowled at the sordid sight.

As Adam reached for the lift button, Sophie instinctively reacted. She grabbed hold of his collar with both hands and kissed him passionately, more lustfully than the kiss they'd just shared. Her breathing was heavy as she wrapped her arms around his neck, pressing her body hard against his, combing her fingers through his hair.

Adam reciprocated, pulling her closer to him. He let out a pleasing groan, urging Sophie to continue. Still embracing each other, lips locked together, tongues caressing, Sophie heard the lift doors close. As soon as she felt the weightless moment of the lift rising, Sophie let go of him, standing back. She straightened her dress and chewed her finger, shuffling from foot to foot.

Sophie hesitantly met Adam's eye. He chuckled, shaking his head.

"The damn lift door wasn't supposed to open. They'd be none the wiser! I was going to–"

"I know." She nervously smiled, concerned her blush showed. Or was the lift hot?

What a kiss. The kiss had been strong. It hadn't felt very pretend, on her part or his.

"And, that then, was for Simon," she said, biting her lip. "Oh, God, that couple – what must they think? I don't usually, you know...what an exhibitionist!" She hadn't kissed like that in a very long time. Heat swelled inside her body, her insides on fire. This evening she'd been dreaming about kissing him again, but nothing so bold.

"I realised."

Sophie was thankful when the lift door opened at their floor. *Much, much cooler in the corridor.*

"You weren't bad," Sophie said, unable to stop herself teasing, as they walked out and headed towards their room. The only way to break the awkwardness the kiss had caused was to joke about it.

"What do you mean, not bad?" Adam sounded outraged.

Sophie giggled in response upon seeing his serious expression.

"So, someone's been on the tequila." Adam grinned back.

"Oh my God!" Sophie covered mouth, astonished he'd tasted the tequila. "Cassie insisted. I did one shot." Adam looked at in

63

disbelief. "Okay, maybe two. Well, you taste of cigars." She pouted, digging him in the ribs.

Was she flirting? Damn, Cassie and her bloody Tequilas.

"I had one with Gareth as we walked back to the hotel." He loosened his tie as they strolled along the corridor.

"Why'd you both leave early, then?"

"Simon tried to set Gareth up with a woman."

Sophie clicked her tongue. "Downstairs – those two women?"

"Yeah. They're the reason we left."

Sophie rolled her eyes. "I am not surprised. He will never change."

"Don't tell Natalie. I made a promise to Gareth."

"I won't."

"I mean it. Apparently, you women talk. He doesn't want Natalie killing the best man before the wedding." Sophie giggled at Adam's worried tone.

They arrived at their door. Adam already had the key card out and let them in. He quickly turned away, walking towards the wardrobe, taking off his jacket. Was he trying to hide his arousal? She'd noticed it, felt it as she'd kissed him. The thought sent delight to her bones. She was thankful, as a woman, she could hide that kind of excitement – but her body pulsed sexual desire.

"I," she hesitated, "I didn't realise I'd have an effect on you." She turned her back on him and winced. *Crikey, maybe I shouldn't have mentioned it.*

"Bloody hell, a kiss like that, the Pope would get turned on!"

"Sorry." She glanced at him and he gave a sly smile.

"Hey, don't apologise – I enjoyed it."

Heat flew to her cheeks again as she blushed. She threw her handbag on the bed and busied herself, slipping off her own jacket and removing her shoes.

Could she keep this up for the whole weekend? She was afraid to admit she was enjoying it, too. It had only been one day. She looked at the bed. They had a night to try yet.

Tonight was a little alcohol induced. Adam had probably had a couple of beers. She'd had a couple of glasses of wine, and a tequila or two. *Sod Cassie!* Enough to allow her to relax, lose some of those inhibitions, give her courage. So she'd reacted upon seeing Simon. Over-reacted more like, the way she'd brazenly kissed Adam. But she'd wanted Simon to see them together.

Proof she was over him. See, she didn't have hang-ups. She wasn't...

She turned and looked at Adam. "I enjoyed it, too," she said, holding onto the pleasant thought of their kiss. "I just didn't think it would feel so..." She shook her head and wandered into the bathroom. Probably best not to have this conversation. She didn't know Adam very well. What if he was very good at... deceiving?

Simon had deceived her.

Adam quickly followed her, hesitating in the doorway. She gave him a smile and he leaned against the doorframe, looking relieved she hadn't told him to go. "Would feel so... what?"

As she removed her make-up, she glanced at him through the mirror.

"It's nothing. We never discussed kissing. And maybe we should have. Obviously, for us to look like a couple in love, we're going to need to kiss." She shrugged. "I never thought..." She hesitated again. Adam looked at her, his blue eyes patient. She frowned and looked back into the mirror, concentrating on removing more of her make-up. "I never thought it would feel like you, uh... meant it."

"It did?" Adam's eyes widened. "I mean, I did. I don't want you to think I'm some sloppy kisser."

Sophie laughed and then sobered. "I'm worried if the truth came out, if James found out."

"He won't, but hey, let's look at it as acting, okay? Actors do it all the time."

"True."

"We both know the score here. Besides this was James' idea, he can hardly judge."

Sophie nodded. He's right. We're just acting. So you happen to enjoy it, a little. It is nice to know what it feels like being on Adam's arm, even if it's a charade. And remember, even though he's kissed me, he hasn't crossed any lines. Not really. Not like Simon. Or had it been in her imagination? Earlier this evening seemed so long ago now, she could barely remember it.

Adam stood there quietly, intrigued, still watching her. Did he want to ask her something?

"What?" She turned to face him.

Adam gently shook himself, as if out of his daydream. "Huh?"

"You're watching me as if a woman removing her make-up is actually fascinating. Surely you've seen plenty of girls remove their make-up, right?" She laughed lightly, looking back into the mirror. She couldn't imagine Adam not having a girlfriend, not when he kissed like that. Dear Lord, what else would he be good at?

Don't even go there.

For a moment he didn't answer. He looked at the floor then glanced back into the mirror to meet her eye. She would never tire of his blue eyes. They were his best feature. Although handsome, his eyes lit up his face, gave it that extra sparkle. Made him stand out from all the rest. And added to his smile... Sophie didn't stand a chance.

"You'd be surprised actually. They seem to want to lock themselves away," he replied, shrugging his shoulder. "I go out with the kind of women who don't like to be seen without their make-up."

"Oh."

Adam stepped into the bathroom, then hesitated. "Sophie, I'm going to sound bang out of order here, but what did you see in

Simon?"

Sophie stared at all her different cosmetic bottles. Every bit of make-up she'd brought with her was in its place. She'd unpacked it on one side of the large vanity area by the sink, while Adam had his toiletries on the other side. She checked some of the caps were on properly, stood up a couple of bottles that had fallen over. She didn't really know how to answer him.

"You're an intelligent woman. I don't understand it." He took off his tie and unbuttoned the top of his shirt. Sophie did her best not to gape. "Look, if you don't want to answer that, then fine. I just don't get it. I'll go make up my bed." Adam turned to walk out of the bathroom.

"I was young, stupid... I don't know." She turned to face him, resting against the sink. "It was my last year in college, just finishing my A-Levels, and Simon kept on asking me out. Eventually I said yes. He was a popular guy in town. Believe it or not, he was a good catch. Maybe I got carried away that he was older. I couldn't really believe he wanted to go out with me, but I agreed, thinking it might stop him hounding me." She chuckled. "A couple of dates, he'd get bored and leave me alone after that."

Adam nodded, letting her speak. He'd moved closer, leaning against the wall with his hands folded in front of him. If she'd been more sober, maybe his handsome looks would have scared her from opening up, but she felt relaxed in his presence. He was safe.

"And on our first date, we hit it off. I didn't even expect it. He charmed me, swept me off my feet. We had more in common than I realised. He treated me like a princess." Sort of, she thought, some of the memories coming back. "He wasn't like what you're seeing now. Our relationship became intense, we couldn't stop seeing one another. We had to be with each other – the whole summer. I thought he was *the one*. And, once I'd truly fallen in love with him, bam. I came home one day and found him in bed

67

with another woman."

And that's when his excuses came. She wasn't good enough, didn't love enough, they weren't compatible. She was too cold.

Adam ran a hand through his hair as she turned away from him. She fiddled once again with things she didn't need to fiddle with. That memory, brought to the surface so quickly, had filled her eyes with tears. She fought to hold them in and it stung. She would not shed another tear over Simon; she'd sworn it a long time ago. She swallowed and with it the pressure behind her eyes ceased. "I know I probably look like I'm overreacting here."

"No, you don't; he hurt you." Adam quickly responded, stepping closer, placing a hand on her shoulder. Before she realised what she was doing, she cushioned her head on his shoulder and he wrapped an arm around her, gently rubbing her back. His scent filled her lungs, his protection enveloping her. It intoxicated her.

"He freaked me out earlier."

"What? How?" Adam made her look at him.

"It's probably my imagination. Forget it." She shook her head. "Look, I need some privacy now. I'll get my pyjamas and change in here; you can change in the bedroom, okay?"

"Yeah, sure." He let Sophie pass. She couldn't meet his gaze. "Hey, Sophie, I'm sorry. It was none of my business."

"No, you need to know, really. You're right. To pull this weekend off, make *us* look believable, you need to know everything." She went to a chest of drawers, pulled out some cotton pyjamas and walked back into the bathroom.

"I'll go get changed then and make up my bed." Adam moved out of the bathroom, closing the door behind him.

Ten minutes later, Sophie emerged from the bathroom, wearing her blue-striped cotton pyjamas, carrying the clothes she'd been wearing that evening.

The lighting had been dimmed. The overhead light turned off, only a lamp by the side of the bed was on. Adam had got some blankets from the wardrobe and was laying them over the chaise longue. Sophie hid her surprised expression. He was wearing some black pyjama bottoms and a dark grey T-shirt. She very much doubted he usually wore anything in bed.

"Hope you don't mind, I grabbed a couple of pillows off the bed," he said, puffing them up and placing them at the top end of the couch.

"Not at all." She placed her clothes tidily on a chair by the dressing table.

"Right, I'll use the bathroom." And he disappeared into the room, closing the door behind him.

Sophie pulled the sheets back to the enormous bed and got in, puffing the pillows up behind her. Adam soon reappeared from the bathroom.

"Night," he said as he got into his bed.

"Adam, you sure you're okay on that sofa?" She watched him try to get comfortable.

"Yeah, I'm fine."

Sophie leaned over and turned the lamp off. She shuffled to get comfortable, pulling the sheets up over her.

She lay there, in the dark. Hotel rooms were always so dark. No streetlights – although a rarity here on the coastal edges of Cornwall – could stream in through the thick lined curtains. Blackness. If it was a clear night, the stars would be on full display. She closed her eyes. Adam on that couch. His feet dangling off the end...

She let out a sigh and switched the lamp back on.

"What's up?"

"Adam, this is ridiculous. We're both two mature adults. This bed is huge. It can practically sleep a whole football team in here, and still have plenty of room."

"Now you're exaggerating."

"Please, get in this bed."

"I'm fine, honest."

"You can't sleep on that sofa!" She jumped out of the bed, her hands on her hips, defiant. "There is so much room in this bed. I won't be able to sleep knowing you're on that thing. I feel guilty enough as it is."

"Sophie, I don't mind."

"Adam, I'm not taking no for an answer. I'm not turning this lamp off until you are in this bed."

"Now there's an offer, a woman ordering me into her bed," he teased. Seeing she was still deadly serious, his tone sobered. "Are you sure?"

"Yes, I am sure," Sophie said impatiently, sighing. "I am sure I'll be able to control myself. How about you?"

He chuckled, shaking his head in defeat. "Okay, okay." He grabbed his pillows and walked around to the other side of the bed. Sophie got back in. He stripped back the sheets that had been tightly tucked in by the maid and slid into the bed. "Happy now?"

"Much better."

Adam pulled the sheets over him. "Okay, I'll be honest – this bed is much more comfortable than the chaise longue."

"See?"

Adam fidgeted for a moment, turning onto his side, and then back. "Do you mind if I take off my top?"

She shook her head and he stripped off his T-shirt and threw it beside the bed. Sophie glimpsed muscular shoulders.

For a workaholic he's certainly well defined.

Stop it.

"You know, I'm not quite use to, well, wearing –"

"I'd guessed that," Sophie interrupted him, laughing.

Once she'd seen he had settled in his side of the bed, she turned off her lamp. Darkness surrounded them.

She turned over to her side and then back towards Adam – not that she could see him. She giggled.

"What?"

She lay on her back, still giggling.

"Am I the first woman you've shared a bed with that you haven't –?"

"Yeah, and if you tell a soul," Adam cut in, chuckling, "I'll make you work on the shop floor for a week, providing all the Oilers cups of tea."

"You can't."

"I can. Best of buddies, me and Mr Thomas."

Sophie laughed loudly. Once she'd controlled her laughter, Adam spoke again. "So what are we doing tomorrow, if the wedding is Saturday?"

"Oh, sorry." Sophie chewed her lip. "I got bullied into it by Cassie. They want to go to the beach. Can you surf?"

Adam let out a groan.

Chapter Seven

Sunlight streamed through a small gap in the curtains. Although subdued by the double-glazed windows, the Cornish wind racing off the Atlantic whistled and howled outside the balcony enough to rouse Adam.

He opened his eyes to the sight of Sophie asleep only inches away. During the night, they'd both managed to find the middle of the bed. She slept on her side, facing him. One of her hands curled round the sheets, the other almost touching him.

Gently, fearing he'd wake her, he rolled over and glanced at his watch, relieved to find it wasn't too early, nearly half past seven. He looked back. Sophie still slept.

He was glad she'd insisted on him sleeping in this comfortable bed; it was large enough he'd felt like he had it to himself. A first, too – sleeping with a woman and not expected to perform, even if she had made a joke about it. Maybe that was why he'd slept so well.

Sleeping, she looked pretty and peaceful. He studied her face more than he'd have dared to if she were awake. Her long, dark eyelashes covered her brown eyes. His mind travelled back to their kiss. He smiled. Her lips were inches away from him, relaxed in sleep. Kissable, soft, full lips. He shifted uneasily. It was morning, and watching her was not helping dull his arousal. He could quite easily kiss her, wake her...

He threw cold water over his thoughts and turned them instead to their conversation last night. Well, now he knew the truth about why she was on edge around Simon. Last night Simon had obviously done something to upset her, although she wasn't letting on what. Keep an eye on him, Adam told himself. Even with what Sophie had confessed, he still couldn't quite understand how a woman like her had fallen for a guy like that. Maybe he'd find out.

Fighting the urge to scoop Sophie into his arms while she lay there, like he would do with any other woman, Adam decided he didn't feel comfortable sleeping in. Not while she slept. Not while his brain resided lower down. If he touched her, she might wake, and that could be embarrassing...or get him into very hot water.

He'd get up, order breakfast and a paper. Yeah, that would work, too. Make the most of the quiet time. Bring himself back to his senses.

***

Sophie awoke, stretching and sighing. Opening her eyes, she realised Adam's side of the bed was empty. Adam was sitting on the chaise longue in his pyjamas, one hand clutching a paper, the other holding a cup of coffee.

"Hey, morning," she drowsily groaned. "Did you sleep okay?"

Adam looked up from his paper and gave her a smile. Would she ever get used to his smile? It made her quiver inside every time. If she were a puppy, she'd be wagging her tail in response.

"Yeah, great, thanks," he said.

"What time is it? How long have you been up?" She rubbed the sleep out of her eyes.

"Not that long. It's about eight o'clock."

"Eight! I said we'd meet Cassie for breakfast at eight." Sophie abruptly sat up.

"Relax. I'm sure Cassie will forgive you. Besides, I thought breakfast in bed would be better."

"Better why?" Sophie scratched her head and stretched again, trying to clear the fog from her brain.

"Think about it. Not being down there, well, can act for us." He gave a sly smile.

"Oh." Sophie blushed, now feeling very awake.

"This way, we can let it work for itself, for very little effort." His tone deepened sexily. "I could be feeding you fruit. Let them think we're at it like —"

"I get the picture!" The thought sent guilty sensations through Sophie's body. Visions of him feeding her grapes, wearing only a short towel tied around his hips, was a very awakening experience; one she needed to bury at the back of her brain.

"And we get to relax, not having to pretend to be something we're not." He smiled reassuringly.

"Though Cassie will tease us about it later, I'm sure." Sophie pulled the sheets back and got out of bed.

"Let her. She'd probably tease you anyway. In the meantime, coffee and a croissant, *sweetheart*?" Adam smirked, leaning across to the low table in front of him and holding up the coffeepot.

She narrowed her eyes playfully. "I thought you'd never ask."

If only she was his sweetheart...

***

During breakfast, they both read the papers delivered with the room service. Adam was glad they could relax in one another's company. He watched her out of the corner of his eye. The

74

deliberation in her face as she read, the way she licked her finger to turn a page. He'd never done anything so normal with a woman. He was captivated, watching her concentrate and read.

He loved women; he'd had plenty of girlfriends, albeit short-lived romances. Some lasted longer than others, but he'd always been honest from the start, never wanting anything complicated or serious. He was too busy for that kind of commitment, and luckily, so were his girlfriends, with their fast track careers. When he started feeling their neediness, he'd nip the fling in the bud, hoping to minimise the damage. Maybe the reason he'd not looked twice at Sophie originally was because his type of woman were immaculate, morning and night, rushing off the morning after with a 'ciao, I'll call you.' They never relaxed, they didn't have time to. That was the way it went. It was his choice. He was happy with his lot.

But was he now?

This felt strange, yet good. Relaxing. Maybe James had been right. He did need a holiday, a change.

Sophie sat in her conservative cotton pyjamas - which Adam found tantalising - her hair still tangled from sleep, not a trace of make-up on her face. Absolutely natural, and there was something so gorgeous about it, it unnerved him.

"What?" Sophie looked up from the newspaper, catching his stare, and frowned at him.

"Nothing." Adam went back to reading his paper. But he couldn't concentrate. "Um, when are we going to the beach?"

"Oh, I'd forgotten about that." Sophie reached for her mobile phone. "Maybe we'd better start getting ready." She sent a text message.

It beeped back a minute later. "We'll meet them down on the beach."

Adam nodded, trying to hide his anxiety. Not so much about

75

the beach, but he couldn't surf, and imagined Simon could, being a local. He had the impression Simon would be trying to show Adam up wherever he could – especially after last night. Was Adam about to be moved out of his comfort zone? He made another note to himself on how to kill James – slowly.

Sophie sighed. "I'm sorry for dragging you down here," she said, obviously spotting his tension. "Especially without letting you know what you were in for. You don't do weddings, do you?"

Adam folded the newspaper. "No, no, I can't say I do."

"You're not sure about marriage, either, are you?" Sophie said. She'd read him easily. His parents' divorce hadn't been pretty, even though he'd been old enough to not be involved. But he'd seen the signs at a young age of a failing marriage. His father working late, his dinner left in the oven. He'd be already tucked up in bed but the arguments kept him awake. He wasn't prepared to risk putting anyone else through that, not with his father's blood running through his veins.

"I do wonder if it's overrated," he replied. "As you said, I'm a workaholic; hardly fair on a wife."

She put her newspaper down, frowning. "Is that what happened? I mean with your parents?"

Was his past written all over him? He could open up but...

"Sophie, it's not something –"

"Sorry." She shook her head. "You're right, it's none of my business." She stood up, grabbed some items from a drawer and headed for the bathroom, closing the door behind her.

Adam sighed. His family wasn't something he talked about.

***

Sophie had lied to Cassie last night. She had brought a bikini with her, in case she and the girls needed a tanning session or a special spa treatment, but not to gallivant around in on the beach.

She stared into the mirror, having a momentary panic at how revealing the bikini was. Yesterday, when Adam had mentioned the pool, she'd dreaded the idea of him seeing her in a costume. It was never going to happen. Until Cassie had this bright idea to go to the beach today and it hadn't rained.

Did she really want to reveal so much flesh? He was a stranger – almost.

Stupid really, as there would be lots of people on the beach and they'd all be strangers and yet she wasn't worried about what they thought.

Sophie emerged from the bathroom with a sleeveless, cotton blouse and denim shorts over her bikini. Adam was ready, wearing a short-sleeved shirt and knee-length shorts. She filled a bag with a beach towel, sun cream and sunglasses, slipped her feet into some sandals and they headed for the beach.

"It's windy today," Adam said, taking Sophie's hand as they wandered along the coastal path from the hotel.

"Yeah, there's a sheltered part on the beach," Sophie said, taking lead on the narrow path. As the tide was low, they could take a short cut onto the beach. She'd been reluctant to let go of his hand, but within five minutes they were walking on the wet sand, strolling towards the sea and her hand was firmly back in his.

It was blustery but not cold, with the sun burning down on them and no clouds in the sky. They soon found their friends on the beach. Natalie, Gareth, Simon, and Cassie were all sitting on beach mats and towels. Cassie had huge sunglasses over her eyes, drinking from a large bottle of water and groaned frequently.

"Ah, there you are. How many tequilas did I have, Soph?" Cassie asked as they approached, her voice hoarse.

"A lot more than me," Sophie said, unable to hide her smirk.

That would serve her right. Sophie's head felt fine, amazingly. Maybe it had something to do with the good night's sleep she had.

Simon was sunbathing on his towel, his surfboard beside him and his golden torso on full show. Yes, he still had his perfect physique. His manual job and obsession with sports and surfing contributed to his six-pack. He was good looking, Sophie didn't doubt that. The thing which made him unattractive – especially now – was he knew it. At least Adam seemed to carry some modesty about him.

Sophie and Adam sat down on their towels.

"Who's for a surf? Adam?" Simon said, looking over, removing his sunglasses.

Adam chuckled. "I don't surf."

"Ah, yes, a city boy."

"I got Gareth to bring down the volleyball net," Natalie interrupted, possibly aware Simon would try to score points against Adam. "I like volleyball."

"Yeah, me too," Adam said.

"I'm in," Simon added, grabbing the net.

While Gareth, Adam and Simon set up the net, Sophie removed her blouse.

"You told me you didn't have a bikini!" Cassie squealed.

"Shh! I wasn't really sure I wanted to do the beach," Sophie said, scowling.

"Oh, I get it. Simon." Cassie was so wrong. "Hun, you have nothing to hide. You're gorgeous, I say flaunt it and let him realise what he's lost."

"I'm sure he hardly cares." Sophie tied her hair back into a rough ponytail and started applying sun cream.

As Cassie opened her mouth, Sophie gave her a warning look. Adam returned to Sophie's side.

"Do you want some help?" he asked.

"Uh, okay, thanks," Sophie nervously mumbled. Adam knelt behind her and gently massaged the cream into her back and shoulders, sweeping any stray hairs off her shoulder, and knowing Cassie was watching, laid a kiss on her neck.

Sophie was turning into some sloppy mess internally. *It's an act. Just an act.* Yet, she could have easily relaxed onto the towel and let him rub cream into her back all day long, his firm hands gently caressing her.

"Can I borrow some?" he said, bringing her back to the here and now. "You can even rub it in." He smiled mischievously. Adam stripped off his shirt and Cassie wolf whistled.

"City boy's giving you a run for your money, Smarmy," Cassie said, giving Adam an appreciative glance. For someone who worked in an office all day, Adam had an equally toned body. Like Simon, Adam had good muscle definition and broad shoulders, and beautiful biceps. "Sophie, you're one lucky cow!"

Adam chuckled and looked at Sophie, who quickly remembered to close her mouth.

"She's right. For a workaholic, when do you find time to work out?" Sophie teased, starting to apply the cream to Adam's back. She so wanted to rub the cream into his stomach and that chest, but realised he could reach those parts himself. *Damn shame...* Sophie licked her lips, for fear of drooling.

"I use my gym regularly, and swim," he said.

"When you're not playing golf."

He grinned, showing off his sexy laughter lines. Sophie wanted to kiss him.

"Right, that's you done." Sophie decided she couldn't take it any longer. She was losing all self-control and forgetting this was pretend.

"Shame, I was enjoying that." He leant in, whispered in her ear, his lips brushing her cheek. Everything he did was for show. And it worked. He even had her convinced. Sophie worried whether she should actually be reacting to it the way she was, and tried not to let on. If Adam realised the effect he had on her, would it turn sour? Or would he play on it further? Hopefully he'd think she was pretending too.

"They want to play volleyball, remember?" She winked.

He stood up, brushed the sand off, then held out his hand to help Sophie up. He held her hand walking over to the make-shift court. It was windier out, away from the rocks, but Sophie was grateful for the cooler air.

The group chose the teams and Sophie, crap at volleyball – it was a sport after all – decided she would stay at the back, out of the way. Gareth and Simon teamed up with Natalie, while Cassie, Sophie and Adam were the opposition.

They played for about half an hour, Cassie's hangover disappearing. Cassie, good at the game, high-fived Adam each time they scored. Sophie loved how her friends got on with him. Simon was starting to become a distant memory, even with him staring her right in the face.

They took time out to have a drink and all sat on the sand, laughing and joking. But Sophie's good mood evaporated when she noticed a couple of women heading their way. One of them was Zoe. Cassie must have noticed her expression, because she put an arm around her.

"Sorry, hun, that's me and my big mouth last night," Cassie spoke softly so only Sophie could hear. "I told some of the girls we were meeting on the beach, and she must have overheard."

***

Natalie suggested they went for a paddle. The lads, Adam included, stayed stretched out on the sand. He didn't want to follow Sophie around like a sheep. A relationship, if it were to look real, needed some independence. Gareth didn't jump up and follow Natalie, so Adam decided to stay put.

They talked to the two new women who'd joined the group, Zoe and Elaine, and started playing volleyball again. When Simon sloped off to join the girls in the water, Adam decided he could still watch him. Again, he couldn't look over-zealous or protective of Sophie. She needed some freedom, too. Thus, Elaine partnered with Gareth, while Zoe partnered Adam, and the four of them played.

After a time, Adam caught the ball, stopping play so they could catch their breath and have a drink.

"We make quite a team," Zoe said to Adam. She stood close to him and offered her drink. Adam politely shook his head. He'd become a little uneasy about her. She seemed to touch him more than necessary. Maybe she was just friendly, but she knew he was with Sophie, right?

"Look at those lot," Gareth said. They all turned. A water fight was taking place at the water's edge, with such a mass of splashing you could hardly make them out. But what caught Adam's eye was Simon. His hands around Sophie, before she turned and slapped him. Adam threw the ball down and strode up the beach. He needed to decide how he was going to play this and fast. How would Sophie want him to act?

***

Cassie started it. Of course she did. She splashed Simon, he splashed her back, the next minute they're all kicking water at one another and laughing so hard, even with the shock of the cold sea. Just like the old days as kids.

81

Luckily, the girls had dumped whatever belongings they didn't want to get wet away from the water's edge. Sophie had even braved taking her shorts off. Adam was playing volleyball, so it didn't matter. When Simon arrived though, Sophie wanted to run back to Adam, but she held firm. She needed to show Simon she was over him and not afraid. She needed to face her fears.

Then, during the splashing, Simon wrapped his arm around her waist. Although his skin felt hot, it sent her cold. She tried to pull away, but he held her firm.

"Sophie..." he said as if to reassure her. But her heart beat faster, from nerves and dread more than anything. Ridiculous, she knew, but she hadn't forgiven him yet. Wasn't even sure if she ever could.

Over Simon's shoulder, Sophie glanced at Adam down the beach playing volleyball. Would he even notice? He wasn't acting like a jealous boyfriend, which was good, showed their (fake) relationship had trust. Sophie nearly wanted to chuckle. She very much doubted Adam had ever been a jealous boyfriend. What did he have to be jealous about? He was more likely the one to make other men jealous.

Her thoughts became serious when Simon moved his hand from her waist to her hip, then her rear, giving it a gentle squeeze. She dropped her smile and removed his hand, glaring at him. "Simon..."

Simon smirked back, whispering in her ear. "Surely you've missed me?"

"No, I haven't actually," she coldly replied.

"Sure you have." He splashed her. "What we had was good."

Natalie and Cassie were in their own little water fight, and had forgotten Sophie standing with Simon. Not technically alone, with a beach full of people, but she felt isolated all of a sudden.

"Oh yes, so good you ended it, remember? It's been a long time. I'm over you."

"You still feel good, you know?" He grabbed her again, squeezing her, pulling her closer towards him, his strong body trapping hers. The scent of sweat, sun and salt on his skin repulsed her when it used to excite her.

She gasped, furious, struggling with him to release her; when he didn't, she slapped him, stinging her palm. "Leave me alone."

Simon wore a shocked expression, rubbing his cheek. Cassie and Natalie stopped splashing.

"Simon, why are you such a prat?" Cassie shouted, striding over and giving him a shove. "Go back to the hole you came from."

Adam must have observed the scene because he paced towards her, his expression grim. Sophie started to shiver, soaked from the water and maybe the shock of Simon's behaviour, too. Adam wrapped her in his arms and held her tight, resting his chin on the top of her head. His hot body warmed her, like a blanket, sending a quiver of delight to every part of her body pressed against his sun warm skin. Once again, she was safe and protected. His scent mingled with sun cream and salt calmed her as she breathed him in.

"I saw what he did." He brushed the strands of hair back off her face. His eyes were fierce and cold. She'd never seen him angry but it fuelled her own.

"How dare he? What's he playing at?"

"What do you want me to do about it?" Adam brushed her cheek.

"Sorry?"

"Well, do you want me to play the jealous boyfriend? Rough him up a little? Give him a warning?"

"Please don't make a scene." She shook her head. "It's not fair on Natalie and Gareth."

"No, I won't. But I might have to do something about it later." Adam glared at Simon, who was staring back – too smugly for Adam, from the way he scowled.

Cassie shoved Simon to make him head back down the beach, following behind, giving him hell by the sounds of things.

"He's touched you before, hasn't he?" Adam asked, as he led Sophie towards her belongings. She picked up her shorts and sunglasses and started to shiver. He hugged her again, skin against skin. Sophie didn't know whether to relish it or be embarrassed.

Whose idea had it been to get soaking wet?

Sophie stared at him, but couldn't answer, then looked away. "Yes, I think so."

"Right, I'm putting a stop to this." He pulled her closer.

"Not now."

"No, but I'll find the right moment. It's upsetting you and he's not going to get away with it."

Sophie smiled nervously. It was nice to hear him being protective. Was he doing it as a friend, or for the lie?

***

Adam had to do something, to look like he wasn't a man to be walked over. For a friend. Because Sophie had very quickly become a friend. She was James and Kate's mate, therefore his and she didn't deserve this harassment.

Shit, even if the woman was a perfect stranger he wouldn't let her put up with this crap.

Luckily, Cassie grabbed Sophie, wanting to know exactly what had happened. Adam wanted to smirk; Cassie had to get the gossip. But she was fun, he liked her and she'd given him the perfect opportunity.

The girls walked on ahead into the hotel, towels wrapped around them.

Simon hung back. *Good.* As they walked towards the lifts, Adam came up behind Simon and pushed him past the lifts and into the gents' toilets.

"Sorry, closed for cleaning," Adam said firmly to an older man trying to walk in behind them. Simon snorted, but the man stepped back, and Adam quickly shut the heavy door. Once closed, he grabbed Simon by his T-shirt, and pinned him against the wall.

"Try another stunt like that and I'll break your fucking nose."

"Hey, I was just mucking around with her." Simon held both arms up, chuckling. "For old times' sake."

Adam released him, stepping back. "She didn't find it funny, and neither did I."

"I'm sorry." But he didn't sound sincere. Adam scowled. The man was about the same height, same build and it had been a long time since Adam had been in a brawl. But anger alone fuelled him to this invincible state.

"Leave her alone," Adam ordered, jabbing a finger into Simon's chest.

"Or what?"

"Leave it, Simon. I'm warning you." He shoved him away and walked out of the toilets, but he heard Simon's last words.

"I'm not afraid of you, city boy!"

Adam ground his teeth, taking the stairs rather than wait for a lift, striding up them two at a time. He paced towards his hotel room, breathing heavily, realising his fists were clenched. All Adam could picture was caving Simon's face in. Repeatedly. He imagined the punch bag hanging in his gym, and how much he wanted to be there, beating the shit out of it. He swiped his key card through the panel and shoved the door open, nearly knocking Sophie flying.

"Oh, God, sorry."

"Hey, where've you been?" Sophie said, nervously smiling at him. She tightened the bathrobe she was wearing. He'd barely registered why, then realised she'd removed her wet clothes. "I was getting a little worried."

The corner of his mouth twitched to a fake smile, but he felt tense, cold even. His foul mood wasn't something he wanted Sophie to see. Forgetting she didn't need to show affection, Sophie put her hand to his cheek, but he took it away. He didn't want appeasing either.

The shit he was dealing with this weekend. *Yeah, James, just chit chat with the old dears – if only it was that fucking easy.*

This was supposed to be relaxing.

A bed of nails would be more relaxing right now.

"I've spoken to Simon. He'll leave you alone."

"Oh, right." Sophie nodded. His anger must have been sending out warning signals, because she kept her distance. "We're going to freshen up then meet in the bar. Natalie's mum and dad have invited us all to join them for lunch." She frowned. "So, are you okay to go? I'll cancel otherwise."

"I'm fine." His tone softened. He rolled his shoulders to remove the tension in his neck. "Whatever you want me to do."

Chapter Eight

"I'm sorry about Simon," Sophie said as they meandered along the narrow streets of Padstow, the nearby fishing town, where they were having lunch.

The sun shone warmly on their faces and the wind had dropped, sheltered by the harbour. He had driven, following Natalie's parents and the atmosphere inside the car at first had been awkward. It wasn't Sophie, it was him. He'd lost his cool, and trying to compose himself in front of her had been hard. Anger swirled around his head like a tornado, destroying every sane thought in his mind. Simon was too cock-sure of himself and needed to be put in his place. What the hell did he want, anyway?

He shrugged in response to her comment, then took her hand. "It doesn't matter. He shouldn't treat you like that. He's done it before, hasn't he?"

"I think so. Last night."

"He's no right to touch you. And besides, you are with me. I should be smashing his face in like a jealous, protective lover."

Just say the word!

"Don't."

"I won't." He reassuringly squeezed her hand, removing her worried expression. "It's not my style. But you're my friend, Sophie. Even if all this is an act, I won't let him treat you with any less respect."

"I'm your friend?" She stopped walking.

"Sophie, I wouldn't be here doing this if I didn't like you. Okay, so I promised James, but if you're a friend of James, you're a friend of mine." He brushed her hair off her face, conscious of observers. "I'm not going to ignore you when we get back to Surrey."

She smiled. "I've certainly learnt never to judge a book by its cover. You're not what I expected...you know, personality wise."

He grinned. "The feeling is mutual." He tugged at her hand, realising they'd stopped following the crowd. "So, the next time he tries something, make sure you tell me." Sophie hesitantly nodded. "I'm serious."

"I know. Thank you."

"So, do you know the restaurant we're going to?" Adam said, taking in the surroundings of the bustling fishing town, with the seagulls crying and the smells of the salty sea air filling his lungs. He hadn't been here before and it had a picturesque atmosphere to it. It really did feel like he was on holiday.

"Oh, um, we're going to my sister's restaurant." Sophie nervously frowned at him.

They walked, away from the harbour and into the depth of the town, Sophie's arm looped through Adam's. He was back to his calm, casual self. He usually didn't stay in a mood long and it wasn't fair on Sophie; she hadn't asked Simon to be an arse. He could see why she hadn't wanted to come to this wedding on her own.

Their gaze met and he could see the anxiety in her eyes. He circled his thumb inside her palm, trying to reassure her. Of course she was nervous. She was about to see her sister and blatantly lie to her about Adam being the boyfriend.

Did she even know? Or had she been like Cassie, assuming? Would Adam being by Sophie's side be a surprise to her?

"I'm sorry, I would have told you sooner, but I could tell you weren't in the mood," she whispered, leaning into his ear. Her breath on his skin stirred delight through his body. "I promise at first I didn't realise we'd be going to my sister's restaurant. I know you're not keen on meeting my family."

"It's okay." His lips brushed her ear and he saw the fine hairs around her neck rise. He liked he could do that to her, that their bodies responded to each other so minutely.

But was it really a good thing?

He had to admit, so far, he'd been enjoying this weekend. But why did he enjoy this so much? Apart from Simon's unwanted attention and the hassle it could bring, there was something devilish about the façade, and yet something natural between Sophie and Adam.

The party entered a small restaurant called 'From Under the Sea.' A man greeted them, smartly dressed with his red tie matching the restaurant colourings.

"Sophie!" he said, hugging her.

"Hi, Robert." Sophie kissed him on the cheek.

"I'll tell Tara you're here. She's busy in the kitchen as always. But first let me show you to your table." He escorted their party of eight to a table already laid out, situated at the back. The restaurant, filled with dark wood tables, cherry coloured cushions on the chairs, had a quaint aura, romantic with candles and small red posies on each table.

Adam was inwardly relieved Simon sat at one end, so Sophie could chose the other, not wanting to be near the man. Adam took the seat opposite Sophie. To even the table up, Cassie had to sit with Simon, but that probably wasn't a bad thing. Cassie constantly teased Sophie. Adam found it funny, but from the way Sophie reacted, blushing and going quiet, she needed a break from it before she burst out the truth. How was Sophie coping with this lie? He hoped she wasn't riddled with guilt. Seeing Simon's behaviour earlier on the beach reassured Adam he should be here by her side, if only to keep that bastard's hands off her.

Robert handed out the menus and lingered at Sophie's end of the table.

"Rob, this is my boyfriend, Adam," Sophie said. Robert's expression showed surprise. "We've only been seeing each other a few weeks." Hopefully no one else was picking up the hesitation in her voice like Adam could. "Robert is my brother-in-law," she said to Adam.

"Good to meet you," Robert said, shaking Adam's hand. "Hopefully Sophie's found herself a good guy at last." Robert sent a darker look Simon's way, making Sophie blush and Simon ignore him. Adam smiled. Rob didn't think much of Simon either.

"I'll let you take your time over the menus," Robert said, as another waitress approached, taking drink orders.

"So your sister is the chef?" Adam asked once the waitress had gone. He took her hand across the table. He could see how nervous she was and tried to use his calming influence on her.

"Yes —"

"There you are, Soph!" A woman came out wearing chef's whites and Sophie stood to hug her. Tara was slightly taller than Sophie and although she had the same hair colouring, it was shorter and tied back out of the way.

"Tara, this is Adam."

"Yeah, Rob just told me. Nice to meet you, Adam." She shook his hand, smiling. Similar brown eyes to her sister, maybe not so dark, but her smile was alike, their resemblance instantly distinguishing them as sisters. "How'd you meet Soph?"

"We work for the same company," Adam said.

"But we met at someone's retirement party!" Sophie quickly added. "And we don't actually work *together*."

"Nothing wrong with working together. Rob and I manage, and

90

actually it's great." Tara chuckled. "If we can make it through to the end of the day without wanting to kill one another."

"Oh, um," Sophie shrugged and looked at Adam. "True."

Adam hadn't thought of the working implications, but it would be another reason to not get involved with Sophie. He didn't do long term; would that make it awkward for them after they'd had their fun? He was best off keeping her as a friend.

"Look, I've gotta go back out to the kitchen, but hopefully we'll catch up Saturday night." Tara hugged Sophie once more. "Nice meeting you, Adam."

"So, uh, that's Tara – my big sister. She got the cooking gene from Mum." Sophie sat back at the table, fiddling with the linen napkin.

"So where does the engineering come from?"

"Dad. He worked in Yeovil, Plymouth, Exeter and then eventually, when the restaurant was going well and Mum needed more help, he gave it all up. Mum was the chef, Dad worked front of house."

"Does this mean you can't cook?" He couldn't resist teasing her. She playfully slapped him on the arm. "Ouch!"

"I can cook, but it doesn't interest me like design. And I couldn't do what Tara does, and cook for the hundreds. Heavens, I think I'd get nervous cooking for just you..." She broke her gaze. "Oh, um, you know what I mean."

Adam chuckled. He lowered his voice, so only Sophie could hear, the rest of the table lost in the discussion over the big day tomorrow. "Yeah. So if you were to cook for me, what would you make?"

"Sausage, egg and chips." She grinned, then rolled her eyes. "I have no idea. Probably something safe like spaghetti Bolognese. Everyone likes pasta...but, oh, maybe that could get messy."

"Relax, it's only hypothetical," he said, softly.

"Of course it is. Then hypothetically you'd get..." She grabbed the menu, and started reeling off complicated dishes from the starters, then the main courses. Adam laughed. "Easy," she said with a shrug, closing the menu.

The food arrived and Sophie talked proudly of her sister and brother-in-law setting up the restaurant. With other celebrated restaurants in the neighbourhood, it could charge prestigious prices for its impressive food. Rob and Tara had worked hard to bring the restaurant up to the status it had, holding its own amongst the best in Padstow. The food was excellent, reminding Adam of restaurants he liked to frequent. He wanted to take Sophie to one of those restaurants. She'd appreciate the food better than some of his previous girlfriends, who were more interested in watching their figures than enjoying the food.

He'd promised himself he wouldn't get involved with Sophie. A presumptuous thought at the beginning of their weekend, it had seemed realistic until last night when he'd witnessed her sexy transformation. Now, getting to know her, seeing how truly beautiful she was – *damn James for being right* – he had to remind himself they needed to stay just friends.

Platonic.

***

"I don't believe it. It is you."

Sophie looked up from stirring cream into her coffee. Harry Chesney, her dad's oldest pal and work colleague headed towards her. A short, portly man, what hair he had left was white.

"Harry!" She stood up and hugged him, kissing his cheek.

"Well, it's been a while since I've seen you. Heard you're working for some robotics company in London."

"Surrey," she corrected. "Thomas Robotics – been there ten months. Harry, this is Adam, my boyfriend."

Adam stood and shook hands with Harry and he and Sophie talked idly, catching up. Then Harry caught Sophie by surprise.

"Look, if you want a job closer to home, all you've got to do is ask. You know I've got my own company, and I can always make room for you."

Sophie laughed. "Shush, Harry. Adam works for Thomas Robotics, too, remember? You'll get me into trouble."

"Yeah, and I'd have to tell Thomas to double her wages," Adam said, grinning.

Sophie elbowed Harry playfully. "He's an account manager, he can do no such thing," she said. "But thank you, Harry. It's kind of you, but I'm fine where I am."

"You look familiar." Harry frowned at Adam. "Are you Thomas' boy? I read about Thomas Robotics not that long ago – the old man's retiring soon." He looked back at Sophie. "But the offer will always be there if you want it. I can't double your wages, but I can certainly match them." He tapped his nose.

"You know I don't want the money."

"I know, sweetheart. Only, your mum and dad would like you closer to home. Well," Harry kissed her cheek, "it was lovely to see you both."

***

Sophie walked into their hotel room, throwing off her cardigan and stepping out of her shoes, groaning.

"I am so full. I don't think I could eat again for a week."

"The food was great. Reminded me of a restaurant I know in Richmond. Maybe I should take –"

Sophie stared at him blankly. He shook his head. She shrugged and went to hang her cardigan in the wardrobe.

"We've got dinner later; not sure I'll be eating all three courses. I've got a bridesmaid dress to fit into tomorrow." What a day, so far.

Considering Simon's annoying antics that morning, the afternoon had been pleasant. At the restaurant, Adam had been the perfect companion, holding great conversation with the rest of the group. But amongst it, he showed Sophie affection, being the loving and devoted boyfriend. But was it too much? She rubbed her forehead. "You know, Adam, I was thinking you could lay off some of the affection."

"How do you mean?"

"At times, I'm worried it looks a bit too much."

"It does?"

"Well, I think so. Maybe I'm not used to being so public with my affection." What was she saying? With Simon she'd never been more public, wanting everyone to know how happy she was.

"But we're supposed to be head over heels in love. It's new. Everything is exciting about the relationship. The 'can't get enough of you' kind. I thought that's how you wanted it played."

"I thought I did."

"We're supposed to have been together for only a few weeks. Usually the first few months are passionate, intense."

Sophie laughed, shaking her head. "You seem to know an awful lot about it, for someone who's never been – oh." Why had she assumed he hadn't been in love? Maybe because the woman would have been crazy to let him go? "Have you ever been in love?"

Adam concentrated on taking off his own jacket, placing it over the back of a chair. He didn't respond.

Sophie watched him, her expression dropped. Had she hit a nerve? She half-heartedly chuckled. "Adam?"

Adam hesitated before letting out a laugh. "When I was younger,

I thought I was in love, but you know how it is with work. I'm too busy. I'm not interested in a relationship," he replied, shrugging, but he never met her eye. "I thought you wanted us to look so unbelievably in love, so that's what I was doing."

"That's it though. Are we believable?"

Adam chuckled confidently. "Sophie, everyone's bought it. Even Simon."

"But what's going to happen in a month's time, when Cassie or someone phones and wants to know how *we* are? What do I tell them?"

"That we broke up," Adam replied, then nervously laughed. "I would suggest that I'd run off with another woman, as I don't mind if I look like the shit in all of this, but considering how your other relationship ended —"

"Yeah, then I'd look like an even bigger fool than before." Sophie flopped onto the bed, suddenly saddened.

"Sophie, tell them what you like. So, okay, you left me." Adam sat beside her.

"They'd think I was crazy! They love you. You're perfect. They wouldn't believe that either."

"Why have you got it in your head I'm too..." He started to touch her hair, but stopped, standing up and placing his hands in his pocket. She frowned, but he shook his head. "Never mind. I'll help you for however long you need me. If you need me to meet some friends back home, then I can do that, too."

"No you won't." Sophie laughed. "I can see you now, cancelling a hot date to come play some farce for me."

"Look, whatever, the relationship is young enough that here we are believably head over heels, and can't see it going wrong. All relationships seem perfect in the early months. They'd believe a few more months down the line our relationship could have fizzled out. Look at you and Simon."

Sophie glared at him.

"I'm sorry, I shouldn't have brought that up. But I'm right, aren't I?"

Yes, he was. Simon had been perfect for four whole months, everything Adam was being now, and then it had gone wrong. Only she hadn't seen it.

"Look, you might have to lie a little longer," Adam said, placing a comforting hand on her shoulder. "And I promise I'll be around if you need me. What are friends for, hey?"

Sophie stared into his eyes for a moment, then blinked. She realised Adam had a wonderful way of making her believe every word he spoke. And she tried not to fall for it. "How do you know about long-term relationships, when you're barely with a woman more than a week?"

"I've been out with some longer than a week." A sarcastic tone laced his voice. "Don't listen to everything James tells you." He obviously wasn't going to tell her if he'd had a long-term girlfriend, if he'd been in love. *He must have. Surely? Had he been hurt, like her?*

"Now if you'll excuse me." Adam walked into the bathroom, locking the door behind him.

The bathroom had become their refuge. The only room where they could escape each other. They hadn't even considered how tough this would be. Their hotel room was the only place the two of them could be themselves together, relax, but even that was hard. The closeness they were having to portray outside of the room and then the close confines of the bedroom, still kept them practically stepping on each other's toes. Two strangers thrown together. Maybe Adam found it tougher. He may have had plenty of girlfriends, but had he spend this amount of time with them?

James really hadn't thought this one through.

She sighed, lying back on the bed, staring up at the ceiling. She had to hand it to Adam though. Whatever he actually felt, he was playing the perfect lover. Had he loved before? Why would he deny it? But he was right. She remembered the days with Simon, practically the whole relationship had been crazy, so alive. They didn't care who saw, just wanted everyone to know how much they were in love. She closed her eyes, the memories flooding back. That's why her relationship with Simon had ended so bitterly, so unforgivably. Because it hadn't fizzled, it hadn't slowly died - not in her eyes. She hadn't seen it coming, because she'd been so head over heels, blinded. But it had ended, quickly. An abrupt screaming end with another woman, a so-called friend, in his bed.

As the years had worn on, she realised what a lucky escape she'd had. If Simon could cheat on her then, would it have stopped him if they were married?

Sophie heard the bathroom door unlock and sat up. Adam appeared, tie removed and the top buttons of his shirt undone. Did he even realise how sexy that looked?

"You're right, I'm sorry." She walked over to him as he opened the wardrobe "We should do it your way. I'm just concerned I'll look like a complete and utter clown." She chuckled, trying to lighten the mood.

"You're not a clown." Adam brushed her cheek.

His touch released butterflies inside her stomach and she laughed nervously. Then meeting his eye, her tone became more serious. "I'm nervous that when we're on show, doing what we're doing," she raised her eyebrows, "for this lie...we've become good friends... I'm worried I'm enjoying being on your arm more than I should." She turned and winced, chiding herself. *Bloody hell, did she really just say that?*

There was a knock at the door. Sophie sighed as she quickly went to answer it, glad of the interruption.

"Hey, you ready?" Cassie peered her head through the door, giving Adam a wink.

"Oh, yeah, sorry, completely forgot." Sophie turned to Adam and wiggled her fingers at him. "I'm getting my nails done. I'll be downstairs in the spa. Might be a couple of hours." Adam nodded as Sophie started to head out of the door with Cassie.

"Aren't you going to give him a kiss goodbye? Bloody hell, woman, I'd be kissing him goodbye!"

Sophie's cheeks burned. She rushed up to Adam. He already wore a subtle smile, mischief in his eyes. She hesitantly placed her lips gently on his. His arms came up around her, holding her momentarily to his lips, then she pulled away. She would never get used to kissing him, how amazing it felt. He was smiling at her, teasingly, not that Cassie would know or be in on the joke. He was enjoying this, wasn't he?

And so was she.

Chapter Nine

Adam had a couple of hours to kill and decided he'd go swimming. He grabbed his towel and strolled through the hotel complex towards the pool, Sophie's words rattled around his brain.

Had he ever been in love?

When he was younger, maybe... He'd dated a girl in uni for a while. Emma. She'd been *the one*. And maybe he was drawn to Sophie because she reminded him a little of Emma. They were alike in some ways. Career minded, intelligent, and, although lacking a little in confidence, sexy as sin.

Must stop thinking of Sophie as sexy – it will lead to trouble.

After Emma, he'd seen lots of girls. He smiled to himself. *Yeah, lots of girls.* Though some may have been more to get Emma out of his head, convince himself he'd done the right thing. He'd been the one to end it with Emma, realising things were getting serious between them. They'd been together a couple of years, and he knew an engagement was expected. But his parents' gritty divorce had been still fresh in his mind and he decided to concentrate on work, painful as the decision was back then. His extensive experiences soon taught him to love and leave them easily enough, knowing not to get involved, to choose women that he wouldn't fall for. For him, women had become about lust, rather than love. But he knew enough about love to know this little act between Sophie and him was spot on.

And he felt lust for Sophie, nothing more.

Would he be glad when this wedding was over? Monday was only around the corner, and they would back to work and reality. So far, their time together had turned out to be good, even with the surprises he'd had. Would he miss it?

He chuckled. James and his 'just sweet-talk a few old ladies'. He'd neglected to mention the ex-boyfriend and a mad best friend to contend with.

But when they both returned to work, would they *see* each other? He never even used to notice Sophie. Would he notice her now? Sure, he'd even go out of his way to say hello.

But would he miss her?

He shook his head. *Ridiculous question.*

Although their relationship was a lie, Sophie knew him without his cash, without his status. She liked him without the knowledge of who he really was. Would it change?

How would Sophie react when she found out he *was* Thomas' boy? Would she be like all the rest?

No. She wasn't materialistic. She was clever, funny, natural... and beautiful. He had to be careful. Too many things about Sophie were attractive.

Arriving at the pool, Adam nearly turned around, any pleasant thoughts disappearing. Simon was there. Unfortunately, he'd spotted Adam, so there was no leaving now.

In the changing room, Adam threw his clothes into a locker, slamming the door, unintentionally, as he locked it. Dread hindered him. Did he really want to face Simon? He'd come here to relax but had the distinct impression that wasn't going to happen. But his middle name wasn't coward either. This could be a good opportunity to make his position clear – don't mess with Sophie.

Just don't drown the guy.

He slung a towel over his shoulder and confidently strode into the warm room, the fresh smell hitting him.

The walls were white with mirrors along the length of the pool, making the room feel larger than it was. The lighting made the water reflect sparkles onto the ceiling. Although small, the pool was big enough to get some lengths in. James' voice in his head dared him to reach fifty.

Easy, this size pool.

Adam flung his towel over a chair and jumped into the pool. Cooler than expected, he ducked his shoulders under to acclimatise.

Simon swam towards him, completing his length. Adam didn't wait. He set off on his own exercise; when he swam back, Simon stood waiting for him, breathing hard, still catching his breath.

"Look, Adam, I'm sorry about this morning," Simon said, holding out his hand.

Adam frowned, but not wanting any trouble, shook it. "It's not me you should be apologising to."

"Yeah, yeah, I'll talk to Sophie." Simon slicked back his wet, dark hair.

"Look, I understand you two had something back then, but it doesn't give you the right –"

"I know, I know." Simon held up his hands. "When I heard Sophie was coming to the wedding, I hoped we could rekindle an old flame, that I could persuade her back." Simon looked at him with distaste. "And then I saw she had a boyfriend..."

Adam's eyes widened with disbelief. "Is that your idea of persuading?"

Simon chuckled, shaking his head. "Anyway, I didn't expect her to be so into you."

He thought he'd get a pushover, Adam mused. That's one thing he wasn't. Adam made a decision and he stuck to it. He needed a lot of convincing otherwise.

"Are you and her serious?" Simon asked, staring at Adam.

Adam stood back, surprised. "What?"

"I said, are you serious about her? It isn't a trick question," Simon repeated with a hint of sarcasm. "Because Sophie needs someone to treat her properly."

Shit. Lie, Adam, it's a charade. "Yes, of course I'm serious about her," he replied, adamantly, glaring back at Simon.

Simon finally nodded.

What an obnoxious shit. As if the cheat knew how to treat her properly. Show some anger. Show you care, even if it's not in the way he thinks.

Adam scowled and started another length, fast and strong, working every muscle in his body. Would Sophie consider taking this prick back? He doubted it. Look at her reactions so far. But then, what if she did want to? Adam wasn't here to stand in their way. But at the same time he needed to look as if he were her boyfriend. To stand down too easily wouldn't fit their current display of the relationship.

Simon leaned against the edge of the pool, keeping his shoulders under the water, waiting for Adam.

As Adam reached the edge of the pool, he stood up, combing a hand through his wet hair. "Look, Simon, Sophie and I have got a good thing going here," he said, choosing his words carefully, "so I suggest you back off. I love her too much to just let her go, so leave her alone." Adam glared at Simon. The 'I'm still prepared to smash your face' look.

Simon nodded and climbed out of the pool. He wrapped his towel around his waist and walked out to the changing rooms.

Adam breathed deeply. Did that man really think he could win Sophie back? Surely not. Maybe Adam needed to be more convincing with his attention to Sophie, if Simon thought he stood a chance. Maybe they did need to act more loved up. Adam could do that.

Obnoxious shit. Adam's skin prickled, anger building inside, his dislike for Simon growing more and more.

He was supposed to be relaxing.

Wait till I get hold of you, James.

Adam stared back at the pool. Fifty lengths it is, to work out how you're going to tell Sophie about this one.

***

Adam walked out of the bathroom as Sophie entered the hotel room. They both jumped in surprise.

"Oh, sorry," she said, averting her eyes. He had a towel around his waist, was freshly shaven and combing back his wet hair. She looked back, intrigued, and then turned, embarrassed. She shouldn't be watching him. After seeing him this morning with his shirt off... She would never tire of that sight. And now, to top it all, he smelled fresh, damp and soapy. Who'd have thought someone, supposedly a workaholic, tucked up in meetings all the time, would have such a great body? You didn't sit in an office all day and get muscle tone like his. He had to work out regularly.

"I thought you were going to be a bit longer, so I jumped in the shower," Adam said, walking to the wardrobe. He picked out some fresh clothes, in no apparent hurry to cover himself up.

Different for men, she thought. They don't care.

Sophie snatched another glance at Adam, who was buttoning a white shirt, hiding away his lovely body. He still had his towel around his waist. "I'll go...um...then." She stepped into the bathroom. "So what have you been up to? Did you make the most of the peace and quiet?" she called out, and checked her make-up in the mirror to occupy herself.

103

"Yeah, I went for a swim. You'll never guess who I bumped into."

Sophie huffed, but she didn't leave the bathroom. "You didn't drown him, did you?"

"No, but the thought did occur to me," Adam joked but then she noticed his tone turn serious. "Sophie, he wants you back."

"He wants what?" She burst out of the bathroom, catching Adam as he zipped up his fly. "Oh, God, sorry." She instantly turned around, her cheeks burning. "What do you mean he wants me back?"

The nerve of that man.

"You can turn around now," Adam said, cheekily. Sophie turned to face him, with an embarrassed frown. He just smirked. "He was hoping to rekindle the flame."

"He can burn in hell!" Sophie snapped. "What did you tell him?"

"Well, of course, I made out I wasn't happy." Adam winked, walking towards her. "I'm assuming I did the right thing. You don't want to get back with this guy, do you?"

"Of course I don't!"

"Good." He smiled wickedly, turning Sophie's insides to mush. "We'll have to make sure Simon knows to leave you alone."

"Why do I get the impression you're going to enjoy it, too?"

"What? Me? Me and Simon are like this." He crossed his fingers. "Besides, what's to enjoy?" He ran a finger under her chin. She swallowed to regain control.

"I know, kissing me can't be particularly easy," she said, trying her hardest to sound blasé. She giggled, then escaped into the bathroom. Flirting with Adam was not good for her health or heart.

She turned on the shower and stripped down, having to do everything daintily not to ruin her French manicured nails – toes and all.

Why would Simon think she'd be remotely interested in him still? What planet was he from? *Planet self-absorbed, obviously.*

And Adam had been her hero again. She was relieved she had him here. How would she have been able to handle Simon's advances without him? Cassie would probably put Simon straight, but letting him think she had a boyfriend probably stopped him being worse than he already was.

She needed to fight her own battles though. This wasn't Adam's problem. She'd talk to Simon, when she got the chance, not wanting to cause a scene at Natalie and Gareth's wedding. This weekend was not about her.

A hint of regret fluttered inside her. Maybe she shouldn't have come? Wouldn't that have been easier? But seeing Cassie and Natalie again, after all this time, that was good, too. She'd been avoiding home for so long now, hiding away when she did visit.

She turned off the shower, and wrapped a huge, soft and comforting white towel around her. It would be so easy to put her pyjamas on, curl up in bed and have a very early night. She wouldn't have to lie, wouldn't have to face Simon.

But on the other hand, she only had until Sunday to make the most of being with Adam. And, oh God, why had she admitted how much she liked it?

Don't get used to it, Sophie.

Tonight they were driving to the church for a rehearsal, then dinner at the hotel with newly-arrived wedding guests. Adam had already proved himself more than capable of charming her friends and family. How hard could tonight be?

Chapter Ten

"Thank, God – I mean goodness that's the rehearsal over," Cassie hissed into Sophie's ear. "Now we can get a drink."

The vicar said his last words of encouragement to Natalie and Gareth as Sophie stood next to Cassie, occasionally glancing to the back where Adam sat.

The wedding party were congregated in the small church, with rows of old pews and kneeling pads, and bibles and hymnals laid out. The florist was already busy preparing the church, hanging flowers on the end of the pews ready for the big day. The wedding rehearsal hadn't taken long. It had been a fast-forward run through of tomorrows events, a bit like she'd once done for a play in drama at school – a way to learn it quickly off by heart. And Adam had sat patiently watching, no complaints. He was just... perfect.

Adam would smile, or wink, when she caught his eye and she'd nervously wave or smile back.

Simon made her nervous, too, being nice. That wasn't fair, she knew. He used to be a nice guy. She wondered if she needed to clarify that she wasn't interested in him. Or maybe with Adam there, supporting her, playing his role, she didn't need to. She hated the idea of making a scene. If an opportunity arose, then she'd talk to him properly.

While Natalie and Gareth spoke with the vicar, Sophie sloped off to join Adam.

"Glad we've got dinner at the hotel now," she said, not knowing what to say. "Even after that huge lunch, can you believe I'm hungry?" She wanted to know what he was thinking. Did he like weddings? Was this his thing? Some men hated all the trappings that went with a big wedding. Would he be someone wanting a small event, a marriage on a beach with a handful of friends, or, like Natalie and Gareth, in its full marital glory, with over a hundred people attending? "Sorry you had to sit through it all."

"It was fine. I don't mind."

With Simon and Cassie walking up the aisle to join them, he took her hand, his thumb circling her palm as he kissed her.

"Let's get some food," Simon said. He looked darkly at Adam, but smiled at Sophie.

Not interested.

"Yeah, I gather there will be quite a few guests arriving tonight," Cassie said, bumping Sophie. "Should be fun!"

Great, more people to lie to.

***

With dinner over, the wedding party was sitting in the busy hotel lounge bar. Newly arrived guests, most of whom Sophie didn't know, lingered and chatted, conversations flowing with the wine.

Huddled on a sofa with Adam, Sophie watched him talk, charming the other guests sitting with them, like he'd done so at dinner. Remaining a quiet bystander, she learnt a little about the stranger she'd come away with; his favourite football team, playing golf practically every weekend, places he'd visited, holidays. He no longer felt like a stranger – there was a connection, something making her feel at ease with him. Natural.

107

She continued to observe, laughing along with the rest of the friends. Did he have them falling for that smile of his? Whatever it was, it worked. She played along when prompted, knowing her cue, when he'd look at her, or give her hand or knee a squeeze. She was filled with guilt, but she certainly found it fun.

"It's wonderful that they're having the ceremony in a church," said an older woman on the sofa opposite, as the barman cleared some empty glasses from their coffee table. "So many use registry offices, or hold the ceremony in the hotel. It doesn't feel right if you ask me. What about you two? Will we be hearing wedding bells soon?" She waited for Adam to answer.

"Um," he replied, turning to Sophie, taking a sip from his glass, frowning questioningly.

Great, he's going to let me answer this one. Oh, joy, his little game, testing her to see what fabrication she could come up with. Or had the woman stumped him? For the first time in the two days, Adam was speechless.

"I think it's early days," Sophie responded, moving closer to Adam, their knees touching. She relished in the small moments of body contact. "Please don't scare the poor man. We've only been together a few weeks." Sophie nervously giggled, then took another sip of her champagne.

"Of course." The woman laughed; seeming happy with Sophie's explanation, she started talking to another lady.

Phew! Sophie finished her glass of champagne. Adam topped up her glass.

"Are you trying to get me drunk?"

"Absolutely. You're funny, and you need to relax." He topped up his own flute, emptying the bottle.

"Remember I have responsibilities tomorrow and don't need to be following the bride down the aisle with a hangover."

"I'm here to look after you, and I will."

Sophie smiled at Adam, reassured, raising the glass to her lips, but she didn't take a sip. She leaned in towards him and whispered, "So, if you were to have a wedding, would you choose a church or hotel for the ceremony? Or somewhere else?"

He hesitated, focussing on his champagne glass and not her gaze. "I've never really thought about it."

"Come on, Adam." She subtly winked, keeping her voice low, not wanting others to overhear. "We've known each other properly, oh, a whole day. Didn't you notice I'm nosey? I want to know."

He took her hand, gently rubbing it, leaning in closer towards her, his delectable mouth inches away. She had to force herself not to steal a kiss.

"I'm not exactly in a position where I want to settle down," Adam spoke softly back, his body language appearing intimate. She frowned, unable to make out what he meant. Was it because his parents were divorced, he feared his marriage could end the same way?

"If the situation was different?" Sophie brushed his shoulder, reciprocating his affection, her hand wandered to the short hairs at the back of his neck. The line between pretend and real blurred. It felt normal to be affectionate towards him. Luckily, he'd think she was pretending and her emotions would be kept safely hidden behind their lie.

"Well, then," Adam hesitated as if confessing a fault, "it would be a church."

Sophie stared in surprised. "I didn't see you as the traditional type of guy."

"I'm not," he instantly dismissed the notion and Sophie noticing, frowned.

He hates giving too much away to me.

"What about you?"

"Me? Oh, I don't know." She coyly smiled.

"I don't believe you. Doesn't every girl have their wedding planned, down to the flowers in the bouquet?"

"Oh, okay, I suppose I always saw myself, as you do at eight years old, marrying in a church, the white dress and everything." She gulped her champagne, knowing she should slow down. "But when I see all the arrangements needing to be made, all of the family and friends; the hassle..." She looked around the bar, the amount of people already arrived for tomorrow's big event. "I quite like the idea of eloping. A nice, remote beach in the Caribbean would be perfect."

"Really? I thought you'd want the big affair."

Sophie laughed loudly, trying to turn it into a delicate giggle, conscious the other guests around the coffee table were now watching the pair of them. Too much alcohol and she didn't have Cassie to blame either. "Do you actually think I will enjoy tomorrow?" She lowered her voice. "I know everyone will be looking at the bride, but I'll still feel like all eyes will be upon me. It's scaring the hell out of me."

"You'll be fine." He placed his arm on hers, giving her a reassuring smile, as the calming, steadying rock that he'd become.

"I'll relax more once the wedding is over."

"So will I," Adam replied dryly. Sophie giggled.

The barman cleared more glasses and Gareth approached.

"Hey, Adam, fancy coming outside for a cigar?" Gareth held out two cigars. Adam glanced at Sophie.

"Go, I'll be fine."

Adam smiled with a sparkle in his eye. Mischief. He leaned in slowly, his hand cupping her neck, and gently kissed her. He lingered, his thumb rubbing the skin below her ear, his tongue softly tracing the inside her mouth. The hot pulse it sent between her legs and through her breasts surprised her. How did he manage to kiss her like that? Did he realise the arousal it caused her? As he pulled away, it left her bereft, wanting more. She watched Adam and Gareth leave the room, regaining her composure, getting her breath back and turned, catching Simon's eye. He'd been watching them the whole time.

***

"Sophie's a great girl," Gareth said, puffing on his cigar. They stood in a wooden shelter designed for the smokers, covered with climbing roses, ivy, and other plants battling to cling to the frame.

Adam nodded, breathing out the cigar smoke slowly, appearing calm and not surprised the subject had turned onto them.

Gareth had wanted a smoking companion who would offer him reassurance – unlike Simon, who would probably tell Gareth he was a fool to get tied to one woman. Adam offered the advice Gareth wanted to hear, and listened, as he'd talked about how excited he was, and nervous.

"You two look good together and it's nice to see her so happy. We haven't seen her in a while, tucked away in Surrey, concentrating on her engineering," Gareth continued, ignoring Adam's silence. "Maybe it will be your wedding next?"

Adam chuckled, not meeting Gareth's eyes. "Early days yet. We're just in the honeymoon period of our relationship, remember? We both want to take it slow. She's been hurt before."

"Yeah, I know. But I just have a feeling..." Gareth stubbed out his cigar and winked at Adam.

Adam had to remember Gareth was making assumptions based on their lie. However, he realised how much he liked being with Sophie, getting to know her better. It felt good, actually. He trusted her. They'd had another great dinner, champagne on tap, although he'd tried limiting his alcohol intake to keep on the ball. He didn't

111

want the lie to slip and certainly wanted to keep an eye on Simon.

Gareth, called away by another guest wanting his attention, left Adam to stroll back through the gardens. A woman walked towards him, her stiletto heels clicking on the cobbled path. He subtly looked her up and down; average height, blonde, fairly pretty, nothing out of the ordinary. The dress she wore accentuated her curvy hips, the neckline plunging to reveal a cleavage. She smiled and he realised she was heading straight towards him.

"Hi, Adam."

He frowned with confusion. He'd seen her before, but couldn't picture where. She laughed, obviously noticing his uncertainty.

"We met on the beach this morning. I was your volleyball partner, Zoe."

"Oh, yeah, sorry," Adam said, shaking his head. "I've met a lot of new faces today."

"On your own?"

"Just had a cigar with Gareth. Think he needed the pep talk."

"And Sophie?" she asked, hinting at... what? Too much champagne addled his brain.

"She's in the bar."

She smiled, as if satisfied. "I enjoyed this morning by the way."

"Yes, it was fun." He slid his hands into his pockets, even jingled his change. His thoughts drifted, wanting to get back to Sophie, his champagne.

"Cigarette?" Zoe pulled out a silver packet, offering them to Adam.

He shook his head. "No thanks. I'd better get back —"

"Oh, you can't leave me standing by myself while I smoke."

"No, I really should —"

"I'll only keep you a few minutes." She tucked her arm through his. He wanted to protest, but deciding it wouldn't cause any harm, allowed himself to be led back to the arbour.

Zoe lit a cigarette and Adam glanced at his watch. How long had he been gone? Would Sophie worry?

"Not sure Sophie deserved you going to her rescue today," Zoe said, her voice soft, exhaling her smoke, edging closer.

"Simon's an arse."

"Sophie deserves him."

Adam frowned with surprise. He'd have to ask Sophie what she'd done to get on the wrong side of this one. He scrutinised the woman. Her make-up was heavy, thick black eye lashes surrounding her blue eyes.

She stepped closer, brushing a hand across his jacket, toying with the collar. He stepped back, brushing her hands away. He could smell her overpowering perfume, tangled with the alcohol and smoke on her breath.

"I think you've got the wrong idea about me," Adam said firmly, walking away.

She grabbed his arm. "Oh, I've got the wrong idea, all right." Throwing her cigarette aside, she moved closer, pulling at his arm.

Adam scowled. "Look, lady —"

"Zoe."

"Zoe. What do you want?"

The woman ran her hands over Adam's chest, looking up into his eyes. "You."

"I'm with Sophie," he said, matter-of-factly.

"I'm a friend of Sophie's."

"Really? She didn't mention you." Adam held the woman's hands away from him, but she kept herself close. "You're not much of a friend if you're hitting on her man."

Zoe giggled. "What? She didn't mention we used to share every-thing?" Her hands snaked around his neck. "Including men." As she tried to kiss Adam, he growled and pulled away. Everything she did said one thing.

"Oh, come on, Adam. Sophie doesn't need to know – if that's what you're worried about."

God, why me? James, wait until I see you Monday.

Adam again tried recoiling but Zoe continued her assault. She toyed with one of his shirt buttons. He batted her hand away.

"I'm very flattered, but Sophie's going to be wondering where I am."

"Let her."

Adam grimaced. Even if he could be with this woman, he wouldn't want to be. Even he had certain requirements Adam didn't want to get angry, but this woman wasn't going to take no for an answer. *Why him?* Maybe another time – if desperate – he might have gone with it, but he certainly knew that while here with Sophie, this could not happen.

He didn't want it to happen.

Then, he caught sight of someone walking towards them.

Shit! Shit!

Zoe had seen her too, because she pounced, mouth over his. Surprised, and off balance, he'd placed his hands on her arms, then shoved her away.

"Sophie, wait!"

***

"Where is he?" Sophie muttered to herself, glancing up at the clock over the bar, conscious she was sitting alone. She didn't like the loneliness – even though the room was full. She looked around. Everyone appeared to be here. Gareth was strolling back, to stand dutifully beside Natalie. Simon? *Oh no, missing.* Had he gone after Adam?

Sophie grabbed her purse and headed towards the gardens.

114

That's where he'd gone with Gareth. Would Adam rough Simon up? No, no, he knew the score. And he certainly wasn't going to do anything to ruin the wedding. Maybe they're talking. Men could be mad at each other one minute, best of mates the next – though unlikely with Adam and Simon. Or maybe Adam was just taking a breather from all this. The two of them had been stuck together since they arrived and the wedding hadn't even happened yet. Maybe he was finding it claustrophobic.

She'd stepped outside, enjoying the coolness of the air and the prettiness of the sun-set sky, light blue merging with pink. She contemplated searching the gardens, then decided to leave him alone. He'd be back soon. Besides, he could take care of himself.

About to turn, she saw two people together by an arbour. The fading light made it harder to see. She shook her head and edged closer, getting a clear view of Adam and Zoe.

Her heart sank to the pit of her stomach, bruising her internal organs along the way. How could he?

And with all the women he could choose to do it with!

Her eyes immediately started to sting, tears forming. Stay strong, Sophie. That woman will not get the better of you. Let them know you're there, and you're mad as hell.

She made her way towards them. Zoe was in Adam's arms, lips locked to his.

She wanted to scream at Adam, but no words could come out. She knew he'd seen her, knew how angry she was. The path forked and she took it.

You're a fool, Sophie Trewyn.

***

"Forget her, babe." The woman tried kissing Adam again, one hand brushing his face, the other draped round his neck. Her softness pushed against him felt so wrong. "Why don't you try me? I'll be much more fun than —"

"Look," Adam pulled her arms off him, firmly, and stepped back, trying to concentrate on which way Sophie had gone, "Zara..."

"It's Zoe," she snapped. Adam pushed her away, letting her go.

"Zoe, how do I put this? I have standards, and you don't reach them."

Zoe gasped, slapping Adam hard across his face. Adam winced, turned on his heel, rubbing his sore cheek.

Shit! Sophie.

He ran after Sophie, seeing her disappear deeper into the gardens, her pace fast.

***

"Sophie! Stop, please!"

She glanced over her shoulder and quickened her pace. Three inch heels weren't good for running.

"I don't want to talk about this." She waved an arm out and shook her head. She felt so stupid. She continued along the path, now lit by little solar lamps. She wanted to escape. The air was cooling and she could hear the sea crashing on the beach below, rhythmic and fierce. The setting sun created an orange glow on the horizon. It was all beautiful but none of it settled her. Her anger felt like the waves, attacking the beach in surges. It kept beating at her chest, tightening her throat.

A part of her hurt, not because of who the woman was, but because whatever Zoe had just experienced with Adam had been real. Adam only pretended with Sophie and maybe now she real-ised she'd like it to be true. She couldn't admit that though, not unless she knew Adam felt the same.

Which he didn't, of course.

Adam grabbed her arm, and swung her around to face him. He swept her hair back off her face and made her look into his eyes, his body unbearably close to hers.

"I swear, she was coming on to me. Seeing you, she launched at me. Literally." He gripped her firmly as if to take control. She glared at the hands on her arms, and he loosened his grip, but he wouldn't let her go. She wasn't going to give in, fall for his bloody charm and his excuses.

Oh, how history repeated itself.

Simon never took the full brunt of her feelings. Adam would, if so insistent to talk about it. She may seem like some shrinking violet but she had toughened up. No way would she let this go unsaid.

"Come with me." Adam took her hand and made her walk, further from the hotel. They came across a gazebo, covered in jasmine and honeysuckle, and in the night air, it carried the scent of those delicate flowers.

Sophie would not be a delicate flower.

She scowled, knowing her tears were visible now. "How could you? This whole bloody lie was about making me look happy, falling for someone too good to be true." She laughed sourly at her own comments. "And it is, isn't it? Too good to be true. Because you've made me look like a fool." Anger filled her, from head to toe she trembled.

"Listen to me. I wasn't, I swear."

Sophie laughed caustically at him. "And I'm supposed to believe you. I know what *your sort* are like, Adam – James told me! A pretty girl only need to smile at you, flutter her eyelashes and you, you, you..." She thumped her fist onto his chest as her eyes filled with tears.

"What? What do I do, Sophie?" Adam raised his voice, pushing her away. "So, I go out with a lot of attractive women. I'm not a cheat. And this weekend I made you a promise, and I take them very seriously."

"Why her?"

"What?"

"Her?"

"Are you even listening to me? What about her? I don't even know who the hell she is!" Adam turned away, frustrated and angry, combing his hand through his hair. He glared back. "Do you want to tell me? Or is this something *else* you've forgotten to let me in on?"

Sophie glared in silence, his coldness shocking her.

"You've got a nerve." Adam's tone chilled her bones. His fists were clenched, his cheeks hollowed with tension and he paced. Sophie hadn't seen him so angry; this morning with Simon didn't come close. "You stood there and let James talk me into coming away with you, knowing full well you were a bridesmaid, I'd be facing an arsehole of an ex-boyfriend and some crazy tart determined to get back at you. What did you do to her?"

"What did *I* do?" Sophie snapped. "I found her in bed with Simon. That's what *I* did!" she shouted. A tear started to run down her cheek. She instantly tried wiping it with the back of her hand, trying to control her emotion. Adam probably didn't do emotional train wrecks, so she needed to get control and fast. Besides, she shouldn't give another man the satisfaction of her tears. "And I had no idea she'd be here."

"Oh, shit... Sophie, I'm sorry." Adam shook his head, moving closer towards her, but she took a step back, not quite finding the trust in him yet. "That explains something she said."

"What?" Sophie sniffed, and took a deep breath. *Control. Breathe.*

"Oh, about you two sharing men." Adam's voice calmed, and

he placed both hands on her shoulders. She let him.

"She said that? Damn, I want to kill her."

"Sophie, I swear, she was coming on to me. If you'd given me one more minute, you'd have seen me shove her away."

Sophie burst into tears, no longer able to keep her emotions in check.

"Hey." Adam gently pulled her into a hug. She wrapped her arms around him, burying her head into his neck, all her anger dispersing, finding comfort in him. One of his hands rested behind her neck and stroked gently. "Just let it go. She's not worth it."

Adam held her tightly, his hand soothing her, and she could feel his strength. Her arms circled around his lean, solid body. He pressed against her, protecting and supporting her. His scent, now her favourite smell ever, calmed her.

"I'm sorry, I should have trusted you. I reacted the worse way possible."

"Look at it this way – you reacted as she hoped, but she's going to be so mad when she sees it hasn't worked."

She looked up at him, trying to wipe away her tears and embarrassment. "I'm so sorry," she whispered.

Adam kissed her forehead. Forgiveness? She closed her eyes, savouring his touch.

"It's okay. In your shoes, I would have responded the same way." He wiped a tear off her cheek with his knuckle.

"Am I forgiven for being so crap at telling you about this weekend?"

"Yes," he said softly, all traces of anger gone. Holding her close, staring down, her heart beat that bit faster again. Would he kiss her? They were on their own. It wasn't needed. Was it? Yet, she wanted him to kiss her, really kiss her. He pulled away, smiling at her. She hid her disappointment by returning a wicked smile.

"Can I rub you right in front of her nose?"

Adam's eyes widened and Sophie laughed, gently wiping her face and realising what she'd just said. *Oh God, she probably looked a mess too.*

"Metaphorically speaking, of course," she said.

Chapter Eleven

Adam let the hotel door shut behind them, placing two snifters of brandy down on the table. He sighed deeply, undoing his tie and removing his cufflinks. This had turned out to be another tough night.

Thank you, James.

Was he making things harder for Sophie? Would she be getting this shit thrown at her if he weren't here?

Once Sophie had calmed, ready to face the guests back at the bar, Adam had made sure they walked back in looking stronger than ever as a couple. He'd held her close, a protective arm around her waist. And when he couldn't hold her, he always made sure he had her in sight.

He'd seen Simon and Zoe talking in the bar. Had Simon put her up to it, hoping Sophie would go running to him? Well, whoever had come up with the idea, their aim to put a wedge between him and Sophie hadn't worked. It was never going to work, although they didn't know that. Adam smirked, remembering why he *was* enjoying this.

Thank you, James.

Sophie had snapped out of her mood quickly, returning to her happier self. Adam admired how she hadn't sulked, but acted as if nothing had happened. She'd seemed so vulnerable earlier.

Seeing her hurt frustrated him, and he didn't know what to do about it. He didn't like failing to protect her. He should have dealt with Zoe quicker; being polite had backfired. His head felt muddled with feelings he couldn't describe and knew they were best kept to himself. Sophie thought his affection was a pretence, and it was, to a certain extent. He never wanted to see her unhappy; those feelings were genuine. However, after this weekend, he had to walk away from Sophie, for her own good.

They had left the bar early. Natalie had already sloped off too, so Sophie had a good excuse, insisting tomorrow was the big day. But the truth was Sophie, conscious she'd been crying and that people could tell, didn't like receiving the attention. Cassie had tried to talk to her and Adam had stepped in, telling her to leave it. He couldn't blame Cassie – she was being a good friend and showing her concern – but it didn't help Sophie's emotions. Neither did the alcohol. He should have watched for that, too.

"Adam, I'm sorry about earlier, jumping to conclusions as I did." Sophie walked out of the bathroom, dressed for bed, her make-up removed. No sign of her previous tears. "I think of that woman and see red."

Adam nodded but wanted to smile. All thoughts of Zoe fled his mind as he considered Sophie's pyjamas. They had to be deliberate on her part, not wanting to wear anything unsuitable or revealing. So Sophie, choosing to blend into the background, like she did at work.

Okay, think about it. She's hardly going to parade around in a silk lingerie. You'd be even worse than you are now.

"So what's her problem with you? I don't get it." Adam scratched his head, trying to remove the image of Sophie in silk out of his head. "I'm not suggesting you would, but considering the circumstances, shouldn't it be you trying to ruin her life?"

"Oh, I don't know. I thought we were friends. We were in some classes together, studying our A-Levels, and she never said she had a thing for Simon." Sophie folded her clothes on a stool by the dressing table, not really looking at Adam.

She had her hair loose, strands falling into her face. Adam wanted to sweep her hair back, but resisted, although he'd never tire of touching her hair, feeling it between his fingers...

"But as soon as I started seeing him, she started spreading horrid rumours. Natalie used to say she was jealous of me, knowing what I wanted to do in life, and having *her* man." Sophie's tone became bitter. She shrugged her shoulders. "And Simon, well, he was a popular guy in town. When I trotted off to uni, Zoe must have stuck her claws in and become hard to resist." She laughed sardonically. "My first available weekend, I rushed home to surprise him. But imagine my surprise! I still think she did it to spite me."

"Why do you say that?"

Sophie let out a sigh, walking towards her side of the bed. "Because as fast as it had started, it was over and Simon pleaded with me to take him back. But once he'd done that, I knew I would never trust him again. However much it hurt, however much I loved him, I wasn't going back to him."

Adam took off his shirt, but noticing Sophie turn her head and blush, realised he should follow Sophie's example with her unrevealing pyjamas, and slipped his T-shirt on over his head.

"Maybe I got the wrong end of the stick – and this doesn't justify how he treated you – but Simon mentioned you getting serious –"

"Serious! He's the one who was serious. Always talking about marriage, kids, you name it. What's so funny?"

Adam stopped smiling. "He said you were the one talking about marriage."

"Did he now?" Sophie screwed her face up with frustration. "Don't get me wrong – I wanted those things, but later. I do want those things." Her voice softened and she looked at the floor.

123

I'm definitely not right for her.

She glared, looking him in the eye. "I wasn't even nineteen. We'd been seeing each other a few months. I wanted my education, career first. I wasn't giving that up. And after Simon had slept with Zoe, I threw myself into it even more. I studied hard. It's what I wanted. I've never looked back."

"Maybe she did you a favour then."

"Do you think I should thank her?" She scowled, then sighed, her tone calming. "Look, she didn't change anything, other than Simon wasn't waiting patiently for me while I studied. Originally, he'd made promises that he'd visit weekends, I'd come home for the holidays. We'd make the relationship work. So that hurt like hell. He hadn't even lasted a month." Her voice quavered. Sophie placed the back of her hand to her mouth, taking a deep breath. He stepped closer, but she held her hand up to stop him. "I went back to uni feeling rather lonely and upset. And even the large amounts of alcohol I consumed – as students do – didn't ease it."

"I'm sorry."

Sophie laughed ruefully and pinched the bridge of her nose. Her eyes were shining, but she didn't cry. "Adam, I apologise. You don't really want to hear all this."

"You're fine." Adam fetched both snifters and handed one to Sophie.

"Thanks," she said, sitting on the bed, sipping her brandy.

"Sounds like you need to get it off your chest." Adam sat on the edge, admiring her delicate fingers holding the brandy glass, with French manicured long fingernails. Nails that could scratch and tease his skin...

Stop thinking about her like this.

It's been two days. Two days! James' words rattled inside his head. *'You two might even hit it off.'* Had that been his plan?

"You know, Gareth said Simon's been this way since splitting up with me." She played with her glass, making the liquid swirl inside.

"He's been an arse that long?"

Sophie giggled, then coughed, as the brandy caught in her throat. "He'd always been a flirt; that's how he caught me. But sleeping with most of the girls in town, from the locals to tourists, wasn't exactly going to make me change my mind about him."

Adam swallowed his brandy. He hated to think it, but maybe Simon and he were similar in some ways. His way to stay detached was to hop from one woman's bed to another, playing the field. He never stayed long enough to get close.

Was Simon punishing himself for letting Sophie go?

"But you're right. Maybe I should thank her. She made me see what Simon was truly made of." Sophie leaned forward, clinking her glass against Adam's before emptying her glass. He gave her a nervous smile. "Because he could have said no, like you."

Sophie put her empty glass down on the bedside cabinet and pulled the bed sheets back. "You know an awful lot about me," she said, getting into bed. She puffed her pillows. "What about you?"

"What about me?" Adam walked around to his side of the bed.

"Aren't you bored of me talking about my miserable teenage years?"

"No." Nothing about Sophie bored him.

"What about you?" she continued. "Why'd you join Thomas Robotics? You've been there a while now, haven't you? Will you leave? I see you as the ambitious sort."

He laughed, making himself comfortable in the bed.

"What's so funny?" Sophie laughed.

He could trust her, right? But what if she changed towards him after finding out who he was? The amount of money he was worth?

He chided himself. Sophie wasn't like that, and he hated keeping secrets from her. She seemed a good person, warm, loving. The past two days she'd constantly insisted on paying for anything and everything. He'd argued a few times, but he'd decided it better to save the argument and work out a different way to make sure she was repaid. She certainly wasn't materialistic, or vain – not in those pyjamas, and the trouser suits she wore to work. Plus, he saw her without her make-up on. How many women had he dated who let that happen?

He should tell her who he really was, before she found out through another source. The hotel might try to contact him. Not knowing how good the reception would be for his mobile, he had left the hotel number with his father, in case he needed to talk about work. And what if Harry turned up tomorrow and he'd done his research? They'd already had enough misunderstandings; he didn't want any more.

"I do need to tell you something."

"What?" She sounded a bit worried.

He sighed heavily. "Adam Reid isn't my real name."

"What?" Her eyes widened and she tensed, edging away from him.

He chuckled, resting a reassuring hand on hers. "Sorry, it is my name; it's just not my full name. Adam *Gordon* Reid *Thomas* is."

"As in..?"

"Yes. Gordon Thomas."

"Gordon Thomas? As in, *the* Gordon Thomas?"

"Yes, Managing Director and owner of Thomas Robotics."

She covered her mouth with her hands. "I'm pretending to be in love with the M.D. of Thomas Robotics' son?"

"Yes." He smiled. Why was he enjoying this?

"Does James know?"

"Yes."

"That bastard. Oh, shit, sorry!" Sophie blushed at her outburst. She didn't curse often, he had only heard her when really angry. "You're worth..."

126

"Yes, a lot of money."

"Oh my God, that explains the bloody car!" Sophie said, exasperated. She sat up in bed. She combed her hand through her hair, scrunching it up and shaking it out. "And my friends are never going to believe this. Never. This makes it even more unbelievable than it already is."

"Sophie, your friends do not need to know. As far as they're aware I'm an account manager."

"Why are you acting as an account manager?"

"My father wants me to work from the bottom up, so I understand every aspect of the business. It's what his father made him do."

"Are you happy about that?"

"I don't mind. It's actually very interesting and I wouldn't have met James, and wouldn't be here with you."

"You say that like it's a good thing, but the last couple of days have been hell for you." She blushed. "I'm sorry. I wish I'd been honest from the start. Shit."

"They haven't been all bad. So I've had a few surprises."

"You're not a man who likes surprises, right?"

Adam chuckled, shaking his head. "Some surprises are okay. Like you."

She waved a hand, ignoring his statement. He was glad; becoming relaxed in her company, he was telling her more than he should. "So when do you take over the role of M.D.? Will you still talk to me?"

He laughed, playfully nudging her. "Yes, of course I'll talk to you. You're my best engineer!"

"Oh, my. Harry, at lunch today – he knew, didn't he?" Adam nodded. "I don't want that job! You don't need to worry about doubling my wages..." She hesitated. "Could you really do that?"

Adam laughed again. "When my father decides to retire, then

I'll be taking over the role. He's not been well these past months, so it may accelerate the hand over. We were going to do it when he turned sixty-five."

She nestled down into the bed, resting on her elbow, pulling the sheets around her. "Now you've told me... are you going to kill me?" She laughed, teasing, remembering the conversation they'd had in the car, when they'd discussed his secret.

Dear God, she was beautiful and didn't even realise it.

He brushed her cheek and kissed her nose. "No, I'm not going to kill you."

He could make love though.

Adam abruptly took off his T-shirt and laid down on his back, tugging up the covers. He switched off the lamp by his bed, dimming the light in the room. Only Sophie's lamp was on.

There was silence between them. He needed to sleep and stop thinking about Sophie. *Hard, when she's fidgeting beside you.*

"I have to hand it to you, Adam, you're good." Sophie broke the silence. Turning to face her, he gave her a look of disbelief, as if expecting a joke. She was going to tease him. And he'd let her. Her confidence was slowly creeping back. "No seriously. You're charming and handsome."

"Thank you."

"Can you dance?"

"You'll find out tomorrow night."

"I'll take that as a yes." She pouted, then continued seriously, "You've convinced my family and friends that we are an item. You know, if you decide the M.D. thing isn't going to work out for you, you could make a career out of this."

Adam's eyes widened. "What? As a male escort?"

"But you're doing such a great job. You could hire yourself out. Women would pay good money for a guy like you." She poked him on the shoulder.

"Is that right?" Adam rolled his eyes as Sophie continued.

"Think about it. Weddings," she listed on her fingers as she spoke, "Christmas parties, retirement parties, christenings, bar mitzvahs, the theatre – all sorts of events where a woman needs a male companion."

"Not bar mitzvahs," Adam replied, a twinkle in his eye.

"Why not?"

"Well, I'm not Jewish for a start." Adam laughed and Sophie chuckled in response.

"Okay, I'll cross bar mitzvahs off your CV."

Adam stared at her in mock horror, his mouth open, speechless.

"I'm joking!" Sophie turned the lamp off and settled down into bed. The room was totally dark, eyes unadjusted to the lack of light. "But if you'd like me to be your pimp..." She laughed just before Adam firmly pushed her out of bed. "Adam!"

Sophie giggled so hard, it was the best sound he'd heard in a very long time.

"I'm stuck! I can't get out," she said between giggles. "Help me."

He turned his lamp on to see the sight and laughed, deep from his belly. She was caught where the chambermaid had tucked the sheets in and, laughing so hard, she didn't have the energy to pull herself back into bed. She'd been dangling, saved by the covers, and hadn't hit the floor with his shove. As he hauled her back into the bed, she wiped tears of laughter from her eyes.

He bent over, almost kissed her, then stopped himself. *What was he doing?* But she'd realised, and it sobered her. Her chest heaved as she got her breath back. For a brief moment he stared into her dark brown eyes, wanting to unbutton those pyjamas, one by one, and feel her soft breasts against his flesh.

Wiping a tear from her face, he gently pressed his lips to her forehead. He moved to his side of the bed and turned off the lamp.

"Goodnight, Sophie."

Chapter Twelve

Sophie was curled up on the chaise longue, eating her breakfast. It was finally Saturday, the wedding day. She agreed with Adam – having breakfast in their room was great. They could relax and let everyone assume what they were up to. She smiled, shaking her head at that thought – she'd never had so much hypothetical sex! But it did work.

Adam had headed down to the pool before breakfast arrived. Probably where he went to get some space, she considered, buttering her toast. The two of them had spent the last couple of days so closely together - the affectionate ways, although nice, were hard. Both of them were on tenterhooks, unable to relax. It felt wonderful to hold his hand, yet strange, because she knew it meant nothing to him. And she shouldn't get drawn into how it made her feel. It had been a long time since she'd been loved. And even now, she wondered if it had been more lust than love with Simon. Because if he'd loved her, would he have treated her so badly?

Then, thinking of last night, teasing Adam, and their brief intimacy, pleasure washed over her like tasting warm, melted chocolate. He'd pushed her out of the bed and they'd had a fit of giggles. He'd let his guard down. For a moment she'd thought he would kiss her, wishing he would. He'd touched her cheek, kissed her forehead...and as quickly as it had started, it finished. He'd swiftly sobered and turned away, saying 'goodnight'. Maybe he wasn't getting attached to Sophie – like she was to him.

Sophie, you are so in trouble. Drop the idea at once.

He doesn't want to get involved.

Had Adam hinted he wasn't the settling down kind, or had James told her? All this pretending – *and wishing it were real* – played on the emotions. Especially as he was gorgeous.

He could hurt her, she realised, but it would be unintentional. It would be *her* fault if she fell for him and he wasn't interested. She'd deal with it. Have to. She couldn't blame Adam if she had this soft spot for him, and he wanted nothing more to do with her after this weekend.

That's going to happen, Sophie. Really, why would he be interested in you?

Good job she was sitting here alone while contemplating these depressing thoughts. This weekend made her want to find love. If only she could find someone like Adam, for real. Maybe she should try to date more, get Kate to introduce her to some of her accounting friends. Someone like Adam though, was going to be hard to beat.

He even turned down Zoe. Sophie's blood boiled and threw her toast onto the plate. Why'd she have to think about her...

Someone knocked at the door.

Sophie jumped from her seat. *Oh, they can't see me like this!* Her hair was ruffled and un-brushed, and she was wearing her pyjamas – the ones that didn't say 'hey, sexy.' At the time of choosing, Adam had been a complete stranger, and she certainly hadn't wanted to give him the wrong impression, so she'd picked the safe option with her cotton, not-sexy pyjamas. Now she wondered if she should have chosen something a little more flattering.

Stop it.

"Who is it?" She scrambled around thinking what to put on; all depending on who was behind the door.

Please be the chambermaid. Please.

"It's Cassie!"

Shit! Cassie needed to see a better, sexier dressed Sophie for this lie to continue. Besides, she'd tease Sophie more for wearing these things than a sexy nightie. She flung off her pyjamas and luckily found a white shirt of Adam's he hadn't put away yet. *Perfect!* He'd been so tidy it almost annoyed her, especially now when she was trying to find something to wear.

She saw the red lipstick mark and scowled. Zoe. She buried her frustration at the thought of that woman – again. She hurried, buttoning it up, leaving a couple at the top undone, and gathered up her pyjamas, quickly shoving them under her pillow.

"Come on, Sophie. What you doing in there?"

"I'm coming. Wait a minute!"

She opened the door, hoping she looked the part of lazing around the hotel room in her boyfriend's clothes. "Sorry. Gosh, you're early. What do you want?" She frowned.

"Did I catch you at a bad time?" Cassie ignored Sophie's question and walked into the room. Taking one look at Sophie, she smiled mischievously at her.

Sophie smiled nervously back, hoping it looked coy more than anything. "No..."

"You sly old fox. Where is he, anyway?" Cassie looked around the room, even checking under the bed. Sophie watched Cassie in disbelief.

"He decided to take a swim before breakfast."

Cassie raised her eyebrows and then pinched a slice of toast. "Thought I'd come tell you the plan," she said. "We're getting our hair done downstairs in the spa at ten, then we'll go back to Natalie's suite to get ready."

Sophie nodded. "Okay, fine."

"That doesn't look like your colour." Cassie pointed to the lipstick on the shirt collar.

"Oh," Sophie tugged at the collar and scowled. "That was Zoe."

"Bitch. No wonder you were upset last night." Cassie rubbed Sophie's arm affectionately. "Uh...did he..?" Cassie nervously looked her in the eye, her face concerned.

"No!"

Cassie shook her head. "Of course he didn't. Sorry. It's just she was bragging last night, but I soon shut her up when I heard your name mentioned."

"Thanks, Cass." Sophie smiled, then frowned. "Why's she here anyway?"

"She's my cousin and her mum and my mum have always been close," Cassie said. "Anyway, her husband couldn't make it so she brought her bitch of a daughter with her instead." Sophie chuckled at her. "You should've told me last night."

"It wasn't worth it." Sophie shrugged. "I didn't want to make a scene. It's Natalie and Gareth's wedding, after all. Besides, Adam and I sorted it out."

Both women turned as the door opened and Adam walked in. His wet, blond hair was slicked back, and his jeans and a tight T-shirt emphasised his toned physique. He looked good even when he wasn't trying.

Cassie winked at Sophie without Adam seeing. Sophie tried not to smirk.

"Morning, Cassie," he said, walking over to Sophie, giving her an approving look up and down. He frowned quizzically at the sight of his shirt, then cunningly smiled.

"Coffee still hot?" he asked, slipping an arm around her waist and kissing her on the cheek. His stubble gently grazed her skin, turning her insides weak. Even chlorine smelled good on him.

Sophie nodded, mumbling a yes.

"How was your swim, Adam?" Cassie asked, her tone having an edge of teasing to it, to Sophie's annoyance.

"Good, thanks," he replied, pouring his coffee.

"I'm surprised you've got the ener –"

"Cassie," Sophie cut in before her best friend could embarrass her, "isn't it time you were going?" She ushered Cassie out of the room, heat rushing to her face. "I'll meet you downstairs at ten."

"Yeah, sure." Cassie waved at Adam over Sophie's shoulder. He waved back. Sophie shut the door after her, turned and rested against the door, closing her eyes and letting out a deep sigh.

So much for a quiet breakfast.

"Nice shirt." Sophie's eyes shot open and she looked down. It rested on her thighs, luckily covering her knickers – thank the heavens! But still too short for her liking, but typically, the sleeves were too long. She got a whiff of the lingering scent of Adam's aftershave; reminding her of the gazebo last night. She made a note to herself to take a closer look in the bathroom to check out the bottle. It was familiar and her favourite. His scent.

"Ah," she hesitated, pulling the shirt down, but it didn't budge. What did she expect? Instead, she fiddled with the top button, doing it up. Then, realising she had no bra on, she folded her arms across her chest as she blushed.

Oh dear God, can he see straight through?

"Sorry. I, uh, um, thought it would look better than my, uh, you know, pyjamas when I answered the door to Cassie."

Oh crap, I feel virtually naked.

"You sure you weren't just trying on my clothes while I was out?" He grinned. Sophie clicked her tongue.

"No, I wasn't." She pulled a face and playfully pinched him on the arm.

"Ouch!"

134

"I'll go take it off. Might as well get showered and dressed." She went over to the wardrobe, careful to not lean too far over, and pulled out some clean clothes.

She looked around, Adam hadn't moved. With a coffee cup to his lips, he watched her. She glowered at him.

"Hey, you can't blame a guy, especially when you're wearing his shirt!"

Chapter Thirteen

Showered and shaved, Adam still had an hour to kill before he even needed to think about getting dressed for the wedding. Maybe he could go for a walk, get some fresh air. A round of golf – now there's an idea.

He still had images of Sophie in his shirt burnt into his brain. It had been a gorgeous view. The shirt had revealed a hint of her nipples, and bloody hell, she had fantastic legs. Okay, he'd seen her legs on the beach, but with her long, chestnut hair tangled, she'd looked like a woman out of a Bond movie. All sexy and tousled, the just-got-out-of-bed look.

She had just got out of bed.

He shook his head and sighed. He'd made a promise to James, and himself, not to get involved. Treat her as a friend, as he would James. Treat her as James would! *Not as James Bond would treat her.*

It was okay to flirt a little, but that was it. The physical side of their relationship was only for show, and only when on show, too. But he kept having visions of helping Sophie out of his shirt, and into that bed…

They'd only shared the room for two days. No woman had had an effect on him like this, not after two days. Sometimes they didn't get past one night.

Golf. Something to take his mind off Sophie.

He grabbed his wallet, car keys and room key card from the dressing table. Closing the door behind him, he headed for the lift.

"Ah, Adam, there you are." Simon walked towards him.

Oh shit, here we go.

"Yeah, uh, Gareth asked if you wanted to join us. I think he knows I'm useless at tying a tie." Simon wasn't exactly happy about this. The lack of eye contact gave it away. Neither was Adam, but he wouldn't let Gareth down, or Sophie.

"Yeah, sure." Adam shrugged.

So much for his round of golf.

They stepped into the lift and Simon pushed the floor button. There was silence between them. The door opened and the tension eased as Simon led Adam to Gareth's suite.

Adam shook Gareth's hand as he walked through the door. The suite was similar to their own room, but larger, with sofas and a table; a separate room led off, and Adam spied a four-poster bed.

"Nervous?" Adam asked Gareth. Partly dressed in his morning suit, Gareth stood awkwardly as if afraid to crease his trousers and shirt.

"No, not really. I'm marrying the girl of my dreams." Gareth winked. "Simon's more worried about the speeches."

They all laughed, some more uneasily than others.

"Here." Gareth handed the two men in turn a glass of champagne and then raised his own. "To the girls of our dreams."

The three men toasted and drank from their glass. Adam thought of Sophie as he sipped the champagne. Was she the girl of his dreams?

In another life maybe.

"And to the other man's girl," Simon said, not so confidently, although glancing at Adam, who watched him.

"Simon, I warned you." Gareth scowled at Simon.

"Sorry," Simon replied. He looked at Adam. "No hard feelings."

"Hey, I don't have a problem." Adam shrugged, trying to keep the smugness hidden. If only Simon knew he had nothing to be jealous about. Although Adam wouldn't let Simon try the slightest thing when it came to Sophie. Hell would freeze over first, and heaven would have to turn a nasty shade of grey.

"Okay, I know it's early. But do you know how to tie one of these things?" Gareth held out a burnt-orange coloured cravat, coordinating with his silk waistcoat.

Do I know how to knot a tie? His father had insisted he learned from a very early age. The kind of schools he'd gone to required he wear a tie.

Adam glanced at his watch. "This is early."

"Yeah, but I want to get to the church and be ready to greet the guests as they arrive. And make sure I'm out of the way so Natalie can leave here and I don't see her."

"Ah, yes, of course." Adam nodded, taking the cravat from Gareth.

By the time he'd polished off his glass of champagne, Adam had the two men looking perfect in their wedding attire. Simon had been bearable; the champagne had helped.

There was a knock on the door and three more men entered, also dressed in morning suits – Gareth's ushers. After brief introductions, Adam saw this as a suitable time to head back to his room, leaving the men to their final preparations.

Suddenly, he had a pang; he wished he could see Sophie. He shook his head, pushing it to the back of his mind.

You're being absurd now.

Still...she was the reason he was here. And they'd been getting along nicely. Great, in fact. Bloody fantastic.

He entered their room.

Sophie turned around and gasped, jumping out of her skin. His eyes widened with surprise, not expecting to see her standing there.

138

Wish granted.

She wore her bridesmaid dress; a strapless, burnt-orange satin dress, which accenuated her figure beautifully. Her hair, pinned up, had white and orange flowers dotted amongst the chestnut locks, with strands of curled hair falling down the sides of her face. She looked...perfectly kissable.

"Oh, hi." She sounded flustered, fiddling with something in her hands.

"I didn't realise you'd come back." He tried to regain his composure, not wanting to show Sophie the effect she had on him. If this was her as a bridesmaid, what would she look like as a bride?

"I forgot my jewellery. Natalie had given us a necklace each. I'm all fingers and thumbs with it – these damn nails! Natalie and Gareth are supposed to be the nervous ones!" She giggled. "Could you help me, please?" She held out a necklace.

"Yeah, of course." Adam took the necklace and Sophie stood with her back to him. He brought the silver chain around her neck. Sophie held the heart-shaped silver locket in place on her chest as he gently clasped the chain at the back of her neck. Her perfume was intoxicating. He had to resist the urge to touch her, stroke her skin, kiss her bare shoulder.

Not appropriate.

She turned to face him and gave a nervous smile. "Thanks."

He nodded, watching her. "You look pretty." He meant gorgeous, stunning...but had to downplay his remarks. Would she read too much into it otherwise?

Sophie rolled her eyes. "Thanks," she replied, but she wasn't taking his compliment seriously. She hadn't all weekend, when he'd been sincere. He wasn't pretending. He did find her beautiful. Never judge a book by its cover, or 'an engineer by her choice of clothes' would be his motto from now on.

She looked nothing like the woman he'd met down the pub

with James.

"Where did you go, anyway?" she asked, nervously holding her hands in front of her, fidgeting.

"Oh, I was going to have a round of golf, if I could. Or at least a few holes, but Simon –"

"Simon?" She scowled.

"It's all right. Gareth had sent him to find me. They were struggling with the cravats, so I never got to the golf course."

"Oh, right." She nodded, and still played with her necklace. "You're dying to play golf, aren't you?"

"Well, I wouldn't say dying as such," Adam replied with equal amounts of sarcasm, and she giggled.

"Okay, I better go. I'll see you at the church. Will you be all right?"

"I'll be fine." He gave her a reassuring smile.

Sophie nodded and leaned towards him, placing a hand on his arm. He caught the sweet, floral scent of her perfume again as he realised she was about to kiss him. He wanted her to kiss him. Suddenly she shook her head, pulling away.

"Sorry, sorry. There's no one here." She playfully slapped her palm against her forehead. He watched her curls bounce. "I'm forgetting myself now." She wouldn't make eye contact with him and hurried out of the door. "I'll see you later."

And then she was gone.

***

Adam made his way into the lavishly decorated old church. Various orange, yellow and white flowers and matching ribbons hung on the end of each pew, making a beautifully decorated aisle for the bride to walk down. By the entrance were two stands holding more flowers. No expense had been spared.

But then it's a wedding. Most people do spend extravagantly on such an occasion, whether they can afford to or not. It's a celebration.

He'd placed himself at the back, on the bride's side, allowing for closer family members and friends to sit at the front. He listened to the hum and rustle, watching as people entered the church; family waving at each other, kissing cheeks and hugging. There were women in hats which complemented their dresses; men in suits, all shades of grey, some more comfortable wearing them than others.

For a moment, as he watched the guests arrive, he allowed the thought to enter his mind – was he missing something here? He pretended to his mates he had a phobia of weddings, but he didn't really. Watching his parents' marriage go down the pan had put him off. If his father couldn't make his marriage work, with his business commitments, could Adam? His mother wanted to see him married off, but his father never showed an opinion. Besides, Adam had got used to playing the field, wining and dining without the fear of supplying the diamond ring.

You don't want this. You're not husband material.

They were ready. All the guests were seated, and the groom and best man stood at the front, waiting patiently. Simon seemed to be sweating more than Gareth. Gareth was the marrying type. A good man, loyal. As for Simon?

It galled him to be anything like Simon.

Two small children nervously walked down the aisle together – the flower girl, possibly no older than four, in her frilly cream dress with a burnt orange sash and the pageboy, of similar height, in his miniature suit. The church fell silent. The odd camera flashed.

The church organ started playing the familiar sound of the bridal chorus. All of the guests stood as the bride, her arm linked through her father's, entered the church. Natalie made a beautiful bride, with her white dress and the veil covering her face. Gareth was a lucky man and by his delighted expression as he watched his wife-to-be join him, he knew it, too.

He watched Sophie, pretty in her dress, alongside Cassie, following the bride, taking her place with Cassie off to the side. With matching dresses and flowers in their hair, they looked almost like twins.

On first impression, he'd never have thought of Sophie as a woman who wore pretty dresses. How wrong had he been?

Adam almost wished he hadn't seen Sophie in her bridesmaid dress now, to see her emerge transformed, like the bride. It would have given him a sense of what Gareth was feeling, seeing.

Poor Sophie, who liked to blend in, was on show. She looked nervous, not used to the attention. She'd been right, yesterday. Even if she wasn't the bride, the bridesmaids certainly did get attention. Eyes were upon them, too. And quite rightly so. Adam needed to convince her she shouldn't hide away. Okay, so he understood maybe why she wanted to hide her femininity at work, to be taken seriously in a male-dominated environment. But out of work, she needed to bloom. And Adam...

Oh God, this was tearing him apart. He didn't want to hurt Sophie. She needed someone stable, reliable, to treat her properly, make her laugh – because her laughter brightened even the greyest of days. She needed the furthest thing from Simon – and him. He couldn't guarantee those things, not if he was anything like his father.

The ceremony went without a hitch. There was a joke made about anyone knowing why they should not be lawfully married. It got a laugh because it was made by the vicar, of all people, with the tone of his voice, and the raise of his eyebrows, looking out towards the full church. Natalie had even winked at Cassie with her fingers to her lips. But it lightened the mood of the guests, removing the intensity, the seriousness of the occasion. Laugh or cry, so they say. Some of the older women had handkerchiefs ready to dab their eyes.

The guests stood up and followed the bride and groom out of the church, played out with the traditional wedding march by the organist, and Adam followed, looking for Sophie in the church's courtyard.

"Are you okay?" she asked, frowning slightly.

"Yeah, yeah, fine. You?"

"I'm starving, but I think we've got to have photographs now," Sophie said, grimacing. "They want some at the church and in the hotel grounds, too." Her tone was unenthusiastic but Adam chuckled, glad Sophie was back on his arm.

Chapter Fourteen

Sophie estimated there had to be over a hundred people seated in the large ballroom. The circular dinner tables were decorated with yellow, orange, and white balloons, and flowers of similar colours. Natalie had thought of every detail, from children blowing bubbles to the table confetti. The room exuded a celebratory excitement from the wedding guests.

The toastmaster tapped a spoon against a glass to silence the guests.

"Ladies and gentleman, please be upstanding for the bride and groom, Mr and Mrs Staplehurst."

The guests stood as Natalie and Gareth entered the room, making their way to the top table, hand in hand. Natalie's dress was beautiful in its simplicity, with its train trailing behind her. Sophie swallowed down the emotions gathering in her tightening throat and blotted a tear. She was glad she'd made it this weekend; she would have regretted missing Natalie and Gareth finally tying the knot. To Sophie, they had always seemed perfect for each other.

Would Sophie find the same as Natalie had found in Gareth? She glanced at Adam and then kicked herself internally for even thinking of him.

This will end in tears. Your tears.

The bride and groom sat, followed by the guests. Finally, Sophie thought, sighing, as she sat back down. She was so hungry; she wanted to eat before she fainted from the lack of sugar running through her veins and the amount of alcohol she'd slowly been consuming. Being a bridesmaid meant champagne was on tap. Or that's how it seemed. Nice but also dangerous; she could easily make a fool of herself.

The photographs had gone on forever. Adam had stayed out of most of them, but Natalie and Gareth had insisted he join them in some of the photos. The 'friends' ones. The lie caught on camera. She'd be lying about Adam for the rest of her life – or one day would have to come clean.

"You okay?" Adam placed a hand on her arm.

"Sorry." She blinked out of her daydream. "I'm fine. My cheeks ache." She rubbed her face gently with her palms. "They hurt so much from smiling for the bloody camera. Everybody's camera! I don't think I've had to smile so much in my life. I dread to think what Natalie and Gareth must be feeling. If one more person asks for a bloody photo…"

Adam laughed. "Here, have this." He handed her a glass of champagne. "This will make you feel better."

See! It was on tap.

She chuckled and took a sip. "Ah, yes, much better. Now I need some food or you'll be picking me up off the floor later."

On the plus side, she certainly wouldn't be able to feel her aching cheeks.

"I'm half tempted to eat the favours." She fiddled with the orange ribbon around the net pouches, releasing the five sugared almonds. "For health," she muttered, popping one of the sweets into her mouth and crunching it, then after a moment, she tapped Adam on the arm, "Were you okay sitting all by yourself?"

"Yeah, why?"

"You looked," she fiddled with her napkin, "I don't know

145

– distant, during the ceremony."

Adam laughed. "No, no. I was just thinking."

"Oh, yeah? What about?"

"Nothing. Nothing." He reached across the table for the pitcher of water.

"I'm doing it again, aren't I?" she said. "I am interested, though, and worried."

"Nothing to worry about." Adam lifted a jug of water and offered it to Sophie first.

She held up her glass, thinking about the champagne Cassie had made her drink as they'd got ready, now regretting it. Yeah, some water would be good. And food. *Where was the bloody food?*

She watched as Adam poured himself a glass, wondering how she could get him to open up, even if only slightly. He knew everything about her now.

"I don't bite, you know," she said.

"I know you don't."

"Well, you confessed last night you're the son of the managing director of Thomas Robotics," she said, keeping her voice low, stumbling on. She still couldn't believe his dad owned the company. Her dad had owned a couple of restaurants, but it really wasn't the same. Adam was worth a lot of money. "So, we're friends right? Don't be afraid to talk to me." She chinked his champagne glass. Sophie decided he needed to drink more, too. That way, she wouldn't look so drunk to him and he might open up.

"Yes, we're friends." His expression was suspicious.

"You must be fed up with my family and friends harassing you, having to idly chat with them. How bad have the interrogations of the new boyfriend been?"

He smoothed his hand through his hair and Sophie thought she glimpsed the hint of anxiety in his expression.

"I feel bad," she said quickly, guilt hitting her, not for the first time this weekend.

"Hey, we've gone over this. It really isn't that bad." Adam placed his other hand over hers. "I'm actually enjoying myself. And you're all right." He winked at her, and she chuckled at his teasing.

The waiters and waitresses came around serving dinner, ending Sophie's conversation, but satisfying her need for food. Adam went into his automatic charm mode. And any doubts or nervousness he'd been showing fell away. She couldn't stop admiring how well he had the other diners at the table all charmed. It was hard to believe he wasn't happy. She hoped he'd be honest with her, of all people.

He'd tell her if things weren't okay, wouldn't he?

***

"Come on, Adam." Sophie pulled at Adam's hand to get him off his seat. With dinner over and the tables cleared, the evening entertainment had started and the guests were heading for the dance floor.

"No, no, Sophie, please, honey." Shaking his head, he placed his champagne glass on the table.

She leaned in towards him, not letting go of his hand. "Come on, show me what a mover you are on the dance floor." She was tipsy – too much champagne and not enough food. Well, not enough food in time before the champagne had truly kicked in. Now she felt confident enough to be cheeky with Adam. And she'd made sure he'd had a couple of glasses of champagne during the meal, too. "Are you my *boyfriend* or not?" she whispered. She gave Adam her best smile, hoping it was as good as his.

Adam narrowed his eyes playfully and allowed himself to be dragged onto the dance floor. Sophie giggled, her eye on Cassie.

"She's a bad influence on you," he said.

Sophie winked at him good-naturedly as they made their way to the centre of the dance floor, where Cassie was dancing with some poor bloke. Cassie had made it her mission to make sure everyone enjoyed the night and as far as Sophie could tell, they were.

Sophie hadn't laughed so much in ages, and Adam proved to be more fun on the dance floor than expected. Maybe the champagne had loosened him up. He kept up the act. Every now and then he'd make sure he had hold of Sophie, spinning her round to the rock 'n roll music, giving her a kiss.

His body, close to hers, swaying in time to the music, left her excited and buzzing. For Sophie the reality was blurring. Her actions felt genuine towards him. Luckily, he'd think it an act. At least that's what she'd say if he questioned it, if he didn't want it to be real.

"Okay, okay, I need to sit down." Sophie finally felt defeated. "And I'm not so keen on this song."

Adam looked relieved, grasping her hand and leading her off the dance floor. They ignored the complaints from Cassie, chuckling with each other as they headed back to their table, their champagne waiting for them.

"Happy now?" he said, sitting down, unbuttoning his waistcoat and loosening his tie. He pulled her into his lap and she giggled.

"Much happier," she said, finishing off her drink. "But now I've got to visit the ladies. I need a wee." Adam chuckled at her. "Oops, probably too much information." *Way to go, Sophie. How to impress the man.* How much had she drunk? She'd hoped the dancing would sober her up.

She reached over him, to the centre of the table and grabbed her clutch bag, then gave him a kiss on the cheek. "Be back in a jiff."

"I'll be here, as long as your Aunt Veronica doesn't accost me again."

Sophie held her hand over her mouth to hide her giggle. Oh God, she felt like a drunken wreck. *Sober up.*

***

Adam shook his head as he watched Sophie walk off towards the powder rooms. He had to admit he hadn't had this much fun in ages. Hell, weddings were fun – he just hadn't been to that many. And it certainly did make a difference if you had the perfect date.

He swallowed.

Was Sophie his perfect date?

Don't go there. Sophie was fun to be with, once she'd let her guard down. She ticked all the right boxes – attractive, intelligent, sensitive and a lot of fun…but would he be any good for her? He pretended to be, but what if he had to do it for real? The act came rather naturally, thinking about it…

He sighed, shaking off those thoughts and took in his surroundings, checking Simon's whereabouts. At the bar. Good. He liked keeping an eye on him.

His smile disappeared when Zoe arrived at his table, with a bottle of champagne in one hand and a glass in the other.

"Refill?"

"No thanks." Adam frowned. But she didn't take the hint, sitting beside him, so he smiled. His fake one. *Try to be nice.* Now *this* was difficult.

He watched the woman, studying her. He didn't trust her or like her. He knew what she was capable of.

"Having fun?" Zoe said.

"Yeah, lots."

"Find it hard to believe with Miss Goodie –"

"Her name is Sophie." Adam turned away, sucking in a deep

breath. He didn't want to waste time on this woman, who was filled with jealousy and spite. He was half-tempted to get up and join Cassie back on the dance floor. Rescue the poor new bloke she'd wrapped herself around.

Adam liked Cassie. Harmless fun. And not once had she tried anything with him. Okay, she flirted, but she flirted with everyone, even Sophie. He glared back at Zoe. This woman meant harm.

"Where is she, anyway? Can't believe she's not draped on your arm. She never used to let Simon breathe."

"She's gone to the ladies. We're not joined at the hip." Adam didn't bother looking at her, watched the dance floor instead, laughing at Cassie's antics.

"You sure?" Zoe said spitefully. "I can't see Simon. I bet she isn't over him, like she says she is."

Adam shot a glance at the bar, not listening to Zoe's malicious words as she continued to ramble. She was right; Simon had gone. He looked around the large room, searching every table and the dance floor. He felt a hand brushing his cheek.

"While the cat's away, babe, why don't the mice play?" Zoe purred in his ear.

Adam shoved the hand away. With a look of disgust, he stood up, revolted to be in her presence.

"Well, I'm definitely not a rat. Go find some other toy to play with."

He walked out of the ballroom wanting to find Sophie. Or Simon. It didn't matter who first. As long as they weren't together.

Chapter Fifteen

Preened, with lipstick and make-up touched up, Sophie left the restroom satisfied. She giggled to herself, realising she'd had too much to drink. Oh, why had Cassie insisted on a couple of glasses of champagne to calm their nerves before walking down the aisle? They weren't the ones getting married.

She couldn't stop herself smiling, thinking of Adam on the dance floor. How much would he pay her not to tell everyone at work? Although she wouldn't say anything really, but she could always use it for her own advantage, when he pulled out the old 'smile' card. Or if she needed a favour at work

Sophie! That's probably the reason he doesn't like people knowing who he is. Probably why he doesn't get attached to women either, thinking they're interested in his money, not him. *Shame on you! You're better than that.*

Here, this weekend, it didn't matter. Adam didn't need his money, Sophie didn't want it. She'd still fancy him, managing director of Thomas Robotics or not.

Oh, Sophie Trewyn, you're in trouble.

As she walked round the corner, her smile dropped.

"Hello, Sophie."

"Simon." She tensed, clutching her bag tighter.

"Look, can we talk?" Simon slowly led her away from the

wedding party.

Hesitantly she walked with him. "I'd rather we went back to the ballroom."

"I just want to talk."

"We can talk in the —"

"Alone. It'll take five minutes."

Her heart beat faster, erratic, and she found it hard to look him in the eye. Why did he still have this effect on her? Why couldn't she act coolly around him? Why did her insecurity creep in? She hadn't forgotten how badly he'd hurt her. He might be a handsome man, but he no longer attracted her. She saw straight through him. She'd find out what he wanted, then get the hell away from him. Maybe he wants to apologise for his behaviour.

He walked her around to a secluded corner. They could barely hear the music coming from the ballroom. She searched for people but there were none. She nervously frowned at him.

"Simon, what's this about? What do you want?"

"I just want to talk to you." He sounded drunk, slurring his words. "I want you back."

"I'm sorry, but I don't want you back in my life." *Why am I apologising?*

"Oh, come on, Sophie. You know you don't believe that." He moved closer; she moved back until she was up against the wall. "I don't believe it, either."

She tried sidestepping but he followed. She could smell the alcohol on his breath and grimaced. She'd made a mistake.

"We can start from where we left off."

"Simon, it's over between us."

"Sophie, please, let me back into your life."

For a moment, Sophie thought he looked rather pathetic, and then, as if he'd seen her guard dropping, he moved forward and placed his hands on her waist.

Sophie pushed at his hands, but each time he placed them somewhere else. Fear had frozen her. She didn't know what to do. She didn't want to make a scene, ruin Natalie and Gareth's day. She could be overreacting.

Think.

"I'm sorry, okay. I did something stupid, I won't do it again," he whispered in her ear, kissing around her neck, a hand brushing her cheek. Hot breath and the stench of alcohol immobilised Sophie. "I promise."

"Simon, get your hands off me!" she snapped, again trying and again failing to shove him away. "You said you wanted to talk."

"I do."

He was way too strong for her, his solid body pressed against hers. Her heart thumped hard inside her chest. She wanted to scream, realising she might be in real danger, but couldn't. Simon wouldn't harm her, would he?

"Look, Simon, please. Adam will be —"

"Forget Adam. Let me remind you of what *we* had." Ignoring her pleas, he gently stroked her face. She closed her eyes for a moment, unable to look at him. Her eyelids stung trying to force back tears. "Remember what we had, huh?" he whispered, nibbling her neck. "We were so good together, babe."

"You said I was —"

"Forget what I said. I wanted to hurt you back then." His wet, drunken kisses plastered her bare skin. Her heart ached with fear, her blood pounded in her ears. She could hear only that and Simon, everything else was deafened. "Does he push the same buttons, babe? Like I use to." Simon groaned, pressing himself harder against her.

He slid his rough, calloused hand gently down from her neck, along her bare skin and rested his hand on her breast, cupping it, gently squeezing, her satin dress giving her little protection. Years ago it would have felt sexy and good; they'd have been fighting to remove each other's clothes. Tonight it made Sophie's skin crawl.

Think.

She tried again, slapping at his hand to push it away, shoving him, trying to escape, but she was wedging herself into a corner. He stayed on her like a leech.

"Simon, please, let me go." She closed her eyes, making a silent prayer. *Adam.* "I don't want this."

"Adam's no good for you." His lips crept from her neck round to her own lips. She felt rigid, too scared to move any further, his strength overpowering hers. "He's no man for you."

Sophie slapped him across his face. "Fuck you, Simon," she snapped. "Adam's so much more than you'll ever be." She knew exactly what Adam was compared to this bastard.

"I very much want to fuck you, Sophie." Simon laughed, grabbing her backside. She gasped as his pelvis rubbed against hers, feeling his arousal. She swallowed down the bile rising in her mouth. She shoved him, fought with him. As he leaned in to kiss her, she screwed her eyes shut, wincing, heart pounding and her throat tightening with fear. Her eyes welled with tears.

She wanted Adam to save her, but this was her battle. She'd wanted not to draw attention to them.

But obviously the softly-softly approach wasn't working.

With all the hate, revenge and anger flowing through her bloodstream, making her body tremble, she did the only thing she could think of; she stamped her heel onto his foot. Hard.

Simon instantly let go of her, yelling out in pain. "Ooww! Fuck! You bitch."

Bastard.

She was so pleased she hadn't slipped her shoes off – three inch heels were a killer.

"Leave me alone!" She saw his fury but now she stood firm.

"How dare you? How *dare* you?" Anger raged through her now. She was finally going to say what she'd wanted to after all these years.

"You," she jabbed him, "you were the one who ended it."

"It was a mistake."

Sophie slapped him. He grabbed her wrist, so she went for the other foot with her heel but he stepped back, releasing her.

She narrowed her eyes scornfully. "You hounded me until I said yes – which I did thinking it would shut you up. And, yes, we hit it off. We spent those precious months never apart. You made all those promises, but you couldn't keep them, not even for a few weeks." Sophie was on a roll. God, it felt good to get it off her chest. Simon was even withdrawing from her. "You called me frigid and cold. You bastard! Don't go on about wanting me back." She was shouting now, not caring who heard, her body trembling with the confrontation. "I'm over you. So fuck off!"

***

Adam hurried along the corridor hearing raised voices, and stopped, witnessing Sophie giving Simon hell. He wanted to grab hold of Simon and smack him into next year. What had the low-life done to cause her to react like this? But Sophie was fighting back and he had to admire the fire in her.

He desperately wanted to intervene, but he held back, realising Sophie needed to do this, to let out the emotion she'd carried inside her all this time. He'd be ready to help if needed.

Unfortunately, Simon saw Adam before Sophie did, so he had to get involved.

"Ah, look, Adam's here to save the day. Get your woman under control."

"You bastard," she said, shoving Simon away. "I should be

pressing charges for bloody assault!"

"Did he touch you?" Anger surged through Adam, realising this may have been more serious. His fists tightened. Maybe he should break the bastard's nose.

"You fucking enjoyed it," Simon bawled.

"I was repulsed."

"Fucking frigid bitch."

Adam launched at Simon, thrusting him against the wall, his fist clenched around Simon's shirt, pushing into his windpipe.

"Adam! I don't want any trouble," Sophie said, shakily. "It's Natalie and Gareth's wedding." She glared at Simon. "He's trying to get the last word, that's all. It's what he's like. Please let him go. It's not like he hasn't called me that before."

Adam released his grip slightly, so Simon could breathe. "All right, you've heard Sophie. No trouble." Then, fuelled by a wave of anger, Adam pushed again and venom laced his words, "But if I see you anywhere near my girl again, I swear, I'll ruin you. You'll have nothing left by the time I'm finished."

"Adam, please...let him go."

Adam did as asked, with a final shove. He wanted to be in Sophie's good books. He was more sophisticated than a drunken brawl – unlike Simon. He needed to walk away. Adam slipped his arm around Sophie's waist.

"You okay?" he asked, and she gently nodded, holding in her tears. He could feel her trembling as he pulled her close.

"Fuck you," Simon shouted.

She's right, Simon has to have the last word.

"You don't like it, do you?" Adam said angrily, glaring at Simon. "You let her go. And now she's returned, more beautiful, made something of herself, standing on her own two feet. She hasn't crumbled at the sight of you. She's too good for you, Simon." *And too good for me.* "Let it go."

Sophie scowled at Simon. "He doesn't like it, because I've found a better man," she said, and they walked away, leaving Simon mumbling some last words, but they weren't interested – though Adam could quite easily have punched the guy.

"My *girl*?" Sophie said, looking questioningly at Adam.

With her arm linked through his, he could still feel her trembling. They walked towards the party, the music getting louder as they got closer. He gave her a squeeze and enjoyed having her close again.

"Well, I want to look like the over-protective jealous boyfriend type. He might get the message that way. Do you think it worked?" He acted relaxed, hiding his anger, trying to push Simon to the back of his mind. It wouldn't be good for Sophie to see him wound up; he needed to be a calming influence right now. And he didn't like being angry in front of her. This was their last night; he wanted her to enjoy the evening.

She nervously smiled. She held out a hand – it still trembled. "Yeah, I think so. God, that was terrible."

"Sophie." Adam stopped their stride and turned her to face him, gently brushing her cheek with his thumb. "He didn't hurt you, did he? Back there...you said assault." Adam tried to control his angry thoughts of knocking his fist into Simon's face.

"Uh..." she shook her head. He could still feel her trembling and she tried holding in her tears. One trickled down her cheek and he wiped it away.

"You were fabulous back there..." he said, wanting to give her some confidence back. Adam's tone became serious again, dwelling on what she'd said. "But did he hurt you? Because I'll go back and –"

"Don't!" She wiped her face and composed herself. After a moment, taking a deep breath, she said, "He was just drunk, and for a moment I didn't know what to do. I was trying not to make a scene."

Sophie fumbled in her handbag and found a small bottle of perfume, which she sprayed around her neck. Adam frowned at her.

"He was all over me," she said, and Adam's jaw clenched. "I don't want to smell of ale and slobber." She shuddered.

Adam sniffed, then kissed her neck, pulling her closer into a hug. Not necessary but he couldn't resist it, and Sophie didn't complain. "You smell fine."

As they approached the party, Sophie hesitated outside the door, pulling her hand out of Adam's.

"Adam, I don't know if I want to go back in there."

"Nonsense. He's not ruining your night. Besides, we haven't got long to go." Adam leaned in towards her, whispering into her ear, "Let's finish the champagne and then we can head up to our room if you still feel uncomfortable."

"Okay," she said softly.

Adam slipped his hand around her waist and they walked back into the party.

Approaching their table, Sophie faltered. Zoe was sitting there. Sophie didn't need this shit.

"Oh, good, you're still here. And there was me worrying you'd leave," Adam said, glowering at the woman.

"Ah, the lovebirds return," Zoe replied sarcastically, ignoring his own sarcasm. Sophie's hand tightened around Adam's.

"You know, Simon is looking for a cheap date," Adam said, taking off his jacket, placing it over the back of a chair. "Why don't you go find him?"

Zoe laughed, but her expression sobered when she saw how deadly serious he was.

"Come on, sweetheart, let's dance," Adam said, tugging Sophie's hand, leading her towards the dance floor. He noticed her smug smile towards Zoe.

Once on the dance floor, Sophie placed her arms around his

neck. The slower songs had begun, meaning the evening was coming to an end. Their weekend, too.

Van Morrison's 'Brown Eyed Girl' started playing. Adam looked at Sophie, and she rolled her eyes.

"My dad always used to sing this to me," she said, blushing, chewing her lip.

Her brown eyes stared back at him. He'd never taken much notice before; how dark they were. And yet, this weekend, he'd been staring into them all the time. He glanced around the room; Cassie winked at him. Zoe sat alone at a table, arms crossed, her keen eye still on them, scowling.

Well, let's give her something to watch. Let's give them all something to watch. He leaned in, his eyes never leaving Sophie's. Gently cupping her chin with his hand, he placed his lips onto hers and kissed her. Letting the music flood over them, drowning out everything else, he naturally inserted his tongue, caressing hers, exploring her exquisite mouth. He closed his eyes. Just Morrison, Sophie, and their kiss.

He knew it was a mixture of adrenalin and alcohol fuelling this moment, but he couldn't help relish it. Kissing Sophie would never be a chore.

She pulled closer, tighter, running her hand through his hair, her bare arms wrapping around his neck as they danced, circling slowly to the music, around and around as they kissed. Adam lowered his arm to the small of her back, and drew her as close as two people could get with their clothes on. It felt fantastic. He held her tight in his arms, hoping she'd forget Simon's assault.

It was a gorgeous kiss; a kiss that could lead to further things. He wanted to guide her to their room right now.

Reluctantly he withdrew, Van Morrison still singing about his brown-eyed girl. But he kept his mouth on hers. He could feel her lips move into a smile. He grinned too, breaking the kiss, opening his eyes, but keeping his hold, keeping her close. She looked up at him, her body resting against his, arms still around his neck. She nervously chewed her bottom lip.

"Are you supposed to be enjoying this?" she spoke softly, still swaying gently with the music.

"I always enjoy kissing a beautiful woman."

"Oh, behave," she retorted sarcastically.

He pulled her close again, and she rested her head against his chest as they continued to dance slowly in time with the music. She felt so natural in his arms.

Cassie came twirling around them, dragging another poor, unsuspecting victim with her. Some other love song was now playing in the background and even more couples crowded the dance floor.

"I got to tell you two this," Cassie slurred, beaming at them in their dancing embrace. She leaned in towards them, unsteady on her feet. "You know, you two look gorgeous together," she said softly, winking at them.

Sophie lifted her head off Adam's chest, laughing off the compliment.

"No, really, you do. Hopefully it'll be your wedding next, right?"

Adam tensed and Sophie giggled.

"Cassie, we've only been together a few weeks! Don't scare the poor bloke," Sophie coolly replied. "Besides, you caught the bride's bouquet, didn't you?"

"Me? Get married?" Cassie snorted with laughter. "Got to find someone crazy enough first!" She looked at the man she was dancing with, who shown a brief worried expression, and shook her head at him. "Anyway, where'd you slope off to when it was being thrown?"

Sophie shrugged. "I think I must have been powdering my nose."

"Well, you missed a battle for the bouquet, but I won it!"

Sophie laughed, shaking her head and Cassie was gone, dragging the poor soul with her around the dance floor.

"She's mad, I tell you," Sophie said. "She was kidding, you know that? It's your smile; it blinds her." Adam frowned. "I mean, you know, you're the one she thinks is gorgeous. If she knew the truth," Sophie chuckled as she spoke, "she'd realise we're like chalk and cheese." He noticed she wouldn't catch his eye, her cheeks were flushed.

Adam faked a chuckle as Sophie rested her head back on his shoulder, and they continued to dance to the music, slowly turning. He liked the feeling of her in his arms.

Were they, really, chalk and cheese? If anything, they had got on famously.

Then she stopped their dance and looked up at him. Her brown eyes, like dark chocolate, staring at him, sent warmth to his bones. She whispered softly, "Thank you, Adam. For everything."

Chapter Sixteen

Sophie stepped out of the elevator, one arm linked around Adam's, her other hand holding a half-empty bottle of champagne. She'd snagged the bottle from the table after the reception had ended, but now wondered if it was a good idea. She was already drunk. Not scrape-her-off-the-floor drunk, but with that warm fuzzy feeling, giving her a new confidence.

The corridor was empty, so she could have released her hold on Adam, but she quite liked the support he provided. His strength. It might be the last opportunity she got to be close with him.

Now there's the champagne talking.

"I told Cassie she should come and see you in Surrey," Adam said.

"Oh, Adam."

"What? I got the impression she'd never visited you," he said. "You could introduce her to James."

"How do you mean? James is happy with Kate. You know that."

"Yes, yes, sorry, of course." Adam sighed. "Still trying to get used to James all loved up with Kate."

"They've been seeing each other nearly a year now; he's going to propose on her birthday."

"Is he?"

"Yes! Hasn't he told you?" Sophie wondered if she'd been told in confidence and had now betrayed James.

"Probably knew I would comment, or talk him out of it." He laughed.

"Why would you do that?"

Adam cleared his throat. "I'm joking. Though, didn't realise they were that serious. Probably explains..."

"What?"

"Nothing. Nothing."

Sophie frowned, then grumbled. "Anyway, why would you want to encourage Cassie to come visit me? I've been trying to put her off."

"Don't you want to see her?"

"Yes, of course, I do, but...what about us? She'd be expecting to see you. If we went out, it would be another night of pretence, and to Cassie, who I hate lying to already." Though the way she felt at this moment, it wouldn't be a charade for her. The line was blurring. Even holding onto him now – she was doing it because she wanted to. The kiss on the dance floor had been the same. "And what about you? Would you be prepared to pretend again?"

He hesitated, fumbling in his jacket pocket, not quite meeting her eye. Was he having doubts? Would he say he didn't want their relationship to be a lie? Maybe she should swig the champagne and numb the pain now.

"Adam?"

"Yeah, yeah, of course. I made you a promise," he replied.

"I'm thinking more short term," Sophie added quickly, sensing the awkwardness. *No, he probably doesn't want to do this anymore.* "If she turns up in a month or something, well...well, I'm not sure what excuse I'm going to make yet to end our *relationship* – hypothetically."

Adam just kept his lips pursed and nodded.

How was she going to end this relationship to her friends and family – without looking like a fool? With another lie, of course.

They reached their room and Sophie leaned tiredly against the wall, waiting as Adam got the key card from his jacket pocket. They both heard voices coming along the corridor, so Adam leaned in towards Sophie, placing his forehead against hers, their noses almost touching. To a bystander, a playful loving embrace.

She slid her free arm around him, under his jacket, savouring the feeling of his physical presence. He was so warm, and firm. She savoured the subtle scent of his aftershave which still lingered around his throat. Deep inside she had an urge to kiss him, press her body against his, but she stopped herself. Did he want it too? His breath, warm on her cheek, and her own nerves made her heart race as they both stared into one another's eyes. Both laughed nervously. The champagne.

She fought her nerves and ever so gently, she pressed her lips against his. *Oh, what the hell?* And to her delight he kissed her back. For the first time in a very long time, Sophie felt aroused, alive. There was nothing more enjoyable than kissing this man, except maybe one thing... something she hadn't done in a while, too afraid to try again. She wanted to make love to Adam. Only Adam.

He released her from the kiss. She no longer cared who the voices belonged to. She took no notice as the people passed them by. He slid the key card down the slot, it beeped and he opened the door. Taking the champagne bottle from her, he tugged at her hand, and once inside, kicked the door closed with his heel. He kissed her again, the champagne forgotten on the dressing table. He was intent and sexy, focussing only on her.

Between hot kisses and gentle moans, Sophie whispered, "Pins... please...out of my hair..." She kicked off her shoes, instantly shortening three inches, sighing with relief. He turned her around, gently removing the pins, kissing her neck and bare back revealed by her dress.

Her hair soon tumbled down her back and on to her shoulders, and she felt relief that her hair was no longer being tightly held in place. His hand swept her curls aside and he pressed his lips to her flesh. She turned, her mouth finding his.

Then, skilful hands unzipped her dress, letting it fall to the floor. Feeling inadequate, she fumbled with the buttons of Adam's shirt as he enticed her towards the bed.

Her strapless bra released and thrown aside, the back of her knees touched the bed, and she tumbled back onto it, as Adam moved slowly over her, still kissing, nibbling, licking. He was an expert in this field; she wanted to beg him take her there and then, the liquid hot pulse deep in her belly, urgent. *Need to make this last, Sophie.* He was attentive, unlike Simon, who had always been urgent, lustful.

Adam's lips on hers, the kiss became more passionate, heated, tongues probing, arousing all her senses. At last, blindly, she had his shirt undone and off, his flesh against hers. She heard the flick of his buckle as he started undoing the belt to his trousers, though his mouth never left hers.

He broke from the kiss, moving down her neck, running his tongue along her collarbone, her nipples hardening under the hotness of his mouth. Then, down to her navel, making her stomach pull in. She moaned as Adam's tongue licked along the top of her satin underwear, reminding her again this wasn't Simon. Simon never teased, never took such care or time.

"Adam..." She gasped. His hands moved over the soft fabric and he looked her straight in the eye. She lifted her hips to aid the removal. Briefly, she worried she'd be no good at this, she'd disappoint him. "Be gentle."

He stared as she lifted her head to meet his gaze. As if touching hot coals, he snapped his hands away.

"Shit, what are we doing? We can't do this!" he said, quickly pulling away from her.

Frantic, he grabbed his shirt from off the floor and tossed it at her. She fumbled to put it on, suddenly ashamed of her body. Her throat tightened, tears stinging her eyes. *Mustn't cry. Mustn't cry. What have I done wrong?* Her body still buzzed with need but it was quickly coming down with cold realisation.

As if he'd seen her mortified expression he was quickly on the bed, cupping her face. "I'm sorry. I'm sorry. You deserve better, Sophie. I made a promise to James."

What promise to James? Damn, James!

She recoiled, leaping off the bed, wrapping his shirt around her. Unthinking, she grabbed the champagne bottle and rushed into the bathroom, slamming the door behind her and locking it.

***

Fuck. Fuck. Fuck!

What had he been thinking? Too much champagne, that's what! Adam paced the hotel room. He'd gone into autopilot outside in the hallway – the way she'd kissed him, his brain had dropped to his trousers. He hadn't seen Sophie, the real Sophie; he'd seen a beautiful woman he must seduce. He'd treated her like any other woman he dated. Wine, dine, then bed. And he'd nearly completed the task too. Her reminder, that she'd been hurt before, stopped him in his tracks, slamming him into a brick wall.

What a mess. What a fucking mess.

He found a T-shirt and slung it on, his brain slowly moving back inside his skull. Taking a deep breath, regaining composure, he knocked on the bathroom door.

"Sophie, please come out." He tried the handle – locked. "I'm sorry." *Fuck. What made me so stupid?*

166

It wasn't as though he didn't want to make love to Sophie, because, oh yes, he did. But she'd see it for more than it was... what it could be... He couldn't commit. Just couldn't. She'd hate him in the end.

She probably hates you now.

"Leave me alone," she shouted through the door.

He noticed the bathroom lock had a safety feature on the outside. Even though he knew he should respect her wishes, he couldn't leave her in there to stew. He had to talk to her. He had to stop her pouring more champagne down her throat. Knowing he was committing a great wrong, he dug in his pocket, found a pound coin, stuck it into the slot and turned, yanking the handle at the same time.

Sophie, sitting on the toilet seat, was drinking from the champagne bottle, black mascara-stained tears streaming down her face. She stood instantly, startled by Adam's entrance. She'd buttoned the shirt but it still revealed her slender legs.

"Go away," she snapped, scowling.

"Sophie, please, let me explain."

"What did I do? What did *I* do?" she hissed. A new flood of tears streamed her cheeks and Adam felt the wrench of guilt he deserved. He rushed forward, took her in his arms, relieved his brain didn't react to touching her.

"You did absolutely nothing wrong. Nothing. Oh, God, I'm so sorry."

She went to drink more from the bottle, but he snatched it, pouring the rest of the contents – which was not much – down the sink, leaving the bottle dumped there upside down. "You don't need any more to drink, either. We've both had too much."

"You speak for yourself. I think I need to be unconscious."

"Sophie, please forgive me. I should never have...misled you."

"Why did you? Am I not your type of woman?"

"Sophie, you are better than my type," Adam said, running both hands through his hair. "I stopped myself because I want us to remain friends. Having sex will complicate things. I don't want us complicated."

"Our relationship is a lie – can't get more complicated than that."

"Our friendship is not a lie." He wiped the tears from her cheeks with his thumbs, then kissed her nose.

"James is my friend and he does not kiss me on the nose," she said coldly, glaring up at him.

Adam removed his hands from her face. "Right. The line is a bit blurry. We have had a lot to drink." Sophie's expression remained grim. For a moment they were silent. "Please... I'm sorry. You did nothing wrong."

She took a deep breath.

Seeing her calming, he said tenderly, "Let's go to bed – as friends. I'll even sleep on the sofa."

Sophie sighed. "There's no need." She wiped her face as she glanced in the mirror. "Just let me wash off my make-up."

Adam left the bathroom, closing the door behind him, and walked over to the wardrobe to hang his clothes up – what clothes he had. Sophie was still wearing his shirt. He picked up her brides-maid dress from the floor where it had dropped... *Really, really need your head examined. James will kill you if he learns about this.* He got a hanger out of the wardrobe and put the dress away, smelling the floral aroma of Sophie's fragrance as he did so.

If I've fucked this friendship up with Sophie I'll never forgive myself.

Adam's head buzzed, angry at himself. He turned Sophie's bedside lamp on, turning off the rest of the lights in the room before getting into bed. It gave enough glow in the room, but his eyes were starting to tire of the bright light. It had been a long day.

He decided not to strip off his T-shirt, instead sinking down in the bed, he hauled the covers up around him. He watched the bathroom door.

What a day. What a weekend. If he'd known the whole truth he doubted he'd have come. Then again, part of him was glad he had. Sophie really shouldn't have come to this wedding on her own with the shit that had been thrown at her. Simon. Zoe. *Me*.

He thought of their last kiss on the dance floor, then just now in the bedroom. He'd been enjoying it more than he should have, otherwise would he have seduced her like that? He didn't want to hurt Sophie, didn't want her thinking he wanted a relationship with her.

He did but it would end in tears. Just like tonight.

Seeing that fiery side of her this evening, as she'd slapped Simon had revealed she wasn't really a pushover. She'd probably been trying to keep patient with him for Natalie and Gareth's sake. But it had given Adam a fantasy in his head, arguing with Sophie, seeing her riled – feisty and sexy, and then making up...

One you need to squash. You almost got yourself into some really hot water tonight.

Adam rubbed his face. He should turn over and go to sleep, but Sophie had been in the bathroom a long time now. He hoped she wasn't stirring things over. It really wasn't her fault.

Should he knock, check she was okay?

Luckily, tomorrow should be easier going for both of them. They needed a breather. Sure, at breakfast he'd have to whisper a few sweet nothings, hold her hand and make little loving gestures. But he didn't think he was going to get an excuse to kiss her again, not like that. Probably for the best, all things considered.

They'd be back to normal, soon.

What was normal? Before this weekend, he had hardly known her. He'd seen her occasionally at work, but had never taken any interest in her, probably said all of two words to her in the whole time she'd been working for the company. *That would change.*

Or would it be best to go back to the way it was?

But James was their mutual friend. They were going to see more of each other. He didn't want to cut her out of his life. They'd become good friends – hadn't they? And how good would that look if he ignored her?

But was it too risky keeping her close? He didn't think he could offer her what she deserved. He worked long hours, longer soon. He remembered his mother, waiting for his father, with a dinner in the oven, then eating alone after she'd sent Adam to bed. He didn't want that for Sophie. But look what almost happened in this bedroom. Would he be able to remain controlled around her?

Visions of her lying on this bed, kissing her soft breasts, the sensation of her firm nipples on his tongue... All the kisses, feelings he should have savoured... *Brain moving south, Adam! Think of something else.*

He started to worry. What's taking her so long? Could she be sick? Or dwelling on what had just happened?

As soon as he decided he'd give her five more minutes, the bathroom door opened. Sophie emerged, still in his shirt, and got into her side of the bed. She sniffed.

"You okay? Really?" he asked. He wanted to reach out and touch her.

"I'm fine." She remained sitting up, but pulled the covers towards her.

"You don't sound fine."

"It's nothing." She wiped her hand across her cheek. "Go to sleep."

Adam sat up. He hadn't liked her tone; she was still upset and he knew it was his fault. "What is it, Sophie? Tell me."

She puffed the pillows, but he continued to look at her until she answered. "It's going to sound stupid."

"Try me. I listen to James a lot," he said playfully. Sophie let out a short laugh, but it died quickly.

"It's just... and this is probably the alcohol talking," she sounded as if she wasn't quite convinced herself, "but I was thinking about Simon."

"Don't waste your time on him," he responded sharply. *Shit, maybe he should have made love to her and obliterated all thoughts of that arsehole.*

"I know, I know," Sophie said, flopping deeper into the bed. "He was my first – and sort of my last. He's my *only* serious relationship." She frowned. "Is he the best I can do?"

In all her life had she only ever loved Simon? He couldn't talk. How many women had he fallen in love with? *Maybe one... none. None.* He moved closer, brushing her hair, unable to resist touching her any longer.

"Of course you can do better than Simon."

"What about you?"

"What about me?" Okay, things had obviously spiralled out of control... Were they going to start confessing feelings? He couldn't afford to be too honest.

"Would you take me out?" she asked. "I mean, you almost... but stopped, so would you?"

Adam nervously laughed. "Sophie, I've really enjoyed this weekend with you –"

"But you've had to pretend."

"Even though I've had to pretend. I'm not pretending now. I like you. I don't have to fake that. But I'm not sure we'd be right for one another. We work together for a start."

"Is that why you stopped?"

"Partly – yes!" Adam breathed deeply, wanting to form the right words before he spoke and put his foot in it again. "But, if what my father has planned, when he retires - I'll be working all hours.

171

I won't have time for a relationship." He lifted her chin, to make her look at him. "And I know that's what you'll want. It's what you deserve. I didn't want us having a one night stand."

"No, that isn't me." Her voice trembled. "Tried that, got the T-shirt – so isn't me." Adam frowned, questioning. "At uni, trying to get over Simon, but it was equally as awful."

"Oh."

"So how is it going to work when we get home, back in the office? Us?"

"We'll still be friends. I'll see you down the White Lion on a Friday evening with James, won't I?"

"I don't know. You tell me. You just said you're too busy – Mr Workaholic." Her tone was cynical. She turned in the bed, her back to him. He hated it and wanted her in his arms.

"Sophie." Adam watched her, not knowing what to say. He didn't love; he wouldn't go down that route. But he had enjoyed this weekend. The show. Being close to her. Kissing her... *Stop! Stop! Stop!*

To his relief she turned back to face him, chewing her lip. "Sorry."

"Come here." He gave her a gentle smile and moved across into the centre of the bed, stretching out his arm towards her. As she turned off the lamp, pure darkness swept over the room. She searched for Adam's arm, and as he felt her lie down, he curled his arm around her, moving her closer to him. He felt the heat of her body against his. She rested her head on his shoulder, easing into his neck, placing her arm over his chest.

He worried for a moment, but it wasn't as if it was flesh against flesh. She had his shirt on. He'd kept his T-shirt on. This is two friends comforting one another. Nothing more. Relax.

'James doesn't kiss me on the nose.'

As they both settled, getting comfortable, with his free hand, he took hold of her hand and held it, with his thumb stroking over the back of it.

"This weekend has been nice. If I'm honest," Sophie said softly. "Thank you."

This weekend, apart from the hiccups with the ex-boyfriend, had been fantastic. But he couldn't tell her. *It's for the best.*

The last couple of nights' sleep had been good. They had slept comfortably apart, albeit in the same bed. Good solid sleep. Adam usually slept well with a woman in his arms, but tonight he wasn't so sure. This was Sophie, his 'brown-eyed girl', and they weren't supposed to do this.

He'd already had one close shave.

But he wasn't going to let her go.

Not tonight.

Chapter Seventeen

Sophie stirred sleepily, remembering the night before. At some point, she'd woken to find herself still wrapped in Adam's arms. She should have moved out of his hold, but considering all that had gone on, she found herself forgiving him – they'd both been drunk. It was probably for the best nothing had happened. Treasuring their last moments of closeness together, she'd snuggled into his chest, feeling its rise and fall and the faint beating of his heart as he slept, and had slowly drifted back off.

Imagine it every night. If only. But he'd made it quite clear...

Opening her eyes, she realised his side of the bed was empty. He'd already got up – like every morning – and she, disappointedly, hadn't woken in his arms.

She laid there for a moment, reminiscing about last night - on the dance floor, the kiss. There was a strange feeling inside her. She did not know if she was happy or sad. Her head was foggy and her heart achy, heavy. The weekend was coming to an end, and so was being with Adam. Before, she'd been looking forward to this day. Now she dreaded it.

She pulled back the covers, knowing she had to get up, though all she wanted to do was stay in the warm bed. A shower would clear her head. She couldn't hear the shower running, and the bathroom door was open. Adam had probably gone swimming.

Was he avoiding her?

She showered quickly, trying to suppress any feelings about Adam. They'd come so close. Did he feel *anything* for her? He wanted to be friends; she had to respect his wishes. She wanted to be friends, too, but this weekend had proved how much she enjoyed having a boyfriend, being in a relationship. Imagine a real one...

As she applied her make-up, Adam walked through the door.

"Hi," he said. "Sleep well?"

"Yes, thanks. You?" she asked, nervous of his answer. *Were they even going to discuss last night?*

"Well, I had this terrible snorer –"

"I don't snore!" She threw the damp towel she'd used for her hair at him. He caught it and laughed. She had to laugh too.

"How's your head?" Adam put the towel back on the rail.

"Fine, thank you. Surprised I actually don't have a headache. How much champagne did we drink?" *Stupid question. Stupid.*

"Enough." Adam didn't look her in the eye then. "What time are we heading down to breakfast?"

"Soon. I'm finished in the bathroom if you need to use it."

Looks like they weren't going to discuss it. Men, and water under the bridge. If he won't brood, neither should she. Time to toughen up.

"It's okay, I showered at the pool." Adam pulled the curtains, revealing the balcony and the clear blue sky, with not a trace of a cloud, only a white scar or two from aeroplanes.

"Ah, perfect for golf," he said, opening the balcony door, letting in a cooling breeze. "The wind's dropped, too."

"Something tells me you're going to get a round in before you leave," she said and Adam looked at her puzzled. "Oh, I forgot to tell you. Last night –"

"Let's not talk about last night. I feel guilty enough as it is."

"No. No, I don't mean about us." Sophie winced, wishing she hadn't said *us*. "Yesterday, I arranged with Cassie to stay with her

175

for a few days."

"What about getting home?"

"I'll catch the train. I'll be fine," she quickly added, seeing his concerned expression. "I think I need to see my sister, catch up with friends. I've stayed away too long." And a trip home with him in the car would be too intense.

"Have you really stayed away because of Simon?"

Sophie screwed her face up, embarrassed, and ashamed she'd been so weak. "Yes. A bit." Then blurted out, "I'd come home for Christmas!" She started brushing her hair, looking at Adam through the mirror. An awkward silence fell between them and Sophie needed to break it.

"Actually, this room is booked for another night – always has been," she said. "Natalie and Gareth are not leaving here till Monday, to catch the flight for their honeymoon. I didn't think you'd want to stay longer, so never mentioned it – but you can."

"I'd love to, but I have meetings tomorrow morning. I can stay for a bit today, but need to head home by this evening."

She nodded, burying any disappointment. As if she didn't know the answer anyway. They couldn't spend another night together, not after last night.

***

Sophie held Adam's hand as they entered the dining room for the first time to have breakfast. Sophie had convinced him to pack later. She wasn't checking out of the room until tomorrow, so he had all day.

Breakfast was a mix of emotions, from the sadness of family leaving to some friends nursing serious hangovers and only touching the coffee – *that would be Cassie.* Not even the hotel's

176

finest Full English could cure her. Sophie managed some toast and cereal, letting Adam and Gareth talk about golf and their handicaps - a conversation going straight over her head. As far as golf was concerned, Sophie was physically challenged.

"Why don't we have a round of golf before you leave," Gareth said to Adam.

"Yeah, okay, I like that idea."

"Oh, us girls are coming too! Let's partner up," Cassie said, suddenly brightening up. "We could do with a giggle."

Sophie internally cringed and swallowed her toast. *Oh, great.*

Allowing the men to carry on talking about their favourite subject, Natalie and Sophie quizzed Cassie on the young man sitting beside her at the breakfast table, wanting an introduction. He wasn't nursing a hangover and seemed very attentive to Cassie's needs. Sophie remembered he'd been the bloke Cassie had been dragging around the dance floor at the end. She wouldn't pry yet as to whether he'd shared Cassie's room.

"This is Dan," Cassie said, her bubbly persona waning.

"I'm a friend of Gareth's." Dan held out his hand and Sophie, surprised, shook it.

"Fancy a round of golf, Dan?" Gareth grinned. "Cassie needs a partner."

"Some fresh air will sort me out. Not." Cassie rubbed her head. "Maybe it isn't a good idea to play golf."

"Oh, you're coming, too," Sophie said sharply. "It was your idea us girls tagged along on this golf lark in the first place."

"Yes, and look what you've done," Natalie said, gesturing to the men deep in sporting conversation.

"If I'm going to look terrible on the golf course, so are you!" Sophie laughed.

They agreed to meet in an hour and headed up to their rooms, Adam taking Sophie's hand once again. It felt so warm and

177

comforting. One more day she had and then it was over. Back to plain old Sophie, lonely and very single.

A part of her would be glad - the intensity of all this pretending was driving her nuts - but the other part was really going to miss him. It had been a very long time since she'd had a boyfriend. Simon. She shuddered. Her only miserable experience with love. At the time it hadn't been miserable, until it came to a crashing end.

But Adam wanted to remain as friends, and she was adult enough to accept his decision. Though she still had these *what ifs* going around in her head.

Back up in their room, Adam silently packed his small suitcase. Sophie put her book down. Distracted by Adam's presence, she'd read the same paragraphs over and over, the words never sinking in.

She stepped out on to the balcony, greeted by the hot sun on her face. Unlike the usual gale force type winds normally coming off the ocean, only a gentle, cool breeze swept through her hair. On the beach, the lifeguards' red and yellow flags, where bathers were supposed to swim, hardly moved.

From here, she secretly observed Adam, who looked the most casual she'd seen all weekend wearing a pair of light khakis and polo shirt and looking extremely sexy. He had gorgeous forearms, Sophie decided. He leaned over and zipped up his case. *And a great bum – especially in those trousers!*

Though she'd realised this early on, it dawned on her now just how attracted she was to him. This wasn't a matter of opinion now, she'd always thought he was good looking. It came from inside her, itching, begging to touch him and be close to him. She ached because she couldn't. Now she'd got to know him, his personality had won her over, he'd become more attractive to her. Could affection grow so quickly in a weekend?

She fancied the pants off him – like a lovesick teenager. Oh God, she was ridiculous.

But she hadn't felt like this in such a long time – since Simon – and it was maddening.

Adam cleared out everything of his from the hotel room, and already it seemed bare, depressing. That heavy, void feeling inside her chest reappeared, tightening all the way up to her throat. Her heart was breaking all over again. It wasn't Adam's fault. It was hers, for stupidly getting attached.

They made their way out to where Adam's car was parked. He opened the boot, put his case in and took out his golf clubs; a satisfied smile crept across his face.

"What?" Sophie asked, trying to hide all emotion. She wanted him to see her happy, unaffected.

"I've been dying to check out the golf course here."

"I'm worried you're going to be competitive at this." Sophie sighed.

"I am very competitive." He grinned cheekily. "So don't let me down."

"Do you even remember our conversation in the car? I'm rubbish at sports."

"I'll teach you. It'll be fun."

This was what worried her. Another session of close proximity with Adam to drive her nuts – all she needed.

"Roller coasters are fun," she said sarcastically. "Well, let's go." She jauntily put her arm through his and they walked through the hotel gardens, making their way to the golf course.

***

Once those who needed to had hired clubs and settled the green fees, they all congregated at the first hole.

Adam observed the party. Natalie and Gareth, the newlyweds,

were unable to keep their hands off one another. Cassie and her new man, Dan, were very similar, albeit a little shyer. Like Sophie and Adam in some ways, not knowing how far to go in such early days of a potential relationship. For Adam, providing these loving gestures to Sophie wasn't exactly hard work. He wanted a relationship with Sophie, just knew it shouldn't happen. His idea of a relationship was very different to Sophie's. So he had a mere round of golf left of her time, then he would have to depart, ending their façade.

Make the most of it, Adam.

But guilt ate at him. He had found himself trying not to overdo the affection. Would Sophie read it wrongly? Would the others realise something was wrong between them? Sophie would have made love to him last night, and she'd confessed one night stands were not her thing. He didn't think they were either, hence he'd stopped at that crucial moment. James had warned him, and rightly so, to treat her properly and he'd been about to break his promise. Having sex with Sophie would not have been a good idea, however much he'd wanted it to happen.

Sophie was different. He dated women all the time, and probably broke a few hearts along the way – usually when he saw things getting serious – but he didn't want to hurt Sophie.

"Is it too late to join in?" Simon called across the green. Sophie scowled, not so much at Simon, but Zoe, who he was dragging along with him. Maybe the woman had taken Adam's advice after all, and sought out Simon last night. They deserved each other.

He automatically pulled Sophie closer towards him. He'd seen Sophie fight with Simon last night – and thoroughly enjoyed watching it, he had no doubt she'd stand up to him again, but he wanted to show them Adam and Sophie were close, united. Sophie responded, too. She obviously wanted to make sure the message was loud and clear. *Good.*

"Yes, the more the merrier," Gareth called, beckoning them over. "We're partnering up. Men take the first hole, then the ladies."

"She's got a big hole," Cassie mumbled into Sophie's ear, but sharply enough that Adam heard too.

"Cassie!" Sophie hissed.

"Well, what's she doing here?"

"I haven't got a problem with it so neither should you." Adam was relieved to hear Sophie say. She frowned at Cassie, her expression sincere, and Cassie shrugged and went back to Dan.

The men took their turns on the first hole, and it quickly became apparent they were all competent golfers. Adam realised Simon would be his closest competition, both taking equal shots. Let's see if Simon can golf as well as he surfs, Adam thought.

Then the girls were up, taking a shot at the second hole. Gareth assisted Natalie, and it was instantly obvious she'd played before, she had her stance right. Her swing was unpractised, but it did the job for this fun morning jaunt. Cassie was up next. She dropped her sunglasses over her eyes and pushed Dan aside.

"I'm just going to give it my best shot," she said, pulling out a club. Dan quickly gave her the correct one and she cringed apologetically at him. She wiggled her bum, poked her tongue out at Sophie, and, after a couple of attempts, the club met the ball, sending it soaring along the fairway into some rough. But it wasn't a bad attempt.

Next up, Sophie. She looked nervous, wringing her hands and chewing her lip. Adam winked, taking her arm and pulling the driver out of his trolley.

Standing behind Sophie, he tucked her body in close, moving her hands with his. With the soft breeze, her sweet scent enveloped him, and her hair caught in his face. He swept her hair back over her shoulder, giving her a kiss on the revealed flesh of her neck. Goosebumps rose on her arms. Adam was riding on a thin line of keeping up the pretence they'd built this weekend, and not giving Sophie the wrong message. He moved his hands from hers, to her hips, softly advising position and stance. He relished being so close to her. His mind wandered, thinking how it would've felt, her soft, naked body against his...if he'd continued last night...

"Come on, you two!" Cassie called out impatiently, but in jest. Thankfully, she liked to tease and it brought Adam back to the present. Maybe Cassie could see how Sophie was reacting, her cheeks flushing pink. And if he wasn't careful he'd have an embarrassing trouser moment. He needed to cool his thoughts down. He did not need his brain moving south ever again around Sophie.

"Adam's making sure I do this right." Sophie replied. "Aren't you, honey?"

"I told you I was competitive." He grinned. Once satisfied he had her in position, he said, "Okay, Sophie, hit the ball as hard as you can."

He stood back and let her take her swing. First attempt, the club hit its target and the ball flew up the course and landed nicely on the fairway.

Sophie squealed, turning around, jumping gleefully, and kissed him. "I did it. I actually did it."

He held her for a moment, mesmerised by her dark brown eyes, and her sunny smile. "I knew you wouldn't let me down." He couldn't stop himself kissing her back, made giddy by her happiness.

Simon tried the same tactics with Zoe, but he obviously wasn't attracted to the woman; he'd used her last night and maybe now Zoe knew it. Although they were trying to imitate affection, there was coldness between them. There was no coldness between Adam and Sophie. Far from it. He might as well be standing at the gates of hell, his feelings and emotions were running so hot.

For the full eighteen holes, this routine continued. Adam

savoured every time he had to guide Sophie. There were some successes, and some blunders in the bunkers, but they all laughed and giggled, and teased each other.

They agreed on a swift pint and some lunch in the clubhouse to analyse the score. With the sunshine blistering, they sat around a large, sturdy, garden table, under the shade of an umbrella.

"Well, out of the ladies, Natalie was the winner," Gareth proudly announced, holding up his pint. "But as a joint effort, I'm annoyed to say - I'm joking! Well done, Adam and Sophie. Soph, you sure you've never swung a golf club?"

"No, never! Crazy golf maybe," Sophie said. "It's all thanks to my brilliant coach." She grabbed Adam's hand and he squeezed it back. "Plus, he's so competitive I was too scared not to do well."

"Rightly so." Adam kissed her cheek, then stood up. "Sorry to say this, guys, but I've got to go."

They all grumbled, except Simon of course. He was going to be glad to see the back of Adam, no doubt.

Slowly, they all made their way towards the hotel, through the grounds, laughing and joking. It had worked; Sophie's friends truly believed Adam and Sophie were an item. He held her hand, dreading the moment when he would have to let her go.

***

Sophie watched impatiently while the group said their goodbyes to Adam and, couple by couple, they went back into the hotel lobby, leaving Adam and Sophie outside alone. Sophie was thankful, because this way she could say her goodbyes and it wouldn't be made-up.

Her friends were so taken with Adam. They liked him, thought he was the best thing for her. Would it be a shock when she had

183

to tell them they were no longer together?

She'd worry about it another day. She could go a couple of months before telling them it was over. That would be realistic – wouldn't it?

"So," she said, Adam finally turning his attention to her. "This is goodbye."

"I still don't like the idea of leaving you here."

"I'll be fine, honest."

"You've got my mobile number?" Adam reached into his pocket to dig out his phone as Sophie nodded. "So text or call me, because Cassie will think it strange otherwise."

"Didn't think of that," she said, frowning. "But what if you're in a meeting or busy?" *With another woman...* The thought brought her breath up sharp. Luckily, Adam didn't notice.

"Don't worry, if I can't be disturbed, I always turn my phone off."

"Okay." She stared up at him, unable to look away from those blue eyes. "Oh, I almost forgot." She handed Adam a little boutique bag she'd been holding on to. "Sorry, it's not much, but I wanted to say thank you for a lovely weekend."

Adam lifted out the bottle of aftershave. "You didn't have to –"

"No, I did. And I noticed you were running low in the bathroom. Not sure if it's your favourite."

But it's now mine.

Adam pulled her close, brushing a hand down her cheek. Were her friends watching? There was no other reason for the loving gestures otherwise – *it's pretend, Sophie. Pretend.*

"Text me, to let me know you got home safe," she said, kicking herself for sounding so stupid and weak. Adam didn't do needy. But she would worry.

He chuckled. "Of course."

He leaned forward, hesitating, a twinkle in his eye, she held her breath. Then he kissed her firmly on the lips, lingering for a moment, before pulling away. She'd wanted it to last much longer, deeper. It would be her last kiss – forever.

"I'll catch up with you in a few days," he said, removing his hand, which was resting naturally on her hip, and walked towards his car. His touch still lingered on Sophie's lips, the bitter taste of the half pint of lager he'd consumed.

What was it going to be like going back to work, facing him, facing normality? Dread filled her.

She waved as Adam pulled out of the car park, and disappeared from view. She sucked in a breath, to stop the tears forming and ease the ache in her chest. Cassie joined her on the gravel drive.

"Come on, chick. It won't be long and you'll be back in his arms again."

"Yeah, I know."

Do I tell Cassie the truth now?

***

Severed.

The only word to describe what he felt. He'd been torn from Sophie, separated, his heart wrenching and aching from the mere thought he wasn't with her.

Could you get that feeling after being with someone for a weekend? Three nights? Four days?

Was he ludicrous?

Had he gone soft?

He'd been driving for ten minutes, winding round the narrow country roads, headed for the main route out of Cornwall. All he could think about was Sophie and whether this feeling was due to knowing he wasn't going to see her for a few days.

Why was he feeling like this?

He'd never felt like this before, not with any of the relationships he'd had. He never let it get to this. Never missing them. Never this empty, black, aching hole inside his chest.

Adam needed to stop thinking about Sophie. Work. Work would get him back to normal, busy his mind. He wouldn't have time to think about Sophie. He'd call his father. Who better to remind him why he could not, and should not, commit to Sophie? His father was the one person who would be in the office on a Sunday.

Chapter Eighteen

"No more! I've got to go to bed," Sophie slurred, perched on a barstool, waving her hand at Cassie.

Cassie had convinced her to have cocktails in the hotel bar, and Sophie had proceeded to drown her sorrows. Now the drinks tasted sickly, her mouth was dry from too much alcohol. Natalie and Gareth had left them to it an hour earlier, but Cassie, the local fish, considering the amount she could drink, had insisted Sophie sit with her. Dan had left, having work the next day, and so had Simon, for which Sophie was grateful.

"Oh, one more," Cassie said.

"No, I can't. I want my bed. I'm exhausted."

Sophie stumbled into her hotel room; her legs like jelly. Glumly she threw her bag onto the dressing table. The room felt so empty without Adam, the bathroom cluttered only with her toiletries, the wardrobe half full.

She was being silly, melodramatic, and drunk. *You're feeling lonely because of the alcohol.* But by God, she missed his touches, his conversations, his teasing. He'd made her feel so alive and happy with life. Now she felt dreary and miserable, with a heavy weight inside her chest, pressing against her breastbone, trying to fight its way out. Tears started to well.

Oh, you are drunk! Well done, Cassie.

She wiped the tears on her sleeve and struggled into her pyjamas. Getting into bed, she plugged her mobile into the charger, and was delighted to see a message from Adam. She'd tried forgetting it was in her handbag, so she wouldn't stare at it all evening, willing it to ring. She opened the message.

Arrived home safely. Hope Cassie isn't getting you drunk.

Sophie hit the reply button and texted back, oblivious to what time of night it was.

Thanks for letting me know. Can sleep peacefully now. Yes, Cassie has got me tasting cocktails.

She wanted to write, 'love Sophie', but paused. She signed it **Sophie x** instead and pressed the send button.

Miss you.

But she couldn't text that. She put her phone down, and snuggled into the bed, pulling the covers around her. It felt so big. So empty. She rolled over onto Adam's side of the bed, and breathed in the scent of his pillow. Damn, they'd changed the sheets. Fresh, smooth cotton, with a trace of the scent of the laundry – and not a hint of him.

She wanted to cry.

Still, she chose to remain on his side of the bed to comfort her. She tucked her arm under the pillow, and to her surprise felt soft material. She pulled it out and turned on the lamp, finding the grey T-shirt Adam usually wore until he got into bed.

She sniffed it, his scent instantly bringing him closer to her. A hint of the aftershave he wore, the one she'd bought him as a parting gift, in a secret way knowing he would keep the scent she loved.

Shrugging off her thoughts, she closed her eyes and silently thanked the maid for leaving it there for her to find. Not caring if she seemed like a small child, using the shirt as a comforter, she hugged it tight. Sophie wanted to cling to Adam that bit longer,

188

and this would be her way.

***

Sophie awoke, clutching Adam's T-shirt.

She realised she would have to return it; she couldn't cling to it forever. What if he asked her if she'd found it? All sorts of scenarios went through her paranoid head. She'd wash it, then return it. She couldn't hand it over unwashed.

It didn't take Sophie long to get ready and pack. She wandered down to breakfast and met Cassie. They had a quick breakfast with Natalie and Gareth, then waved the happy couple off as they departed in a white, vintage Rolls Royce, decorated and trailing the traditional old tin cans and ribbons.

"Hope they don't come across a tractor," Cassie said, waving frantically.

Sophie sighed. The end of the wedding, and the weekend. She'd agreed to have a few days with Cassie, but a part of her wanted to go home straight away, to find Adam, to let him know how she truly felt – how did she truly feel? She understood why he hadn't wanted to have sex, maybe even thankful he had stopped if he only saw it as lasting one night, not long term. If Adam had been interested, wouldn't he have said? She'd already made a fool of herself once with a man; she wasn't prepared to put her heart back in front of a firing squad again.

"What are you sighing about?" Cassie said, poking Sophie's arm. "You'll be back with him soon. I won't keep you long."

"I want to spend time with you. I haven't seen you in ages."

"And why is that?"

"You know why. I've been too afraid to return and face Simon."

"Well, the less said about that bastard the better." Cassie looped

189

her arm through Sophie's. "Let's check out and I'll take you to my house."

"Great idea. And we're not drinking anything stronger than coffee – you hear? I need to give my liver a rest."

Cassie laughed. "Oh, you're no fun."

***

"You know where the second bedroom is?" Cassie pointed up the stairs. "Go unpack your stuff while I put the kettle on."

Cassie dumped her own luggage – not having as much as Sophie – in the hallway, and Sophie headed up the stairs. It had been a twenty-minute drive along narrow Cornish country lanes as Cassie lived a few miles inland, in the nearest main town to Tinners Bay.

Her small semi-detached house, decorated in a modern style for the age of the house, suited Cassie in a nutshell.

In the guest room, Sophie only unpacked what she thought she'd need, hanging them in the oak wardrobe. She rummaged through her handbag to find her phone, checking for texts. No messages. Still clasping the phone, disappointed, she headed back down the stairs, solemnly deep in thought, and into the kitchen where Cassie was pulling mugs from a cupboard while the kettle boiled.

"You're really missing him, aren't you?" Cassie said.

Sophie swallowed. "I can't believe I can feel like this after one weekend."

Cassie frowned. "How'd you mean? Oh, you didn't realise how much you loved him, and now you do?"

Sophie's stomach turned to ice. "Well, we've only been seeing each other a short while. I wasn't sure if he was the one but..." God, Sophie really was digging this lie deeper. No one would believe her when she announced she's broken up with Adam.

"But now you do." Cassie handed Sophie a mug of tea. "I knew you two were perfect for one another. I'm sure Adam feels exactly the same."

Sophie wanted to blurt out the truth but she couldn't. One day, in years to come, when Sophie had found someone she was blissfully happy with, and like Natalie, tying the knot, maybe then she'd come clean. *'You remember that hot guy at Natalie's wedding? Total lie...'*

She slipped her phone into her jeans pocket.

"Babe, text him," Cassie said. "Don't feel you can't talk to him because I'm here."

Sophie pulled out her phone and started a text message, hoping Cassie wouldn't see what she put.

Hello. Sending text to keep Cassie happy. Love you.

She added a smiley with its tongue hanging out to emphasise the 'love you' was really in jest. *Yes, it was.* Or at least she hoped he would read it that way, and not literally that she loved him... because she didn't...too early to say what she felt, wasn't it? You couldn't fall in love over one weekend – could you?

***

Adam noticed his mobile vibrate as the meeting ended. As he walked out of the conference room, he looked at the message.

It was from Sophie. It gave him such a thrill that it made him instantly want to bang his head against a wall. He was a grown man. It was a new experience – or a very old one. Maybe he'd forgotten how it felt. He didn't get excited like this about any other woman. Why Sophie?

He smiled at the 'love you' and the smiley, pressing the reply button.

"Adam! Can you spare a minute?" Adam looked up to see his father calling from his office. The message would have to wait.

"Yeah, sure, what is it?" Adam slid his phone into his pocket and walked down to his father's office. By the time he'd entered the room, Gordon was already sitting behind his mahogany desk.

"Sit down, sit down," his father said, gesturing towards a black leather chair opposite him. These past few months, Adam had noticed him aging quicker. More grey scattered amongst his brown hair, deeper lines around his eyes. He looked tired. "I thought we could run through a few things to make this hand over go smoothly."

Adam nodded, and listened to his father. All business, no pleasure. The man hadn't even asked if Adam had enjoyed his weekend away. If they took the business away, the two of them would have nothing in common. He turned sixty next year. Adam had assumed Gordon would run the company for another ten years, as his grandfather had. How would his father cope with retirement, especially now he was being forced to take it early under his doctor's advice? Gordon's days revolved around work and golf at the weekends – which usually aided business ventures.

After he'd left Adam's mother, Gordon had gone through a string of girlfriends. Adam remembered most of them, all beautiful because his dad could attract the finest of women. He probably still could, even now. Back then he had the mixture of good looks, style and money, but none of the girlfriends stuck around for long, tiring of the lack of attention. Gordon was too busy with work to commit to a relationship. He couldn't give them the time they needed. It meant Adam wouldn't be able to either. He never wanted to make a woman as miserable as his own mother had been. Sophie deserved better.

Adam swallowed and tried to listen to his father as he showed him charts and future projections for the company. Why did all of a sudden this become a problem? Adam had known his future before, and was happy with his lot. He loved his job, this company.

Why did Sophie run through his mind so much?

"I want you to handle the Jerrisons' contract," Gordon said, bringing Adam's focus back to work. Gordon pushed the paperwork across the desk. "You're more than capable, and I need to take a backseat. This way I'm still around if you need some advice, but I'm confident you can deal with this without me."

Adam perused the documents. He didn't have time to think about Sophie, he had work to do.

***

After a quick pasta dinner, Sophie and Cassie were sitting outside at a black aluminium bistro table in her small garden. Tea lights flickered in the middle of the table, hopefully to keep the midges away. With the sun setting late at this time of year, it wouldn't get dark till around ten. They laughed and giggled through a good majority of the bottle of wine standing in a wine cooler on the table.

"You and Adam are made for each other, like Nat and Gareth," Cassie said, pouring them both another glass of white Zinfandel, finishing the bottle. Sophie clicked her tongue, tiring of this conversation.

"Well, they've been together a hell of a lot longer. I don't want to count my chickens. Look at Simon – I thought he was the one!"

"Simon's an arse. Bloody hell, you found him in bed with that bitch. What a bastard."

Sophie could tell they were drunk, or getting there; Cassie swore more. "I'm still not going to count any chickens," Sophie said.

Cassie clucked like a chicken, making her arms wave like wings, then burst into laughter. Sophie found her infectious, giggling with her. She decided to change the subject. Talking about Adam was actually making her miss him more. *Not good. Not good.*

"So what about Dan?" she asked, raising her eyebrow at Cassie and sobering their conversation.

"He said he'd call," Cassie said, sipping her white Zinfandel. "But I won't hold my breath. They always say they'll call."

"I'm sure he will," Sophie said, nodding positively. "He was a really nice guy, and seemed very into you when we were playing golf."

Cassie sighed. "He's a great guy. God, I hope he calls. And I didn't sleep with him that night."

"Really?"

"All right, all right, I know what you're thinking. Yes, he did come back to my room, and yes we did have a good smooch, but I really liked him, and didn't want to blow it the first night – if you'll pardon the pun." Cassie sobered, looking Sophie in the eye. "My mum always said men don't like to marry the women they sleep with on the first night."

"Yep, my mum says that too. But look at Nat and Gareth."

"Touché." Cassie chinked her glass against Sophie's. "How right you are. But they are different. They were kind of friends and flirting with each other before the first date."

"True."

Maybe if she'd slept with Adam it would have felt like the first night, too. Probably for the best they hadn't. It wasn't as if they'd been on a date. Sophie started making a mental note not to sleep with Adam unless they'd been on a few dates.

As if.

"Anyway, for some reason, call me superstitious if that's what it is, I didn't want to ruin it. Besides, I was so bloody drunk, couldn't tell my arse from my elbow. Poor guy could have been there all night, and I never would have – well, you know?" Cassie laughed and snorted, which made her laugh more, and Sophie was back in a fit of giggles again. She'd missed Cassie. It was so good to catch up with her, even if she was harbouring a lie.

She'd come clean – honest. One day.

***

After a lot of laugher and some coffee, Sophie insisted upon heading up to bed. She checked her phone. No message from Adam.

A nagging voice inside her head rang. *You are being ridiculous. Grow up!*

As she got into bed, her phone vibrated on the bedside cabinet and she snatched at it. Adam. Pleasure buzzed through her like an excited teenager.

Sorry was in a meeting when I got your text. Busy day. Hope Cassie is looking after you. A.

No kiss. Nothing. Not even a 'love you' in jest. But he'd texted her. So he valued her friendship, didn't he? Should she text him back? It was a bit late, but he had just messaged her. Of course, you never knew how long these things took to come through; he could have sent it at five o'clock.

She should reply tomorrow. Best not to look too eager. Or needy.

She pulled out his T-shirt, and sank into the pillows, closing her eyes.

***

Sophie extended her stay to a week. It wasn't like she didn't have holiday to use up – she did, and the few days she stayed with Cassie flew by so quickly, she couldn't bring herself to leave. She caught up with friends and family, popping back to Padstow to see her sister and brother-in-law. But Sunday arrived quickly, her week in Cornwall ending.

As Cassie and Sophie ate lunch, the phone rang in the kitchen. Cassie answered it, nodding and talking quietly – unlike Cassie – and Sophie heard her saying something about Thursday.

She watched Cassie put the phone down and saw the instant transformation; calm vanishing, excitement replacing it.

"That was Dan! He's asked me out! I'm meeting him on Thursday. Oh my God, oh my God!"

"Great. I knew he'd call you."

"Yes, he apologised; he's busy at work, and has been meaning to phone," Cassie said. She beamed, her cheeks glowing, happiness plastered all over her face. Sophie's own heart swelled with joy for Cassie. At least one of them might have a happy ever after from this wedding. Cassie *had* caught the bouquet.

Oh please not another wedding – yet!

Sophie's mobile buzzed. She looked to see a text from Adam. She'd told him earlier in the week she'd decided to extend her stay, and he'd encouraged it, said there wasn't a problem with work – what would two more days be? It had put her mind at rest with the decision, hoping the time apart would help squash whatever her feelings were for him.

What time does your train arrive? I'll collect you.

No need. I'll get a taxi. She quickly texted back.

The next minute her phone was ringing. She didn't even need to see the caller ID to know it was Adam.

"Sophie, I'll pick you up. I want to make sure you get home safely."

"There really is no need."

"I took you to Cornwall; I was meant to bring you home."

"It wasn't your fault I changed my plans," she said, trying to hold

196

in any exasperation. The last thing she wanted was him meeting her at the station. She needed to put space between them, of that she was certain.

"What time is the train?" His tone turned stern.

She sighed. "I'm coming from Bodmin on the three-seventeen. I have to change at Reading and I have no idea what time it gets into Chertsey - I think it's around eight-thirty." She glanced at her watch, as if it would tell her.

"Okay, I'll see what I can do."

"If you're not there, I won't worry. I'll get a taxi."

Sophie sighed when she hung up. Cassie frowned at her.

"You don't look happy."

"Oh, it's nothing," Sophie replied, shoving her phone in her pocket. "We'd better get a move on or I'll miss my train."

***

"Promise me, you won't leave it so long next time," Cassie said, pulling Sophie into a hug.

Sophie's throat tightened as they said goodbye. She'd miss her friend, even though they were good at keeping in touch by phone or email. And now Sophie had returned, she'd be able to do it again. Simon was well and truly forgotten.

"And you and Adam can always come and stay with me for a weekend."

Sophie smiled, hiding her internal anxiety. "Yes, of course."

The train journeys passed uneventfully and she read most of the time. But a romance novel wasn't the best choice. She found herself more tearful when it looked like the hero was leaving the heroine forever, even though she knew there would have to be a happy ending.

Yeah, happy ever after happens in fiction, not in real life.

Over the past week she had thought what if they'd just done it, had sex, and got it out of her system? She wished she knew what it would feel like to make love to him.

But that's it. Make love. She couldn't have a one night stand. It did not sit well with her conscience. Or her confidence.

It was late but still light when her final train pulled into her station. Fearing Adam could be waiting on the platform, her heart rate increased and her palms grew hot. She hauled her luggage out with great difficulty, swearing under her breath. The case was awkward and cumbersome and she was irritable through tiredness.

She headed off the platform, when she heard her name. Turning, she saw Adam. Her heart rate went up a notch further and her head buzzed with confusion. Was she pleased or not? She'd wanted to see him again. But here, now? He walked towards her, looking all business like – and sexy. His smile turned her insides to goo. He looked even better in the flesh than she'd been imagining all week.

Flustered, she dropped her holdall, trying to pick it up while pulling her suitcase along as well. "Oh, have you been waiting long?"

"Ten minutes at the most." Shaking his head, he grabbed the case. "Let me take your bags."

"I could have got a taxi."

"I didn't want you getting a taxi."

They didn't have far to walk to his car. Sophie didn't wait for him to open the door, getting in as he put the luggage into the boot.

"So, did you have a good time with Cassie?" Adam asked, as he drove.

"Yeah, it was nice. But I'm glad to be home, no longer having to pretend."

"Why did you have to pretend at Cassie's?"

"You're joking, right?" Sophie snapped. She *was* tired. "Cassie

198

wants to know everything, the finest details." She sighed heavily. "I did my best to change the subject most of the time. I'm just fed up with it now."

Adam chuckled.

"It's not funny. I wish James hadn't suggested you coming along with me."

"I'm glad he did!" Adam said. "Someone needed to keep an eye on you with your ex on the prowl."

"Forget about bloody Simon! This was a bigger lie than I realised. Cassie's invited us to go and stay a weekend. What am I to say?"

"You can say I've had to go away that weekend."

"I'll be ending our 'relationship' way before I have to go visit any of my friends – thank you!" She sounded grouchy, but she was upset. "If only I didn't have to..." She stopped herself in time, realising she was talking out loud.

"What?"

"Nothing."

Thankfully, the journey didn't take long. She was relieved to see her home; it felt like a decade had passed since leaving it. She couldn't get out of the car fast enough. She loved being with Adam, but knew it was futile. She needed distance.

Adam fetched the case out of the boot and started towards her flat.

"What are you doing?" She went to grab the case, trying not to struggle with the holdall and her handbag, but he wouldn't let her take it.

"I'll take it up to your door." He walked towards the entrance.

"I can manage." She followed him, glad she'd put on some sensible shoes and wasn't teetering on uncomfortable heels.

"I know, but I thought –"

"You thought what?"

"Sophie, what's got into you?" Adam frowned, and still, to her frustration, carrying her case to the front entrance of her building. "I'm trying to help."

"Help? Do you think this is helpful in any way? I'm confused. I don't know how you feel about me or anything." *Sophie, shut up!* "What happens now? Do I fade back into the background as the boring engineer?"

Adam shook his head with a puzzled expression.

"Didn't just a part of you enjoy being with me? Because..." She looked at her shoes, hesitantly continuing, "because I enjoyed being with you."

"Sophie, I can't. I just can't."

"Can't what?"

"I'm not good at relationships. Real ones." His hand gripped the handle of the case tighter, his knuckles whitened. "Pretending is fine, I can do that. But I will let you down."

"How do you know until you try?"

"I just know."

"So why are you here?" her voice quavered.

"I wanted to make sure you got home safely." He started to head up the stairs with the case.

"Leave it. I will take the case! Go, please." *Before I burst into tears.* "I am home safe. No one will mug me climbing one flight of stairs. I'll see you at work tomorrow." She carried the case up the stairs, determined to make it look easy and not like the heavy, awkward lump it was. It didn't help when her handbag slipped off her shoulder, making her curse with frustration. Adam had gone back to his car but she knew he could still see her through the windows on the stairwell, so she had to keep up the pretence that she could manage just fine and dandy.

Fine and dandy. Yeah, keep telling yourself that, Soph.

If she'd learnt one thing this weekend, it was she missed being in love. She wanted Adam to run up those stairs, grab hold of her and kiss her. They'd stumble into her flat... She shook herself. What a daydreamer she was becoming. Stupid chick flicks she'd sat through with Cassie.

She was angry she'd stupidly opened her heart up to him and he'd turned her down flat. Had the 'no good at relationships excuse' been his polite way of saying she wasn't his type? Too plain. Not striking enough. Not model material.

Adam deserved model material – let's face it.

He needed someone with equally good looks and fine bone structure. Maybe someone taller, too. Though Sophie didn't consider herself short, around five foot seven, Adam could rest his chin on top of her.

Dull engineers were not his type, obviously. He needed someone from advertising or marketing. Someone with flair, panache.

She was irritated, and just plain bitchy now, fumbling for her keys, conscious he was still outside watching she got into her flat securely.

Door open, she hurried inside. The air was hot and stuffy – *like her mood* – from being shut up. She opened some windows, closing the curtains as she went, and noticed his car pulling away. Tears trickled down her face, and annoyed, she brushed them away with the back of her hand. She'd apologise to him tomorrow, and tell him to ignore the fact she'd blurted out stuff about a relationship. She didn't want one either – at least she'd tell him that.

Chapter Nineteen

"Soph."

Sophie jumped, looking up to see James peering over her monitor.

"James! You scared the life out of me."

"Hello, stranger." He grinned, placing a cup of coffee onto her desk. This was her regular treat; he'd stop at the local café down the road on his way to work and get a takeaway. It might not be Starbucks but it was a delicious kick to a Monday morning and beat the coffee machines at work.

Sophie fumbled with the paperwork in her in-tray. It didn't look too bad actually – at least it wasn't spilling out over the tray.

"What have I missed?" She hoped James wouldn't notice the extra make-up she was wearing, and the new outfit, not so plain. It had nothing to do with if she bumped into Adam. She'd done some shopping with Cassie, that's all.

"Not a lot. The meeting in Manchester was dull, and nothing you need worry about on your first day back," James said, still smiling. "Adam said you both had a good time and it wasn't that much work, just chatting to some old ladies. How'd he do?"

"Oh, of course they loved him." Adam hadn't mentioned her being a bridesmaid, or Simon? Or their 'near sex' experience? No, he wouldn't discuss that, even with James. He wouldn't kiss and tell. Not that she would either. Probably easier not to mention anything. Nothing happened.

Nothing did happen. Kissed a bit. And cuddled...occasionally. For show! For show! Apart from that last night in bed... That was only the two of them. But nothing happened!

"He behaved himself though – with you? I made him promise me no funny business. I know what he's like, you see." James' expression became deadly serious, which was quite rare for someone with such a happy disposition. It stunned Sophie. Had he read her mind?

Sophie laughed, hoping it didn't sound nervous. Explains all the '*I promised James.*' "No, there was no funny business. He was the perfect gentleman."

"Good. I thought I could trust him. I didn't want him thinking you were one of his usual dates. You two got on though?"

"Oh, yeah, we've become good friends."

"Well, you look great. The time off did you the world of good."

"Oh, thanks." She brushed a hand down her jacket. *Bugger. So, James does notice these things...* "Is Adam in today?" She tried to make the question sound as innocent as possible. She had wandered past the marketing office, hoping to bump into him. She hadn't spotted either the BMW or the standard company car in the staff car park.

Oh hell, you do have a problem.

"No, he's out the next couple of days with various meetings. I think he's got a busy week ahead of him."

Sophie's heart dropped; she really needed to stop this yearning for Adam. This would never do. Would it be Simon all over again? No, Adam was better than Simon. The week away had made things worse, not better.

James grabbed a chair and wheeled it around next to her. "Did he tell you..." he kept his voice low, "uh, anything, about himself?"

"Yes," she said, softly. "And what were you thinking? If he's like the next M.D."

"Shhh... I knew he'd be the perfect date, don't let his job description bother you. Adam's a good guy. Just needs some direction," James mumbled the last line more to himself. "But it looks like his father might be retiring sooner, rather than later."

"Oh, right." Sophie swallowed.

"Yeah, Mr Thomas had a bit of a health scare a few weeks ago, and well, has finally decided to take his doctor's advice to take it easy. He's taking a back seat and giving Adam control."

Sophie sipped her coffee as James brought her up to speed on the projects they were working on.

Sophie was soon back to her old routine of work. She spent the week catching up with her in-tray and getting back to her designs. Her priority was the new QB20s. The memory of Adam talking about getting sales for them, which seemed so long ago, brought home how important these designs were. Manufacturing had to be kept on schedule so they didn't disappoint customers.

Throughout the week, one thing lingered, making her heart heavy. She missed Adam. Hopeful, she still wandered past his office – busy with the sales and marketing team but not him. Her in-tray reduced but her longing to see Adam didn't. Her last words to him had been snappish and ungrateful, and she hated herself for it. She wanted to see him, to apologise. The last thing she wanted was him thinking badly of her; it was important he at least liked her. But she couldn't bring herself to phone him, or even text. She wanted to talk to him face to face.

"Coming down the pub?" James said, switching off his PC. Friday already, and five o'clock had arrived. One week down and another weekend to endure without seeing Adam.

Huddled under James' umbrella, she walked over the road with him to The White Lion. Due to the rain, the pub was crammed, but they found a small table to sit around and chat.

"I picked up the ring the other day," James said, and continued eagerly to tell Sophie about his marriage proposal plans and Kate's birthday arrangements. "I'm going to take her somewhere special in the morning, then in the evening we can celebrate with our friends."

Sophie nodded, then smirked. "She will say yes, then? You're confident."

"Yes, otherwise it will be a commiseration party." James chuckled. "We've been talking about it. She's just waiting for me to pop the question traditionally and all that."

"I'm really happy for you both." She clinked her wine glass against his raised pint.

"Thanks." James smiled. "You can make Kate's birthday?"

"Of course."

"Good. She's popping in here once she's finished work, so don't mention her birthday!"

"I won't." She patted his arm reassuringly.

"She's been asking how you are, says you should come over for dinner one night. Maybe I'll get Adam round, too."

She swallowed. Was James suggesting setting them up or was it because now they were all friends?

"That would be lovely," she said as sincerely as possible. *Her idea of embarrassment hell more like.* How was she supposed to act around Adam now? She still didn't know, till she saw him. It wouldn't be kisses and loving gestures. Would she know how to act normally around him amongst friends?

James leaned over the table, closer to Sophie. "You know, I had hoped you two would hit it off."

Sophie nearly spat her drink out, but managed to gulp down the liquid quickly, burning her throat and coughed. "What? You were trying to set us up?"

"The man needs a good woman."

"And you think I'm her?"

"Why not? Sophie, have you looked in the mirror lately? You're gorgeous, and smart. And you're a nice, grounded girl. Someone Adam needs – even Kate agrees with me." Sophie shook her head at James in disbelief, but he continued. "Listen, hear me out. I had my day too. Used to play the field. Not quite to the standards of Adam – haven't got his looks or his money - but since meeting Kate, I don't miss it. And I don't think he would either. He just doesn't realise it yet."

It wasn't instantaneously obvious, like with Adam, but James was good-looking in his own quirky way. Very tall and lanky, he had a wonderful smile, always happy, sharing his positive disposition. His hair had this mad unkempt look. Nothing could tame it. But she didn't doubt he'd had his day.

"James, really, stick to your day job, because matchmaking is not working for you. He's not interested."

"So you are?" He raised inquisitive eyebrows.

"No! I learnt, you know, we talked, about stuff generally, getting to know each other," Sophie babbled. *Dig yourself out of this one.* "And he said relationships weren't his thing. Not long-term ones, anyway."

"Yeah, that's what he thinks." James shrugged and drank some of his pint. "But I'm telling you I used to be the same. I'll get Kate to organise an evening around ours, after her birthday, so he can get to know you better –"

"No!" Sophie pulled a face. "We got to know each other, James," she said sternly. "It's hard not to, going away together for a whole weekend. I won't come if I think you two are trying to force us together. It won't work. I swear he's not interested in me."

"Okay, okay, sorry." James nodded, then pointed to the bar. "Ah, speak of the devil, here's the man himself. I won't say another word on the matter." Sophie turned and saw Adam at the bar, ordering some drinks.

Adam – with his arm around another woman. Three-inch heels making her as tall as him, a red dress hugging her slim figure, bouncy blonde hair, and glossy red lips.

Sophie swallowed, her stomach churned and knotted like she'd been kicked. This reaction to seeing him with another woman caught her unaware and it wasn't pleasant. This felt nothing like seeing him with Zoe. She gulped her wine down, and grabbed her bag as she stood up. This was too much. James and his match-making, Adam and his new girlfriend.

I can't compete.

"I, uh, um, got to go," she said. James stared in surprise. "I've still got some stuff to do at home, and really need an early night."

"Don't you want to see Adam?"

"It can wait till Monday. He looks busy." No way in hell would she apologise to him here now. Do it in the office on safe ground. Or call him.

Coward.

"And what about Kate?" James looked perplexed, still holding his pint half way between meaning to drink it or putting it down.

"Arrange something. Call me. But no meddling!" And with that, Sophie shot out the back door of the pub faster than a catapult could have launched her, preferring to exit via the garden and not bump into Adam heading for the front door.

Coward.

James always walked her home, or Kate would pick them both up and give her a lift, but it was a summer evening, and her flat was within walking distance. There was enough light to walk home. And luckily it had stopped raining, otherwise that really would have brightened her mood – not.

She'd thought about turning back, realising she was being

childish. It could be innocent on Adam's part. But he'd had his arm around the woman's waist, hadn't he?

He'd held you around your waist too... maybe it comes naturally to him?

Sophie closed her front door, hanging up her coat and slipping off her shoes. All the time, her hands trembled. She hadn't anticipated how it would feel to see him, let alone with another woman.

She went into the kitchen and switched on the kettle. She didn't want any more wine; drowning her sorrows would not be wise. She'd take a long hot bath, and soak, read a good book. Finish the romance she'd started reading – like that would make her feel better. Maybe start a thriller then. Something with gore, guts, and a good bloody murder.

She ran the bath, putting extra bubble bath in for a full foam effect, indulging herself, then went back into the kitchen and made her tea. Re-entering the bathroom, she smelt the scent of the bubble bath, ginseng and jasmine, and it made her relax. Twisting her hair, she clipped it up with a large butterfly clip.

In the bath, she couldn't focus on the book, her mind travelling back to Adam. She found herself thinking of the dance floor, Van Morrison playing, his kiss. A memory she replayed constantly in her head. It caused a lump in her throat, trying to rise and cause tears every time. She would not cry. She sighed heavily, and closing her eyes, sank into the bath, the bubbles rising around her, fizzing.

The doorbell rang, and Sophie sat up, startled. She'd go mad if it was her bloody neighbour again, locking himself out. He'd want to borrow her phone, because he wouldn't have his mobile on him.

It rang again.

"All right, all right." Sophie got out of the bath and wrapped a large bath towel around her, and then grabbed her dressing gown. Her neighbour was not catching her in just a bath towel.

She opened the door in an exasperated tone, "Mark, you really need to stop – oh." She was staring at Adam, who leaned against the wall, as if to ring the bell again.

"Who's Mark?"

"My neighbour. He keeps getting locked out."

"Why'd you leave the pub?" He sounded strangely annoyed.

"I wasn't feeling too great."

"That's not what you told James."

What had she told James?

"In fact, he said you took one look at me at the bar, gulped your drink down and shot out of there. Said it was weird because you wanted to speak to me."

Great, she could rely on James to fight her corner - not. She had to remember he was Adam's friend before he was hers. They stick together. Or was this him meddling again? She thought she'd told him his matchmaking days were over.

"Can I come in... please?" he said, tagging the please on as if remembering his manners, and trying not to be angry with her.

"Sure, come in," she said, wrapping her dressing gown tightly around her, praying the flat looked tidy. "Did you want a drink?"

He shook his head. "I wanted you to meet Lauren tonight."

"Why?" She internally winced at how sharp she sounded. But why the hell would she want to meet his new girlfriend? How insensitive was that?

"She works for Jerrisons in Manchester and they want us to design a robot for their manufacturing plant. A modification to the QB20. I said you could do it."

Now I feel stupid.

He stepped closer; she could smell the alcohol on his breath, mingled with his aftershave and dewy rain.

"I'm sorry. I, uh..." she shrugged, "I don't know, I felt I needed to leave." It was a free country the last time she remembered. If she wanted to go home from a pub early, she could, couldn't she?

"Come back to the pub now. It's still early."

"No."

Adam glanced at his watch, frowning. "Were you in bed?"

"No, the bath."

He stepped forward and fingered a couple of damp strands of hair. She looked him in the eye. Would he kiss her?

She wanted him to kiss her.

Her heart pounded so loudly she was afraid he could hear it.

"Come on, Sophie," he said, with his persuasive tone. The corners of his mouth twitched, but she was glad he resisted a full on smile. She gently shook her head, not able to find words to fill her mouth. "Okay, well, be prepared to travel with me Monday. We're going to Jerrisons for a couple of days. Pack an overnight bag." She opened her mouth to protest but he held his hand up. "You've got to come. I'm not taking no for an answer."

"And that's you telling me as my boss?"

"Yes. I would have come and told you in the office today, but we didn't get back in time – damn accident on the M40. So I thought we'd come over to the pub to discuss it - you could meet Lauren and she wouldn't need to spend a boring evening in a hotel. I'll have to entertain her now." He fixed his eyes on hers. Was he looking for a reaction? What was this? He knew how she felt about him, or must have a good idea. Did he want to make her jealous?

"I'm sure you've had plenty of experience in entertaining pretty young women. I doubt you'll find it hard. Why would you want a boring engineer to cramp your style?" She stepped towards her front door, but he grabbed her arm.

"Sophie, I find you far from boring."

"What do you *find* me, Adam? I'd like to know." *No you don't. Live in denial – the best way. Bury your head in the sand and wait for it all to pass.*

"Last weekend... it was special. You're special." He kept his hand on her arm. "But we're better off as friends. I'd let you down otherwise. My father is retiring soon –"

"Yes, I know." He looked at her, scrutinising. "James told me," she said, feeling the need to confess. She shrugged off his arm, and opened her front door. "If you please, I'd like to get back to my bath." Adam glanced at her thick dressing gown. "Go! I'll see you Monday. I'll come prepared."

She closed the door behind her – tempted to slam it – then headed back to her bath, topping it up with more hot water.

Her brain was even more frazzled. She couldn't stand being near him and not being able to touch him or hold him. They had to be 'friends' now. She preferred pretend lovers, if she couldn't have it real.

What did she have to do to find love? Because that's what she wanted more than anything now. She wanted to love and be loved.

Maybe Kate should set her up with one of her friends. Would Adam get jealous? He didn't really react to Simon, but it had all been a game. Now he liked her, thought her *special*. Whatever that meant. How special? Would he go into a burning rage, turn into the green-eyed monster if he caught sight of her with another man? Was that what she had to do?

She shuddered at herself and those thoughts. Not exactly a nice quality. Maybe Adam wasn't right for her. And she had to accept it. Being friends was better than nothing, right?

But the spark. Her whole body had responded to him when he touched her hair. Like magnets. He was her north, she his south, and her body would have leaned into him, stuck to him, only she fought the force to stay put, keep her distance.

No. She didn't want any other man.

Chapter Twenty

Adam waited outside the small cottage, rocking on his feet. For some reason his body tingled with anxiety. His mother was going to ask yet again whether he had a girlfriend, or had 'settled down.' She always did. And he'd disappoint her.

"Hello, love," Adam's mother, Pam, said, opening her front door. "Sorry to keep you waiting; I was in the greenhouse." She removed her gardening gloves, and gave him a kiss on the cheek then let him into her house.

The house wasn't huge, but big enough for her. It had been her settlement out of the divorce, plus his father had settled an income to keep her comfortably and not have to work. Maybe it was guilt for being such a lousy husband – and father.

A hectic work schedule with his father meant he hadn't called in on his mother since before the wedding, two weeks ago. He usually visited his mother's at least once a week for lunch, or dinner, worried she was lonely. However, nowadays she had a better social life, busy with hobbies and charities, and he actually did wonder if she had a man on the scene – but she hadn't said anything yet. Pam was in her early fifties and looking good, so James told him. Adam couldn't see her in any other way than as his mother. She still had a good figure, dressing fashionably, and always looking after her appearance. She wouldn't be seen without her make-up, or with a hair out of place.

Adam had inherited his blond hair and blue eyes from his mother. She'd been stunning in her day - that's why his father had fallen for her.

His parents had been divorced fifteen years now, but he still remembered, as a kid, his mother sitting at the solid oak kitchen table, eating alone with him while his father's dinner dried in the oven, keeping warm.

They walked through into the kitchen and as his mother switched the kettle on, she asked, "Tea?"

"Yes, please." He took a seat at the same solid oak table – only in a different kitchen.

"So, tell me how the other weekend went, the wedding you attended?"

"Fine." *What had he told her about that weekend?*

"Adam, what is it? You don't seem fine?" She gave a concerned frown and he shrugged his shoulders, then combed a hand through his hair.

What was bothering him? Sophie? Twice now they'd ended on a bad note. She'd been honest about her feelings for him. That wasn't supposed to happen. He wasn't good enough for her – he'd be just like his father once handed his role running the company. Too involved for a relationship.

Pam sighed. "Are you worried about taking over from your father?"

"No, I knew it was coming."

"Well, your father should have listened to a doctor years ago. He's never delegated, never trusted people to run, or manage, or whatever they do. He kept things too close to his chest. And that's made him sick. You'll do a better job."

"You've got a lot of faith in me, Mum. I'm not sure I will."

"Sweetheart, you are not like your father. You don't need to let

213

that job eat you up like it did him. Yes, I know it's a family business; it's been with the Thomas' for years. But your grandfather managed the business with far less stress."

"It's changed a lot now though. The company has expanded."

She placed a mug of tea in front of him and a tin of biscuits, before sitting opposite.

"So, have you met a nice girl yet?" Adam looked up suddenly. "What about the girl you went to the wedding with? When am I going to meet a girlfriend?"

"Mum." Adam gave her a warning look. *Here we go again.*

"Adam, your father will want to know there is an heir to the throne." She was right, and he knew it.

"I don't want to make the same mistake Dad did." Adam sighed. "I still remember growing up and him never being home, you waiting for him to return. I'm not sure I want to put another woman through the same things you went through."

Adam's father hadn't been very paternal towards him. Even now, their relationship was purely business. Occasionally they'd play a round of golf together, but they would always end up discussing the company and contracts. If they took the business away, and the golf, Adam had nothing in common with his father.

"You listen here." Pam prodded the table with her finger. "You are not like your father! How many times do I have to tell you? You don't have to be like him."

"But he was so busy he couldn't even come home to the woman he loved."

His mother coughed, tapping her chest until she'd swallowed her tea and composed herself. "Is that what you think?"

"You two were in love once. I thought you divorced him because of the way he treated you, never coming home, never being the husband you deserved."

She sighed. "Look, Adam, there's something I've been meaning

214

to tell you for a long time now, and I suppose at thirty-three you are old enough to know the truth." Adam frowned at her. "I'd just turned nineteen when I met your father, and within a month I was pregnant. Your father did the honourable thing at the time and married me – quickly. He was like you are now, flitting from one woman to the next, choosing the wrong women." She scowled. "I was one of those wrong women, attracted to the wealth and the status. He was that bit older, which had an attractive quality about it, too. A good looking man, your father, and at the time we thought we were so in love it didn't matter."

"You don't have to tell me this."

"Oh, yes I do!" she snapped, meeting Adam's gaze. "Anyway, you were born, and he was thrilled to have a son – the next heir. But it didn't take long for the honeymoon period to end and realise we were stuck with one another. I wouldn't leave your father, not with a son to bring up – I didn't want to raise you in a broken home. But after a while, the coward found it easier to stay at work, let it take over and consume him. We lived separate lives, only under the same roof. Once you were off to university, I knew I could leave him properly."

Adam swallowed. All his life, his mother had led him to believe his parents had been happy. He thought all those lonely evenings were part of the deal, in sickness and in health, that she loved his father to stick by him - yet she'd been doing it all only for Adam.

She patted his arm. "Adam, please, I know you usually have a string of girlfriends, but if you're worried about making the same mistakes as your father, you're going the right way about it."

"Mum." He took his arm away.

"I'm just saying, if you get one of these women pregnant –"

"I won't."

"That's what your father thought!" she said crossly.

"I'm not careless."

She ignored him, holding up her hand. "If you get one of these girlfriends pregnant, and you feel you have to marry her, you *are* making the same mistakes. History will repeat itself!" She hugged her mug of tea, as if finding comfort from it and calmed herself. "Please, Adam, find a woman you love, want to be with the rest of your life – as best you can at least. I suppose there never is certainty." Pam stood up, keeping her eyes fixed on Adam. "But if you carry on with some of those *women* –"

"That's it. I'm not listening to this." He stood up, his chair scraping the floor. He knew she'd wanted to say something less polite. It's why he'd rarely brought any of them to see his mother. He'd made the mistake once, a lot younger then, and he'd seen the disapproving look in her eyes. That particular girlfriend had been materialistic, vain, and two-dimensional. Pretty though, and great in bed, which had been the reason Adam dated her, but he could hardly tell his mother that at the time. She'd been a bad choice to introduce to his mother. He'd never done it again, not wanting to see her disappointment. He wanted approval from his mother, more than he ever did from his father. He hated he'd disappointed her. "Not all of the women I date are like Michaela," he said angrily.

His mother snorted with disbelief, tipping her tea down the sink. "I'm only saying this because I'm worried. Worried you'll make the same mistake, and then you will be following your father's very own footsteps. It'll make you miserable. Don't be afraid –"

"I'm not! I've got a girlfriend." *What was he doing? Trying to please his mother. Getting her off his back.*

His mother paused. "You have?" Her face lit up with surprise, her tone softened. "Why didn't you say?"

"Yes, Sophie." *Oh, please forgive me.* "She's the one I went to the wedding with. We met at Ted's retirement a few weeks back. She works at the company. We've been keeping it quiet."

"Oh, wonderful! Well, you'll have to bring her around tomorrow for Sunday dinner. I want to meet her."

"Oh, uh ... Mum, I'm not so sure. We're supposed to be taking things slowly."

"I'm not taking no for an answer. The fact that you've been seeing this girl over a month – and not told me – must mean it's serious. It'll give me an excuse to cook a Sunday roast."

"Uh... okay, I'll check she doesn't have any plans." Adam finished his tea and pulled out his car keys from his pocket.

"Where are you going? You can stay for lunch if you like, and tell me more about Sophie."

"I've got a busy morning and also need to let Sophie know about the change of plans for tomorrow." He gave her a kiss on the cheek. He might need the whole afternoon to convince Sophie.

"Change of plans?"

"Yeah, well, we weren't doing much, but I need to let her know." Adam didn't like lying to his mother. It had been easier lying to Sophie's family and friends. "What time tomorrow?"

"Come over midday. I can get to know her a bit, then." She sounded excited.

Adam nodded as his insides turned cold. Great. What had he done? Now he really had to persuade Sophie to help him keep his mother off his back.

But what if she won't do it?

After that weekend, she had to help him. She had no choice. One good turn deserves another, and all that.

***

"Oh, Tara, why didn't you tell me at the wedding?" Sophie had slumped onto her sofa, talking to her sister on the phone. She'd

217

almost not heard her telephone ring, being in the bathroom scrubbing away, with her music turned up so loudly. Her housework needed doing, and besides, it kept her busy so a certain person didn't creep into her thoughts.

"Rob and I wanted to wait until I'd had my twelve week scan. But look, if everything goes to plan, you're going to be an aunty, little sis!" Tara never counted her chickens until they'd hatched – like Sophie.

"Everything will be fine. Congratulations!" Sophie found herself squealing with excitement, as if they were teenagers again.

"I wish you were closer to home."

"So you'd have a guaranteed babysitter?" Sophie chuckled, hiding the regret that maybe she should be closer to home. What was keeping her here, other than her job?

Tara laughed. "Not at all. I'd love you closer to home, you know that, right?"

"Of course."

"But you have Adam."

Sophie swallowed. She hadn't fixed the lie – yet. Probably wouldn't for a while. *Must add to the to-do list.*

"Yes," she replied, cringing. Good job her sister couldn't see her face.

"Shame, because you could take up Harry's job offer."

"I know, I know. But I love my job here, too."

"Would Adam move?"

"Oh, um, it's not something we've discussed."

"Maybe you should." Tara laughed. "Anyway, I've got to go – restaurant still needs to open."

"Make sure you take it easy." Sophie returned to her housework, turning the stereo up loud. Her sister was having a baby. How exciting!

She had something happy to think about.

***

Adam pulled up outside Sophie's. Every window in her flat that could open was open, and music escaped them. He was relieved she was home. He'd thought of phoning, but that would have been forewarning and besides, if he'd asked her on the phone she could easily say no. To his face, she'd find him difficult to refuse. He'd make sure of it.

He climbed the stairs, guilt playing on his mind. He knew Sophie had a soft spot for him. She'd been honest, and he shouldn't use it to his advantage. She'd never forgive him, and he didn't want to lose her friendship. He didn't like the thought of her not being in his life. He shook his head and rang the doorbell, not wanting to probe further about that feeling.

He wasn't right for Sophie. She deserved better. His mother wasn't right.

The music could still be heard, and it didn't sound like Sophie was coming to answer the door. Maybe she hadn't heard the bell. He rang again, trying not to let his impatience get the better of him. He had to remember how he'd left here last night; their conversation heated. It hadn't gone according to plan. He'd really wanted her to come back to the pub. James seemed to think she'd interpreted Adam arriving at the pub with Lauren in the wrong way. With the pub being busy, Lauren had taken his arm to stop them being separated, and he'd automatically put his arm around her, forgetting himself. *Stupidly*.

Lauren appeared interested in him, but he'd kept her at arm's length. She was a client, and he shouldn't mix business with pleasure, though it hadn't always stopped him before. Thankfully James and Kate had been at the pub; he'd used their excuse of going home and had dropped Lauren off at her hotel early. He'd turned down the invite of a nightcap in her room, saying he needed early night. For some reason, being with another woman felt odd, as if wrong. With Sophie in the back of his mind, it felt like he was cheating on her. *Which was ludicrous.*

He rang again, and held it for a bit. He didn't want to appear rude, but he wanted to be heard. Sophie needed to help him, otherwise he was stuck. Or he'd have to find someone to pose as 'Sophie'. And considering some of women he knew, he doubted they would pass his mother's inspections.

But would Sophie?

What if his mother hated her?

The music stopped. He rang the bell again to make sure he'd be heard.

"Okay, okay, I'm coming," Sophie called from behind the door. The door opened, and Sophie appeared, her eyes widening. "Oh. Adam." She instantly became self-conscious, reaching up to push her hair behind her ears, only to find it wasn't there, but tied back in a scruffy ponytail. She wore not a grain of make-up, and was clad in a pair of denim shorts and a vest top. She had nothing on her feet, revealing burgundy-painted toenails. Beads of sweat formed along her hairline and she had flushed cheeks – she looked hot. Hot as in heat, though he had other hot thoughts, too. He really did need to get a grip. She looked so natural, and showing off so much flesh brought back pleasant memories.

"Sorry," he said. "I didn't mean to ring so many times, I wasn't sure if you heard me."

"How long you been standing there?"

"Not long." Adam smiled.

"I wish you'd called." She rubbed her hands down what material covered her thighs. "I could have got changed."

"You look fine. I'm here because I need to ask you a favour."

"As my boss again?" She scowled, placing a hand on her hip. She'd sniped last night about him being her boss. And he was, or would be soon.

"No, as a friend."

"You'd better come in then. Sorry, I was doing some housework." Sophie wrapped the cord around the vacuum cleaner standing by her dining table. The room was a large lounge-diner. Adam hadn't taken much notice the night before. Maybe he'd been distracted by the fact she'd stood there in her dressing gown, with only a towel underneath. All thoughts of this woman being naked distracted him.

Adam followed her to the small kitchen, and stood in the doorway; it wasn't big enough for the pair of them to enter, he'd get in her way. She filled the kettle and switched it on, and pulled two mugs out of an overhead cupboard, her vest top rising as she did so and revealing more flesh. Adam inwardly groaned. Why on earth was he fascinated watching her do the most mundane things?

"Tea or coffee?" she asked.

"Don't mind." He shrugged. She pulled the jar of coffee forward, and put a teaspoon full into each of the mugs.

"Sorry, it's instant. Probably not what you're used to."

"I can drink instant."

"Sugar?"

"No thanks. Sweet enough as I am." He grinned, but she frowned at him.

He'd have to lay on some charm at this rate.

They sat on opposite sofas, Sophie curling a leg up underneath herself. Although the flat was warm with the afternoon heat with only a light breeze coming through the open windows, she hugged her coffee as if cold.

Did he do this to her? Put her on edge? She'd become snappish and automatically defensive. All that weekend they were fine together. Now home, they couldn't act properly with one another.

"So, what's this favour?" She raised her eyebrows.

Adam placed his mug on the coffee table in front of him. He winced. "I kind of told my mother I have a girlfriend."

"No, Adam." Sophie jumped up, almost spilling her coffee, so she put it down, too. "No way."

"Please, Sophie, she wants to meet my girlfriend tomorrow for dinner."

"Get Lauren to do it. Didn't you go out with her last night?"

"I can't ask Lauren – she's a client! And no, I didn't go out with her, actually."

"What possessed you to tell your mother you have a girlfriend?" Sophie paced the lounge floor.

"She was hassling me about stuff, and I blurted out I was seeing you – to make her happy. I can trust you, Sophie."

Sophie threw her arms up. "I can't do this pretending any more."

"Come on, you owe me, remember?"

"So there were strings attached," she said, her eyes narrowing.

"No, but as I did you a favour, I thought you'd oblige and return it – if I asked!"

"But it's your mother!"

"I'm not asking you to pretend for a whole damn *weekend* – just one afternoon," he said, his voice rising, his fists clenched. She'd scowled as he'd mentioned the weekend. Damn, he wasn't doing very well at sweet-talking her. "Please, Sophie. Don't make me beg."

Try the puppy dog approach.

They stood in silence, Sophie glaring at him, Adam trying his hardest to look desperate. In some ways, he was desperate. No one would pull this off better than Sophie. They'd had a weekend practising and they'd fooled all of Sophie's friends and family. There was a closeness his mother wouldn't see through, and then she'd give him some space to work things out.

His mother was probably planning a dinner this very minute, out shopping for it. He couldn't break her heart, letting her know he'd lied to her. He could bring Sophie over, share one afternoon, then he could tell his mother it hadn't worked out.

He liked Sophie – a lot. All he could think about was seducing her, but this time definitely getting her into his bed. It was only the thought that she deserved a better guy that stopped him. However, thinking of Sophie with another man didn't sit well with him either. Of all the women he'd dated, none of them had complicated his thoughts as much as Sophie. But he was the 'not the settling down' type. It wouldn't be fair. Sophie seemed the sort of girl who would fall – shit, look at her ex and what he did to her – and Adam didn't want to hurt her, didn't want to be anything like that prick. He'd rather have her as a friend for life than share a brief intimacy before wrecking it all.

He sighed. "Sophie, I just need her to... to think I'm coming around to her ideas. Please help me."

"What would I have to do?" she asked, then quickly added, "Not that I've agreed or anything!"

"Just be yourself." He stepped closer, taking her hand, pulling gently, teasing her to step forward. He kept his eyes firmly on hers. "So will you do it?"

She went to take her hand away, but he wouldn't let her; pulled her closer. He could lean in and kiss her. "Please, Sophie?"

She frowned. "I don't know."

"It won't be like the weekend. We're hardly going to need to be on full display." He wouldn't get to kiss her again, he regretted. "It's my mum. Dinner and holding hands at the most."

Sophie groaned. "Okay. Okay, I'll do it. Just this once."

He grinned, grabbing her face with both his hands, planting a kiss on her lips. "Thank you."

She stood eyes wide, startled by the action, quickly recovering. "What time do I need to be ready?"

"I'll pick you up at eleven forty-five."

"What?" she said, exasperated. "You said dinner!"

He winced. "I meant Sunday roast. Mum will do it for about two-thirty probably. She wants us over early so she can get to know you." He finished his coffee, which was lukewarm, but drank it anyway, and started for the front door. She'd agreed. Best to get out while the going was good, before she changed her mind.

"What am I supposed to wear?"

"You'll think of something, and whatever it is, you'll look great. You always do." And with that he gave her an appreciative glance towards the summer attire she was wearing. He wanted to ask what she was doing tonight; they could go for dinner. But then he thought better of it. He couldn't get in too deep with Sophie. He just couldn't. "See you tomorrow morning."

Chapter Twenty One

Sophie stared into the full-length mirror in her bedroom, fretting. Would she do? If Adam really was her boyfriend, she'd be keen to impress, but would it make it easier on Adam if his mother wasn't impressed with her?

What if Sophie liked his mother? Or didn't like her?

What if Adam's mother liked Sophie? Or disliked her?

That would truly be a nail in the coffin where Adam was concerned. Not that he'd date a girl only for his mother's approval; it sounded like Adam's mother didn't like the types of women he dated.

She blew her hair out of her face. Another hot July day was forming outside, so she'd chosen a floral summer dress; she'd even opted for sensibly heeled sandals. But she wasn't plain either – she wouldn't become the dowdy engineer again, even in the office – she would be herself. Because, at the end of the day, she was done with lying. His mother would see her full personality; the only lie today would be the part about her being Adam's girlfriend, heart wrenching as it was, because she would love for it to be true. And he knew it, too. That's how he'd wrapped her around his finger. His seductive blue eyes looking deep into hers, he'd turned on his gorgeous smile and she'd found it impossible to say no.

You do owe him, too.

He had one day. This one favour. Then it would be all over. She had to travel to Manchester with him on Monday, but that was business – she'd have a separate hotel room.

She glanced at the clock by her bed. Eleven forty-three. He'd be here any minute.

***

"Here we are," Adam said, pulling into his mother's block-paved driveway.

"Oh, why did I agree to this?"

He grasped her hand, feeling its warmth, and they walked up to the front door. Adam didn't need to knock, as the door flew open, and his mother beamed at the both of them.

"Sophie, this is my mother, Pamela," he said.

"Pam! Everyone calls me Pam." His mother waved them in. "Lovely to meet you, Sophie. Come in."

As Adam walked Sophie through to the lounge, he could see his mother sizing her up.

"You're not as tall as I imagined," Pam said. "Or blonde. I was expecting you to be blonde."

Sophie chuckled, squeezing Adam's hand tighter. "I have my blonde moments," she said. "You know, like walking into a room and completely forgetting why I walked in there."

"Oh, yes, all the time. But then, I *am* blonde," Pam said, laughing, gesturing to her stylishly bobbed hair. "Although, not so natural nowadays." She checked her hair as she passed a mirror. "Right, well, I've decided against the idea of a roast dinner. Rather hot today, don't you think? Thought we'd have a salad and make use of the garden."

"Sounds fine, mum."

226

"So, would you both like tea or coffee, or something cold?"

"Coffee, please," Sophie said.

"I'll have the same, please, Mum."

Okay, his mother seemed to approve but they'd only been in the house five minutes. His mother left them alone, and he smiled at Sophie, and rubbed her hand. She gave a nervous, unsure expression. "You're doing great."

"I'm not sure what's going to be worse, if she likes me, or hates me."

Adam heard his mother coming back into the room, so quickly kissed Sophie's hand, lacing his fingers tighter through hers.

Sophie shot him a stern expression before turning to his mother and smiling. "Do you need any help in the kitchen?"

"No, you're all right, dear." Pam smiled then turned to Adam. "Why don't you take Sophie out to the garden? It's shady, and so much cooler than in here."

Adam led Sophie into his mother's cottage garden, full of nooks and crannies, hollyhocks, sweet williams and lupines, towards a patio. A big umbrella shaded the chairs, padded with cushions, around a garden table. He held out a chair for Sophie, then sat beside her.

His mother soon appeared with a cafetiere and three cups on a tray. The conversation flowed steadily, Pam asking Sophie most of the questions, and for most of it, Sophie answering them truthfully.

His mother was quite taken with Sophie. But then who wouldn't be? She had a natural charm about her and her confidence had grown since the wedding weekend. Was that why she was being so honest, letting her feelings for him be known?

"You know he's rich, don't you?" Pam said.

"Mum!" Adam's cup clattered on its saucer.

Sophie glanced at Adam and put her cup down. "Yes, I know he's rich." She smiled at his mother. "Though I only found out

227

at the wedding."

"You did?" His mother sounded surprised.

"Yes, before I thought he was an account manager at the company."

"Ah yes, you're using my name, aren't you, dear? I wanted the name to be double barrelled – you do when you're nineteen – but Gordon wouldn't allow it, so I insisted Adam had Reid as a middle name." Adam rolled his eyes. He'd heard this story a few times.

"I'm not interested in his money," Sophie said, suddenly defensive. "I fell for his charm and that smile of his."

"Ah, yes, his charm. I believe it's due to him being an only child; he was pretty good at getting his own way. Would pull one of his adorable faces and I found myself unable to say no." Pam stood up, laughing. "Time to get my own back. Let me show you some old photographs."

"Mum, please, not the family photos." But it was too late, she headed off toward the house. Adam groaned.

Sophie chuckled. "Oh yes, please." She nudged him, and knowing his mother was out of earshot said, "Blackmail material at work, I think."

"You dare."

His mother promptly returned, armed with a couple of photo albums. Adam hid his face behind his hand, shaking his head.

"You'll scare her off."

"Nonsense. I haven't had a chance to do this ever," his mother said, then turned to Sophie. "You're the first girlfriend he's ever brought home. Oh, except once, some strumpet – too busy filing her nails to have a conversation with me."

"Mother!" He shot her a warning glance, but Pam ignored him. Handing an album to Sophie, she huddled next to her and pointed out the pictures. Sophie said 'oh cute' a lot, and giggled, too, as his mother told her some anecdote about the picture.

Eventually his mother glanced at her watch and said, "I'd better sort out lunch." She left Sophie and Adam sitting under the umbrella.

"Has Pam only met one of your girlfriends?" Sophie asked, flicking through the pages of the album.

"She's met some at family occasions, but after Michaela, I tried to avoid it at all costs."

"Were they as bad as your mum makes out?"

"No! She assumes they're all as bad as Michaela, but they weren't." He looked at her earnestly.

"I believe you." Sophie smiled then her turned attention to a photograph he couldn't see because she'd tilted the album. "Oh, this one I need to copy and take to work," she said excitedly. "James would like to see this one."

"Which one?" Adam said, frowning.

"Not showing you." Sophie held the book to her chest. They stood, and she ran down the garden, giggling. He chased after her, catching her quickly, grabbing her around her waist. He knew his mother had a great view from her kitchen window. Would she be watching?

Adam pulled Sophie around to face him, and she put the album behind her back, still laughing. She quickly sobered as Adam looked at her, a cheeky smile forming. He tugged her towards him, his lips landing on hers. He had longed to kiss her, probably since picking her up at the train station. Sophie relaxed into him, the tip of his tongue parting her lips. Lost in the kiss, his hands slid around her waist, resting on the small of her back, pulling her closer, crushing her body against his, and then he found the photo album.

He snatched it from her grip, pulling out of the kiss and grinned. "Ah-ha!"

She huffed. "That was not fair."

He cupped her neck, stroking her soft skin with his thumb.

229

"Sorry, had to give my mother something."

"Shall we go see if she needs some help?" Sophie slipped her hand into his.

"Yeah, all right," Adam replied. She pulled, and he resisted, she turned and frowned. "Thank you, Sophie."

"For what?"

"For pleasing my mother."

"I'm just being myself. The only pretending I'm doing is being your girlfriend. And that's not really hard."

Adam quickly hid his surprise, hearing her sincerity. It wasn't hard. But it didn't mean they were right for one another.

***

Sophie walked into Pam's kitchen with the intention to help. Sophie wanted to show Pam the type of girl she was, wanting to be liked. It could backfire, though. What if Pam didn't want help, wouldn't like her for it? Too many chefs... Well, she'd try at least.

"Need a hand?"

"Actually, you could chop up those tomatoes," Pam replied, then frowned. "You do know how to use a knife?"

Sophie chuckled. "Were his previous girlfriends really that bad?"

"You don't know the half of it. I dare not share it with you either, otherwise you might scarper. And I like you."

Sophie gulped at Pam's honesty. It would be Adam's mess to deal with after today. Not Sophie's this time.

Sophie breathed deeply, shaking off her guilt, and set to work with the tomatoes, then the peppers, cucumber, and carrots, making some decorative as her mother had once shown her. The two of them chatted casually, while Adam was sent back and forth to lay the garden furniture out.

"Oh, my, you can cook!" Pam said, noticing the salad. Sophie could argue that a salad was hardly cooking, but she knew what Pam meant.

"My mother's a chef. So is my sister."

"But I thought you were an engineer?"

"I am, but my mother didn't let me go to university without some basic skills."

"Basic skills are how to use the microwave for beans on toast."

"I also worked in Mum's restaurant during the summer holidays while at uni," Sophie said. She'd hidden herself more like, insisting on helping in the kitchens rather than waitress, for fear of seeing Simon. How silly did that seem now?

Adam walked back into the kitchen and Pam turned her attention to him. "Adam, this woman is a keeper. Not only is she beautiful, she can cook, too."

Sophie blushed, handing Adam the salad bowl. He looked anxious - maybe he realised lying to his mother wasn't a good idea. Pam was friendly and passing compliments left, right and centre. Sophie modestly shrugged them off.

By the time they'd finished in the kitchen, Sophie had swapped recipes, and they were laughing and joking like old friends. Adam had gone quiet. Maybe he was already trying to work out how he was going to tell his mother Sophie and he were no longer an item?

"And she eats," Pam had commented during lunch. By now, Adam was glaring at his mother for her constant digs at his previous old flames. Sophie couldn't help but giggle.

"Well, that's a good thing," Pam had continued. "Think of money well spent when you go to fine restaurants and she actually enjoys the food, rather than playing with it because she's too concerned about her figure." Pam winked at Sophie.

Pam insisted they stay longer and play cards, teaching Sophie how to play Cribbage – and lose, even with Adam's help.

It was actually wonderful - and another thing Sophie missed. Family involvement. She wanted to be part of a family. She had a family, of course, but they felt so far away. And her life was settled here – wasn't it? She loved her job. Yet, Harry's offer milled around in the back of her mind.

If only Adam would see sense. Maybe he would after today. They were relaxed with one another. It became normal to Sophie to touch him, pat his arm, and give him little kisses. Were they fake on his part, though? Did he still see it as a lie?

The afternoon drifted on. Birds sang their evening songs, and crickets chorused in the garden among the long grass in a part Pam kept natural. Too full from the lunch, Pam served cheese and biscuits, then a huge gateau for dessert. Finally, Adam insisted he take Sophie home, promising his mother she would see Sophie again.

A promise he'd have to break, because Sophie would not be doing this again. She'd enjoyed the day, enjoyed Adam's company and loved meeting his mother. But if it couldn't be for real, she needed to move on. She hadn't got over Simon and regained her confidence to let it be stifled over a relationship that wasn't ever going to happen.

Besides, guilt had eaten away at her at the wedding, lying to her own family and friends, and now today, meeting Adam's mother, she hated being part of this deception. It was happening all over again, but this time her family weren't the ones being fooled.

Adam stood outside Sophie's flat. Despite her protest, he'd insisted he walk her up to her front door.

"You should never have promised she'd see me again," Sophie said.

"I know." Adam's hand combed through his hair, and his forehead creased with a frown. "At times, today was really tough. It's not great lying to your mother."

232

"Now you know how I felt at the wedding. I didn't have to lie to my mother's face, but I had to make up a story over the phone. And Cassie – I hated lying to her."

"I haven't got my mother off my back, have I?"

Sophie wrinkled her nose. "No, probably not. But you'll have to tell her something. Maybe the truth. You're not ready to settle down." She sounded annoyed, but he needed shaking or thumping, to come to his senses. Hadn't today felt as right for him as it had for her? They fell into a natural rhythm with one another. Comfortable, and happy with a spark of life she'd never felt before.

"She's going to kill me. She really likes you. I was hoping in some ways – and no disrespect – she wouldn't, so we could've been out of there early. But no, you lay it on thick and she loves you."

"Hey, don't you blame me. You said be yourself. So that's what I did."

"Sorry. Of course, my mother was always going to like you, that's what I love about you," he said, stepping forward brushing her cheek. She froze. Her heart sped up. "And it's why I asked you. Thank you for today."

That's what he loves about you. About you. Not loves you. Remember.

Sophie shrugged, coolly. "You're welcome. Considering what you did for me at the wedding, I suppose it's the least I could do."

Adam looked at her, a look she knew. He leaned forward, head tilting, lips parted, moistened. He kissed her. And she let him. He was a superb kisser. Heat pulsed through her body, landing deep in her belly, tingling. As her body leaned into his, wanting to relax into his arms, comb her fingers through his hair, he pulled away. Suddenly she felt stupid. Why did she let him kiss her?

"I'll see you tomorrow. Remember an overnight bag," he said, too casually for Sophie's liking.

"This is business, isn't it?" She sucked a breath in deeply.

233

"Of course."

"Right, well, I guess we're square now," she said. A lump formed in her throat. Wasn't this where he said, 'What the hell, I've had a great day with you. Let's just give it a go?'

"Yes, we're square." He nodded.

They no longer owed one another a favour.

She chewed her lip, finding the courage to speak. "You know how I feel about you, so don't ask me to do this again."

"I won't." He had the audacity to shrug his shoulders.

Feeling tears welling in her eyes, she hurried into her flat. Before closing her front door, she said, "Then, never, never kiss me again – unless you mean it."

Chapter Twenty Two

Monday morning arrived far too quickly, and Sophie made her way into work with a small overnight bag. Not sure what to expect from the trip, she'd dressed up a little and wore more makeup than she would usually for the office. She'd kept her hair down, and conscious she looked different than her fellow engineers were used to seeing, her stomach fluttered with anxiety.

They're blokes, they won't notice.

She heard a whistle of approval. James was looking over his desk. "You're looking very smart."

Great. What was it with James? He's not a normal guy. Maybe Kate had trained him to notice the finer details, which was a great quality for a guy to have, but not today. Not for Sophie.

"I have a meeting with one of our customers. I'm going to Manchester with Adam," she replied, trying not to sound defensive, or fiddle with her hair. She casually switched on her computer, to check emails and do as much as she could before Adam appeared.

"So this look is for the clients, not Adam?"

"Definitely not for Adam." She was certainly getting closer to the devil every day, the amount of lies leaving her mouth. In her defence, she'd wanted to look her best for the clients, too. It *was* for the clients. She didn't give two hoots what Adam thought – really.

Last night she'd made a decision. She could no longer stay at

Thomas Robotics, however much she enjoyed her job and the people she worked with. She couldn't watch Adam from the side, out of her reach. Out of sight would be better to get him out of her mind. She would miss James but they could stay in touch. And if she stayed, would she be asked to pretend to do this, and pretend to do that for Adam? She wouldn't be used.

She'd called Harry and found his offer still stood. Open indefinitely, he'd said on the phone. She would move closer to home. With her past firmly behind her now, she was no longer afraid to go back. And her sister was having a baby. She was going to be an aunt.

"Did you see Adam over the weekend?"

"Why?" Sophie blushed. What did James know? Should she be honest with him?

"He couldn't play a round of golf with me Sunday," James said, wandering over to her desk, leaning on the partition. "Said he was busy. I hoped he was busy with you."

"Does he know you're trying to push us together?"

"No! I'm not." James grinned. "But don't you tell him."

"Of course not." She screwed up her face and tapped his arm. "How embarrassing does that look? Because he's certainly not interested in me."

"I need to bang his head against a wall."

"It's no good trying to force something that can't happen. Besides," she looked at her computer screen, unable to look at James, "I'm thinking of leaving."

"What?" James said, shocked. "You can't. Does he know?"

Sophie shook her head. "I'll tell him while we're in Manchester. My father's friend has offered me a job, and my sister is pregnant. I think I want to move back home."

"You think? You're not sure?"

She huffed and tried to sound more positive. "No, I do."

236

"Oh, right. Well, congratulations to your sister." James rubbed his head. "Would you stay though, Soph, if Adam asked you to?"

She frowned, and swallowed. Could he read her so easily?

"You like him, don't you?"

"There is no point continuing with this conversation, James. Go back to your desk."

"Please promise me you'll talk to Adam."

"I will. And I'm sorry. I would've liked it to have worked out too."

Sophie turned her attention to her PC, feeling her eyes prickle. She did not need to cry now, not in the office. James went back to his desk, mumbling about it being a shame, then picked up the phone and dialled. She started to answer some emails, and soon became engrossed in her work, calming herself and forgetting about a certain person called Adam.

"Are you ready?"

Sophie jumped in her seat, as Adam appeared at her desk. His blue eyes locked onto hers, and he smiled.

"Oh, um, yes, I think so," she said, pressing send on an email she'd been typing.

"Just waiting for Lauren to arrive," he said. "Come with me and get a coffee. I'll bring you up to speed on the meeting we're having this afternoon."

Sophie got up from her desk, feeling eyes upon her. James. He was going to be thoroughly disappointed; not only had his little matchmaking ploy not worked, it had probably driven Sophie away. But she needed to escape Adam's presence if her heart was to remain in healthy shape and beat normally. In the meantime, she would have to endure its erratic behaviour in Adam's presence.

Instead of walking to the coffee machine down the corridor, Adam directed her into an office containing a single desk and an oval table with six chairs tucked underneath. Newly furnished, a faint furniture polish aroma, and photographs of their equipment hung on the wall as if they were fine pieces of art. There were even fresh cut flowers on his desk.

"My new office," Adam said, proudly. "There will be an announcement soon about my father retiring."

"Oh, right." Sophie looked around, dumbfounded, while Adam poured coffee from his very own coffee machine, freshly made. He handed her a cup. "Please take a seat." He gestured to the table.

She sat, cradling the coffee mug, warm in her hands, as Adam joined her.

"Do I need to take notes?" she asked, aware she'd not brought a notepad or pen with her. Adam shook his head and talked business, explaining the meeting, running through his pitch for Jerrisons' large contract. No mention of the weekend, his mum, nothing. Anxiety rose up Sophie's spine, dreading how to tell him she was leaving.

"I thought the meeting today would be a good opportunity for you to meet the company you'd be making the design for," Adam said.

Sophie nodded, putting down her coffee cup, for fear of dropping it.

"Lauren came down to see our factory here on site. But she also wanted to spend the weekend in London," he continued. "So she's returning to Manchester with us today."

"Okay."

"Sophie, are you all right? You've gone quiet on me again."

No, she was not all right. He seemed to think she could fake being his girlfriend, kiss and cuddle, then switch it all off. Not any more. Couldn't he see how much she'd been affected by this?

"This work is all very well. A great proposal to our clients. However, I must make you aware I am thinking of leaving, taking Harry up on his offer."

"What! Why?"

She winced at his startled expression and angered tone. "Because ..." She chewed her cheek. "I've let things get personal between us. For me. For me things are personal between us. And I think it will be better if I leave."

"Sophie, you're the best engineer Thomas Robotics has got. You're a real asset to this company. I'll double your pay if I have to. I wasn't joking at the wedding and I'm not joking now."

"It's not about money," she said, glaring at him, angry that he thought he could buy her. All he needed to do was love her and she would stay.

A knock at the door interrupted them. Lauren waited, and smiled.

"Hi, Lauren." Adam opened the door and Lauren bounded in, her long blonde hair clipped back.

"Good morning. Sorry I'm a bit late," she said.

Sophie thought she'd made an effort in her appearance, but she hadn't even tried compared to Lauren. She was wearing killer heels – if Sophie wore four-inch heels all day, every day, they'd kill her. A wedding maybe, or a night out, but not for work. Lauren's heels accentuated a grey, fitted trouser suit. With her perfect, slim figure, Lauren looked sophisticated, and gorgeous. She meant business, carefully planning every minute detail of her appearance.

She was everything Sophie wasn't.

She was everything Sophie thought Adam would want.

"No, you're fine. Gave me time to talk to Sophie about the meeting," Adam said, smiling at her. Sophie noticed it wasn't the genuine article Sophie usually received, giving her a very small vote of confidence. Although she'd just told him she was leaving, so that could be the reason his expression was tense.

"We'll continue our *discussion* later." He directed this comment to Sophie.

"Maybe James would be better off –"

239

"No, Sophie. I want you at this meeting," he said, scowling briefly. "Shall we get on the road, ladies? Traffic being good, we've still got a three and half hour journey ahead of us."

Sophie agreed to meet Adam in the car park and went to get her things from her desk, shutting her PC down. Making her way out of the building, Sophie bumped into Lauren on the way, coming out of the ladies' room.

"Is he single?" Lauren asked. Sophie frowned. "Adam?"

"Oh, uh, yes, I think so."

"What's he like?" Lauren whispered. "Nice? Or head up his own backside. You know, guys who know they're good looking tend to be utter bastards."

Sophie swallowed. "No, he's a good guy."

Or was he? No, Adam hadn't done anything intentional to hurt her; she'd done it all by herself.

"Might have to have another crack at him then." Lauren winked at her. "He seemed all business Friday night. Maybe I can get him to unwind."

Sophie gulped. Would Adam unwind with Lauren? Very likely. If Pam's discussions were anything to go by yesterday, Adam preferred blondes.

Somehow, in those four-inch killer heels Lauren had passed Sophie and got to the front passenger door of Adam's BMW while Adam loaded their bags into the boot. Sitting in the back was probably a better idea – she could stay out of the conversations. Let Lauren take her crack at Adam.

Once seated and buckled into the back of the car, Sophie realised her mistake. She'd sat behind Lauren, meaning Adam had a better view of her whilst driving, and could catch her eye in the rear-view mirror. She couldn't switch seats now. How obvious would that look?

"Did you have a good weekend in London?" Adam asked Lauren,

pulling out of the Thomas Robotics car park.

"Fantastic, thanks. I went to the National Gallery, The Tate, and even managed to get tickets to the theatre Saturday night."

Sophie's insides turned cold as she listened to Lauren talk about her weekend. Not only was the woman gorgeous, she was intellectual. Sophie had assumed Lauren had been to London to shop. And once she'd finished shopping, she'd done more shopping, or visited a beauty salon. *She did have beautifully manicured nails.* But no, she'd done the tourist things, visited the galleries, museums, places of interest. She'd done all the things Sophie enjoyed doing.

"Sorry I couldn't show you around. Busy weekend," Adam said, glancing at Sophie in the rear-view mirror. She wanted to hide; instead, she rummaged through her handbag aimlessly.

"You'll have to make it up to me," Lauren said, chuckling, giving him a nudge, and to Sophie's annoyance, Adam grinned at Lauren. The heart-stopping-turn-insides-to-goo kind. Lauren giggled again. Sophie didn't need to witness this. Really, she didn't. She kept her reactions concealed, hopefully, as Lauren wasn't aware of Sophie and Adam's history.

What history? That's the point! There is no history. Give it up, Soph!

Sophie felt sicker by the minute. Not car sickness, but jealousy. If Lauren did actually take a crack at him, Adam wouldn't say no. Not to a woman like her. He'd be mad otherwise.

Maybe he'd even fall in love.

That thought left a horrible metallic taste in her mouth. She swallowed.

If Lauren had been the materialistic kind, like his mother seemed to think he dated, then Sophie wouldn't have cared. Lauren would have no future with Adam. *Very much like Sophie.* But no, not only did Lauren have the model looks and style, she had the brains, too. Any hopes of Sophie and Adam living happily ever after were doomed.

During the journey, Lauren talked about her favourite artists, art exhibitions, her fascination for the architecture, history of London. Sophie even joined in, discussing her favourite attractions in the city, actually liking the woman. However hard she tried to find a fault with Lauren, there wasn't one. She was actually very nice.

Adam occasionally glimpsed at Sophie through his mirror, seemingly when she'd been staring at him and got caught. Otherwise he concentrated on the road, or Lauren.

"Are you all right in the back, Sophie?" Lauren swivelled around best she could in her seat to look at her. "Sorry, I should have asked if you'd be all right in the back, only I get terrible car sickness. You're not feeling sick or anything?"

"No, no, I'm fine." Sophie sat up straighter, fiddling with her hair, hoping it hadn't become suitable for birds to nest in. "Sitting in the back makes me sleepy, that's all." She yawned.

How do you confess you're plotting to murder a perfectly nice woman who's about to steal your man?

She's not stealing your man. He's not yours.

Lust-filled thoughts of Adam mixing with the knowledge that Lauren could have him whilst she couldn't had turned her quiet. She'd let Lauren and Adam control the conversation in the end. Turn inwards, try to become invisible. It was what she did best.

Relieved to get out of the car when they arrived at Jerrisons Ltd in Manchester, Sophie slammed the car door. It had been a laborious four-hour journey watching Lauren flirt with Adam. It grated on her. She refused to let herself be jealous. *Ha! But you failed.*

Adam should have taken Lauren to see his mother. He wouldn't have been lying then. Pam would like Lauren. The woman was probably a better cook, too.

Once signed in and given passes at reception, Lauren led them straight through the tall glass atrium, full of tropical plants and palms, and into a meeting room where three men waited. Sophie was hungry, as Adam hadn't stopped apart from a quick 'stretch the legs' break. To her relief, a finger buffet had been provided and they worked through their discussions as they tucked into their late lunch.

Adam sat next to Sophie, instantly sending heat up her neck into her cheeks. She wanted to fan herself or go check the air-conditioning level, but thought better of it. Lauren took the chair on the other side of him. A thorn between two roses, though Sophie considered herself more like a dandelion compared to Lauren. She observed the three other male attendees. An attractive man, similar age to Adam, called Nick Sallico, was smartly dressed and had a friendly disposition. He knew Adam well, going by the way they slapped each other's backs, laughing heartily and shaking hands at the initial greeting. The other two were senior members of the company, both in their fifties, and looking like they'd spent too much time in the office, both with portly figures.

They wanted a Thomas Robotic's engineer to work closely with them, to design a piece of equipment based on the QB20 for their factory. It needed some alterations and specification changes to suit their company's needs. Confidently, Adam declared Sophie was the engineer for the job and would be working on their project.

Sophie saw a solution to her problem, which would mean getting away from Thomas Robotics for a while without leaving the company, which deep down she didn't want to do. But it would mean she'd be further from home.

"I could be seconded here to work on the specifications with Jerrisons more closely," she suggested. The others around the table mumbled and nodded.

"Sophie, this project won't just take a couple of weeks. It could take months," Adam said. She'd tried throughout the meeting not to let him distract her, with his aftershave – her favourite – wafting her way.

"I know. But I'd be happy with it."

"It sounds like a great idea," Nick interjected. "Probably would save a lot of time and travelling if Sophie was prepared to do it. Could reduce the project time, too."

Sophie nodded her agreement. She could do this one job and then move back to Cornwall. That way all parties would be happy. Adam wouldn't be losing his 'best engineer' for this job.

"I'm not sure about it. Although Sophie's work priority would be with Jerrisons, the plan was never to transfer her to Manchester. I'd still like her based at Thomas Robotics because there may be other projects she needs to oversee."

"James could deal with those," Sophie said. "If there's anything he's not sure about he can email me and I can take a look from here."

"We're a friendly bunch. We'd look after her," Nick said, smiling at Adam, then Sophie. But Adam's expression was hard, disagreeable.

He doesn't want me to leave, yet he doesn't want me. Sophie's hackles rose. She would deal with it later, though. This meeting was not the place to start shouting at Adam.

The meeting ended, unresolved on whether Sophie should work from Thomas Robotic's offices or at Jerrisons.

"Tomorrow morning, we'll show you around the site and discuss time frames," Clive, one of the senior manager said, shaking Sophie's hand, then Adam's.

Nick approached them. "Have you got plans tonight? Would you like to go out for dinner?"

Sophie, about to say she was happy to stay at the hotel and catch an early night, was interrupted by Adam agreeing and arranging the details with Nick.

Oh, great.

"We'll meet you there, say seven-thirty?" Adam said, and Nick nodded. Lauren looked pleased. Sophie wondered if she could make up an excuse to leave early. She did not fancy watching Adam and Lauren hitting it off.

Once Sophie was inside the car, this time in the front seat, Adam glowered at her, his expression grim and his knuckles white as he gripped the steering wheel.

"What the hell were you thinking?" he said. Fury laced his words as he started the car, yet he didn't move it out of the parking space. Instead, he glared at her, his face reddening.

"This morning I told you I was leaving. This way I get to leave, without leaving the company. Both of us are happy."

"No. I would not be happy about this arrangement." He banged the steering wheel with the palms of his hands. "This contract was never to have you based in Manchester. You'd work from our offices."

"Adam, I can't stay around you and make a fool of myself. You know how I feel about you. And I can't see it changing with you under my nose. I want a future. I want what Natalie and Gareth have. My sister is pregnant; I'd like to have children too, one day. And I can't see it happening if I cling on to the hope you might change your mind."

"Sophie, I can't. I just *can't!*"

"So why do you want me to stay?"

"I don't know." He sighed.

"You can't have it all. You can't expect me to stay, if you don't want me."

"We will find a solution."

Sophie laughed with an edge of anger to it. "How?"

"I don't know yet," he snapped and crunched the car into gear with force.

"I have to leave. You have to let me go. In fact, you cannot stop me."

"Great. Helping you out at some fucking wedding has cost me my best engineer. For fuck's sake, why did you fall for me?"

Sophie stared in shock. She'd never heard him swear, not in front of her like that. Not at her.

"I shouldn't have sworn at you," he said. "I'm sorry. I'm angry."

Sophie was equally fuming. *Who the hell does he think he is?*

"No, I'm sorry. It wasn't intentional," she snapped, sarcastically. "I should have realised you're one hell of a liar, Adam."

He drove, in silence, to their hotel. They were checked-in, given their keys. Neither spoke a word unless it was necessary. Sophie knew if she opened her mouth she'd say something hurtful or spiteful, and she had to be careful. He *was* her boss.

Not for much longer!

She heard her father's voice. '*Never burn bridges.*'

They found their rooms – next to one another. Adam opened the door to his hotel room with the swipe of his key card. He still hadn't calmed down.

Tough. He cannot have it all.

This was about Sophie preserving herself. The only way to get over Adam would be to separate herself from him. Hadn't it worked with Simon? And the only way Adam would keep Sophie was to commit.

She wasn't expecting a promise of lifetime commitment. She was a realist. Sometimes relationships faded, or came to a shocking abrupt end – like Simon. Yet, wasn't it worth a try, rather than to never know?

"Be ready for seven-fifteen," he said, then entered his room. She jumped as his door slammed shut.

She slammed hers just as hard.

Chapter Twenty Three

The hot shower hadn't calmed Adam, and, as he threw on a fresh shirt, all he could think about was Sophie leaving. And how to stop her.

But what hold did he have on her?

As her boss he could offer her a pay rise she couldn't refuse. Except in the short time he'd known her, he'd learnt money would not be of interest to her. She wasn't that kind of person. That's why he liked her.

Now he really wanted to kill James. Why'd he ask him to go to that stupid wedding? If Adam hadn't gone, he and Sophie would have remained strangers, work colleagues. He wouldn't have all this mixed up shit going on and he wouldn't be on the brink of losing one of the best engineers Thomas Robotics had managed to employ. His father, if he learnt the truth, would go ballistic.

Never mix business with pleasure.

Well, he hadn't – technically. They'd attended the wedding as strangers, becoming comfortable with one another. Unfortunately, the Sophie he'd met down the pub that first time hadn't been the real Sophie; not the one he'd gone away with. He could relax with Sophie, didn't have to put up some pretence about who he was and what he did. Ironically, their façade in front of her friends and family had made them at ease with one another.

His father would agree to Sophie being based in Manchester – if it meant not losing her from Thomas Robotics permanently. And deep down he knew it was the best business decision, too. But for some reason this really wasn't sitting easily on his conscience. Adam growled, raising his fist. He stopped himself punching the mirror he stared into and slammed the wardrobe door shut instead. Breaking glass, and his fist, would not provide a solution.

He liked the idea of Sophie being only an office away, situated in the same building, down at the pub on a Friday night, living locally. He wanted her near in case he needed her. So he could... What? Use her?

No. He had to let her go.

Still infuriated by this thought, he slipped his watch on, checking the time as he did so, then grabbed his wallet and room key.

Adam knocked on Sophie's hotel door. He leaned against the wall, drumming his fingers on it, sucking in his breath, trying to regain some patience. But his mood made him want to bang the bloody door down, angry with Sophie for falling for him. Which was ludicrous – he should be flattered. It had added a complication to their relationship. But what did he expect? Their weekend together had been wonderful, if you forgot about the ex-boyfriend. He'd go back in a flash to how they were, only the two of them in each other's company. He missed it. A part of him wished he'd made love to her. And that's why he didn't want Sophie going away, because it would confirm he'd never feel this way again – whatever *this* was. Never have it again. He liked the idea there was some hope. He'd lose it if she went.

Ridiculous.

Sophie opened the door, zapping the breath out of him. Wearing a red evening dress with thin spaghetti straps, she looked stunning. Her hair was pinned up, not as precisely as when she'd been a bridesmaid, revealing her slender, kissable neck... He knew what it would do to him if he kissed her, just behind her ear.

"Wow, what a dress. The colour suits you," he said, eventually finding some words as he stared.

She fumbled with a sparkling red clutch bag, smoothed her dress and smiled, her gaze not ever meeting his. "Thanks, I bought it with Cassie."

Another quality of Sophie's – she lacked confidence. She didn't realise how beautiful she truly was, and it made her all the more special. Women moaned that men could be bastards, using their good looks. Yet women knew how to use their looks, too. Even Lauren, a nice enough girl, knew she was attractive. He'd noticed her flirtatious behaviour in the car today. Some women flaunted it so much they lost their appeal.

"I thought you didn't like shopping." He smirked, his anger taking a back seat. A sort of calm came over him at the sight of her. He couldn't stay angry at Sophie for long.

"You know full well I don't like shopping. Cassie dragged me around. We'd gone out for lunch. She spotted the dress and insisted I buy it."

"Glad she did."

"The sad thing is she thought I should buy it to please you," Sophie said, lifting her chin as she shut her door. She strutted down the corridor, not waiting for Adam and he stared admiringly. Cassie was right; the dress did please Adam. Sophie's curves filled the dress magnificently, it accentuated her bum – and fantastic legs.

Where Sophie lacked confidence in her appearance, she'd gained in asserting herself. Ever since she'd buried Simon. Adam liked this fiery side. She'd become someone who stood her ground. Adam imagined lighting that fire, having a blazing row, so he could apologise and make it up to her...making love, taking that passion into the bedroom.

But because Adam respected her, and wanted to keep her at

249

the company, he kept his brain inside his head and not down in his boxers. Well, he at least tried to. His brain could quite easily move south, as he stayed back and groaned, watching Sophie sashay. Shaking himself out of his reverie, he strolled after her, secretly enjoying the view.

Even his mother liked Sophie. Had he messed up there, letting his mother meet Sophie? She'd telephoned this morning, reiterating how wonderful she found Sophie, wanting to see her again. And reminded him if he continued with his fatal string of romances, he would follow the same path as his father. Adam had argued, of course.

"If you love her, hold onto her," were his mother's last words to him this morning.

Maybe Sophie transferring to Manchester would be a good way to end their so-called relationship. It would let Sophie off the hook with her friends and Adam could use it as an excuse to appease his mother.

But there the icy feeling was again, churning away at his insides. He didn't want Sophie moving away. He liked her where he could see her – *especially wearing that dress!*

Outside the hotel their taxi waited. Adam slid into the back beside Sophie, yet she remained silent. For the first time, he felt a frosty aura around her. Her legs crossed away from him, her body twisted, her back to him as she stared out the window. Adam wasn't sure whether opening his mouth would charm her or annoy her, so kept it shut. Did he really want to get into an argument about her leaving? He needed to think of a solution – and fast! One where she didn't move to Manchester or Cornwall, never returning to Surrey, to him.

At the restaurant, they were shown to their table by the waiter. A bar stretched along the back wall, with bartenders polishing glasses or shaking cocktails. Everything gleamed like it was brand new.

Nick and Lauren were already seated opposite one another, so it forced Sophie and Adam to do the same. This was much to Adam's annoyance, though he knew it evened up the table; Sophie sat next to Nick. The four of them talked, but if Adam tried to get into the conversation with Sophie, she wouldn't allow it. She'd give closed answers, shutting their exchange down where possible. However, Nick had her full attention.

Adam unclenched his fist, hidden under the table, and smiled, falsely.

With each course served, the wine flowed and Adam wished Lauren and Nick would disappear, wanting Sophie to himself, to sort out their problem. Not that he'd worked out a solution, yet.

"Shame you're not here for a couple of days, could have shown you around," Nick said, topping up the glasses of wine, emptying the bottle.

"I would've liked that," Sophie replied. "Sounds poor, doesn't it, but this is the furthest north I've ever travelled."

"What? You've not been to Cumbria?" Lauren said, then sipped her wine. Sophie shook her head. "Manchester is a great city."

"Ah, yes, what a city," Nick added.

"Oh yeah," Adam couldn't bite his tongue, sarcasm lacing his words, "Nick can show you all the clubs and bars he knows." He laughed and Nick joined in heartily with him.

"Okay, so I know a few." Nick played along, taking Adam's digs in jest.

"I'm sure you have some stories to tell for each club."

"Hey, pot calling the kettle – I'm sure you do, too. You've seen a few with me!" Nick chinked his glass against Adam's and chuckled again.

"This could be where I'm going wrong." Lauren frowned. "To catch a classy guy, I've got to go clubbing." She winked at Adam.

"Get your heart broken, more like," Sophie mumbled. Adam's

expression sobered.

"So, when did we last do the clubs?" Nick asked Adam, changing the subject slightly. Adam shrugged, not wanting his antics in Manchester discussed in front of Sophie.

Adam had known Nick a couple of years now, going out for drinks when he had meetings at Jerrisons. They got along well. Nick wasn't much different from Adam when it came to women. He was another prime example of a man making the most of his good looks. What was Nick's interest in Sophie? Purely business? Or could he have other intentions?

Nick would not be right for Sophie. Any more than Adam would.

"So, if you move to Manchester, will we need to show you the nightlife?" Nick said, resting his arm on the back of Sophie's chair. "Are you a secret party animal, Sophie?" He nudged her shoulder.

She put her glass of wine down and shook her head. "No, it's not really my thing."

"No, Nick, the girl's got some class," Lauren said, pushing her plate away.

"Yes, sorry. I'm rather boring," Sophie said.

"It's not boring," Lauren said. "I tell you what I find boring. Shopping."

"Agreed." The girls chinked their glasses together.

"No problem. I don't like shopping either," Nick said, and they all laughed. Except Adam. He chuckled, trying to play along but jealousy bubbled below the surface, and he concentrated on keeping it in check. He had no right to be jealous.

Simon was different. He had felt no jealousy where he was concerned. But Nick – he was a threat.

"But you've got gorgeous clothes," Sophie said to Lauren.

"I'll let you into a secret," Lauren said, softening her voice and Sophie leaned across the table. "I have a personal shopper."

Sophie giggled. "Sounds like heaven. I should do that."

As the night progressed, and the dinner finished, they walked up the street to a small club Nick knew, insisting Sophie got to see at least one club. Sophie and Lauren found a table, while Adam went with Nick to the bar.

Nick put the drinks on the table, but didn't sit.

"Sophie, will you dance with me?" Nick asked, before Adam could even suggest it. He'd been planning how to separate the two and thought whizzing her off to the dance floor the best option. But the bastard got there first.

"Sure," Sophie replied. She looked Adam in the eye, then let Nick lead her down to the dance floor.

"Would you like to dance?" Lauren asked Adam, interrupting him from his envious reverie.

He grimaced. "No, I'm not much of a dancer." *He was. But not with Lauren.*

***

The music slowed in pace and Nick took Sophie into his arms, slowly dancing. They'd been talking, laughing, and now dancing together the whole evening. It felt strange to Sophie, yet good.

And so what if Adam had to watch her with Nick? She'd sat through a four-hour car journey listening to Lauren's, at times, flirtatious chit-chat. Adam had been chatting with her all night, too. Although that could be largely due to Sophie ignoring him.

She felt awful actually. She'd been topping up Lauren's wine glass all night, and only a little of her own, hoping the more Lauren drank, the less attractive Adam would find her. Unfortunately, Sophie had been trained by the best – Cassie – in topping up drinks. Though, Cassie usually filled her own glass up too, and got equally as drunk. Tonight Sophie remained sober.

Poor Lauren. She actually was a lovely woman. Sophie liked her, but she didn't want her having any hope of success with Adam.

Sophie Trewyn, you should be ashamed of your behaviour.

"Is anything going on between you and your boss?" Nick whispered into Sophie's ear breaking her thoughts.

"Uh, no." *If only.* She glanced over Nick's shoulder as they turned, and sure enough, Adam watched them. "Why?"

"He's looking over here like he's praying I'll spontaneously combust."

Sophie giggled. "He's a friend. Maybe a bit protective. But I'm not *with* him."

Maybe the green-eyed monster in him might make him come to his senses. Instantly, she felt bad about using Nick. But she wasn't, really. This was her trying to get on with her life and not dwell on Adam. Besides he'd made her angry today and this was her way of dealing with it. And If Nick wanted to pay attention to her, she would let him. This was real. None of it fake. They genuinely liked each other and could hold a pleasant conversation.

"Good. Because, I mean, you know, if you get to work with us, then maybe you and I could hang out more?" Nick smiled at her. He was handsome, yet in an opposite way to Adam's light features; he had short, spiky, coal-black hair and dark brown eyes, but his smile didn't have the same effect as Adam's.

"It would be nice. I'd appreciate the friendship."

He didn't smell as good as Adam, but then she was biased on that score too. And they didn't gel in the same way she had with Adam on the dance floor at the wedding.

"I thought more –"

"Let's see if I get the job first, huh? I'd rather we concentrate on being friends." *But a date wouldn't be out of the question – if it meant trying to forget a certain person.*

"Of course. Hope he doesn't put his foot down and insist you stay in Surrey."

"He won't. He'll go with whatever is best for the company."

"James doesn't give you enough credit."

"James?"

"Uh, oh." Nick winced. "I've been sprung."

"Did James put you up to this?" Sophie stopped dancing and frowned, but Nick twisted her around, keeping her moving with him. *What was James up to?*

"You know, he needn't have bothered. I would have asked you to dance anyway." Nick pulled her closer, whispering in her ear. "He asked me to look after you, show you a good time."

"Good time?"

"Oh, but he said if I tried to get in your knickers he'd be up here in a flash ripping my head off." Nick grinned cheekily. Sophie stared, taken aback. "Look, he's concerned, and wanted me to boost your confidence. To be honest, I'm not sure what he was going on about. The way he talked I thought you had two heads or something."

"So are you pretending to like me?" she asked warily, easing away from him. *Great, can't even find a man to really like me. James still has to intervene, yet concerned for the welfare of my knickers it seems.*

"No, no, no!" Nick said. He tugged her closer, then brushed his thumb along her cheek – it didn't feel as good as when Adam did it. "On the contrary, like I said, I would've chatted you up anyway. You're a catch."

***

If he tries to kiss her...

"Are you sure you don't want to dance?" Lauren said.

Adam tore his attention from Sophie and Nick on the dance floor and looked at Lauren. She leaned closer into him. He could smell her perfume mingled with the alcohol on her breath. Poor girl, he'd hardly been company for her.

He shook his head. "No, I think it's time we headed back. I've ordered a taxi."

"We?" Lauren's eyes lit up.

"Sophie and I. We've got an early start with the meeting, remember? We need it to end on time so we can head back home in the afternoon." And he couldn't sit here any longer and watch the woman he loved in the arms of another man.

He loved?

"Oh, right. Yes, of course." Lauren flustered.

Adam strode over to the dance floor and tapped Nick on the shoulder. If he'd been a Neanderthal caveman, this would be where he dragged his woman back to his cave by her hair– after punching this guy's lights out. But Adam wasn't prehistoric; his mother had brought him up to have manners, and Nick was a client.

"We should head back to the hotel – early start tomorrow," he said over the music. "The taxi will be waiting outside."

"I don't mind escorting Sophie back if you want to leave early," Nick said, still not removing his arm from around Sophie's waist, which really annoyed Adam. He clenched his jaw, then released it, trying to relax. Nick wasn't to know he was treading on Adam's toes.

"I need to talk to Sophie, and there's no point in taking two taxis," Adam said, his expression stern, and Nick frowned. "Besides, someone needs to take Lauren home." Adam gestured towards Lauren, still at the table.

"It's okay, Nick. I'll go with Adam," Sophie said, to Adam's relief. "It does make sense to get the taxi with him." As Nick let go of Sophie, Adam placed his arm around her. Sophie scowled at him. *Fight – make love – fight – make love.* Let her scowl.

256

Nick assisted Lauren out of the club, Adam and Sophie following. Adam got into the back of the taxi with Sophie, yet she sat as far as she could from him, staring out the window, in a similar way to how they'd arrived.

"So your sister's pregnant?" Adam said, trying to break the silence.

"Yes, but if I move to Manchester I've buggered up moving closer to home," she said, her tone cold, still unable to look at him.

He wanted to say 'You are not moving to Manchester.' But he kept that to himself. He would clear it up in the meeting tomorrow.

"Did you have a good time tonight?" He tried again to drum up some conversation. He'd been aware how little she'd said to him all night, another thing he'd loathed. Her lack of interest in him hurt his pride. "You seemed to get on with Nick."

"Yeah, he's a nice guy."

"He's a rat."

Sophie's eyes narrowed as she turned to face him. "Oh my God. You *are* jealous."

"I am not jealous of Nick."

"So why have you been staring at us with your face like... like thunder." Her cheeks were red, matching her dress, her fists clenched.

Stoke the fire.

"He's no good for you. He's like Simon."

"He is nothing like Simon!"

"Then, he's like me."

"He's nothing like you, either."

"He won't commit, Sophie." Adam tried to keep his tone calm. "He's looking for a roll in the hay, then he'll be gone. I know, when we've gone out for drinks, how he likes to smooth talk women."

"And so what are you now? My bloody fairy godmother? So what if Nick's a rat? If I have to find out the hard way, I will."

257

The taxi pulled up outside their hotel. As Sophie tried getting out of the car elegantly, her tight red dress making the process slower, Adam tried giving her his hand. She slapped it away.

"I can manage," she hissed.

In the lift she stood silently, and her chest heaved. Her eyes were glistening, trying to hold in tears. He'd seen that look so many times, and it wasn't a trick; she didn't turn them on or off like a tap. He knew there were genuine tears forming.

"I'm sorry. It wasn't my intention to upset you," he said, stepping forward, trying to take hold of her hand.

"Don't touch me." She snatched it away and the lift pinged. They were at their floor.

The doors opened and he gestured she exit first, then followed. She stopped and turned on him.

"How dare you? How dare you?" she said vehemently, pointing at him, her other hand clutching her handbag tightly, showing the whites of her knuckles. "Why can't you even admit you were jealous?" she dabbed at her eye, then started to walk off.

"All right, I was jealous," he shouted, striding after her. "All night you haven't paid me the slightest bit of attention and I've hated it. Happy now?"

She paced towards her room, fumbled with her purse to get her key card out. She swiped it down the panel in the door, and opened it. "No, I am not happy." He opened his mouth to speak, but she held her trembling hand up to stop him. "And I don't want to shut you out, but what choice do I have? Good night." And she disappeared behind the door, it closing before he could jam it with his foot.

He'd bottled it. He was going to tell her how he felt. But she was gone.

He entered his own room and paced. Was his mother right? Would he never know until he tried? He certainly didn't want to make the same mistake his father made, even though he was the product of that mistake. He didn't want to wind up with a pregnant woman he didn't love, having to marry her – however careful he usually was. But who's to say a woman wouldn't do it? He was rich. Ridiculously rich. One way to lay claim to him would be to have his child. Then he would be lost, unable to share his life with Sophie.

And his mother was right. He was a better delegator than his father. He'd already been working towards hiring the right people, training existing staff so they could take on responsibility. With a good secretary, he could organise his time. He could make time for Sophie.

He already knew he didn't want to lose her.

And he certainly didn't want her with another man.

He loved her.

He couldn't wait six months, get his life sorted at the company, then go find her. She'd be gone. Someone as wonderful as Sophie would be snapped up – look at Nick! It wouldn't take long for some guy to come along and see through her plain, placid disguise and realise the full warmth of her character, her fire and passion.

Watching her with Nick had done him good. The anger and jealousy coursing through his veins tonight had made him realise he could not stand the thought of Sophie being with anyone else but him.

Anything he did from now on would feel worthless without her beside him.

What have you got to lose?

Sophie.

Chapter Twenty Four

Adam knocked hard on Sophie's hotel door.

"Sophie, please open the door. I need to talk to you."

When she unlocked the door, it was like the air he needed, preventing him from suffocating. He took a deep breath, relieved she'd actually opened the door. He wasn't sure what he would have done if she hadn't.

"Thank you," he said, taking in every detail of her face. She'd removed her make-up, yet her skin, in its purity, still looked beautiful.

With no hesitation, he leaned in and pressed his lips on hers, easing his arms around her waist, tugging her towards him. She responded briefly, then jerked away, and slapped him.

"I told you never to kiss me unless –"

"I mean it!" Adam said, his eyes never leaving hers. "That's why I'm here. I mean it."

With both hands, he clasped her face and kissed her again, this time with an urgency, a need. This kiss had to convince her his feelings were real.

Her arms wrapped around his neck and her body pressed against his, her soft breasts pushing against his chest. She believed him. Without letting his mouth leave hers, he walked them inside her room, the door automatically closing behind them.

"I'm sorry," he said between the kisses, her soft moans making him delirious. "So sorry. I've been such an idiot."

He felt every curve of her body; from her rounded, firm bum he'd admired all evening, up to her shoulders, and down again, until he found the zip on the side of her dress and started to guide it down. He wanted her naked – right now.

Fight – make love.

And oh boy, he wasn't going to mess this up a second time.

Suddenly Sophie tore herself away, pushing at him.

"What? What's the matter?" he asked anxiously. "I thought you wanted this."

"Stop, Adam. Stop," she said, breathless and flustered. She held her hands up and backed away as he stepped towards her, wanting her back in his arms. "I can't do this."

Oh God, he had to convince her that she could.

"Why?"

"Because everything I've done with you has been a lie. We technically haven't even had a date." She zipped her dress, and tugged at it, to regain its position and her composure. "Not a real one anyway."

"Sophie, what I feel for you is far from a lie – you have to believe me."

"It just doesn't feel right." She hugged herself, still keeping her distance.

Adam smoothed down his ruffled hair. She wanted him to do this properly. He adjusted his shirt and prayed his erection would disappear soon.

Thank Calvin for boxer briefs.

"You're right. Absolutely right. You deserve better than me waltzing in here. I've mucked you around. We'll go out, some place special." He looked past Sophie and frowned. She stood in front of the bed he'd been planning to make love to her on. On the bed lay her suitcase – open. "Were you packing?"

She turned to the case and shut the lid; he quickly flipped it back open. "You *were* packing."

"We leave tomorrow."

"But..."

"Adam, I can't stay around you." Sophie sighed. "Yes, okay, I was thinking of leaving."

"We have a meeting tomorrow. And not only that..." he glanced at his watch, trying to keep his anger in check, "it's nearly midnight. Where were you going?"

"I don't know. Another hotel. I had to get away from you. I probably would have come to my senses, if you hadn't knocked on the door anyway."

"Is this what you do? Run away from trouble?"

"No."

"You ran from Simon."

She slapped him. For the second time that evening, he reminded himself. This fight-make-love dream he'd been revisiting over and over inside his head turned out not to be as great as it was cracked up to be. The fighting actually hurt.

"I did not!" Sophie said, raising her chin. "I was already at uni. It made it easier to put Simon out of my life by not returning." He could see her tears welling, her eyes sparkling with moisture. "I thought the easiest way to forget about you would be to move on, too."

He took hold of her hand. "I don't want you to leave me. I can't bear the thought of us being apart. Tonight proved it." Carefully, he kissed her forehead. Then, because he couldn't resist, he kissed her cheek, then, gently, her lips. "Wednesday, seven o'clock, I'll pick you up. I'll take you out to dinner. It'll be our first date."

"You're just saying that because I said –"

"Sophie!" Adam looked her in the eye and smiled. "You're right.

262

However much everything between us felt real, it was all based on a lie. I want to do this properly – for you."

She nodded hesitantly.

"I mean it. I'll see you in the morning," he said, and she nodded with a smile. "And do my blood pressure the world of good – stay away from Nick at that meeting."

She laughed, but wiped her eye with the back of her hand as she did so. He kissed her again, gently, not wanting to risk getting carried away. He could so easily get carried away. He hated the idea of them sleeping in separate rooms, separate beds. However, unlike the wedding, he didn't think he could trust himself to just cuddle. He'd be tempted even more than before. But he wanted to do this properly.

***

Sophie stared at the suitcase on her bed. What the hell had she been thinking? Yes, fine, move away, leave, but don't look like you're running for heaven's sake.

She had to endure working with him while she found a solution, not run.

In her anger, she'd grabbed her case, and started packing, her argument being she wanted to be ready for an early off tomorrow morning. Then she'd boiled over, so frustrated with Adam she'd convinced herself to leave the hotel that night.

Ha! That would show him!

She would have come to her senses, realising the wine she'd drunk at dinner was giving her Dutch courage.

But she didn't have to leave now. Adam would take her out on a date. She would see how this went. Heavens, he kept saying he wasn't good enough for her. But was she good enough for him?

263

All day she'd been thinking Lauren was the one perfect for him.

He could change his mind; he had a couple of days to think it over. What if his conscience took over once again? She pushed all negativity to the back of her mind, needing to stay positive.

Ready for bed, she slipped in under the covers, shattered as she was. Her emotions had been up and down like a lift in shopping centre. She had nearly, very nearly, made love to Adam in this very bed. If she hadn't come to her senses, she would have done it. Twice now she'd come so close... She wanted it. She didn't doubt it. Having Adam in her bed as a permanent fixture was her dream.

But if Wednesday night went well, she shouldn't let him in, not straight away. They both needed to get to know one another properly. Because once she made love to Adam, that would be it. It would be hard to recover. If things went wrong, then she would be running from him. The only way she could heal her heart.

***

Adam held her hand as they walked to breakfast, kissed her fingers before letting go of her hand, and paid her heart-warming compliments. It felt surreal. It was like their weekend away, only this time they weren't acting. She did not care he was showing his affection publicly. It was hard to control her own love towards Adam, worried she'd become overbearing and seem heavy, but she felt rather loved up – *just a smidgen!*

She sighed, rather loudly, staring at her bowl of fresh fruit.

"What?" Adam stopped buttering his toast.

"Nothing, it's embarrassing."

"Tell me." His knife clanged on the plate.

"To think yesterday, I got myself so worked up in the car; believing Lauren was perfect for you –"

264

"Lauren?"

"Yes, because she's beautiful, stylish and clever."

Adam chuckled. "But you're those things too."

"I'm terrible."

"No you're not."

"I am." Sophie leaned on her elbows. "Because I got Lauren drunk in the hope you'd find her unattractive." Adam chuckled. "Don't laugh, it's not funny. I have to apologise."

"Sophie, honey, Lauren really doesn't need to know. We all drank the wine."

"Not as much as her! I don't want her feeling embarrassed. She's really nice – even if she was trying it on with you."

He held her hand, thumbing sensuous circles into her palm. "You really had nothing to be jealous about. Where as I –"

Sophie waved it off. "Nick was just being friendly."

"I know what he's like."

"Let's say no more on the matter. Deal?"

He leaned over the table, tilted her chin up, and gently kissed her, his mouth tugging at her bottom lip for a brief moment. Good job she was sitting down.

"Deal."

***

They attended the meeting together and were shown around Jerrisons' factories, demonstrating where Sophie's expertise was required. Throughout the day, Adam remained professional, and so did Sophie. This is where they would have to draw a line between their work and their relationship. Adam, about to become the Managing Director, needed to be taken seriously. But it worked. Sophie happily concentrated on her work, and tried not to be distracted by his occasional cheeky smile and wink in her direction when no one was looking. *Roll on Wednesday night.* The day spent not touching Adam drove her to distraction.

She refused to avoid Nick. After all, he'd done nothing wrong. James had been the one interfering, though Nick confessed to liking Sophie anyway. So she made sure she didn't give any wrong impressions, although deep down, she wanted to shake his hand and thank him for paying her attention last night. It had woken Adam up to a reality Sophie delighted in.

"Have you had any more thoughts on Sophie joining us here, Adam?" Nick asked, as they were finishing the meeting.

"I have discussed it with Sophie, and I would rather she stays at our offices," Adam replied, in a professional manner. *And as sexy as hell.* Sophie stayed quiet. If she and Adam worked this out, there would be no reason for her to move on. She still carried doubt, and wanted someone to pinch her. A part of her still couldn't quite believe it was happening.

***

"Sophie, honey, you're home." Adam nudged her gently, as she'd fallen asleep, unable to keep her eyes open.

She stretched and yawned, realising they were parked up outside her flat.

"Oh, heavens, did you drive all the way? I would have taken over some of the journey."

"It's all right. I'm used to it. Even like it." Adam unclipped his seatbelt.

"Don't get out of the car," Sophie said, waving a finger at him. "Why?"

"I don't know. It's not our date. You're dropping me home from work, remember?"

"A gentleman should still see a lady to her door."

"But will you be a gentleman when you get to my door?"

"Of course."

She giggled at his teasing. She kissed his cheek and went to leave, but he grabbed her hand and pulled her back.

"That wasn't a kiss."

"You'll have to wait for *that*, too." She winked. God, what was she doing? Would playing hard to get backfire on her?

"But this morning you let me kiss you." His lips were inches away, the heat of his breath touched her lips, she smelled his aftershave – *her aftershave* – and had to fight her own struggle to not kiss him.

"They were pecks, and besides, I've had all day to think about this."

Adam grumbled. Sophie smiled, wickedly. This would be fun – if she could hold out long enough. Or Adam didn't get bored.

"What are we going to do about work?" she said, frowning, all of a sudden worrying what she was supposed to do around him in the office.

"What do you mean? I'm not going to be secretive about it. What's the point? We'd get found out in the end." He grinned. "We'll have an open but professional relationship in the office."

She smiled agreeably, then kissed him on the lips, and regretted it, pulling away quickly before he could take a hold – his tongue in her mouth did all sorts to her insides. Butterflies back flipped deep in her belly. His kiss could set her knickers on fire; he was so damn hot.

"See you tomorrow," she said, getting out of the car sharp-ish. Adam got out his side. "I said stay in the car!"

"I'll prove to you I'm as good as my word." He opened the boot, took her luggage out and carried it towards her flat.

"I don't doubt you're good," she said, pouting at him as he gave her a sexy smile. She walked as fast as she could after him, remembering the last time he'd tried taking her luggage to her front door and how it had ended. She wanted tonight to be much better.

He dropped the bag outside her door.

"I will try to stop by your desk, Miss Trewyn." Sophie snorted a laugh at him. "But otherwise, I'll be here at seven tomorrow evening."

She laid her best, sexy voice on thick, praying she didn't sound stupid. "I look forward to it."

He pecked her on the cheek, then headed back down her stairwell.

"Boo! That wasn't a kiss."

He chuckled as he walked back towards his car.

Once inside her flat, she closed her eyes and swallowed, trying to slow her breathing and her pounding heart. She worried whether she'd just played that cool enough, or too cool.

Was this really happening? Or would she wake up tomorrow and find Adam had changed his mind?

Chapter Twenty Five

"Morning, James!" Sophie said in a sing-song voice, entering the office bright and early. She couldn't sleep and knew her inbox would need assistance. Besides, the quicker she got the day over with, the quicker the evening would come.

"You're early." He frowned, looking at his watch. He was the only one in the drawing office; none of the old-timers, as he called them, were in yet. "Is something wrong?"

"Nope. Everything is absolutely fine and dandy."

"You do seem in a good mood, come to think of it."

"I am in rather a good mood, yes." She leaned against a filing cabinet beside his desk, beaming like a Cheshire cat.

"Did Nick..." James cleared his throat, "um, look after you?"

"Yes he did, actually."

Oh, this was going to be fun, letting James sweat it out. Then she'd give him a hug and kiss for pure genius, and his meddling. But she'd enjoy pulling his leg for a bit first.

"He didn't –?"

"No, you're okay. He didn't get in my *knickers*." She looked him sternly in the eye.

James winced. "I'm sorry. I thought... uh, and how did Adam react?"

"Not very well actually, James." Sophie sobered her expression.

"Did you tell him you were thinking of leaving?"

"Yes," she said leisurely.

"Oh, shit, it backfired, didn't it?"

"No!" Sophie threw herself at James, smacking her lips on his, hugging him. "You and your meddling may have worked."

James hugged her back. "Oh, thank God! You had me worried then. I thought Nick had over stepped the mark. Or you'd fallen for him instead."

"Don't tell Adam –"

"Don't tell me what?" Adam walked into their office, suspicion across his face.

"I'm hugging his girlfriend," James said, releasing Sophie. She stepped back, brushing his chest, and James playfully nudged her, like they were some Laurel and Hardy act.

Girlfriend? The word sounded odd. But nice. Very nice.

"Do you mind if I borrow Sophie for a moment?"

"No, Boss, she's all *yours*." James winked at Sophie.

"What was all that about?" Adam asked Sophie as they strolled towards his office.

"I'll let James tell you another day," she said. She didn't want to ruin anything. What if Adam felt manipulated – would he change his mind about her? She hadn't been aware of it; she'd been a puppet also. And he could still change his mind regardless, Sophie kept reminding herself.

"So, what did you want to see me about?" she said walking into his office.

He pulled her into his arms and kissed her, surprising her. "I'm in meetings all day. I just wanted to see you before I got snowed under."

"What would your father say?" She edged away from him, to tease him.

He followed. "I'm not going to tell him. Are you?"

She backed into his desk and laughed coyly. As he bent to kiss her again, she turned her head; he planted a kiss on her cheek, and groaned with frustration. She noticed Adam's calendar was open on his computer screen, and from seven o'clock he'd blocked it out with Sophie's name in the box.

"I've got till midnight, have I?"

"You could have me all night, but I didn't want to be presumptuous." He smiled cheekily, and Sophie's insides turned to jelly. "And in case you're wondering, I blocked it out so that Joan didn't book a dinner with a client or something."

"If you say so." Her lips parted as she gazed up into his passionate blue eyes.

"I say so." He moved closer, pinning her against his desk, giving an alluring growl as he swept a hand across her cheek and down her hairline, cupping her neck. He leaned in, lips moistened, ready to kiss her again. She would need all the willpower in the world not to fall into bed with him on the first night. Which sounded daft considering they'd shared a bed. But she wanted to do this properly. Not jinx anything.

When had she become so superstitious?

"Careful," she said, placing her hands on his chest, bending back so his mouth couldn't touch hers but her hips pressed against his, feeling the stir in his groin. "You'll be late for your nine o'clock." She twisted and pointed at the screen, and he looked. "See?"

He let her go, moaning sexily. His gaze smouldered as he watched her straightening and regaining her composure. Yes, she'd need a lot of determination to keep this to the not-on-the-first-date-rule. He was number one in seduction and she was only human.

Finding her legs still worked, albeit slightly wobbly, she walked around the oval meeting table to safety – it really would not be appropriate to be caught snogging by his secretary – as he sat

271

behind his desk.

"I'll have to remember to lock my office door in future – when alone with you." His voice was provocative.

She giggled, reining in her excitement. "I'll see you at seven."

***

"Are you all right?" Adam said, looking over his menu at Sophie.

She'd been gazing at the menu but with her brain worrying, she might as well have stared at a blank page. Was this where Adam Reid Thomas wined and dined all his girlfriends?

"I'm a little nervous."

Sophie had totally forgotten to ask what to wear, floundering in front of the mirror, wondering whether the electric-blue satin dress was suitable - its length, resting above the knee, showed off her legs. It was another posh frock bought on a shopping trip with Cassie. But the doorbell rang, spot on time, so she didn't have time to change.

Adam's appreciative smile had comforted her decision on the dress. His grey, tailor-made suit, with a silk dress shirt, reassured her she wasn't overdressed either. She'd swallowed, struck by how handsome he looked. She'd nearly said there and then, sod the not-on-the-first-date-rule.

Sophie focused on the present, nervously looking around the restaurant. It was elegant and chic, and only a low hum of voices and waiters walking back and forth broke the peaceful ambience. Candles flickered on the table. The restaurant had several private nooks and crannies, and Adam had a table in one of those hidey-holes.

This too-good-to-be-true feeling kept creeping over her. She wanted to pinch herself. She loved him. Did he feel it too?

"Why are you nervous?" His forehead creased with a frown.

"I know it's ridiculous. I mean, we've spent a whole weekend with one another." She rubbed her upper arm. The restaurant was warm, but she still had goose bumps. "Everything you're doing, saying...feels so great. When we were pretending it was like it came from a script... Now I'm improvising, worried I'm going to say or do something wrong."

He took her hand into both of his – hands Sophie never stopped admiring, knowing what they could do to her, and hoping they'd touch her again.

"Sophie, when I think about it, everything I did with you then, I enjoyed. It wasn't a lie. Okay, so we were pretending to be a couple, but the kissing and the touching, I wanted to do. I wanted to make love to you."

Breathe, Sophie. At this rate, she'd be breaking that rule!

She used the menu to gently fan herself. "I enjoyed it too. I wasn't sure you were."

Adam's response was interrupted by a waiter appearing.

"Good evening, Mr Thomas," he said, "and good evening, Miss." Sophie detected the little surprise in the waiter's expression upon seeing her sitting at the table, too.

After the waiter had taken their order and disappeared, Adam said, "I usually dine here alone."

"Oh, so I'm not one of many then," she said, teasing gently, but a sense of relief waved over her. No girlfriends before, therefore no expectations. No one would be judging her. Would she be Adam's first love, last girlfriend?

"No, I never bring a girlfriend here. This place is my sanctuary."

"I feel privileged."

"I want to share everything with you. In fact, I don't really like calling you my girlfriend. Maybe I'll have to change it to fiancée?"

Sophie blushed again, heat rose up her neck. She gulped her

water, wishing the waiter hadn't taken the menu so she had something to hind behind. "Look, let's take it one step at a time. I don't want to rush anything." She'd been rushed into everything with Simon, and look how it had ended.

They ate and shared a bottle of wine and conversation. Sophie told Adam about her stay with Cassie mainly, as they hadn't properly talked since she'd returned. Sophie couldn't wait to see his mother again, although they'd agreed to keep the lies they'd told between them, for the time being.

"The *lie* might be a good story for the best man speech," Adam said, chuckling.

Sophie dabbed her mouth with her napkin. "Will you stop talking about marriage," she said, her tone light. "At this rate you'll be beating James to it."

"Good point. Let the man have his day. But you're right. I don't want to be far behind him."

"Adam, please, you're moving this too fast." She chewed her lip. "Of course I want a future with you, but I'm realistic. I want to enjoy the early stage, the getting to know you, not rush into it. Simon −"

"I'm not like Simon. I make a promise and I'll keep it."

The end of the evening came with a taxi ride home. Adam and Sophie stood outside her front door kissing.

"Do you want to −?"

"Nope. First date." He shook his head determinedly. "I would love to come in, but we know it won't be just coffee. Are you free tomorrow? I can pick you up at seven again."

"Oh, heavens, I'm running out of dresses."

Adam laughed, seeing the panic in her expression. "Wear jeans. I'll take you to a place where they do great pub grub. I know you'll appreciate it." He brushed her hair, and cupped her face, kissing her again.

Finally, he pulled out of the kiss. "Oh, this *is* murder leaving you," he said, his arms sweeping around her back and holding her close. She rested her head on his shoulder.

Willpower.

Then, finding it, she stepped back as he released her, found her key and unlocked the door. "I'll see you tomorrow."

***

Thursday evening wasn't too dissimilar to Wednesday. They were sitting in a cosy pub eating again. She pushed her plate away, leaning back and resting her hand on her stomach. At this rate, Sophie would need to get herself down the gym with the amount of calories she'd consumed.

"Was it okay?" Adam studied the plate, and some of the food Sophie had left and then up at her, frowning.

"I can't eat another thing."

"Not even dessert?"

She shook her head. "If I keep eating like this I'll be the size of a house – and then you'll hardly find me attractive." She giggled, trying to make a joke of an insecurity she didn't realise she had. Adam's girlfriends before her had probably been waif like, tall and thin. She didn't see her keeping her figure if she carried on eating out like this.

"What I love about you is that I can come to somewhere like this and you'll appreciate the food." Adam put his cutlery together, also finishing and pushed the plate to one side so he could lean towards Sophie. "I made the mistake of bringing someone here, and she turned her nose up. Never did it again. A complete waste. I might have money, but I don't like to throw it away. Or good food."

"Okay, fine, but we can't do this every night. I'm going to need to join a gym or something."

"I can think of the perfect exercise."

"I bet you can." Sophie's whole body sizzled internally, it wouldn't surprise her if she glowed beetroot red at this particular moment.

"I like taking you out, and showing you off. I like spoiling you." Adam stood, picking up their drinks. "Let's sit outside."

They chose a picnic table with an umbrella and watched the boats, large and small, sail past on the River Thames, sending small waves lapping to the water's edge. Ducks quacked and swans glided past on the water with their cygnets following. July's warm, light evenings let them sit out, soaking it all up, talking, touching and kissing, until the sun disappeared and the crickets started singing.

Sophie felt consumed in her own bubble, unaware of and deaf to the rest of the patrons around her. Lost in Adam's world. The blue of his eyes kept her mesmerised, her heart light. Nothing else mattered at this moment in time. She kept pushing away that small voice of doubt.

"Come on, I better take you home," Adam said, taking her hand. "I've got to think of something special for the third date. Are you free tomorrow?"

"Oh, I promised James I'd go over to The White Lion with him. You're more than welcome to join us."

"Okay, I'll meet you over there. Mustn't exclude friends."

"Especially as he's the one who gave us both the push we needed."

Adam looked at her puzzled.

"Haven't you worked it out? James has been meddling from the start, wanting to set you up with *his* idea of the *right* woman." She licked her bottom lip, watching for a reaction. "Whether I am that woman, well, time will tell."

"I've no doubt you're the right woman."

***

Sitting in his office, Adam had his arms behind his head, smiling to himself, remembering every detail of the night before. Sophie, gorgeous, with her dark brown eyes, dimples when she smiled, intelligent – she wasn't called Thomas Robotics' best engineer for nothing – and a grounded, down to earth attitude. Nothing materialistic, uninterested in his money. She was easy going, but lacked a little in self-confidence, which charmed him. It meant he could shower her with compliments, make her blush the perfect pink, and, more importantly, witness her regain her confidence.

Last night Adam had dropped Sophie off and, like the night before, tore himself away, resolute he wouldn't enter her flat. He wanted to take this slowly for Sophie. They could have quite easily have jumped into bed with one another by now. He wanted to wait a little longer. Their passion bubbled below the surface, and he wanted to do things properly for her. He got the impression Simon had rushed her, even the sex.

Concentrate.

Adam's priority for the morning was to browse through his emails before his first meeting. Scrolling down, he noticed one from Nick Sallico, Jerrisons. This would get his attention first. His brow knitted together as he read, making him sit forward. Cursing, he hit the print button.

He walked outside his office to his secretary's desk. Joan had worked for his father and would now continue to work for Adam. She was extremely experienced, and felt more like a family friend than an employee, she'd worked so long for the company.

"Joan, please can you call Sophie Trewyn to my office as soon as she arrives." He looked up at the clock; it was eight-thirty. She might not be in, yet.

"Certainly. Anything else?"

Adam shook his head. "No thanks, I'll call you if I need you. When Sophie comes, don't let us be disturbed." Joan nodded and he went back to his desk to continue reading his emails. Ten minutes later, Sophie knocked and entered.

"Summoned by your secretary now. Whatever next?" she said, smiling. Unfortunately, Adam wasn't in the mood to appreciate her light sense of humour.

"Sit down, Sophie," he said. "Have you had a chance to grab a coffee?"

She shook her head, sobered by his tone, and he poured two cups of coffee from his filter jug. He joined Sophie at the oval table in the middle of his office.

"I've got some good news and some bad news, I'm afraid."

"Oh. Are we talking business...or personal?"

"Both." He pushed the printed email towards Sophie, letting her read it for herself. "Nick's sent this email, this morning. We've won the contract, on the proviso you are seconded up to Manchester for six months."

***

"It's my fault, isn't it?" Sophie finally broke the silence.

"He may have come up with it all on his own eventually, but you did put the idea in his head."

"I'm sorry." Sophie swallowed. Everything really had been running too smoothly, hadn't it?

"I'm sorry. If I hadn't been such a prat, you'd never have made the suggestion. Shit!" Adam slammed his hand down on the desk and Sophie jumped. "Sorry." He placed a hand over hers, squeezing it. "I can't screw this bloody contract up. My first one, and we need this contract. My father won't hand over the company if he thinks I'm incapable of making a bloody decision."

"Adam, I'll go. Of course. It does make perfect sense as. I understand your commitment to this business and I wouldn't expect any less of you. I'll do it for you and Thomas Robotics."

His expression didn't soften, he only nodded his acknowledgement. "How long do you think it will take you to actually get the designs finished?"

"I wasn't going to admit this in the meeting, but I don't actually think they'll take six months. It's a design modification to the existing QB20 and if I put extra time in – I mean, what will I do up there on my own, other than work?" She smiled at him. "I reckon I could have it done within three months."

Adam nodded, pulled a pen out of his inside pocket and scribbled some notes. "I'll get an adjustment made to the contract. We'll agree to six months maximum – just in case things go wrong along the way – but if you finish sooner you can return."

Sophie drank her coffee, cupping it with both hands, and fidgeted, watching Adam make his notes. He looked up, obviously sensing her attention was on him. "What?"

"What about us?" She sounded needy, and hated it. Was she about to lose the one thing she'd wanted so much? Had it all been too good to be true?

He took the cup out of her hand and rubbed his thumb in her palm. "Nothing changes about us."

"I'd understand if you wanted to put *us* on hold. Start over when I got back."

"If I have to travel up the M40 every single weekend to see you, that's what I'll do."

"I don't expect you to."

"I'll work it out. Let me think about it. At the moment I'm pissed at Nick for suggesting this, but my brain will clear and I'll think of a solution."

Chapter Twenty Six

Sophie sat in The White Lion's beer garden, feeling glum. Her stomach knotted and it felt like the whole world rested upon her shoulders. James tried to cheer her up, but the thought of moving up to Manchester horrified her.

You made your bed; you have to lie in it.

"Six months will fly," James said, clinking his glass against hers.

"Yeah, I know. It's my fault. I put the stupid idea into Nick's head." She finished her wine. She really needed to take it easy, otherwise she'd be a drunken mess by the time Adam arrived.

"Want another one?" James stood up, finishing his pint.

"Yeah, all right." *No, no, no.*

"Sorry, James, but do you mind if I steal Sophie away from you early?" Adam strolled up to their table, still wearing his work suit, though with tie removed and his collar open. Sophie's innards became weightless. "I've got a table booked at seven-thirty."

"I said no more restaurants," Sophie said.

"This one is special."

"Have I got time to go home and change?"

"No, you look fine as you are." He squeezed her shoulder, reassuringly.

James smiled agreeably. "All right, just this once. But remember – Friday's she's my drinking partner."

"Hey, just this once, I promise." Adam clasped James' hand and shook it. "And as long as we keep our games night."

James grinned. "Remember Wednesday night, okay?"

"Why Wednesday?" Adam frowned.

The way the corner of his mouth twitched, wanting to smile, Sophie saw Adam was teasing, but James couldn't. She playfully slapped his arm. "Stop pulling his leg. You know it's Kate's birthday Wednesday."

"Yeah, and I've got the week off so I can't nag you," James said. "Remember it's at Rendezvous at seven, right?"

"Got it," Adam said, tapping his temple, then took Sophie's arm, helping her as she stood from the picnic bench, being the perfect gentleman. Sophie would never get used to this. "We'll be there, James."

***

"So, where are we going?"

Adam grinned at Sophie, pulling down a side road. They were in Virginia Water. On either side of the road stood large houses with metal gates closing off their huge driveways.

"I'm taking you to my house." He stopped in front of a pair of tall wrought iron gates and took a remote from the glovebox. As the gates opened, revealing his home, Sophie's mouth became that wonderful 'Oh' shape. He wanted to kiss her perfect mouth, but instead, smiling, he drove into the sweeping gravel driveway, and parked.

The house wasn't that old, only ten years at the most, but built in Georgian style of sandstone with a slate roof and white sash windows.

He opened the front door, and Sophie gasped as she stepped

inside.

"Wow, how the other half lives," she said, admiring the magnificent staircase climbing up the centre of the house, the hallway leading off either side. Like the rest of the house, cream walls and wood flooring gave it a spacious and bright feel. The outside of his house may appear old, but the inside had an uncluttered modern style – a bachelor pad. Maybe one day Sophie would get to add her touch, add some womanly warmth to the place.

"Come on, I'll give you a tour later." He grabbed her hand and walked her through the house to the kitchen; the sweet smell of potatoes baking made her turn to face him.

"We're having dinner here?"

"Yes. You were worried about eating out all the time, so I thought I'd cook." He pulled her closer, loving how she felt in his arms, like she fitted into place, his missing jigsaw puzzle piece. "It's not much; salad, jacket potatoes, cold meats. I'm not really much of a cook, more because of time. But I thought we could sit outside while it's still warm."

"When did you do this?"

"Before I came and got you from the pub." He grinned mischievously.

"I thought you had a meeting."

"I did – till five-thirty, then I came straight here." He tugged at her hand, and led her into his games room.

Pool table, dartboard, pinball machine, a large flat-screen TV hanging in the corner to watch the sports, and a huge black leather sofa along the back wall. On another wall hung a blackboard, scored with chalk down the middle, James and Adam's names written at the top with a tally. Sophie spotted it and laughed.

"He's beating you!"

"Yeah, if only we kept a tally of our golf games."

She chuckled again. "He's not great at golf, so he tells me. When does he come over?"

"Tuesdays usually. He brings the curry; I supply the beer and the entertainment."

Adam led her through the French doors and Sophie again gasped. They'd entered the conservatory, which contained his swimming pool. You couldn't train for the Olympics in it, but it was enough for him to get his morning swim, or unwind after a long day hunched over his desk.

She turned, brushing her hands over his chest. "Explains something," she said, toying with a button. "I did wonder how you'd find the time to get to a gym."

"The gym is upstairs," he said, and her face lit up with surprise. "Well, what do I need five bedrooms for?"

He led her past the sun loungers in the conservatory and took her out onto the decking. He'd already laid the table – white linen, scented candles, a small posy of pink carnations, zinnias and roses, cut from his garden – and made her sit, even though she protested she wanted to help. He watched her take it in, all the things he took for granted, as he saw it every day. The garden always looked impressive at this time of year, flowers full in bloom, trees fat with leaves. A small pond with a fountain near the decking provided the relaxing sound of water trickling over rocks. Music for the garden, his mother would always say.

"Your garden is beautiful."

"I do have some help. My father's gardener comes over here a couple of days a week."

"Does your father live far away?"

"No, he's in Wentworth."

"And you didn't fancy living there, close to the golf course?" she teased.

"Wasn't sure I wanted my father as my neighbour. Bit close for comfort. I work with the man, too, remember."

Adam brought everything from the kitchen, insisting Sophie remain, admiring the garden with a glass of pink champagne. She wanted to help but he enjoyed waiting on her. He'd never done this before, entertained a woman at his house. Yes, he'd brought them home for a drink, and bed, but never dinner. Never simply relaxing and soaking up the peace of his own home.

They talked. It came so naturally and he found himself daydreaming, wanting this to be every day, imagining the rest of his life, sitting in this garden with Sophie, growing old together. The lawn full of children running around. How many children would she want? It was something he realised he wanted so much more now. It had never occurred to him before meeting her, loving her. He'd been so adamant it wasn't a life for him; he was a player, wining and dining women, never wanting commitment.

As the night air chilled, they retired to his living room, drinking champagne with strawberries floating in the glasses, feeding each other the fruit. The talking had ceased, replaced with kissing and cuddling. He was lost in the sensation of her tongue caressing his, her hands running through his hair. He'd pulled out the clip holding her hair in place, and combed his hand through her long, chestnut hair, like silk ribbons between his fingers. He wanted them both to be naked on this sofa, but he held back, taking it slowly. The most he did was undo a couple of buttons on her cream blouse, so he could stroke her neck and collarbone, or cup her breast.

"Should I call you a taxi, or would you like one of my bedrooms?" he said, between the kisses as he caught the time on the clock; almost midnight. They'd fallen into lying on the sofa cuddling.

"I'd like to stay in *your* bedroom, please," she whispered.

"My bedroom?"

"Yes."

All he needed to hear. He tugged her into his hold, stroking her face, around her hairline as he kissed her. He'd been taking it easily earlier, cuddling and kissing; now, as he had permission, he wanted to move it up a notch.

Without his mouth being far from hers, he unbuttoned her blouse, teasing it off, discarding it. Next to go were her trousers, easing her out of them, kissing, nibbling her soft skin. He cupped her breasts so they spilled out over the cream lace, rubbing and pinching her nipples so they formed hard buds, then licked and sucked them, like they were cherries on top of ice cream. She moaned, throwing her head back. The sound vibrated through his chest, down into his belly and along his hardening groin.

He needed to get her off this sofa. This was not where he envisioned their first time. Standing up, he gently pulled her with him, leading her up the stairs. They got as far as the landing, Sophie fumbling with the buttons on his shirt, but he soon made her forgot what she was doing. One flick, he undid the clasp and her bra loosened, he removed it with great delicacy. Both hands trailed up to her shoulders and pushed the straps down her arms, tossing it aside. They heard the light spatter of fabric landing on the wooden flooring, and Sophie giggled, kissing him, pressing her soft, freed breasts against him.

They reached his bedroom door, which stood ajar, and Adam, so hard he ached for her, elbowed the door open and guided her towards his bed.

***

Sophie, stripped down to a pathetic piece of lace material, landed on the soft bed, her mind and body like jelly. His expert hands had caused ripples of pleasure across her skin as he'd removed her clothes.

The minute she'd said the word, given him the green light, he'd pushed every single button. Inside her a fire now roared. All she could concentrate on was wanting him, inside her, making love, like her body had been neglected for all these years. Between her legs, she throbbed. She wanted her knickers *off!*

She pulled at his shirt he'd looked so damn sexy in all night, desperate to feel his hard muscular chest against her flesh. Heat against heat. On the landing, she'd failed miserably to remove it, distracted by his brain-melting sensations. He helped her now.

He pulled back the sheets, and she knelt on the bed, still kissing, touching, helping him with his trousers, pushing at his boxers. All she wanted to do was show him how much she loved him.

Her hand found his cock, stroked, gripped, and he shuddered and groaned.

Gently, blindly, he removed her hand. "Sophie, honey, for me to last, you need to not do that."

He kissed her; she mumbled some agreement, letting him take control.

He's the expert.

Starting at Sophie's mouth, Adam moved his kisses down her body, from one breast to the other. Slowly, carefully, covering every inch of her body. She gave soft moans at his touch. She didn't know what else to do but lie there, relishing a mixture of bliss and torture, her body longing for his. He moved down further and further, running his tongue along her hip, up the inside of her thigh, pulling off her knickers.

This was where they got to last time, but this time he wasn't stopping.

With fingers and tongue running along the inside of her legs, he parted them, and kissed, licked and sucked. She gasped again, her hips naturally moving in time with him. Liquid warmth pooled deep inside her. Then, before his tongue sent her over the edge, as slowly as he'd descended, he returned, kissing her lips, hovering over her.

"Are you sure want to do this?"

"Yes – oh wait!" she said frantically, placing her hands on his chest. "I'm not protected. I'm not on the pill."

"It's okay," he soothed. "It's already taken care of. But are you sure? I can wait." His patient tone made her heart swell with love she held for him.

"Yes, I love you, of course I'm sure," she whispered, her hands cupping his face, pulling him towards her. She didn't care what happened after, she wanted, needed him now.

"I love you, too."

She felt his hardness sink into her. She tilted her hips to deepen his thrusts; she couldn't get enough of him.

They started out frantic, new, excited, lustful for each other, then, gaining some control and moving as one, slowed, finding a perfect rhythm. Heat flew to her belly. Delight and pleasure rippled through her body with every hard thrust inside her, lost in the oblivion of the two of them joining as one. Never wanting to lose him, or leave him.

When she could control herself no more, digging her fingers into his shoulders, pulling his body tighter to hers, she pushed him in deeper and her body shuddered. Over and over. An uncontrollable ecstatic cry escaped her. She scratched along his back, and he groaned, and she felt his final thrust and the pulse inside her as he too could no longer hold on.

They relaxed in a damp, luscious heap, hot from exertion, breathing irregularly. Adam, still lying on top of her, his lips pressed against her neck, groaned sexily. She held onto him, tightening her grip with legs and arms, not wanting him to move, not wanting to let him go. His naked, gorgeous, delicious body could sleep there for all she cared. She didn't care if the house caught fire - she wasn't moving from his bed. Sex like that - she was surprised the bed wasn't burning. As her breathing calmed, she felt him softening inside her, withdrawing.

He quickly dealt with and discarded the condom with ease and skill. *When did he put it on?* She really was an amateur. She must have been looking at him quizzically, or worried, because he smiled, and tapped his head and said, "Little trick I know, while you were distracted. I can put those things on blindfolded." The sexiest grin spread across his face as he knelt over her.

Distracted? Then a thought occurred, him licking, nibbling and kissing her all the way down, and she blushed. Excitement as quick as electricity spread to every nerve ending. Oh, she couldn't wait to feel it all over again.

"Were you all right? You were very quiet." He lent forward, brushing her hair back. She hoped she didn't look like Medusa or worse.

"Was I not supposed to be?" Sophie looked at him nervously. He was so experienced, and she felt a novice. Did he want her screaming his name from the rooftops at the height of pleasure? She thought that was a movie thing.

"No, no, just me worrying, I suppose." His lips found hers, and he tumbled on to her, tightening his hold. "I don't think you realise how much I love you. I want you all over again."

"So soon?" She raised a hopeful eyebrow.

He sexily growled, nuzzling into her neck. "Oh, hell, yes."

"You're ready again?"

He shrugged, and grinned cheekily. "Well, give me five minutes."

***

He'd had the best night's sleep ever before waking up with Sophie in his arms, in his room. Horny and allowed to be. He didn't need to get out and hide his arousal any more. This morning he hoped to be able to use it. Sex first thing in the morning with Sophie... he was having a hard time thinking of anything better to do.

He exhaled, stroking Sophie's hair, then down her back, memorising her curves as he spooned into her. He rarely got to do this – it usually felt awkward or false the morning after. But last night, making love, had felt so different. At first, he'd been worried, thinking she was unhappy, or he wasn't satisfying her. Then he realised; they'd been consumed within one another, only interested in pleasing each other. She wasn't the type to dramatise the sex. Bloody hell, his mother was right, James was right. This was how it was supposed to be. The good stuff.

Never let her go, he thought, squeezing her more tightly.

Sophie stirred, and turned, opening her eyes, squinting as she adjusted to the sunlight.

"Good morning," he said, plying her with kisses, nestling into her neck, inhaling her scent. Her sweet, floral perfume still lingered, plus a little of him, their sex. She reached to touch his face, and he placed a kiss in her palm. She sighed with pleasure.

She stretched and sat up, looking around the room. "Oh my... is this your bedroom?"

"No, it's the guy next door's."

His bedroom was rather impressive, his own personal space. Well, his whole house was private, but no one really saw this room. The master bedroom. All straight lines, contemporary style fitted wardrobes, dark wood against pale walls. A dressing table stood in one corner, which he never used, though it would be Sophie's now, and a white, leather sofa sat in front of one of the sash windows, where he usually threw his clothes.

"Last night," she nudged him, "I wasn't really taking much

289

notice, but it's huge."

He looked under the bedcovers suggestively at his hardening erection. "Why, thank you."

She giggled, slapping him lightly and he grabbed her arm, pinning her beneath him.

"I need to do one thing before I fetch you breakfast." He kissed the hollow of her neck.

"And I wonder what could that be?" She wrapped her legs around him, pulling him towards her. He stretched, reached for another condom and skilfully rolled it on. Then, unable to help himself, he teased her with his finger, rubbing, then inserting it. She gasped, tugging him closer with her legs, and he ran a hand up, holding her delicious thigh up, as he entered her, penetrating deep, her lips covered his, kissing, moaning. She opened up to him as a flower does to sunshine.

"I...love...you..." Her voice breathless, urgent, made him want to please her more.

***

Lying there, sated, they both sighed, getting their breath back. Adam, leaning on his elbow, trailed a finger around her nipple, then her breast. He gently kissed her, then said, "I'll be two minutes – do not move."

He strolled away from the bed and Sophie watched, unable to take her eyes off his naked body. As he walked across to a set of drawers and pulled out some fresh underwear, she admired his strong thighs, and tight buttocks – and blushed as she remembered how she'd held on and dug her nails in – then his narrow waist, spreading to a muscular back and shoulders. Athletic. How much swimming did he do? All he needed was wings sprouting from those shoulder blades and he was her angel sent from heaven. She'd never be able to picture him the same with his clothes on, now she knew what lay underneath – and she would always desire him undressed.

Once he'd left the room, Sophie pulled the covers up around her and sighed. She wanted to squeal. She was in Adam's bed; they'd made love; he'd said he loved her. All her wishes had come true.

Her plan had been to take this slower, but last night, here in his house, she couldn't wait any longer. And besides, it's not like she hadn't got to know him already. Simon had encouraged her into bed on the second night, stealing away her innocence. She hadn't really been ready, Simon being her first, but he'd insisted, said she was just nervous, and then their relationship had steam-rollered from there. Thinking about it now – and she wasn't sure why she was – she realised she might not have been in love with Simon like she'd thought. Because what she felt for Adam was a hundred times stronger. Magnetic energy coursed between them with the slightest touch.

Adam – naked, bar his boxers – arrived like a god, carrying a tray.

"I'll get us some coffee in a minute," he said, placing the tray beside her.

Sitting up, she saw croissants, jam, toast, and orange juice. "I feel like a princess. Thoroughly spoilt."

He grinned. She wouldn't grow tired of his smile. "So, after breakfast, what would her Royal Highness like to do today?"

She leaned in towards him, and kissed him, making sure her tongue licked his top lip and he groaned. "Stay in bed with you, please."

***

291

Having finished breakfast, Adam had pulled Sophie into his bathroom adjoining the bedroom, and they'd showered together, still unable to stop touching one another. Massaging, lathering soap onto each other, exploring each other's bodies again. Adam washed her hair, raiding another bathroom for some conditioner – otherwise, her hair would have been like straw and impossible to comb through. She'd tried to wash his, standing on tiptoes, but his strokes up her body had been far too distracting.

She'd spied a large roll top bath, and fantasised about it with her, Adam and a lot of bubbles. *Another time.*

Both of them prune-like, Adam turned the shower off and handed Sophie a bath sheet and another smaller towel for her hair. As he wrapped a towel around himself, she tugged at it, smiling cheekily. He went to grab hers, but Sophie ran out of the bathroom, giggling. Adam, right behind her, still after her towel, bumped into her as she stopped abruptly, squealing.

A woman stood in Adam's bedroom, looking as shocked as Sophie felt. Sophie rapidly tried to cover herself up with the towel Adam had dislodged. Her heart thumped inside her chest. The woman looked in her mid-fifties, casually dressed, with short silvery-grey hair.

Adam peered around Sophie. "Oh, hi, Audrey. Sorry." He covered Sophie up and secured a towel around himself. "This isn't your usual day?"

"Sorry, I had a day off in the week, remember? Said I'd call in today."

"My fault. Yes, sorry, clean forgot."

"Anyway, I saw you had company…" She meant Sophie's clothes all scattered downstairs. Sophie blushed and looked at the carpet. "And assumed you'd be in another bedroom. I was dropping off some clean towels." She placed them on the dressing table's chair. "I won't stay long at the house as I can see you're busy." Audrey turned and scurried out of the room.

"Audrey's my housekeeper. I'll properly introduce you when you've got more clothes on."

"What did she mean about another room?"

"Well, let's just say, you are the first to sleep in *my* bed."

"I don't understand."

"Sophie, I don't want to have to draw diagrams," he said, trailing a finger down the towel, from between her breasts to her pelvis. She swallowed at the sheer sexiness of it, wanting to remove the towel and jump his bones. *How on earth could she be thinking about sex again? Her body should be exhausted.* "And I don't really like reminding you – or myself for that matter – I've had a shady past with women. But those women have never slept in this bed. For some reason, I knew it was just sex, so I used to use another room."

"Oh." Sophie stood dumbfounded, still getting used to the idea she was indeed special. Not that she thought Adam would treat her like his past girlfriends; it had been his reason for not committing initially, thinking he couldn't give Sophie what she deserved. And thinking he didn't want it. But all these little things were, well, lovely.

"I suppose I was afraid of them getting close, getting to know me. I didn't want them getting to know me." He dried himself off and quickly dressed in a pair of shorts and polo shirt. "I'll go put the coffee on," he said. Sophie coughed suggestively and looked down at herself, still wearing the bath sheet as she towel dried her hair. He smirked. "And I'll get your clothes."

She found her knickers and slipped them on, then spotted Adam's cream shirt by the bed. It smelled of him, his aftershave, musky and masculine – her favourite. She grinned as she put it on, remembering Adam's reaction the last time she wore his shirt and made her way downstairs. She heard voices, and the front door shutting, and realised, with relief, it was his housekeeper leaving.

293

Phew! Yes, would prefer a proper introduction another day – with clothes on.

She tiptoed into the kitchen, sneaked up on Adam as he spooned coffee into the machine, and putting her arms around his waist, snuggling her head against his back. He turned and cuddled her, one hand fingering her damp hair, pushing it behind her ear, the other sliding under the shirt, down her hip, tucking into her knickers. He breathed out an appreciative sigh and kissed her. Their foreheads still touching, lips still hovering over hers, he said, "Think we better take the coffee upstairs."

Chapter Twenty Seven

Adam walked Sophie to her door late Sunday night.

Rising on her toes, she kissed him goodnight. As they separated, her heart ached so much at the thought of goodbye she thought her chest would burst open. She'd see him tomorrow – this wasn't *goodbye* goodbye – but the thought of not sleeping with him hurt. This really was what love felt like. They hadn't left each other's side all weekend. Lounging around his house, snuggled up watching television, or swimming, reading, sleeping...making love.

Sophie had been the one doing the reading, though she'd found it hard to concentrate on the book she'd pinched from his study, watching Adam, shirtless, practising his golf swing.

Dear God, he was gorgeous.

"Can you stay here tonight?" She looked up to see his reaction, fingering the collar of his jacket.

He grinned. "Yes, I can. I like that idea. But I will have to leave early tomorrow morning."

Relieved she would spend another night held in his arms, she fumbled with her keys, opening the door.

It being late, she led him straight to her bedroom, welcoming him into her bed. Spooning in behind her, Adam kissed her neck, the soft spot by her ear, his tongue licking along her shoulder, while he caressed her breast, hip, and thigh. With him pressed against her, she felt far from tired, and with a moan of delight, turned in his arms to kiss him back.

Their lovemaking remained slow, sensual, making the most of each other. But while they kissed, gently rocking, clinging together, the dread of work came to her mind. Jerrisons. Manchester. How much she would miss Adam overwhelmed her. The tightness in her chest became uncontrollable. She stilled, unable to stop the prickling sensation in her eyes, and as he met her gaze, her tears trickled down her cheek.

"Sophie, what's the matter?" Adam stopped, and gently rubbed her cheek. "Am I hurting you? Do you want me to stop?"

He started to pull out, but she clasped him tightly and shook her head. "No." The last thing she wanted was separation.

"Then what is it?"

She sucked in a breath, too afraid to speak, but she needed to be honest with him. Her fingers stroked his temple, her eyes fixed on his. "I don't want to go to Jerrisons. I don't want to leave you." She tried her hardest to contain the sob.

"Hey, I promise you, I'm working on it." He wiped her tears. "You may still have to go, but I'll find some sort of solution, okay? Because I don't want you to leave me, either."

"Okay." She nodded.

They still made love like it might be their last time.

***

"Sophie," Adam said softly, sweeping her hair off her face. "Love, I've got to go." He perched on the side of her bed, fully dressed. He would have loved to get back into bed, but had important work to do, especially concerning Sophie.

She rubbed her face and yawned. Her eyes widened with the

296

realisation he was dressed. She sat up with a start.

"What time is it? Am I late for work?"

He chuckled and shook his head, stopping her from getting out of bed. "No, it's only six o'clock. I've got to run though. I probably won't see you until Wednesday evening, as I have meetings galore. Plus our issue to sort out."

She nodded at him. He kissed her, hating the idea of leaving her, finding it difficult to stand and leave the bedroom.

He'd throw himself into work. He wouldn't have time to think about her.

"I love you," he said.

"I love you more."

"We'll argue about it Wednesday."

***

The last three days had been the slowest of her life. She hadn't seen Adam since he'd left her flat early Monday morning, and here she sat, now Wednesday, staring at the clock, willing five o'clock to appear. She still had another thirty-five minutes to go.

She felt empty and void, as though half of her was missing – the part with her heart.

She'd received the odd text from Adam, answering her silly messages reminding him she still existed and loved him. Hopefully he wasn't finding her neediness annoying. What if he decided she really wasn't for him, that the past weekend, albeit bloody fantastic, was too much? Maybe it wasn't so bloody fantastic for him. Maybe he found her clingy, annoying, and not really pretty enough ...

He'd said before he would let her down, that he wasn't right for her. What if he hadn't changed his mind, and realised he couldn't commit? Or worse, bumped his head and awoken to reality. *Because, let's face it, it's too good to be true.* She had all these stupid, pathetic little doubts in her head, because he wasn't there, physically, in her life. She couldn't touch, kiss, or cuddle. He was only at the end of a telephone and that didn't seem real. He'd been out for the last three days in meetings; even his secretary hadn't seen him. It made the time spent in his house feel like it had been a dream and she now lived her nightmare.

Sophie thumbed her mobile again, desperate for some kind of communication. Every five minutes she'd stare at it, willing the arrival of a text message from him. To hell with it. She'd text him again, with good reason. Try not to sound needy, clingy, or pathetic, but practical.

Hey, you. Are you picking me up tonight, or am I meeting you there? Love Sophie x

Should she have sent the love and the kiss? Frustrated, she tucked the phone into her trouser pocket, worried that lost in the depths of her handbag she wouldn't hear it if it beeped. She looked at her PC again; only five minutes had passed. James wasn't even in the office to chat to, so she had to knuckle down and concentrate on some work, tie up some loose ends. Might as well, as she was sure she'd be travelling up to Manchester soon to start this contract. At that thought her belly turned cold, sickening her.

Life without Adam for six months. She swallowed and blinked, fighting back the stupid tears which were trying to form. She couldn't even handle three silly days.

It wouldn't be so bad, she knew. They'd travel weekends, he had said. But what if he couldn't? What if his work demanded he stayed in Surrey, he was too busy to get away? What if he decided their relationship should go on hold? Oh, she hated these doubts.

Her phone beeped and vibrated in her pocket. She yanked it out, her heart lifting, then falling rapidly into a black abyss.

James.

Make sure you're there before 7:30pm don't be late. P.S. she said YES!

She texted back, congratulating him and not to panic, she'd be there, then closed her PC down. Sod it, she was going home. It wasn't like she'd never done extra hours. She was taking some time back. She was too miserable to work right now, and besides she'd be slogging her guts out in Manchester. She couldn't stay up there – alone – for six months.

***

Wrapped in a bath towel, Sophie thumbed through her wardrobe of freshly dry-cleaned dresses. Adam had seen them all, but which one did he like the best, and which one would suit this surprise party for Kate?

Her phone beeped and she threw the dress she held onto the bed, reaching for her mobile. A momentary blast of excitement flew through her bones, seeing a message from Adam.

Sorry can't pick you up. Will have to meet you there. Love Adam x

Throwing her phone aside, she slumped onto her bed. Well, at least he was coming. She'd been fretting all day he wouldn't be there. Then it really would look like a lie, that being Adam's girlfriend was all a big fantasy.

She texted him back, reminding him of the timing, then called for a taxi and got herself dressed.

***

Stomach rumbling, Sophie huddled in a dark corner of the dance floor, surrounded by people. Some faces from work she recognised, others she didn't. She fiddled with an earring, then pulled at the hem of her black dress.

They were all gathered in Rendezvous' function room above its restaurant. The room was strewn with balloons over the circular tables surrounding the dance floor, saying 'Happy Birthday' and 'Congratulations'. The disco was ready and waiting to light up and burst into song as soon as Kate arrived.

James' plan was to propose in the morning, spend the day together doing special things, then say he'd treat her to a meal out at her favourite restaurant. He would arrive at Rendezvous with Kate, and the group would shout 'surprise' and celebrate her birthday and – hopefully – their engagement. All very sweet actually. James had put a lot of thought into this, and all day, Sophie had hoped Kate would say yes. James, from the beginning with the planning, had been confident it was a sure thing, but Sophie felt relieved when she'd seen his text message earlier. Through the chattering amongst the friends when she'd first arrived, Sophie learnt that James had texted other friends too.

Although Sophie knew some of the people and they all had a common connection in James and Kate, she felt lonely without Adam by her side. The group was whispering amongst themselves, general conversations including 'what's the time?' making Sophie glance at her watch. It was nearly seven-thirty and still no Adam. She'd hated arriving alone, looking very single. She rubbed her arms and hugged herself, even though the room was warm and stuffy.

"Shhh!" a voice in the crowd hissed.

"They're coming up the stairs," someone else, who was keeping an eye out near the door, whispered. They ran back to the group. The door opened, and Sophie almost burst with delight, seeing

Adam, handsome as ever.

"Sorry, sorry. False alarm," he said, entering. She ran into his arms.

"I was worried you were going to be late."

"Sorry, I got held up." He kissed her, lips full on hers, heat bolting through her body by his simple touch. She would have liked to have deepened the kiss, but quickly realised they had an audience – all eyes were on them. Someone coughed.

"You're here now, that's what matters."

Another person from the group hissed at them to be quiet; somebody even clicked their tongue. Sophie grabbed Adam's hand and pulled him into the crowd.

Before she could tell him how much she'd missed him, how much she loved him, the person watching the door was whispering again. "They're coming! Quick. Silence, everyone."

A little hum of whispers, a hush from the crowd and the group silenced. Adam squeezed Sophie's hand. She looked up to meet his gaze, and smiled. He was real. He was here. It hadn't been a dream.

A waiter came through the door first, followed by James and Kate. She wore a party dress and James was the smartest Sophie had ever seen him. He did own a suit, and actually had a tie on.

"Surprise!" everyone chorused. The DJ hit the flashing disco lights, the glitter ball turned, the traditional song, Cliff Richard's "*Congratulations*," exploded from the speakers. Kate, mouth open with surprise, flung her hands to her face, then held them out to embrace the first of her friends who went running to her. Everyone huddled around James and Kate, shaking his hand, kissing her, and demanding to see the ring.

James, holding Kate's hand, walked over to the DJ and took the mike from him, wanting to make a speech. Everyone gathered around the dance floor.

"Thanks, everyone, for coming," James said, his voice amplified by the microphone. "Luckily, she said yes." The crowd roared with laughter, and clapped. "I'll get this all done now - I'll be too drunk later." More cheering and clapping. "So, to my darling fiancée, happy birthday!" Kate tossed her straightened blonde hair back over her shoulder and kissed him. She was wearing heels, and James still needed to bend a little to receive his kiss. "The wedding is next year, the 17th July, so save the date. You're all invited. And Adam – where's Adam?" James squinted, searching, the lighting making it hard to find anyone in the darker areas.

"Here." Adam waved, tall enough to stand out from the crowd, his other arm still firmly around Sophie – and that's where it was staying. The way she'd been feeling the last three days, she wanted to chain herself to him. He stepped forward, so James could see him, Sophie moving with him.

"Ah, there you are. Would you do me a favour, mate? And be my best man?"

"Love to." He glanced at Sophie; she hugged him excitedly.

"Thought I'd ask now you're not nervous of weddings," James said, chuckling. Sophie giggled.

"Is *that* why you put me up to it?"

James grinned across the dance floor at Adam. "I wanted you to see what you were missing. And if I'm not mistaken, it worked." James gestured to Sophie, and Adam pulled her closer. "Right, everyone, I've talked enough. Food will be served soon. Let's celebrate!"

James handed the microphone back to the DJ and grabbed Kate, swinging her around the dance floor, blissfully happy. The music started as their friends joined them.

An hour into the evening, James and Kate made their way over to Adam and Sophie. "Sorry. Been meaning to get to you two sooner, but family and other friends have got in our way," James said, shaking hands with Adam, and hugging, playfully slapping each other on the back.

"Let me buy you a drink," Adam said to James, then turned his attention to Sophie and Kate. "Ladies, more champagne?"

"Yes, please!" they agreed, raising their glasses.

"I'll join you at the bar in a minute, mate. Just want a word with Soph," James said, and Adam nodded, walking off towards the bar. Kate made an excuse to visit the ladies so the two of them were alone.

"All right?" James said, awkwardly.

"Yes, why?"

"I can't believe my interfering paid off," he said. "So glad I don't have to get Kate to set you up with one of her accountant friends."

They both chuckled. Yes, Sophie was glad James' matchmaking had worked.

"How much did you meddle, though?"

"Oh, I've been thinking of trying to get you two together for a long time now, and Kate would tell me to leave well alone, but when I found the wedding invitation, and learned you had no date, nothing could stop me."

"Did you really think it would work?"

"I thought it hadn't, when you said you were leaving. I was really worried I'd screwed up royally. So I called Nick, knowing you'd meet him and what type of guy he was."

"Yes," she said, scowling. "I'm still not sure about that. I thought, 'great,' even James has to get Nick to pretend to like me."

"Don't be angry with me, Soph."

"I'm not, really. You're lucky it worked though." She nudged him playfully.

"Did Adam bloody good. And I've never seen him like this with another woman. And I've seen him with a few – oh!" James cringed. "Sorry, but honestly, Soph, tonight, he's not left your side. He's mad about you."

"I've missed you so much," Adam whispered into Sophie's ear, as they slow danced. His warm breath on her neck sent a tingle of delight down her back.

"I've missed you, too." She tightened her hold, tucking her head under his chin. This was as close as they could get without removing clothes. *And boy, did she want to remove his clothes!*

Public place. Lots of people. Not cool.

"So, do you want the good news or the bad news first?" Adam said.

"I've dreaded asking you about Manchester all evening, so give me the bad news." She looked up, meeting his gaze; his blue eyes had her bewitched.

"The bad news is you're going to be seconded to Jerrisons." The corner of his mouth twitched, as if he wanted to smile. "But for no more than six months. I've stipulated it in the contract."

"Yeah, I know, the quicker I get the job done, the quicker I can come home." She sighed, then frowned. "So what's the good news?"

"I've been busy these past few days, meeting customers with my father, as he's handing over the reins and it's given me a chance to talk to him." As Adam spoke he stroked her back, and she tried really hard to concentrate on his words, and not on what his hands were doing. She'd missed his touch. Her body – and her heart – yearned for him.

"A few months ago, he was preparing to expand our Manchester factory and he wanted me to oversee it. Then he put it on hold, with his health scare, realising I'd be needed here more. Once I'd been running the company for a while, I could then think about the expansion again." Sophie nodded, not really having a clue where it was leading. She'd drunk too much champagne and couldn't even blame Cassie this time.

"Anyway, our secretary, Joan, is going to make sure I get anything that's too stressful for my father to handle. He's agreed to help me by remaining in the office for the next six months – he didn't really want to retire yet. Joan promised me she'll make sure he goes home on time, and he's promised to take it easy."

"And what are you going to do?"

"I'm going to move to Manchester, and expand our factory."

"You're coming with me?" She couldn't hide the excitement in her voice, though she still felt hesitant. Was that what he was actually saying?

"Yes, and if you like, we can get a place together between the two companies for ease of commuting and I'll make a desk for you in our office, so you have office space there – in case you need to get away from that ghastly Nick."

"He's not ghastly."

"He is if he goes anywhere near you."

She playfully slapped his arm. "You have no reason whatsoever to get jealous. I'll set him straight."

"Good." His lips found hers, and his kiss melted her bones. If he hadn't been holding her, Sophie would have positively wobbled to the floor.

Once they'd stopped kissing, realising they were still in public, she chewed her lip, frowning. "But this means you're putting on hold becoming the new M.D.?"

"Yes, but as I said, my father wasn't actually happy about retiring early. I will still have a lot of responsibility, supporting him," he said seriously.

"Is this what you really want?" She looked up into his eyes, and he strengthened his hold around her, pressing her body close to his.

"Yes. You're what I want."

She smiled, then nervously worried. "What if it takes longer to expand the factory?"

"Then, as I said, you can work from our Manchester office. But I hope, all things going to plan, to have it wrapped up in six months at most. But whatever, we'll make sure we get you home to see your new niece or nephew regularly."

He'd remembered. She tried to kiss him, but he put a finger to her lips.

"And one day – not today, can't steal James and Kate's thunder, and I'd like to do it properly – but if I asked you," he raised his eyebrows, his voice casual, "would you marry me?"

"Yes!" She kissed him. They held one another tightly, the kiss deepening.

He pulled away, his sexy grin spreading across his face. "Good. Just remember that answer for when I ask you again."

Bonus Material

Coffee's On Me

"We've been here before," said a gravelly voice from behind me. My heart leapt to my mouth, then dropped into my stomach and my cheeks burst into flames.

I swallowed and turned, my fears confirmed; Carl. How could I not recognise Carl's deep voice with its sexy rough edges?

Why him, of all the men in the department, company, city, country even? Hadn't he left?

He took a chair beside me, and fire coursed through my body. We wouldn't need the heater on, I was generating enough heat to warm the whole building – all five floors.

"Looks like we're on the night shift together again," he said, grinning. Well, he seemed chirpy, considering the last time we'd done this shift together it had been a total disaster.

More for me than him.

"Just try to keep your clothes on this time."

Yes, that's why it had been a disaster.

"I will." I pursed my lips. I wanted to remind Carl he'd been the one removing my clothes.

"Coffee?"

I shook my head.

"Oh, yeah, I suppose you don't drink coffee anymore?" His smile was so annoyingly flirtatious and he smelled amazing – all male and musk aftershave. He was torturing me. If I told him how I felt, would he laugh in my face?

Possibly, after last week.

"No, I've just finished one, thanks," I replied, as cool as a cucumber, then stared at the monitors in front of me. Just empty offices and corridors. Nothing moved. Trying my hardest not to show any reaction to him, I looked him in the eyes – and regretted it, my insides turning to jelly.

"I thought you were leaving," I said.

"I was."

This job was some extra cash. All I had to do was watch some monitors and walk the corridors of a swish company on some business park. I'd started University late in life, but it was only now I knew what I wanted to do, and this worked around my studies nicely, paying better than bar work. Carl was probably ten years older, ex-soldier – the Paras I believed, hence his fantastic physique – and was trying to find his own niche in life too, settling back into civvy street. He hadn't said why he'd left the army, and I didn't want to pry.

"What happened about that personal trainer job?" I asked, my focus still glued to the security monitors, rather than looking him in the eye.

"It fell through."

"Oh, sorry to hear that. So you're back here?" I glanced at him.

"Never left. Not that stupid." He winked. "And you? How's the studying?"

"Fine, thank you."

"Need a nude male model?"

I coughed, sitting up straighter. God, if I'd been drinking coffee again, it would have been all over me, just like last time. Carl just grinned at me.

Why an earth had I told him I was studying an art degree?

That's what we'd been talking about before the incident. I'd had a life class that day.

I reluctantly smiled at him. "No, I don't need a nude male model, thank you."

Mind you, what I would do to see Carl naked…all that muscle definition…posing like Adonis. Pretty sure I wouldn't be able to concentrate on drawing him though.

As it was, he'd seen me down to my bra and knickers. Actually, as hot coffee landed in my lap, I hadn't any choice. The soldier in him reacted instantly, stripping me down, ripping my blouse open. Buttons flying off as if in some passionate clinch – I'd wished! Once he'd unzipped and removed my trousers, he'd dragged me into the nearest toilets, and started dabbing the red patches on my thighs and stomach with cold water, using paper towels. I'd been too stunned to tell him I could manage, and that he might be overreacting.

The most embarrassing day of my whole twenty-five years of existence, and yet, dealing with the whole situation calmly, while I stunk, and stung of coffee, he hadn't so much as batted an eyelid. He'd obviously seen much more horrifying things in his time in the army than non-matching underwear.

The real indignity of it all was I'd been trying to be poised and cool, flirting with him, trying to be impressive – but it had backfired. How I'd managed to get a whole cup of scalding coffee in my lap I would never know.

So embarrassing.

Then again he was probably the cause of the spill. For some stupid reason, I turn all fingers and thumbs with him around. I'd been thankful it hadn't landed over the equipment and wiped out the security systems. At least the event was just between us. I was sure he hadn't told a soul. No one else had said anything, or made teasing remarks.

I'd sat, mortified, with my jacket wrapped around me the whole evening, patches of my skin still stinging, until my uniform had dried. Carl had done the walks along the corridors, and he'd cheekily grinned and pulled faces into the cameras as he passed them. I'd been too miserable to laugh at him.

The following morning, the shift ending, I'd left the premises swiftly, with a coffee-stained blouse, tightly buttoned where some remained, and knotted at the bottom. I couldn't get out of the building fast enough. My trousers, luckily black, looked better for wear, albeit still damp. I'd zipped my coat right up, endured a bus ride, paranoid the other passengers could smell the aroma of eau-de-*Nescafe* which followed me everywhere, but at least relieved I would never see Carl again.

Or so I thought.

"I thought Matt was on with me tonight?" I said, frowning.

"He was, but he needed to swap shifts," Carl said, watching the screens. "I'll go do the first patrol. You sit tight." He placed a strong hand on my shoulder as he got up and gave it a squeeze. I wanted to lean into his hand, feel it on my cheek but instead stayed rock solid, resistant.

He's not interested in you. It's your head playing games with you.

And I wasn't about to make an idiot of myself for the second week running.

Left alone to watch the screens, my tension ebbed away as I saw Carl come into the picture and go. Although black and white, and not as crisp as my telly at home, at one point I got a good look at Carl's backside as he walked away from the camera.

What a fit bum. Tight, black uniform trousers doing it justice. Solid, muscular thighs, a narrow waist that flared out to broad powerful shoulders...

And then his face. He had bright blue, dazzling eyes and a cheeky grin. Always closely shaven, not a trace of stubble. His

311

light brown hair was longer than if he'd been in the army, but still short, gelled into a fashionable spiky style. Lips I wanted...

"Did you miss me?"

I jumped clean out of my seat. "Bloody hell, Carl, don't do that to me!"

"You *did* miss me." He was beaming. "Here, I got you a Coke from the vending machine." He handed me the bottle. "Careful how you open it. I don't think I can cope with seeing you in your undies twice in a row."

"Can you please stop reminding me?"

"Why?"

"Because that was the most humiliating thing to happen to me – ever."

"Really?"

"Yes! I think being dumped by Jason Becket at my school dance, in front of all my classmates, was less embarrassing."

"The boy was a fool."

I frowned. What did he mean? Carl was good at being nice. Another attractive quality. "Well, I know now we were much too young, and yes, I can see he was a git." I shook my head. Why was I telling him this?

"Are you seeing anyone?" he asked, so matter-of-factly, I was taken by surprise.

"What?"

"Well, you're at uni now. There must be young men, tongues out and tails wagging, trying to get a sniff of you."

"Pardon?"

"So...you're single then?"

"Yes. And sadly, living back home now I've decided to go back to university."

"Beautiful woman like you, single. Outrageous. Have to change that."

Beautiful woman?

"Carl, did you get a bump on the head or something? Have we had intruders and you're not telling me?" I looked around. "Hey," I yelled, sarcastic, cupping my hands around my mouth, my voice echoing around the large room. "Can we please have the real Carl back!"

He chuckled at me. "I'm being serious, Izzy."

"What? You saw me in practically my birthday suit, and... nah." I pushed my long hair behind my ears, irritated I'd forgotten a band to tie it back. Was he suggesting, what I thought he was? I stood, and my hands trembling, I slid them into my trouser pockets.

"I'll go take a look up on the top floor," I said, and walked off before he could argue.

I took my time patrolling the fifth floor. Too scared to confront Carl. Surely, after last week, he would've been put off. He was probably joking. Or felt sorry for me.

Unable to hide up there forever, I returned to the security room.

"I thought you were avoiding me," he said, teasing, his blue eyes piercing through mine. "What took you so long?"

"No, I thought I heard something, so had to check it out."

"Oh, yeah, I saw." He frowned, gesturing towards the monitors. "What could possibly be up on the fifth floor?"

"Nothing." I smiled.

"So, you going to let me buy you breakfast after this shift?" Carl flicked out his wrist to look at his watch. "Only a couple of hours to think about it."

"Um…"

"Go on, Izzy. Don't break my heart. If breakfast goes well, I promise I'll take you to dinner, too."

I swallowed. My chest wanted to burst open with the delight - he wanted to take me out.

Me.

He grinned, laying on his charm, his voice thick with persuasion. "Come on, least I can do after last week. I'm sorry I overreacted."

Yes. Of course, it's yes!

I giggled and nodded, trying to keep a firm grasp on what felt like a big kid inside of me, trying to break out and scream with excitement.

"Alright. Breakfast would be good," I said, as calmly as possible, all things considered. "Thank you."

He leaned towards me, looking from my lips to my eyes, his hand gently stroking my hair from my temple, to behind my ear. My body responded, blood pounding crazily from my toes to my ears. I swallowed. Was he going to kiss me?

"And – I don't want you thinking I'm jumping ahead of myself here – but if I do get to peel off your clothes again, I promise to take it slower."

Printed by RR Donnelley at Glasgow, UK